Victor Pemberton was born in Holloway, in the London Borough of Islington, in the early 1930s. His first job was as a Fleet Street postboy but after two years' National Service he went to work in the travel industry and wrote his first radio play 'The Gold Watch' which was broadcast by the BBC and has since been repeated five times. He went on to write radio and tv plays full time and in 1971 became script editor for the BBC's 'Dr Who' series, later writing for the series himself. In recent years he has been a producer on Jim Henson's 'Fraggle Rock' and has set up his own production company, Saffron. In 1989 he won the International Emmy award for a documentary programme he produced. He continues to write for TV and radio. His trilogy of radio plays, 'Our Family' in which he first told his family's story, was originally broadcast on BBC Radio 4's 'Saturday Night Theatre' in January 1989 to great acclaim, eliciting over 2000 letters of appreciation to the BBC. Victor Pemberton now lives in Essex.

Also by Victor Pemberton

Our Street
Our Rose
The Silent War

Our Family

Victor Pemberton

HEADLINE

'Keep the Home Fires Burning' by Ivor Novello and Lena Guilbert
Ford. Reproduced with kind permission of Ascherberg, Hopwood
& Crew Ltd. 'The Honeysuckle and the Bee' © 1901, Sol Bloom,
USA. Reproduced by permission of Francis Day & Hunter Ltd,
WC2H OEA. 'Just a Little Twilight Song' © 1925. Reproduced by
permission of B. Feldman & Co Ltd, London WC2H OEA. 'Take
me back to Dear Old Blighty' © 1916. Reproduced by permission
of B. Feldman & Co Ltd, London WC2H OEA. 'Knees up Mother
Brown' © 1938. Reproduced by permission of Peter Maurice Music
Co. Ltd, London WC2H OEA.

First published in 1991
by HEADLINE BOOK PUBLISHING PLC
10 9 8 7 6

ISBN 0 7472 3383 7

Typeset by Colset Private Limited, Singapore

Printed and bound by
Caledonian International Book Manufacturing Ltd, Glasgow

HEADLINE BOOK PUBLISHING
A division of Hodder Headline PLC
338 Euston Road, London NW1 3BH

In love and admiration of Letty and Oliver
and
for our family:
Stan, Audrey, Jonathan, Lesley and David

Chapter 1

The River Thames at Woolwich glistened in the sunlight. After a severe thunderstorm the night before the early afternoon sun burned relentlessly out of an azure-blue sky, and the surface of the water dazzled the eyes of passengers crossing the river on the free ferry. In the nearby Plumstead Road, the pavements were so hot the puddles of rainwater from the previous night's downpour were steaming like boiling kettles: many had dried up completely. Despite the heat, the road was as busy as ever. People were bustling in and out of the little shops, the women in cool three-quarter length summer dresses and straw hats, the middle-aged men enduring raw necks from their hard collars and ties. As it was Thursday afternoon quite a lot of the shops were closed, but the market stalls were there in force, selling everything from second-hand shoes and rabbit pie, to 'penny thriller' booklets and eels and mash. The petrol ration meant there wasn't much traffic around, just the occasional double-decked tram or open-topped bus, a few cars, and some horse-drawn carts and vans: thanks to 'Kaiser Bill', the war was still going strong after almost two long years, and the sacrifices being made at home were hurting.

A short way south of the river the brightly coloured shop and stall awnings of the Plumstead Road were dwarfed by the enormous shadow of a sinister-looking building, thick black smoke curling out of its tall, narrow chimneys. Some

1

people said it looked more like a prison. Those who worked there said it felt like one. But once you approached the large iron gates from the short, depressing walk past the rows of little terraced houses in Burrage Road, there was no mistaking that it was a munitions factory. The main building of the Royal Woolwich Arsenal was a great, lofty hall, dark and forbidding from the outside, with high fanlight windows and massive sliding steel doors. When it was first built, it probably must have stood out elegantly against the Thameside skyline. But the dirt and black grime of the years had taken its toll of the façade, and it was now impossible to see the colour of the original bricks.

In the shell-filling workshop, an annexe to the main building, lines of young girls and women wearing respirators and white overalls and caps were busily stuffing exploder bags into the tops of shells. The air was filled with chatter and giggles, the smell of machinery oil and TNT powder. Male factory workers rushed back and forth delivering new supplies of shell-caps, others arrived every few minutes with wooden mallets to tap the powder compartments delicately into place. But it was organised pandemonium, with the rituals carried out quickly but cautiously.

Most of the girls found the work boring and monotonous, but at the third bench from the door Letty Edginton was almost enjoying herself. Every time she finished lowering an exploder bag into a shell she stood back and admired it as though it were a work of art. It was obvious that she wasn't used to doing manual work in a factory, a fact that her next-door neighbour, had just pointed out.

'Don't be silly, Vi,' Letty replied, pulling her cap firmly over her head. 'I'm as capable of doing a hard day's work as anyone here.' She adjusted the respirator covering her mouth and continued filling the shell with TNT powder, ignoring the sniggering of the other girls working at the crowded bench.

'Well, I don't care what yer say, Letty,' insisted Vi. 'A munitions factory is no place fer a girl like you ter be workin' in. You're a square peg in a round 'ole. Anyone can see that!'

Letty Edginton and Vi Hobbs were different from each other in every conceivable way. Vi was nineteen years old, a year older than Letty and a good five inches taller, and she towered over the frail-looking younger girl. But in the two short weeks since the two girls had met, they had become close friends.

'As a matter of fact, I like this job,' said Letty, unconvincingly, her voice muffled by the respirator. 'It's interesting.' Not in a million years would Letty ever admit how she really felt. Working in such a place was so different from anything she had ever done in her middle-class life before. The hours were long and tiring, and it was hard to get used to being shut up all day in a dark factory, with a respirator clamped to her mouth, and noise and smells that pulverised her.

' 'Scuse me, Duchess,' interrupted one of the girls at the other end of the bench in a phoney toff's voice. 'What time is yer chauffeur collectin' you this evenin'?'

A gale of muffled laughter filtered through the dozen or so other respirators.

'Leave 'er alone, Rita,' snapped Vi, 'or I'll come down there an' give yer a bleedin' fourpenny one!'

Rita didn't say another word. She knew that Violet Hobbs meant what she said. Vi was a strong girl from a tough family, used to getting into scraps with her four brothers, who were all in the building trade.

'It's all right, Vi,' interrupted Letty, calmly. 'I'm perfectly capable of taking care of myself.' Her soft blue eyes flickered along the bench, as she searched for a reply as quick-tongued as those of the other girls. 'I don't need a chauffeur, Rita. I always go home on the tram.'

Letty's feeble response only caused the girls to snigger

again. Suddenly she wished the floor would open up so that she could fall in. Oh, she thought, if only she could snap back the same way that Vi did. Vi was tough, and could give far more than she was ever prepared to take. These two weeks that Letty had been working at the factory had seemed the longest of her life. Not only was it her first job ever, but also a hard, manual one, something she'd never been used to. Since leaving school, most of her days had been spent sitting at home sewing with her mother, or reading books out loud every evening to her young brother, Nicky. But everything about her life here in the factory was different – especially the other girls. Why did they have to make fun of her all the time? Why couldn't they be friends with her, like Vi? After all, *they* were the ones that were being stand-offish, not her. But though she thought these things, Letty had been taught never to answer anyone back. And, she told herself, to do so now, with girls who were far tougher than she was, would be inviting trouble. The only course that seemed open to her was to pretend she was no different from anyone else in the factory. And that was clearly failing. Oh God, she thought, as she loaded her umpteenth shell, why did her mother put her in such a place? Did she do it out of spite, merely because Letty had repeatedly begged her to let her get a job just like any other girl of her age? Just to show her what real life was like?

The air was suddenly pierced by the sound of someone ringing a hand-bell. In an instant, there was a frenzied dash for the ten-minute afternoon tea-break in the canteen.

'I tell yer again, yer shouldn't be 'ere, Letty,' sniffed Vi, pulling down her respirator to reveal her long pointed chin. 'You're not like the rest of us. Someone like you shouldn't be doin' manual work.'

'I don't know what you're talking about, Vi.' Letty pulled down her respirator, and wiped the sweat from her forehead.

She had a small dimple right in the middle of her chin. 'We've all got to do our bit to end the war, haven't we? Although I must say, I dread what'll happen to all these bullets and shells we're making.'

'We're at war!' Vi wiped her nose on the sleeve of her overall. 'If we don't kill the Boche first, it's our boys that'll suffer.'

Letty sighed deeply. 'Yes, I know. But it still seems so wrong.'

The two girls made their way out of the now deserted shell-filling shop, winding their way between the rows of empty shell-cases, wooden mallets, and foul-smelling TNT. They looked an odd couple, one tall and lanky, the other small and slight.

'Yer know, I could kill that old cow of a muvver of yours,' growled Vi, leading Letty through the Howitzer short-field gun shop, where only a few moments before, hundreds of girls had been working shoulder to shoulder, with barely enough room to stand. 'She oughta' be chained to a cart-'orse that one!'

Letty snapped back her protest. 'Vi! I wish you wouldn't talk about my mother like that. I don't like it. Anyway, it's not her fault. Well – not really.'

'What're yer talkin' about! Yer said yerself, yer wanted ter do typewritin' or somefink.'

Once again, Letty found herself trying to justify her position. 'I told my mother I wanted to do my bit for the war effort. After all, my brother Tom joined up, so why shouldn't *I* do something.'

'So she puts yer in a place like this?' Vi snorted scornfully. 'Luvvly!'

'It was *my* fault, Vi. Please don't let's talk about it again.' But the more Letty thought about it the more she was sure that her mother's decision to put her to work in a totally alien environment was a spiteful act of revenge. Revenge, because Letty had had the audacity to want to do something for herself.

As the two girls entered the canteen, they could hardly hear themselves talk, for the air was drowned by the sound of female chatter and laughter. Over a thousand women and girls were sipping their tea in a great sea of white – caps, overalls, chunky chipped mugs and plates. Even the walls, if a little grubby, were painted white, but at least they were relieved at intervals by large posters which proclaimed Mr Asquith's words that if the war was to be won, then the home effort was vital. Looking around the vast interior, it was easy to see that women and girls *were* the home effort, for most of their menfolk had been enticed into the Army, and were using the very weapons their wives and sweethearts were making back home.

'I still say, if *I* 'ad a muvver like yours, I'd kick 'er up the arse!' Vi was yelling above the din as she pushed her way to the front of the tea queue. 'Yer shouldn't let 'er boss yer around, girl. I mean, just look at yer. She won't even let yer wear make-up.'

'I don't like make-up.' Letty was getting a bit embarrassed.

'Why not?' Vi was already at the tea-urn with two chipped mugs. 'Yer'd be surprised what yer can cover up wiv' a dab of face powder! Not that yer can afford much on the mingy wages they pay yer in this dump! D'yer know, the uvver day, I 'ad to swap two ounces of marge fer a lipstick – "Parisienne Scarlet". It's beautiful!'

Letty laughed as they looked around for somewhere to sit. 'There's a place.' She made her way towards a bench where one of the last few men left in the factory was sitting quite alone. He was a pale-faced little man, who looked older than his years, with thinning grey hair, and metal-rimmed spectacles which seemed too small for him.

'No, Letty.' Vi took Letty's hand and tried to lead her off in a different direction. 'That's Mr Greenslade. 'E's best left alone.'

'But why? There's no one sitting at his table.'

'He just lost 'is son, Billy. In the trenches somewhere up Front.'

Letty's face crumpled. 'Oh no. The poor man.' She turned to look sympathetically at Mr Greenslade. But he didn't notice her, for he was staring aimlessly into his half-drunk mug of tea. 'We shouldn't leave him alone. We ought to try and comfort him.'

'No, Letty.' Vi held firmly on to her arm. 'He don't want no company at the moment. Everyone 'as their own way of dealin' wiv fings.'

Letty took a last look back over her shoulder at Mr Greenslade, who briefly raised his eyes and tried to smile. Letty smiled back, then followed Vi through the mass of white overalls.

'Come an' sit wiv us, Duchess!' The harsh Cockney voice calling to Letty came from a group of young girls who were turning to look at her from a table she was just passing. 'We've scrubbed the seat for yer, love. Yer won't get yer knickers soiled.'

The girls screeched with laughter, until the joker suddenly found her mug of tea in her lap after receiving a sharp jab in her back from Vi's elbow.

'Sorry, love,' purred Vi, smiling falsely, and fluttering her eyelashes. 'Can't see where we're goin'. We've 'ad too much champagne.'

The girl, her lap dripping with hot tea, immediately leapt to her feet as if in challenge. Vi's smile disappeared abruptly, and she stared the girl straight in the eyes. 'Yer will forgive me, won't yer – *love?*' The girl weakened very quickly, and sat down. Vi and Letty moved on to a nearby table.

'Why do they keep teasing me?' Letty sighed despondently. 'What have I done wrong?'

'Take no notice of 'em. They're jealous of yer, that's all.'

'Jealous? Of what?'

'You're educated. Most of this lot can't string two bleedin' words tergevver. They're ignorant. You can talk proper. They resent it.'

Letty was bewildered. She didn't feel she was particularly clever at anything she learnt. She looked the same, walked the same, she breathed the same foul factory air that the other girls breathed. And yet, apart from Vi, none of them would accept her no matter how hard she tried to say the right things.

Vi leaned forward and squeezed Letty's hand reassuringly. 'Stop worryin'. Nobody'll pick on yer while I'm around. But I still say yer shouldn't be 'ere. Why did your old woman put yer ter work 'ere of all places? A munitionette! Yer should be wiv' people of yer own kind.'

Letty suddenly felt indignant. Turning to look around her, she replied, 'There are other people like me here. I'm not the only one. What about Lady Winterton over there.' She turned to look at a middle-aged woman, who was chatting quite merrily at a bench nearby. Unlike Letty, she seemed thoroughly relaxed, and she looked no different from any of her work-mates. 'Her husband runs a bank in the City. She's much more educated than I am.' Letty turned back to Vi again. 'Honestly Vi, there's no such thing as class when there's a war on.'

Vi gave up. In the two short weeks she'd known Letty, she had very quickly discovered that her new friend had a will of her own. She sighed loudly. 'Yer know your trouble, don't yer, girl? Yer don't get enough fun out of life. What yer could do wiv is a nice boyfriend.' Vi reached into her overall pocket, and took out a small, broken piece of looking-glass.

'There's nothin' like a good slap and tickle once in a while.'

Letty, thoroughly embarrassed, blushed deeply, and took a quick gulp of hot tea, which burnt her lips.

Vi was pouting her cupid's bow lips in the mirror. 'You'll never find yerself a decent 'usband if yer don't get out an' meet people.'

Letty sat up straight, something she usually did when she was embarrassed. 'I don't need to do that, Vi,' she said, confidently. 'When my brother Tom comes back from the war, I'll meet all the people I want.'

'A bruvver's not a boyfriend, Letty.' Vi took a quick gulp of tea, and left a heavy lipstick mark on the chipped mug. 'An' anyway, fer all yer know, 'e might be layin' dead in the bottom of some trench by now . . .'

Letty's soft blue eyes suddenly turned to ice, as they shot Vi a look of piercing anger. 'Don't you *dare* say such a thing to me, Vi Hobbs! Don't you dare! Tom's alive, d'you hear! He's coming home – I know he is!'

It was a difficult moment, for Letty rarely talked about her odd-sounding family, and hardly ever about her older brother, Tom. The idea that she would never see him again clearly filled her with deep despair. Vi was completely taken aback by Letty's outburst, and for once she didn't know what to say. 'I . . . I'm sorry, Letty . . . I . . . didn't mean to . . .' She was floundering awkwardly. 'Of course 'e's alive.'

Luckily, the hand-bell rang again, and the tea-break was over. The mass of white overalls rose from their tables, and, like a swarm of butterflies, fluttered back into their different factory workshops.

Letty drained the tea from her mug, then got up. Vi watched her anxiously. 'I really am sorry, Letty – 'onest I am.' She looked upset, ashamed of her stupid, insensitive remark. Letty smiled back at her friend. After all, she didn't really believe that Tom might never come home again. Or did she? There had been no word from him since he went to the Front nearly three months ago, and sometimes Letty had to admit to herself that she was worried. But the two girls were soon engulfed by the swarm of white overalls. As she and Vi fluttered with them, Letty turned to peer over her shoulder: Mr Greenslade was still sitting at his table, staring into his mug of tea.

Two hours later, the swarm of white butterflies had changed colour. Caps and overalls were replaced by summer hats and ankle-length dresses, and one or two of the more well-to-do munitionettes were even sporting parasols. The warm, late afternoon sunshine was a welcome relief for the mass exodus of girls and women who had been locked up all day in the stifling atmosphere of the Royal Arsenal. Some of them took a deep breath of fresh air, others just closed their eyes and smiled gratefully up at the sun, which they had only seen filtering through the factory windows.

'Night, Duchess!' A chorus of girls was yelling at Letty as she and Vi followed the mass exit of workers, swarming out through the factory gates. Vi's response to the teasers was to give her usual 'V' salute with two fingers, but Letty ignored them, and adjusted her shining black straw hat, which had a taffeta-ribbon bow sewn on one side. Even though she was only slight, Letty looked smart in the drab, navy-blue cotton dress her mother had made her buy, clearly, Vi thought, to make her look unattractive to potential boy-friends. Walking by Letty's side, Vi had so many frills on her coloured dress she looked like a peacock.

The two girls finally cleared the factory entrance, and started to make their way towards the tram stop on the main Plumstead Road. Behind them, thick palls of black smoke were still billowing out of the factory's giant chimneys, a constant reminder that if the war was to be won, the furnaces

10

for the making of weapons had to be kept going day and night. Vi took out a Woodbine cigarette from a packet of five which she'd got out of a machine in the workshop. Letty was astonished at the way Vi lit up without caring if anyone was watching her. She had been brought up to believe that cigarettes were only for men, and strongly disapproved of women smoking, especially in public. Vi, on the other hand, thought nothing of it. As she said, she reckoned that if her father and brothers could smoke, why shouldn't she?

'See yer termorrer!' Vi called, as she parted from Letty at the corner of Plumstead Road. It was Thursday evening, and for Vi that always meant stewed eels and mash at the Pie Shop, followed by a penn'th of gin with the dockers at The Crown and Anchor down by the river. 'Don't do anyfin' I wouldn't do!' Then in a moment, she was gone, leaving a trail of grey Woodbine smoke behind her.

Letty walked on. Suddenly she felt alone. Her evening was clearly going to be nothing like Vi's. In fact, by the time she got home, there was usually very little left of it. The journey from Woolwich to Islington never took less than two hours, for it involved taking two journeys by tram, and one by bus. By the time she reached the tram stop in the Plumstead Road, two brightly painted red double-decked trams were collecting a long queue of women and girls from the factory. Letty got on to the second one, which, much to the ridicule of most of the male passengers, had a woman driver and a woman conductress. To her relief, Letty found a seat by the window on the top deck, and within a few minutes the noisy old vehicle was scraping its way along the rails towards the main Woolwich Road. As it went, Letty watched people rushing out of office and factory buildings everywhere, all eager to get home as soon as possible. Every evening, she noticed how few young men there were around: most of them had clearly been caught up in Lord Kitchener's

11

patriotic call to arms. However, when the tram passed the gates of Southwark Park, Letty did catch a glimpse of a unit of khaki-clad young soldiers being drilled to exhaustion by their sergeant major. Fifteen minutes or so later, Letty got off the tram at London Bridge, and changed on to an open-topped omnibus. The railway station was, as usual, bursting with activity, with hordes of servicemen, laden down with rucksacks and suitcases, rushing to catch trains that would start their perilous journeys back to the battlefields of Belgium and France. How Letty hated stations, especially in wartime. The platforms were stained with nothing but tears and farewells, and echoed to the sound of soldiers cheering, or singing wartime songs. She'd loathed saying goodbye to Tom, she'd hated the way their grief had got lost in everybody else's. It had all become so impersonal. She shuddered at the memory.

Although it was only a short journey from London Bridge to her next change, Letty, again, climbed the open steps to the top deck. There was a nice cool breeze up there and she had to make quite sure she held her straw hat on with one hand. She paid her penny to the middle-aged male conductor, who clipped a ticket for her on his shoulder machine, then quickly disappeared down to the lower deck. Along this stretch of the journey, Letty could smell the river close by. And what an invigorating smell it was – a wonderful combination of salt, and steam boats. When she alighted, she walked across Blackfriars Bridge, pausing half-way to breathe in the fresh air, and take in her favourite views of London. Behind her was Big Ben and the Houses of Parliament, and stretched out before her, the majestic sight of St Paul's Cathedral, and the City of London, where her father William Edginton, had his gunsmith's firm. But even as Letty stood there, marvelling at the wonders of her beloved city, she couldn't escape being reminded of the war. On the

12

river below, a small naval gun-boat, its funnel belching out black smoke, hurried from beneath the bridge, and raced off at speed along the river towards Tower Bridge, Woolwich and the Thames Estuary. A few minutes later, Letty made her own way on foot along the Victoria Embankment, where she paid a penny for an early evening edition of the *Star*. It was, of course, full of war talk, with a headline story telling of the Boche Army's preparations for a battle near a river in France called the Somme. The name meant nothing to her, but she was sure it couldn't be nearly as beautiful as her own lovely Thames. She was just in time to catch a Number 38 tram, and by the time she had settled herself on the upstairs deck, the vehicle was scraping its way through the dimly lit curves of the Kingsway Tunnel, heading for the Angel, Islington. It was after half-past seven in the evening before Letty finally got home to 97 Arlington Square.

Arlington Square was one of the more affluent areas in the borough of Islington. The elegantly designed terraced houses had been sturdily built of grey brick during the early part of Queen Victoria's reign, and most of them had large, attractive windows which overlooked the gardens in the middle of the square. Each house had ample accommodation for a large prosperous family, and the staff were usually allocated small boxrooms on the top floor. The gardens in the Square were delightful, and well-kept by a veteran of the Boer War, nicknamed 'Smudge'. By the time Letty arrived home, the old boy was just locking up his timber storage shed for the night and, after exchanging a quick wave with him, she hurried through the front garden gate, and into the house.

Sylvie, the new parlour-maid was waiting for Letty as she came through the front door into the hall. 'Your mother's been askin' for you, Miss Letty,' she whispered. 'If I was you, I'd go straight in.'

'Thanks, Sylvie,' replied Letty, quickly taking off her hat, and hanging it on the large oak coatstand beside the sitting-room door. The two girls were roughly the same age and they liked each other. Nowadays Letty was beginning to use Sylvie as her accomplice whenever there was the possibility of trouble with Letty's mother. This was clearly such an occasion, so Letty paused to take a deep breath before she went into the dining-room on the other side of the hall.

'And about time too!' As usual, Letty's younger brother, Nicky, who was playing cards with his mother at a card-table by the window, was the first to pass comment as she came into the room. At the age of fourteen he was a typical teenage mischief-maker, and whenever he had the chance to get Letty into trouble, he would. 'Seems to take you a long time just to get from Woolwich.'

Letty ignored him, and went straight to her mother. 'Sorry I'm late, Mother. The Number 38 got held up in Rosebery Avenue. There was a big Pacifist demonstration.'

'Oh yes.' Nicky was still sniping. 'Pull the other one!'

'Oh shut up, Nicky!' Letty turned on him irritably. '*You* only have ten minutes' walk to your school.'

Beatrice Edginton completed her hand of cards. 'Your supper is on the table,' she said, without looking up at her daughter. 'Mrs Simmons has laid a place for you.'

'Actually, if you don't mind, Mother, I won't have anything to eat tonight.' Even as she was saying it, Letty felt guilty. 'I had a big lunch in the canteen today.'

Beatrice looked up. She had a pallid, oval face with a flawless skin, and brown hair that she parted in the middle and combed severely into a bun at the back of her head. 'I'm glad to know you're getting the type of food you prefer.'

'I don't prefer it, Mother. But it's a long day. I have to eat something.'

Beatrice got up from her seat. She was really quite a small

woman and most of her family seemed to tower above her, even Letty. 'Nicky,' she said, 'go and tell Mrs Simmons to clear the dining-table.'

Nicky, already playing cards with himself, groaned. He was in danger of becoming a podgy boy, and his metal-framed spectacles were beginning to look too small for him. Irritably he got up from his chair, went to the kitchen door, opened it, and yelled. 'Mrs Simmons! Mother says clear the table!'

Beatrice covered her ears. 'Nicky! Will you stop that shouting! And go upstairs and do your homework.'

'But Mother! You said we were going to play whist with Father tonight.' One look from his mother was enough to tell him that there was no point in arguing. He slammed down the cards he was still holding in his hands, and made for the hall door, making quite sure he glared at Letty before he went.

As Nicky left the room, Mrs Simmons entered from the kitchen, carrying a large silver tray. She was a tall, burly West Country woman, who was not a particularly good cook, but certainly looked the part in her black widow's dress and white apron. Furthermore, she was the only one in the house who didn't feel intimidated by Beatrice. Going straight to the dining-table, she lifted the metal cover off the one remaining plate, to find that her cold boiled beef and new potatoes were untouched. As always, however, she said nothing, merely shook her head reproachfully at Letty, sighed, cleared the dishes, and retreated back into the kitchen.

Letty watched her mother collect the playing cards together, put them back into their packet, and tuck them into the card-table drawer. 'Would you like to do some sewing tonight, Mother?' she asked, gingerly, trying to suggest something that would get Beatrice out of her mood. 'Or would you like me to read to you?'

Beatrice moved to the dining-table, and cleared the silver salt and pepper pots. 'At this hour of the evening, I would have thought the last thing you would have is any spare time for me.'

'Oh but I do, Mother! Really I do!'

Beatrice took the salt and pepper pots to the heavy oak sideboard. 'Then why not try getting home on time for a change?'

Letty sighed. In the two weeks since she had started working at the factory, each evening her mother had complained about her time-keeping. But it was a very long journey from Woolwich to Islington, and Beatrice couldn't seem to understand that it just wasn't possible for Letty to get home before the family finished their supper. 'It wasn't my idea to go to work in a factory, Mother,' she sniffed, defiantly.

Beatrice turned to look at her. 'No. But at least you're doing your bit for the war effort.' Then she smiled sweetly for the first time. 'That *is* what you wanted, isn't it, Letty?'

Letty didn't answer. She just lowered her eyes as her mother swept past her towards the hall door. But as she was leaving, she called back over her shoulder. 'Fifteen minutes then. A little sewing, I think.' She paused briefly, and turned. '*After* you've had a bath, and changed into a clean dress.'

Letty paused a moment, then followed her mother out into the hall. They were met by Beatrice's husband, William Edginton, who was just coming down the stairs. 'Ah, there you are, Letty!' he beamed. 'And how were things at the Royal Arsenal today?'

Letty kissed him eagerly on both cheeks. 'Fine, thank you, Father. It's hard work though.' She was surprised to see him dressed in his new grey suit and patent leather shoes. He was such a distinguished, elegant man, tall and willowy, with a

16

fine bushy, military-type moustache, and he looked smarter than ever tonight.

'Just make sure you don't work too hard, young lady. I don't want my girl burning herself out too soon!' He kissed her affectionately on the forehead, bringing a warm glow to her face. Then he turned to Beatrice. The smile he gave her was weak, and formal. 'I shall be out for the rest of the evening, Beatrice. There are quite a few things I want to catch up with at the office.'

Beatrice merely nodded her head in acknowledgement.

Letty looked from one to the other of them. There seemed to have been so little contact between them these past few months. 'Nicky thought we were all going to play cards tonight.'

William gave her an awkward smile. 'Some other time, my dear. Work comes first.' He collected his trilby and grey felt gloves from the coat-stand, and made for the street door. Before leaving, he stopped and turned briefly. Beatrice was already climbing the stairs. 'I may be rather late.'

'I'll tell Mrs Simmons not to lock up,' Beatrice called back over her shoulder before disappearing into her own bedroom on the first floor.

William waited for her go, then opened the street door. 'Goodnight, my dear,' he called, quietly, to Letty. 'Sleep well.'

Letty looked miserable. Her father always seemed to be out every evening these days. 'Goodnight, Father.'

William went out, but just as he was about to close the door behind him, he poked his head back in again. 'By the way. There's a letter or something for you. I think it's from Tom. Sylvie put it in your room . . .'

'Tom!' Before her father had even finished speaking, Letty had already sprinted up the stairs to her bedroom on the second floor. The envelope was propped up on her

17

dressing-table, and it had a British Army postmark. She threw herself on to her bed, and ripped it open. Inside was a snapshot of Tom, looking every bit as handsome in his uniform as Letty had expected, and accompanied by a laughing group of his Army pals. On the back of the snapshop, without any clue as to date or whereabouts, was a short message: 'Dearest Letty, These are some of my mates. They would all like to meet you. Some hopes! See you soon. Lots of love to you, Father, Nicky (and Mother, if she still remembers me!). Your old bruv, Tom.'

Letty lay back on her bed, and sighed. Tom's postcard was the only thing that had made her really smile all day. Her favourite brother had been away for over three months, and this was the first time she'd heard from him. How she missed him! Ever since he went away she had had no one to confide in, no one to talk over her problems with. It had come as a great shock to Letty and all the family when Tom decided to volunteer for the Army. Her mother had never forgiven him and had virtually banned him from the house. But Beatrice had always treated her eldest son with indifference, and Letty knew only too well that there were other reasons why her mother resented not only him, but also Letty herself.

After a quick bath and change of clothes, Letty was downstairs again, joining her mother in the sitting-room for two wearisome hours of sewing and one-sided chatter. Letty never understood why her mother wanted her to go through this boring evening ritual, for Beatrice hardly ever spoke a word to her as they sat opposite each other in armchairs in front of the empty fireplace. But at least Letty had the ticking of the family's grandfather clock to keep her company. It also gave her the opportunity to think things over, like where her father went to every evening, or how many boyfriends Vi was drinking with in The Crown and Anchor.

And Letty was a passionate daydreamer, picturing all the things she would like to do with her life, like having a home of her own one day. Not that she wanted to get married – well, not yet anyway. Every so often she would flick her eyes up to look at her mother, half-framed metal spectacles on the end of her nose, engrossed in her cushion-cover sewing. It wasn't a happy face, Letty thought. Oh no. It hadn't been for some months now. Why couldn't she tell them all what was wrong? Letty had her own shrewd suspicion, but she knew her mother would never admit what was upsetting her so much. Why did she have to live her life in such an insular and self-centred way? Letty remembered the times when the family were together of an evening, and there was talking and laughter, and games and songs at the piano. But not any more. As she glanced around the room at the elegant furniture and richly embroidered curtains, she wondered if it was really worth having such expensive things, if it meant sacrificing happiness.

Only when the grandfather clock struck ten did Beatrice speak, 'I think that's enough for one night,' she announced, putting down her sewing, and taking her spectacles off her nose. As usual, Letty handed over her own sewing, and, after her mother had inspected it, waited for the traditional reply. 'Progressing. Slow. But progressing.' Both of them rose simultaneously, and after Beatrice had put the sewing away in the needlework-cabinet, Letty kissed her on both cheeks, and watched her make for the door with no more than a passing, 'Good night, Letty.'

A few minutes later, Letty was back in her room again, and tucked up in bed. She wanted to read a little, for she still hadn't finished re-reading Harrison Ainsworth's *Windsor Castle*, one of her favourite ghost stories. But she was too tired and, after turning off the electric light switch by the door, and opening her window, she snuggled down for the night. As usual, it took her a long time to get to sleep: her mind seemed to take forever to slow down. She thought about the day she had just had, and the one she would be getting up to in just a few hours' time. She thought about Vi, and all the other girls in the shell-filling shop at the Royal Arsenal, and why they didn't like her, and what she had to do to become one of them. For nearly an hour she tossed over and over in bed, having imaginary quarrels with the girls who were so stand-offish to her, telling them, in her mind, how she was every bit as good as, if not better, than they. As she finally did drift into sleep, Letty was determined to put things right, to make herself more popular with her workmates. The only thing she hadn't thought out was how to go about it.

It was another hot morning, so Bert Greenslade decided to take his tea-break in the back yard outside the Royal Arsenal canteen. It wasn't the most relaxing place to be, littered as it was with wooden packing cases, discarded blank cartridges, and rusting Howitzer spare parts. But at least he could get away from the mass chatter and laughter of the factory workers for a few minutes, and feel the warm sunshine.

'Much better out here, isn't it, Mr Greenslade? You can't hear yourself breathe inside.'

Greenslade, sitting on an old, upturned packing case, looked up to find a young girl standing beside him. She was holding two mugs of tea.

'I thought you'd like some tea. It's got two sugars.'

Greenslade looked puzzled, and stared at her for a moment. Then he took the mug she was offering him. 'That's very kind of you, Miss.' His voice was barely audible. 'Thank you.'

'My name's Letty. Letty Edginton. Mind if I join you?'

Greenslade moved over, and made room for her to sit on the edge of the packing case beside him.

Ignoring Vi's advice, Letty had decided that someone should at least make the effort of talking to the poor man. In her opinion, no one should feel alone when they're faced with a tragedy. 'Mr Greenslade,' she said, awkwardly. 'I was very sorry to hear about your Billy. It must have been a terrible shock.'

Greenslade lowered his head without answering.

'How old was he?'

Greenslade took a sip of tea before replying, 'Seventeen.'

Letty momentarily closed her eyes in horror. 'How terrible.'

Neither of them noticed that Vi and some of the girls from Letty's work-bench were anxiously watching them from the open side door of the canteen.

'Do you have any other children?' Letty asked, determined to find something else to say.

'No.'

She sighed, and quickly took a sip of her tea. 'I hate this war, and the people who started it. They have no right to take loved ones away from us.' For the first time, she turned to look at him. 'You must be very proud of him?'

Greenslade turned to her. His face was tired and drawn. He had clearly slept very little these past few days. 'Proud?'

'He was your son. He died for his country.'

The man's eyes suddenly lit up, and stared straight at her. 'No, Miss. If you must know, my Billy didn't die for 'is country. 'E died because his country couldn't give 'im a decent livin'. 'E died because 'e 'ad nowhere to go except the Army. Try tellin' my missus ter be proud of 'er one an' only kid, whose lyin' six feet down in some blown-up Froggie field. Try tellin' 'er that 'er son's life was only worth one King's bleedin' shillin'!' He leapt up from the packing case,

21

threw his tea on to the ground, and shoved the mug back at her. Then he started to walk back towards the workshop.

Letty felt stunned, and completely out of her depth. 'Mr Greenslade!'

Greenslade stopped walking, but didn't turn.

Letty put down the mugs and went to him. But she didn't really know what she was going to say. 'I didn't mean to . . . what I meant to say . . . what I was trying to say. You see, my brother – his name's Tom – he's in the Army too. He's only a year older than your Billy.' She bit her lip nervously. She realised her first approach to Greenslade had been naïve in the extreme, and the response had completely devastated her. 'If anything happened to my Tom – I don't know what I'd do.'

Greenslade stared at her for a brief moment, then smiled gently, and came back to her. 'Thank you for the tea, Miss Edginton,' he said. 'I really appreciate it.' He held out his hand to her.

Letty was almost in tears. But she took hold of his hand, which he covered with his other, and shook it firmly.

By the time the day shift finished work at five o'clock that evening, Letty's meeting with Bert Greenslade had become quite a topic of conversation with the girls in the shell-filling workshop. Even Vi told Letty how impressed she was by what she had done, assuring her that she was the only one who'd had the guts to try and comfort the poor man. But Letty denied that she had done anything to help. In fact, the more she thought about it, the more she felt she had made a big mistake by intruding on personal grief. Whatever Letty thought, however, during the afternoon tea-break, Bert Greenslade was no longer left alone at his table. And for one brief moment, a couple of the girls had even brought a smile to his face.

22

'Night, Letty!'

Without realising it, Letty had effected a general change of attitude towards both Bert Greenslade and herself. Now as she passed through the factory gates with Vi and the rest of the girls, suddenly there were frequent calls from her workmates, and none of them hostile. The 'Duchess' had clearly lost her title.

A few minutes later, Vi was heading off for her Friday evening gin, and fish and chips with yet another date she'd picked up in The Crown and Anchor. 'See you on Monday!' she called to Letty. 'Have a good weekend!'

'You too, Vi!' As she watched Vi hobbling off in high-heeled shoes that were too small for her, Letty knew that there was absolutely no chance at all of her having anything of the sort. In fact, all her weekends were the same. Card games with Nicky, Saturday evening pianoforte with Mother and some of her boring women friends, and enforced Sunday afternoon silence while Mother slept, and Father read the newspaper. She turned into the Plumstead Road, where two trams were as usual collecting the long queue of muni-tionettes. Just as she was about to join them, however, some-body called to her from behind.

'Letty! Letty – wait for me!'

She stopped, and turned. A young man was trying to push his way through a crowd of giggling young girls. Letty was puzzled. She couldn't make out who it was, and thinking it must be a mistake, joined the queue.

'Letty! Don't go! It's me!'

She turned with a start. Suddenly, the voice sounded familiar. By now, the young man was waving his cap and jumping up and down behind the giggling audience. Finally, he pushed past them, and she saw that he was wearing a soldier's uniform.

Letty burst into delirious excitement, 'Tom!'

To the amazement of everyone around, the young soldier rushed at his sister, dropped his kitbag to the ground, and caught her as she leapt up into his arms. The onlookers immediately burst into laughter, cheers, and applause. By now, Letty was half-laughing and half-crying. 'Oh Tom! Tom! What are you doing here? How did you find me?'

'The new maid told me. What's her name – Sylvie? Not bad huh? Quite a good-looker!'

Letty laughed. 'You went home first?'

'I went to the house first – yes.' His correction was quite deliberate. 'There was no one there except Sylvie.'

Quite oblivious of being watched, Letty just hugged and hugged him. 'Oh Tom! I've missed you so much!'

'I've missed you too, Letty!'

The shining brass buttons on Private Edginton's uniform were pressing into Letty's face. But she didn't care. Tom was home. He was alive! And in a few moments, they were travelling on the top deck of the tram together. For Letty, *this* weekend was going to be very different.

Finsbury Park was not the largest park in London, but to Letty's mind it was the nicest. Bordered on three sides by the Seven Sisters Road, Green Lanes and Harringay, it was a small haven for grey squirrels, pigeons, nannies pushing expensive perambulators, and anyone who just wanted to get away for an hour or so from the hustle and bustle and endless anxieties of wartime life. It was Tom's idea that they should leave the crowded train outside the entrance and grab an hour of peace together in the park where as children they'd stood on the footbridge over the main London-Scotland railway line, mesmerised as the great train engines of the London Midland and Scottish Railway Company passed by on the track below. But Letty's favourite area was the Boating Lake. It wasn't very big, but it did have a little island

24

in the middle which was taken over by birds of every shape and breed. When they were younger, Letty and Tom had often moored their rowing-boat and explored the island, but only when the park attendants were out of sight. It was always worth the risk, for they often saw ducklings hidden in their nests, and anyway a rowing-boat on the lake was the one place that Letty and Tom had always felt free from the rigours of life at home.

'You know, Tom, the last time you took me here, I was still at school. Nicky was with us.' Letty was deliriously happy to have her big brother back again. For her it was like old times, lying back in the rowing-boat, enjoying the warm evening sun, guiding the rudder only when absolutely necessary.

'That's right,' puffed Tom, sweat pouring down his forehead as he tugged away at the oars. His cap was off, exposing his short back-and-sides Army haircut, and he was stripped down to his khaki shirt and braces. 'I seem to remember splashing you both with the oars or something.'

Their laughter echoed across the lake, scattering a flock of screeching seagulls who were skimming the surface of the water. When all was quiet again, Tom stopped rowing, allowing the boat to drift aimlessly. Looking straight at Letty, his smile faded as he said, 'What are you doing in that munitions factory, Letty? Was it her? Was it Mother?'

Letty's smile also faded. She lowered her eyes, and bit her lip uneasily. She nodded.

'Why?' growled Tom angrily. 'What the hell does she think she's up to now?'

Letty replied with a sigh. 'I just don't know what's going through Mother's mind these days. She's so – unpredictable.'

'The woman's mad!' snapped Tom. 'The idea of putting someone like you in a munitions factory. It's wicked!'

'Oh, it's not that bad,' said Letty, trying to sound

25

reassuring. 'Actually, there are really some very nice girls working there. I've made lots of friends.'

'But you're not cut out for manual work, Letty. I always thought you wanted to be a shorthand-typist or something.'

'I do.' She stopped trailing her hand in the water, and wiped it on her dress. 'Mother wouldn't hear of it. In a funny way, she seems to resent the idea of me being able to use my own mind.'

Tom wiped his brow on his shirt sleeve, and put on his cap. 'Well, I won't let her do it! It doesn't matter if she hates me, but I won't let her ruin *your* life!'

'Mother doesn't hate you, Tom,' sighed Letty. 'She doesn't know how to love anyone, that's all.'

Tom wasn't so sure. Ever since he was a child he'd felt unwanted by his mother, the real odd-boy out in the family. He always knew that if he wanted to get anywhere in the world, he would have to go it alone. And a month or so away from his nineteenth birthday Tom Edginton had, like so many other boys of his age, joined the Army – regardless of the risks involved. He had to get away from home, from his mother. She despised her eldest son, and Tom knew why. It was because he was too calm, independent, and defiant. In other words, he was just like his father, William. As he stared down at his own reflection shimmering on the surface of the water, Tom could see again all the awful moments, all those maternal humiliations that had been inflicted on him. Like the time when he was no more than five years old, and she'd mocked him in front of a party of her smart friends. '*Such a pity Tom has large ears*', he remembered her saying. '*If he's not careful, he'll take off!*' Thank God for Letty, he thought to himself. Without her all these years, he'd never have survived.

A slight breeze was slowly edging the boat towards a bank covered with lupins, hollyhocks, and a splash of coloured

26

summer flowers. Letty's fingers were dangling in the water again, forming a gentle rippling pattern as the boat drifted. 'You know something, Tom. I have a feeling that – Father has a mistress,' she spoke without any emotion.

'What!'

Letty didn't look at her brother. She just stared in the water without any expression. 'Of course, I'm not absolutely sure, but I've suspected it for a long time – ever since he's refused to come down to the shelter with us during the air raids.'

It took Tom a moment to take this in. Although he'd known for years that his parents were merely acting out their marriage, the possibility of another woman had never occurred to him. Covering his eyes with one hand, he asked, 'D'you know who she is?'

'I think it's Amy Lyall, in the pawnbroker's shop in Upper Street. She was divorced about a year ago. I've seen Father going in there several times.'

'Amy Lyall! But she must be at least twenty years younger than Father.'

Letty quickly tidied her hair, and repositioned the large pin in her straw hat. Her reply was cold. 'I'm sure Father has his own reasons.'

'Oh God, Letty!' Tom was quickly putting on his tunic. 'If only I'd known you were going through all this.'

'Oh it's not myself I care about. It's Mother.' Letty was beginning to feel just a little chilled, so she pulled her shawl around her shoulders. 'She can't help the position she's in. Whatever she's been like to us, I can't stop feeling sorry for her.'

'*Sorry!*' Tom felt the anger rising in him so much that he picked up the oars again and started to row energetically. 'I still haven't forgotten the time when she slapped you in the face, just because you answered her back.'

27

Letty smiled at her brother, because she knew how protective he was towards her. 'What does it matter, Tom?' she said affectionately. 'I don't worry how Mother treats me any more.'

'The best thing that can happen to you, Letty, is for you to meet a nice young bloke who'll take you away from home and love you.'

'*Me*!' Letty roared with laughter.

But Tom refused to join in with his sister. He stared straight at her. 'Now listen to me, Letty. Over the years, you and I have been the best of friends. We've shared a lot of good times together – and bad times. But when the war's over, we'll both be going our own separate ways, because – well, that's the way life is. I've got a lot of things I want to do, people to meet, places to go. But you . . . you're different.' He took hold of her hands and looked at her seriously, with affection and admiration. Tom had always thought of his sister as someone who had so much capacity for love, so much to give. 'Believe me, Letty,' he continued, 'one of these days, you're going to find a good bloke who'll take care of you.' He paused. 'Don't you want to have kids of your own?' he asked tenderly. 'I know I do.'

Suddenly Letty grew serious. 'You do?'

'Well, of course. It's only natural.' He leaned forward and took hold of her hands. 'As a matter of fact, there is someone. I'd like to tell you about her.'

To Tom's surprise, Letty tensed and pulled her hands away. 'It's getting late, Tom.' Her voice was suddenly very formal and she sat up straight. 'You know how Mother hates us being late for supper.'

Tom looked down, hurt and started to do up his tunic buttons. 'I'm not going home. I don't belong with the Edginton family any more. That's one of the things I came to tell you. I just don't fit in. There's a Serviceman's Hostel

28

just near Victoria Station. I'm going to spend my leave there.' He looked up to give his anxious sister a reassuring smile. 'Don't worry. We can meet every day if you like.'

Letty was close to tears, angry tears. 'Don't you dare say such things to me, Tom Edginton! You're my brother, and you've got every right to stay in your own home.'

Tom was shaking his head, and rowing again. 'It won't work, Letty. Mother will never forgive me for joining up as a foot soldier. You know how she bolted the door on me when I left. She'd never let me inside the house. It'd be one long argument between us. Can't you see?'

Letty straightened her back defiantly. Tom recognised the look. He knew that, in her own way, she could be just as obstinate and determined as their mother.

'You're coming home, Tom,' she insisted, as she took the rudder again and steered back towards the Boat House. '*Your* home!'

Chapter 2

It was nearly nine o'clock by the time Letty and Tom arrived home at Arlington Square. Mrs Simmons told them that the Master and Mistress and young Nicky were almost finished supper, and that the Master in particular was very anxious that Miss Letty was not yet home. Letty took off her hat, and quickly arranged her hair in front of the large hall mirror near the coat-stand.

Tom took off his cap, dropped his kitbag on to the floor, and looked around. Nothing had changed in the three months since he'd gone away. Although Number 97 Arlington Square was an elegant house, it was still just that – a house, not a home. 'We're making a big mistake, Letty,' he said, feeling that he was not part of the place any more. 'It's far better that I stay at the Hostel.'

'No, Tom. You'll do no such thing!' Letty was still in a determined mood. 'Once Mother knows you're here, everything will be all right, you'll see. Now just wait there a minute. I want this to be a surprise.' She made her way towards the dining-room door, but before entering, turned and whispered, 'Oh Tom, Mother and Father are going to be so excited!'

Tom smiled wryly as he watched Letty disappear into the dining-room. He did not share her optimism.

'Letty! My dear child, where have you been? I was just about to go to the police station to report you missing.' It was easy to see that William Edginton was Letty's father. He had the same colour eyes, and a dimple in the middle of his chin. But in all other respects he was the living image of his elder son, Tom, who looked even more like his father now that he'd grown a moustache.

'I'm sorry I'm late, Father,' said Letty, quickly kissing him on the forehead, then doing the same to her mother, who was sitting at the opposite end of the dining-table finishing her dessert of stewed pears. 'The thing is, something rather important came up.'

'Young lady,' said Beatrice, delicately dabbing her lips on her table napkin, 'may I suggest that you sit down and have your supper. The staff are not on duty all night.' She put down her napkin, and with one hand, checked to make sure that her bun was still neatly in place.

'Don't have the kedgeree,' groaned Nicky. 'It tastes like carbolic.' Behind him nearby, Sylvie glared at him disapprovingly.

'Mother! Father!' Letty was bursting to get Tom into the room. 'I've got a wonderful surprise for you! There's someone waiting in the hall. Someone – very special.'

Beatrice exchanged a rare look with her husband.

'Letty,' asked William, uneasily. 'What's this all about?'

She had already rushed to the door, and opened it. In a moment of silence, Tom entered the room.

'Tom!' Nicky was the first to react. He leapt up with excitement from the table, and threw himself into his big brother's arms. 'You've grown a moustache!' shrieked Nicky, immediately tugging at it.

'Tom! My dear boy!' William had left the dining-table to greet his son, clearly overjoyed to see him.

'Hallo, Father,' Tom said, awkwardly. 'It's good to see you again, sir.' He stretched out to shake hands, but William threw his arms around the boy and hugged him.

There were tears in his eyes as he said quietly, 'Thank God you're alive, son.' For a brief moment they just stood there, smiling affectionately at each other. Though William was at least thirty years older, standing side by side they could almost have been taken for twin brothers: the same height, tall and willowy, the same glow in their blue-grey eyes, and now the same bushy moustache.

'How many of the Boche did you kill, Tom?' inquired Nicky, who was proudly trying on his brother's Army cap. 'I bet it was thousands!'

Tom smiled half-heartedly. 'Not quite as many as that, Nicky.'

'How long are you home for, son?' William was deliberately leading Tom towards his former regular place at the table.

'Just seven days, sir.'

'Seven days!' gasped Letty despondently. 'But you've been away for months.'

'There's a lot going on Up Front. Things seem to be hotting up out there.' Tom sensed the anxiety emanating from both his father and Letty. Awkwardly he added, 'Of course, if it's not convenient, I could put up at the Army Hostel at Victoria.'

'Army Hostel!' William was shocked by such a suggestion. 'Don't be absurd, my boy! This is your home. We've missed you so much.' He turned to Beatrice, who was still seated, and said, 'Isn't that so, my dear?'

Beatrice pretended she hadn't heard. She merely picked up her table napkin, and started to fold it.

William looked embarrassed, then annoyed. 'Beatrice!' he repeated, this time quite firmly.

Beatrice looked up. Her face showed no emotion. 'I'm relieved to see you are home without injury,' she said flatly.

Everyone watched her as she rose from the table. 'I'll get Mrs Simmons to make up your bed.'

As she turned and made for the door, Tom intercepted her. 'Thank you, Mother,' he said, kissing her formally on the forehead. 'It's good to be home again.'

'Good,' replied Beatrice, the ends of her mouth curling up into the suggestion of a smile. 'Then may I take it you'll be discarding that uniform before taking supper?'

Without waiting for an answer, Beatrice left the room. Tom lowered his eyes in despair, but the moment his mother had gone, the others surged forward, hugging and holding him in relief, excitement and affection.

In the hall outside, the rapidly fading light of evening was shining through the stained glass panels of the main front door. Beatrice turned on the electric light switch, eliminating most of the shadows. Electricity was an innovation in Arlington Square, where most of the other houses were still lit by gas. She made her way upstairs to her personal bedroom on the first floor. She and William had separate rooms, for they hadn't slept together since the night when they'd finally admitted that they had never really loved each other. That was nearly twelve years ago.

Once inside the privacy of her own room, Beatrice turned on the light. For a brief moment she stood with her back against the closed door, feeling tired and strained. Bleakly she looked around. Although the furnishings in the room were heavy, she'd spent time ensuring everything looked attractive. Beatrice knew she had inherited her late mother's good taste. She walked over to the windows, peered out briefly to see Old Smudge, the gardener, just locking up the gates to the communal gardens in the Square. She quickly drew the curtains, and went to her dressing-table, where she sat down and looked at herself in the mirror. She took the combs out of her bun, then shook her hair, which was brown and long, and tumbled down over her shoulders. Suddenly she paused, and took a closer look at a grey hair. Quickly she found a pair of scissors, and removed the intruder, then sat back in the chair, studying her reflection more in despair than admiration. Deep in thought, she was only half aware that her hand was opening the dressing-table drawer. She took something out, and looked at it. It was an oval sepia photograph of a small boy dressed in a sailor's uniform. Beatrice Edginton sighed deeply, and tears of relief immediately swelled up in her eyes. The photograph was of her eldest son, Tom.

* * *

Take me back to dear old Blighty,
Put me on the train for London Town,
Take me over there, drop me anywhere,
Liverpool, Leeds or Birmingham – well I don't care.

The famous Miss Ella Retford was on stage, belting out the song that she had made famous. The audience loved it, especially Letty and Tom, and Vi Hobbs and her boyfriend for the evening, a muscular young man with tattooed arms, named Sid, whom Vi had met in a Docklands pub the evening before. And, as usual, a lot of the audience that night was made up of soldiers home on leave, together with their wives or girlfriends, and the highlights of the evening were, as always, the sing-songs.

I should love to see my best girl,
Cuddling up again we soon shall be,
Whoa! Tiddley iddley ighty,
hurry me home to Blighty,
Blighty is the place for me!

Letty adored joining in the chorus with everybody. She had never been to a Music Hall before. It had such a wonderful atmosphere – all red plush and gold tassels, and there was the glorious smell of fish and chips and vinegar all around the gallery upstairs, and the air was thick with the blue haze of cigarette smoke that only the long stage spotlight could cut through. In fact the only time Letty had ever been inside a theatre was when her parents had taken her and Nicky to the West End to see a play by someone called Bernard Shaw. But her father fell asleep in the first act, and Nicky made so many smells after eating a whole bag of humbugs that their mother had insisted they leave at the interval. No, Letty had never experienced anything like this. The Music Hall was something different – oh, so different from life in Arlington Square. There were singers, and dancers, and jugglers and comedians, and everyone and everything seemed so alive!

'So what d'yer think of the Finsbury Park Empire, Letty?' Vi practically had to shout to make herself heard above the roar of soldiers singing their heads off.

'I think it's the most wonderful place I've been to in my whole life!' Letty yelled back, deliriously happy. 'We're having such a good time, aren't we, Tom?' Her brother, who had discarded his uniform for the evening, ignored her. He was too busy joining in the chorus, and admiring Miss Ella Retford's ankles, just visible beneath her three-quarter-length stage costume.

'I don't know what I'd do without my three penn'th of gods every week,' said Vi, clapping in time with the rest of the audience. 'It's the only way you can get through this ruddy war!'

Letty wanted the evening never to end. But with a wave and a patriotic smile, Miss Retford left the stage to tumultuous applause, cheers, and whistles. Then the red plush curtains closed, leaving a pretty young chorus girl to change the Act number to 'Six' on the programme easel at the side of the stage.

The lights dimmed, followed by a roll on the drums. The orchestra in the pit, or rather the band of eight ancient performers, was conducted by a splendid white-haired man in full white tie and tails with a red carnation in his buttonhole. Known to the regular patrons as 'good old Reggie', he raised his baton as though about to conduct a symphony concert, but what followed was a jolly little song which introduced the star turn of the evening, the legendary comedian, Harry Tate. And as the funny little red-faced man found his way through the red plush curtains, he was greeted with a roar of delight from the audience. Within seconds he was going through his repertoire of jokes, some new, some old. Everyone laughed and yelled and cat-called, especially Vi, whose raucous laugh could be heard above everyone. She particularly liked the rude jokes, and nudged Letty so many times that Letty was sure her arms were going to be bruised black and blue in the morning. At first Letty wasn't certain how to react to some of the jokes, and she even found herself blushing once or twice. But she was easily won over, mainly because it was such a joy to hear so many people enjoying themselves.

It was only when Harry Tate was going through the popular part of his act which poked merciless fun at Kaiser Wilhelm and the Boche, that events took an unexpected turn. Stepping forward to the footlights, the comedian bellowed out one of the war's most popular catch-phrases: 'Anyone here know what's a good Hun?'

Quite unexpectedly, Vi's friend Sid stood up and shouted out at the top of his voice: *'A dead 'un!'*

Once again the whole audience erupted into cheers. Everyone that is – except Tom, who suddenly covered his ears as if in agony. The deafening noise of shouting, whistling and cat-calling continued throughout the Hall for several minutes, until he could bear it no more. Picking up his straw-boater hat from the floor, he turned to Letty and said 'I'm going outside for a smoke.' Letty was taken by surprise, especially as everyone around seemed to be smoking. But before she even had time to reply, Tom had left, much to the irritation of everyone in his row of seats who had to let him pass.

On the stone steps outside the gods, leading down to the exit, Tom lit his cigarette from one of the gas lamps, and made his way to the street outside. Although it was getting late, the sun had only set a short while ago, so there was still plenty of light. With his boater on, he leaned against a lamp-post to smoke and take in the cool evening breeze after the stifling atmosphere inside the Finsbury Park Empire. He was glad to be alone for a few moments. So much was going on in his mind.

'Tom! Tom, what is it, dear? What's wrong?'

He turned with a start, to find Letty hurrying towards him. Suddenly, he felt consumed with guilt. 'I'm sorry, Letty,' he said, taking a deep puff of his cigarette, and trying very hard to avoid her anxious look, 'I just felt like a smoke, that's all.'

Letty knew something was wrong. She had never seen such torment in her brother's eyes before. 'But you could have smoked all the time if you wanted to. Everyone else did.'

Tom's instant response shocked her to the core. He suddenly threw down his newly lit cigarette, and stamped it out angrily on the ground. 'For God's sake, Letty!' he snapped with his back turned towards her. 'I'm allowed to do what I like you know. I'm not your husband!'

Nothing could have hurt Letty more. The last thing in the world she wanted to do was to expect Tom to be answerable to her for his actions. A burst of audience laughter and cheering could be heard from the theatre as she said, after a deep breath, 'I'm sorry, Tom. I didn't mean to—'

Before she could move away, Tom suddenly took her hand, and threw his arms around her. There was an anguished tremble in his voice as he said, 'Oh Letty, don't listen to me. Don't listen to anything I say. I ought to be ashamed of myself for saying such a thing – to you of all people.' Then he held her at arm's length, and for the first time looked her straight in the eyes. 'Forgive me?'

'Don't be silly, Tom. There's nothing to forgive.' She was relieved, but still concerned. 'Didn't you enjoy the evening? Did I do something wrong? Don't you like Vi or her friend?'

'I loved the evening, Letty. I loved everything about it. Especially being with you and your friends.'

'Then what's the matter? Please tell me.'

Tom hesitated for a moment, then started to walk her a few steps to the street corner. 'It's people, Letty. People everywhere. They don't think before they say things.'

As they reached the corner and came to a halt, a lamp-lighter arrived. It took only a few seconds for the mantle to ignite in the street gas lamp, and almost immediately the natural evening light was being replaced with artificial light and shadows.

'How can you possibly say that the only good person – is a *dead* one?' Tom asked. 'How can you actually laugh at such a thing?'

Letty looked puzzled. 'But they weren't laughing at *anyone*, Tom,' she said, the gas light now flooding her face. 'They were laughing at the Boche.'

'Boche! Huns! Germans! What does it matter what you call them. They're flesh and blood, just like you and me. They're some mother's sons or husbands or sweethearts, just like our lads – just like me. It's not right, all this killing.'

Deep down Letty knew she felt exactly the same as her

brother but somehow she found herself repeating what she had heard practically every day from her workmates at the factory. 'The Boche are our enemy, Tom. They started this war. Either we kill them, or they kill us.'

Tom suddenly grabbed Letty by the shoulders and glared at her. '*Kill*, Letty?' he said, in a low, intense whisper. 'Do you know the meaning of the word? Do you know what it actually means to take the life of a man? Have you any idea what it's like to look at the face of that man *after* you've killed him, to know that because of what you've done, he'll never see his family or friends again, he'll never enjoy all the good things in life that would've been waiting for him.' He released his hold on Letty's shoulders, but carried on staring at her. 'Don't talk about killing people,' he said, swallowing hard. 'You don't know what it's like.'

For a brief moment Letty stood motionless staring into Tom's eyes, which were glistening with tears. Suddenly, her big brother was looking much older. As he turned away, Letty knew – oh how she knew! People occasionally called her psychic, because of her insight. Even so, it was hard for her to accept the reason for Tom's anguish. He *had* killed someone himself – had taken another man's life. She didn't know who, or where it had happened, but knew it had. Letty had always been told that to kill someone meant that you were a murderer. But this was war, and you were a hero if you killed the enemy.

The sound of the National Anthem could be heard filtering out from the Music Hall. It was being sung with such gusto by the audience, with such pride. Letty took a deep breath, and put a comforting arm around Tom's waist. It was hard to think of her big brother as someone who had actually taken a man's life. But to her, he was no murderer. He was still the same little boy who took Letty's part time and time again against their mother. 'It's not you, Tom,' she said reassuringly. 'It's this horrible war.'

Within seconds the exuberant Music Hall audience was streaming out on to the previously quiet and deserted streets. Some were laughing and joking, some were still echoing Miss Ella Retford's rendition of 'Take me back to dear old Blighty'. Letty and Tom clung on to each other, completely engulfed by the surge.

'Where d'ya get to?' Vi was calling to them as she and Sid approached from the gods-exit. 'Didn't you like 'Arry Tate, Letty?'

'He was bloody marvellous, after you left,' laughed Sid, slapping on his cap. ' 'E told a marvellous one about the Kaiser gettin' piles!'

Letty did her best not to sound a spoilsport, and joined in their laughter. 'Sorry we had ter leave,' she said, trying to cover up. 'Tom had a terrible headache. He's had them since he was little.'

'Oh, what a shame,' replied Vi, pushing one of her curls back beneath her hat. 'What 'e needs is a nice glass of Guinness. Why don't we all go ter the Eaglet down Seven Sisters Road?' she suggested eagerly.

'I don't think so,' replied Letty, quickly. 'It's a bit late. We'd better be getting home, don't you think, Tom?'

'Er – yes. Yes, I think so.' Tom had now composed himself, but made quite sure he remained in the shadow thrown by the street lamp.

'That's a shame,' sniffed Sid, who was wiping his nose on his shirt sleeve. 'They do a good brown at the Eaglet.'

'Never mind. Some other time,' said Vi, grabbing hold of his arm. 'See you at work t'morrow, Letty.'

'Yes, Vi,' replied Letty, smiling gratefully. 'We had a lovely time, didn't we, Tom?'

Tom took a moment to respond, then said. 'Oh – yes. Terrific. Thanks a lot, Vi.'

'Pleasure,' said Vi, flirtatiously, much to Sid's resentment. 'By the way,' she asked. 'What regiment did you say you're in?'

'Seventh Middlesex,' replied Tom.

'The Shiny Seventh!' she squealed. 'At least, that's what my brother Olly calls it.' She was rapidly being pulled away by an impatient Sid. 'He's in the same one.' Suddenly, they were almost lost in the crowd as Vi managed a last shout. 'Night, Letty!'

Letty and Tom stood for a brief moment, allowing themselves to be jostled by the hordes of happy revellers from the show. Then Letty steered Tom away and, without saying a word, they moved off with the human tide.

Within half-an-hour, the lights of the Finsbury Park Empire were extinguished, and the audience had gone home. But the echo of Miss Ella Retford's war songs still clung to the warm night air.

Chapter 3

Tom had made up his mind. Today was the last day of his leave, but before he left he was determined to get Letty away from the munitions factory. Ever since he arrived, Beatrice had deliberately avoided him. Either she was too busy harassing Mrs Simmons and Sylvie about the state of the house, or she was locked in her room having one of her endless afternoon dozes, which seemed to last from lunch to tea-time. On one occasion, Tom thought he might talk the matter over with his father, but William had been absent from the house every night, giving substance to Letty's suspicions that he had a mistress. But Tom was absolutely determined that it was now or never. Beatrice had to be persuaded that Letty was not cut out to be a manual worker. He chose his moment carefully.

Beatrice was playing her pianoforte in the sitting-room. It was the one activity that clearly gave her pleasure, and she was an accomplished player. During her early days at Miss Hailsham's School for Young Ladies in Willesden, Beatrice's parents had been keen that she should take up a career on the concert platform, for she had surprised them all by learning to read music at a very early age. However, it was not to be. Although she never lost her love of music, as she grew older she'd realised the idea of using it to earn a living did not fit into her plans for a comfortable future. These days, she found greater inspiration in the genteel but popular songs, usually singing them in a pleasant contralto voice to her own accompaniment. But if Tom thought this had put his mother in a receptive mood, he was mistaken.

'A shorthand-typist? Out of the question!' Beatrice rose quickly from the piano stool, brushed past her son, and started to busy herself with any unnecessary job she could lay her hands on. 'Letty is just not suited for a clerical position.'

'But why not, Mother? How can you say that, when you haven't even given her the chance to prove herself?'

'Letty couldn't possibly cope with the strain of office life. She's a practical girl. She has to do practical things.'

'That's not true, Mother. Letty's very intelligent. She's always reading books.'

Beatrice waved her hand dismissively. 'She's always reading newspapers. It's undignified in a young girl. Newspapers are for men.'

Tom groaned despondently. 'Mother, that's ridiculous! Girls have the right to know what's going on in the world as much as anyone else. Lloyd George is asking them to help the war effort too, you know.'

Beatrice continued to bustle around pointlessly. 'I really don't want to discuss the matter,' she said irritably. 'Letty's career has nothing to do with you.'

'Career! You call it a career to get up at crack of dawn every morning, travel to the other side of London, then slave away all day in a hell-hole of a place where you can hardly breathe for the smell of oil and gunpowder?'

Beatrice ignored him. She put on her metal-rimmed spectacles which were hanging around her neck, made for her armchair, then calmly picked up her petit point and started to sew.

'Mother,' said Tom urgently, sitting directly in front of her. 'Have you seen how tired Letty is? And you should just look at her hands sometime. They're absolutely burning with blisters!' His voice was filled with anxiety. 'Working in a munitions factory is very dangerous. There have been so many accidents. Letty could be killed or injured at any minute.'

Beatrice was still unmoved. 'I do wish you'd stop exaggerating, Tom.'

'Mother, why are you doing this to Letty? She should be using her mind, not her hands.'

Beatrice finally lost her patience. She took off her spectacles, and slammed down her sewing on her lap. 'Now listen here, young man,' she asked, with eyes glaring straight at Tom. 'Did I interfere with *your* choice of career?'

Tom met her glare. 'Fighting a war is not a choice, ma'am,' he snapped formally. 'It's a necessity.'

'Was it a necessity that forced you into becoming a foot soldier?'

Beatrice's icy reply was only too familiar to Tom. He had heard it so many times since, on impulse, he had taken the King's Shilling. He had wondered if he should feel guilty for not having consulted his family, but knew only too well that his mother would never forgive him for refusing to apply for officer training. He replied with a deep sigh, 'We've been through all this before. I don't want to be an officer. I don't want to be responsible for sending men into action.'

Beatrice was appalled that a son of hers could come out with such a statement. Doesn't want to be *responsible*! Ever since the day Tom was born, she'd expected him to be the best in everything he did, a leader of men, someone in whose glory she herself could bask. But it had never happened. He had not turned out to be the son his mother had wanted. And therefore Beatrice felt she had failed doubly, for she had tried to mould Tom into the kind of man she had been unable to turn William into. William, like his son, had always refused to give in to her domineering ways, a refusal Beatrice interpreted as weakness. If her family was to thrive, she felt she *had* to have complete control over them all. However, things had not turned out like that and they were getting worse. In the last year or so the members of the Edginton family were beginning to develop minds of their own. Even Letty and young Nicky were frequently challenging their mother's opinions. This was not what Beatrice had anticipated. They were betraying her.

'Don't you think I don't know why you left this house?' she now asked quietly, but with tension underlying her every word. 'You ran away because you couldn't bear the thought of living under the same roof with me and your own family.'

Tom looked at her with incredulity. 'Mother! I love my family. You know I do!' Even as he spoke, however, Tom found himself questioning what he had just said. At the back of his mind, he wondered just what sort of a family he really belonged to. He knew that his father had some affection for him, but when Tom was a child, William had never once taken the boy's part. No. Nicky was the real favourite, and everyone knew it. He was young, cheeky, and at times made Tom laugh with his wicked behind-the-back impersonations of their mother. Tom didn't resent it, but he did often wish that he hadn't been born the eldest. If it hadn't been for Letty, his life at Number 97 Arlington Square would have been intolerable. She was the one person he could always turn to when he was at his most despondent, who would actually enjoy talking to him. She had always been a friend as well as a sister to him. Tom knew that Letty, too, yearned for just one day when she could actually feel she belonged to a normal, loving family. But that day had never come.

Beatrice rose quickly from her chair. 'I see no point in continuing this conversation.' Although it was only mid-morning, the room had become very dark, for a thunderstorm was gradually approaching. As she turned on the electric light switch beside the hall door, a crystal chandelier immediately burst into life. Then she called back to Tom over her shoulder. 'If you love your family so much, I'm amazed you want to spend your time in a trench with men whom you have absolutely nothing in common with.'

Tom watched his mother in despair. How could he tell her that since joining the Army, his life had taken on a completely different meaning. For the first time he had a sense of belonging, of being part of a family that *really* cared for him. Finally, he took a deep breath and said, 'Mother. I think you should know that the men I've been sharing those trenches with are amongst the finest people I've ever met in my life. In there we're all together, there's no such thing as who we are or where we come from. We're just one person.'

Beatrice let the curtain fall back into position again, and turned slowly to face him. 'My goodness,' she said quietly, and without emotion. 'You sound just like a socialist.'

They stared at each other in silence and dislike and, for a fraction of a moment Tom felt as though he were drowning, as though he could see his whole life flashing before him. He knew Beatrice had always resented having children, *William*'s children. She had done so only because it was expected of her. Even when little, he'd known how much his mother had hated him. In every way he was too much like his father, a man whom Tom was sure his mother had never loved. Now, the only way to release her frustration was to take her spite out on both Tom and Letty. For the first time Tom could see this clearly. Nicky was more fortunate. Nothing anyone did seemed to worry him, and he hadn't an ounce of sensitivity. He couldn't care less how his mother treated him, and perhaps this was why he was Beatrice's favourite.

Tom finally broke the silence. 'I'm leaving for France again this morning. Please don't let me go remembering you like this.' Beatrice suddenly tensed. Even she couldn't disguise the look of anguish in her eyes. 'It doesn't matter what you think of me,' continued Tom, 'but I beg you – don't take it out on Letty. She's a fine, intelligent girl, with so much love in her.'

Beatrice rubbed her eyes with a thumb and one finger, as if they were sore. 'Love,' she said, with a wistful, distant look, 'is a very overestimated word. Some have it, some don't.' She took one last look at Tom. This was her own son, her own flesh and blood. She wanted so much to throw her arms around him, to show him that she really did care, to beg him not to go. But she couldn't do it. That other 'self' inside her forbade it. 'Goodbye, Tom,' was all she could manage as she left the room.

For a moment, Tom stared at the door as though mesmerised. Then he wandered across the room to look out of the window. On his way, he stopped at Beatrice's piano, and casually glanced at the sheet music of the song she had been playing. He read out the ironic title, quietly to himself: 'Love's Old Sweet Song'.

Old Smudge was just emerging from his shed as Tom, khaki-uniformed and carrying his kitbag, entered the gardens in the Square. The first part of the thunderstorm had passed over, leaving the brick paths and early roses with a good shower of rainwater which now glistened in the quick bursts of sunshine. Smudge was much loved by all the residents in Arlington Square. Now in his late seventies and a veteran of the Crimean War, he still recalled stories about those dark days to anyone who would listen.

'Just came to say cheerio, Smudge,' called Tom, as the old man drew nearer.

47

'Blimey, Mr Tom! You ain't bin 'ome a week already, 'ave yer?'

'I'm afraid so,' said Tom. 'Seems like no time at all.'

Old Smudge shook his head knowingly. 'Back to the same place, is it?' Well, I wishes yer the best o'luck. I takes my 'at orf to you young fellers. I for one knows it can't be no picnic out there, that's fer sure.' Old Smudge knew only too well what it was like to be in the Front line. He still carried the scar from a Russian bayonet, a souvenir, as he called it, from the Battle of Balaclava in 1854. 'You take care of yerself, d'yer hear?' he added, taking off his flat cap, and holding out his hand.

Tom took the old boy's hand, and shook it affectionately. 'Don't worry, Smudge. I will.'

'Ere, before yer go, just 'ang on a minute. I got somethin' for yer.' He reached into his jacket pocket and took out a pair of scissors. Then he turned round, and after scanning the countless array of rose bushes, carefully selected the best deep crimson flower he could find, snipped it off and offered it to Tom. 'This is fer luck. Take it wiv yer, Mr Tom. Remind yer of Old Smudge – and 'ome.'

Tom took the rose, and smelt it. He was deeply touched. 'Thank you, Smudge,' he said, swallowing hard. 'I'll keep it pressed inside my Bible.'

'Tom! Tom! Oh Tom!' Letty, close to tears was shouting and waving as she entered the gardens and rushed straight up to him. 'You weren't going to leave without saying good-bye, were you?'

'Of course not, Letty,' said Tom, holding her close. 'Whatever gave you such an idea?'

Using an old piece of rag which he always carried around with him, Old Smudge wiped the rain water off one of the garden benches. Then he discreetly returned to his hut, and closed the door.

Tears were now streaming down Letty's cheeks and on to her lips as she struggled to speak. 'Don't go, Tom,' she sobbed. 'Please don't leave me.'

'Now listen to me, Letty Edginton.' Tom put his arm around Letty's waist and led her to the bench. As they sat, a quick burst of sunshine caused the sycamore tree above to engulf them in a deep, web-like shadow. 'You've got to be strong, Letty,' he said firmly, taking her hands and looking straight at her. 'When the war's over, I'm going to come home and take you away from all this.'

There was a glimmer of hope in Letty's eyes. 'Will you? Will you really?'

'I'll get a job. I don't know what. Maybe something to do with canals. 'D'you remember how you and me and Nicky used to take walks after Sunday school?'

'Oh yes!' Letty remembered, wistfully. How could she ever forget those magical walks along the banks of the Islington canal at New North Road, watching the old barge-horses trotting along the straight canal paths, pulling their great cargoes to all parts of the country.

Tom drew closer to Letty, and with one finger wiped the tears from her eyes. 'Times are going to be good for us one day,' he said, reassuringly. 'When I get married and have kids, you're going to come and live with us – that is, until *you* get married and have kids of your own.'

Letty looked up with a start. *'Married? You?'*

'Well, of course,' said Tom, with a broad smile. 'Everyone wants to get married sooner or later. Don't they?'

Letty bit her lip anxiously, unable to reply. *Get married? Tom?* It was something she had never thought about before. In Letty's mind, *she* was the only girl Tom really knew. At least, that's what she had always taken for granted.

Tom drew closer again. Then, after quickly looking over his shoulder to make sure no one could hear him, he whispered, 'D'you remember that game we used to play when we were young? When we used to tell each other things – private things – that we didn't want Mother to know about?'

'*Secrets*,' Letty replied, almost inaudibly.

'That's right – *secrets*.' Tom lowered his voice even more. 'Letty,' he whispered. 'Can you still keep a secret?'

'Of course I can!'

Tom took a deep breath before telling her, knowing he'd tried before and been rebuffed. 'Well,' he said, without realising that he was squeezing her hands. '*I* am going to get married.'

She gasped, and quickly pulled her hands away. Suddenly, her mind was troubled and confused. She felt consumed with resentment, even jealousy, as though Tom had betrayed her. If he got married, it would mean he'd leave the family, leave her. She'd have no one to confide in. Tom married! Letty felt her face flushing with irritation and anxiety. What a mean thing to do to her! What a mean, thoughtless, inconsiderate thing to do to his own sister! For one brief moment, she even became aware that not only was she pursing her lips sternly like her mother, but she was actually *thinking* like her.

'Her name's Marguerite,' continued Tom, excited that his secret was at last being shared. He then unbuttoned one of the top pockets of his tunic, and took out his wallet. 'I've got a photograph of her. She's a year older than you. Not as goodlooking, mind you. But you'd like her, Letty. You'd really like her.' He showed her the photograph.

Letty wiped her hands on her dress, then paused before taking the photograph. It was actually an old, rather tattered portrait, which seemed to be of a schoolgirl, not a young woman.

'It's not a very good picture,' Tom rambled awkwardly. 'It

was taken a few years ago, when she was still at school. But she hasn't changed much. Well – not really.' He was watching his sister nervously. 'What d'you think, Letty?'

Letty studied the photograph without any expression on her face whatsoever. Inside, she was having to admit that the girl who might one day be her sister-in-law looked utterly charming, with the most scintillating smile and large, laughing eyes. 'She looks very nice,' she said, with great difficulty.

'I met her at this farmhouse. She and her family were hiding from the Boche. She can't speak any English – not yet anyway. But I'm learning French. Just a few words here and there.' Tom paused from his excitement for a moment, then looked at the photograph himself. 'I love her, Letty.' He was staring at his sister now with such intensity. 'I knew the moment I saw her. It's not like the way I love you. With Marguerite – it's different.' He was desperately seeking approval. 'You two are going to be such good friends, I know you are.'

Letty returned the picture, and tried to smile. But no matter how hard she tried to hide her feelings, the tears trickled down her cheeks. She seemed so vulnerable, so lost.

Tom smiled with understanding at his sister, then took out his handkerchief and wiped the tears from her face. 'Come on now,' he whispered gently in an echo of the words he'd used to his mother, 'Don't let me go away remembering you like this. It won't be long before we're all together again.'

Letty sniffed, and nodded.

'What was it you've always said to me? Every cloud . . . ?'

'. . . has a silver lining.' Letty answered quietly.

'Every cloud has a silver lining.' Tom laughed affectionately. For years he had teased her about her favourite saying. 'Yes. That's my little sister. Nothing's going to get us down, is it?'

'No.'

'And whatever happens we'll always be friends, won't we, Letty? You, me – and Marguerite.'

Letty sniffed, took a deep breath and smiled as best she could. 'Yes, Tom. Always!'

From the distance, the first rumblings from the next approaching storm could be heard. After Letty and Tom had left the Square, their seat was quickly drenched in a pool of rainwater and falling leaves.

Chapter 4

The night sky above the River Somme in the North-west of France was pulsating with the glare and rumble of artillery gunfire. Lush golden cornfields were trampled down or prematurely harvested by machine-guns, and any corn still standing was pitted by the glowing faces of red poppies. Ever since the great British offensive started on 1st July, the air had been filled with the smell of rotting corpses. British Tommies, Australian Anzacs, German Boche – no one was spared and, as someone remarked, they all smelt the same. Hand-to-hand combat had turned men into fighting animals. But then not even animals escaped the human conflict, for cows, sheep, and wild birds were caught in the crossfire, too, or blown to pieces by shells and land-mines. For almost two weeks, the deafening sound of war was relentless. The moments of silence were rare, and when they came seemed unreal.

'Obbs. Oliver 'Obbs. Most people call me Olly.'

'Pleased to know you, Olly,' whispered Tom to his companion, shaking hands with him.

A dug-out in the middle of a French cornfield seemed an odd place for introductions. But Tom and his soldier companion had just been put on look-out duty while the rest of their division got some shut-eye, and this was the first time they'd actually met.

'It's bloody dark out there,' whispered Oliver, adjusting

his tin helmet, and cautiously peering over the top of the sandbags, out towards Jerry's lines on the far side of the field. 'What d'yer fink those bleeders are up to?'

'Probably the same as us,' replied Tom. 'Watching and waiting.' Tom couldn't see Oliver in the dark, for the moon that night was very firmly trapped behind thick dark clouds, which made the lapping waters of the great river beyond an even more eerie sound.

'What about a fag then?' suggested Oliver.

'Good idea. Have one of mine.'

'What yer got?'

Tom pulled out a cigarette from his packet, 'Players,' he replied.

'No thanks, mate,' said Oliver, retrieving a dog-end from behind his ear. 'Players are too lah-de-dah for me. I'm a Woodbine man meself.'

Both men lit up, using their tin helmets to conceal the match-glare from the top of the trench.

Oliver took a deep drag on his fag, swallowed the smoke for a moment, then exhaled. 'Where yer from?' he asked, spitting out a piece of loose tobacco.

'London,' replied Tom, who inhaled far less smoke. 'D'you know Islington?'

Oliver turned with a start. 'No kiddin'? You're from Islington?'

'Yes. Arlington Square. Just off the New North Road.'

'I'm not far from there meself,' said Oliver eagerly. 'Just up by the Archway.'

'Really? My God it's a small world!'

'Blimey!' Oliver just couldn't get over the coincidence. 'Yer come all the way out to France, and who d'yer share a dug-out wiv? Someone from yer own back yard!'

Both men laughed softly as they pondered over this unexpected link with home. 'How long have you been out here,

Olly?' asked Tom, after blowing smoke through his nose. 'I don't remember seeing you when we were digging in?'

'Nah,' sniffed Oliver. 'We've been hung up at Delville Wood, just down the road – waitin' for reinforcements. Only got in a coupla hours ago.' He blew the ash off his fag and took a brief look out at the darkened fields beyond, through a slit between the sandbags. 'So what pubs d'yer use in Islington then?' he asked in a low whisper. 'D'yer know the Eaglet – just off Hornsey Road?'

'Can't say I do.'

Oliver quickly stifled his smoker's cough. 'It's my favourite,' he spluttered. 'Me *and* my bruvvers. I've been pissed in that pub more times than I've 'ad 'ot dinners.'

Tom laughed to himself. But something was going through his head that he couldn't quite work out. Oliver's voice. It sounded vaguely familiar. Maybe it was the chesty smoker's cough, or just his companion's way of taking a quick breath before each sentence. Tom had a good ear; his companion definitely reminded him of someone, but whom? 'Olly,' he asked suddenly. 'What did you say your surname was?'

'Obbs. Oliver 'Obbs.'

'Hobbs?' Tom was thinking hard, 'Wait a minute. You're not by any chance related to someone called Violet, are you?'

Oliver turned with a start towards Tom, even though all he could see was a dark shape. 'My sister Vi! 'Ere – 'ow d'you know that?'

'Good lord. How incredible!' spluttered Tom, trying to move his feet around in the squelching mud. 'I've met her! I've met Violet. She works with my sister Letty – at the Woolwich Arsenal. We all had a night out together at the Music Hall.'

'Blimey!' The remains of Oliver's dog-end suddenly burnt his fingers, and he reluctantly flicked it into the mud. 'I must be dreamin' all this!'

Simultaneously, both men slid their backs down the sand-bags to rest on their haunches. 'She's quite a girl your sister,' said Tom. 'She certainly likes a good laugh.'

'Yeah,' sneered Oliver dismissively. 'At uvver people's expense, crafty cow!'

Tom was taken aback. 'What d'you mean? Don't you get on with her?'

'Violet's a bleedin' mischief-maker, always 'as been. Never stops makin' trouble for me and my bruvvers wiv our old man.' Oliver suddenly realised that he was raising his voice, so he quickly reduced it to a whisper again. 'You tell your sister to watch her step wiv Vi. What d'yer say her name was?'

'Letty.'

'Dinky-dink, is she?' Oliver was using one of his made-up expressions.

'Pardon?' asked Tom, puzzled.

Oliver explained himself. 'Is she a good-looker?'

Tom smiled gently to himself in the dark, then answered, 'Oh yes. Letty's a good looker all right. When we get home again, you must meet her.'

'*If* we get 'ome, more like.'

Tom didn't reply. He was thinking of home. In fact it was all he had thought about since returning to the Front after his leave. Home! Not the cold, tension-ridden house where his mother lived, but the home he would set up with Marguerite, his French girl, who would one day be his wife. Oliver was thinking about home too, in a rough back street in north London, where he slept on the bare floorboards of a so-called bedroom with his three brothers, all of them builder's navvies. Oliver and Tom couldn't have come from more contrasting backgrounds, and yet here they were sharing a common home – a mud-filled trench somewhere in the middle of a god-forsaken battle-field.

'You two men!' Tom and Oliver were suddenly shaken from their reflections by a young officer, who was squelching his way towards them from the far end of the trench. 'I want one of you to reconnoitre that wood on the far side of the field. We're pretty sure the Boche have got a machine-gun position waiting there for us when we go over the top.

'Which one of us d'you want, sir?' asked Tom.

'I don't care a damn! Just get a move on!' The officer disappeared as quickly as he had arrived.

'It's OK, mate,' said Oliver immediately. 'Leave this one ter me.'

'Oh no you don't,' replied Tom, quickly stopping Oliver from scrambling over the top of the sandbags. 'We'll toss for it.'

'Don't be a nark! What's the point? There's no time.'

'No, Olly!' Tom insisted. 'It's only fair. We'll toss.' He reached into his pocket and took out a farthing, his lucky coin which he'd had since he was a child. 'Light a match, Olly.'

Olly sighed, but took off his helmet to shield the glare from the match he was striking.

'Heads I go – tails you.' Tom flicked the coin. 'Sorry, Olly.' He blew out the match, then pressed the farthing into the palm of Oliver's hand. 'Hang on to that 'til I get back. OK?'

Oliver didn't like being a loser, but as he quickly shook hands and watched Tom's dark shape scramble over the top of the sandbags, he had a strange feeling inside him. In the few minutes that they'd met, he'd actually come to like the bloke. The two couldn't have been more different – rough and smooth, Oliver thought to himself. And yet, Tom was one of the few people Oliver had felt he could talk to straight away.

'Be seeing you, Olly!' Tom's hushed voice was calling from

57

the other side of the sandbags. 'Give my regards to Lord Kitchener!'

Oliver couldn't see his companion as he disappeared into the dark field beyond. But without realising it he was squeezing Tom's farthing into the palm of his hand.

Just before Oliver and the rest of the division went over the top the following morning, someone pulled something out of the mud where the two soldiers had met during the night. It was a pocket-book copy of the Bible. Inside was a crushed red English rose.

'Take cover! Take cover! Zeps comin'! Put out yer lights!'

The sound of Jimmy Hinckley's bugle pierced the night air, and at times like this it seemed the most unmusical instrument ever invented. Nevertheless, it was the one sound everyone in Arlington Square responded to, a sound which warned of the approach of one of the Kaiser's hated airships.

Arlington Square was one of the more affluent areas in the borough. The working-class districts of Holloway and Finsbury Park seemed miles away, even though they were literally just down the road. And as for the neighbouring boroughs of Shoreditch and Hackney, they were simply unmentionable as far as the residents of the Square were concerned. They ignored their very existence. One thing they did not ignore, however, were the air-raid warnings.

'Take cover!' yelled Jimmy over and over again, his face blood-red from the awful bugle-blowing. The son of a police constable in the New North Road, he took his duties very seriously. Every evening he waited for the first signal from the local police station that a Zeppelin air raid was on the way, and within minutes he was on his bicycle, roaming the surrounding streets, his bugle-call alarm echoing around the neighbourhood. He knew everyone relied on him. Jimmy Hinckley was eleven years old.

'Boy!' yelled Beatrice from her upstairs bedroom window at Number 97, 'will you stop that dreadful noise!'

'Better take cover, Mrs Edginton,' bellowed Jimmy. He was wearing his father's old flat cap, which was at least three sizes too big for him. 'There's a Zep on the way over.'

'I don't care about the Zeppelin!' Beatrice was shaking with indignation. 'I do not intend to leave my bed in the middle of the night for . . .'

As Beatrice spoke, the Maroon Warning Signal exploded nearby, shattering the hot night air like a deafening cannon shot. She screamed. Within ten minutes she was on her way to the air-raid shelter with Letty and Nicky.

Essex Road tube station was just a stone's throw from Arlington Square, no more than ten minutes' walk along the busy New North Road. Beatrice hardly ever used the tubes, but when she did she made quite certain that she travelled first class. Before the start of the Great War in 1914, ninety-six stations of the London Underground railway system had opened, and most Londoners were changing the habit of a lifetime by deserting the horse-drawn omnibus in favour of the much faster means of transportation. Already the Underground trains were being referred to affectionately as 'the tube'. To Beatrice, their platforms smelt of mouse urine and unscrubbed navvies. But this was an emergency: keeping alive was more important than pride.

By the time she had reached the station with Letty and Nicky, the platform was bustling. Ever since that night over a year before, when the Kaiser's Zeppelin bombs had rained down on the neighbouring East End streets, people had been nervous of what to expect next. A giant airship would just slip silently in and out of the clouds, like a great cat stalking its prey. In the streets below, there was so little time to hide or run away. A loud explosion, a fire, then screams everywhere. For many, the only place to take cover was in the bowels of the earth, on the tube platform.

'This way, mother,' called Letty, above the chatter. 'I can see somewhere for us to sit.'

'I want to go home,' grumbled Nicky. Although it was not yet ten o'clock in the evening, he hated being hauled out of his bed when he was still half asleep.

'Oh shut up, Nicky!' snapped Letty, as she led her mother and young brother to the last place available on the platform floor. As they went, a small baby was bawling its head off nearby. Older children were chasing each other in and out of the shelterers, a dog was barking, and people everywhere were coughing and spluttering in the air, made stifling by the thick curls of smoke coming from cheap tobacco and rolled cigarettes. At the far end of the platform, an elderly blind man was attempting to extract some kind of tune from his mouth-organ. Everywhere, yawns competed with anger and frustration. Kaiser Bill would not have been welcome in Essex Road that night.

Beatrice shrieked as a distant explosion in the street above reverberated along the darkened tunnel.

'Why don't yer shut up, missus!' yelled an angry man's voice from somewhere amongst the shelterers. 'You're scarin' the daylights outer my kids!' Everyone agreed, whilst some jeered at Beatrice and some laughed. The small baby wailed again.

'Take no notice of them, Mother,' said Letty. Even so, she was embarrassed by her mother's hysterical behaviour every time they took shelter like this. She knew it wasn't only the Kaiser's bombs Beatrice feared, it was the prospect of mixing with the lower classes as they drank, slept and snored, and made disgusting personal smells without any shame whatsoever. And Beatrice made her feelings perfectly plain. Letty hated it all, and was positive that one of these nights, her mother would get a much deserved slap round the face from an irate fellow shelterer.

Just as Letty was spreading out a blanket for the family to sit down on, a rush of cold air followed by a rumbling sound was heard in the distance. Within seconds, a tube train burst forth from the tunnel, and snaked its way to a halt. Letty wished it could be the last one, but there was no hope of that until just after midnight.

'Mind the gates, please!' As soon as the warning was yelled, a horde of passengers filed on and off, and the platform immediately became a bedlam of yet more noise and chatter.

Beatrice leant back against the cold tiles, her eyes looking up towards the curved, unfriendly ceiling above the platform, as though in prayer. 'Dear God, when will it all end?' she sighed. 'What are we doing in a place like this, like rats in a sewer? No air to breathe, not even a seat to sit on!'

'Ack-ack guns! That's what we want, dearie!' The laconic advice was offered by an outrageously fat old woman, still wearing her kitchen apron, who was perched alongside Beatrice on a stool much too small for her. She smelt heavily of carbolic soap, and was sprouting a few whiskers from the second of her two chins. 'Defenceless, that's what we are. Give us some ack-ack guns. We'll soon bring down those bleedin' gasbags!'

'If we're not all killed first,' yawned Nicky, who never missed an opportunity to scare the daylights out of his mother. 'If there was a direct hit on this station, we'd all be buried alive! Owch!' He flinched, as Letty twisted one of his ears and told him to shut up.

Most of the departing passengers were now on the train and closing the gates behind them. After the train had rushed off and disappeared into the tunnel, a curious, weary silence descended upon the platform. Then, from the distance, an old blind man started to play a tune on his mouth-organ: 'Keep the Home Fires Burning'. One by one the crowd joined in, and soon everyone was either singing, humming, or whistling. It was a gentle, moving sound.

'Oh no – not again!' Beatrice felt another of her headaches coming on fast. 'Why is it that whenever the lower classes are faced with a crisis, they always have to sing!'

Letty didn't answer. She loved the song, and she loved to hear the people all around her singing it. She sensed only too well what they were all feeling. War was so ugly. It brought only grief and despair and having a sing-song together was a way for people to express what they felt. As she squatted down and closed her eyes, she soon found herself joining in the rest of the chorus. Nicky did so too, and much to the irritation of his mother, he knew every word.

When the song came to an end, a strange silence once again descended upon the platform. Some people tried to settle down to sleep, others just snuggled up to their loved ones, hoping the night would pass quickly.

Although Letty's eyes were closed, she was wide awake. She was thinking about what would happen when Tom came home from the war. Would he really ask her to go and live with him and his French wife? Then her mind started to panic. What would happen if Tom's wife didn't like her? Suppose this French girl – this *Marguerite* – insisted that Tom went to France to live? Letty could feel herself becoming resentful of someone she hadn't even met, and she hated it.

'I wish Father were here now,' sighed Nicky, who was tired and bored. 'At least he could tell us some good jokes.' And before Letty could stop him, he asked of his mother, 'Why does he always have to go out in the evenings?'

Nicky's question was innocent enough, but it quickly provoked a tense response from Beatrice. 'I've told you,

Nicky. Your father has business to attend to.'

'What – every evening?'

Beatrice didn't answer this time. She turned away and tried not to think about where her husband was at this moment. All she knew for sure was that William was in another woman's arms and not her own.

'Have a bullseye, dearie.' The old lady with the whiskers on her chin was holding out a bag of sweets to Letty. 'And what about the nipper?'

Nicky didn't have to be asked twice. In a flash his hand was digging into the bag of sticky sweets, and Letty popped one in her mouth too.

'They should reserve part of the platform for first-class passengers,' snapped Beatrice irritably. 'Letty, I do wish you wouldn't talk to people like that. You're becoming more and more like them every day.'

'I don't mind, Mother,' replied Letty. She added wryly, 'After all, I do work with them, remember.'

As Letty spoke, a loud explosion from the street above caused a cloud of dust to come fluttering down from the ceiling. Then, to everyone's horror, the lights went out, and the platform was plunged into darkness. Beatrice was the first to scream, immediately starting babies crying and dogs barking. Soon, nearly everyone was on their feet, calling or shouting out each other's names.

When the lights suddenly came back on again, there was a loud sigh of relief from everyone along the platform.

'Was it a direct hit?' asked Nicky, relishing the drama. 'Are we trapped?'

Beatrice gasped, and looked as though she were going to faint. All along the platform people were nervously asking what had happened. Rumours, counter-rumours – everyone had their own idea of where the Zeppelin bomb had dropped, or how close it had been. Despite the station manager's calls for everyone to keep calm, some people made a rush for the exit, anxious to find out whether their own homes had been hit. Others were shaking their fist at the ceiling, shouting abuse at Kaiser Bill and everything he stood for. There was anger everywhere, but Beatrice was the only one still panicking. If the Boche thought that they were going to break London's morale, they were greatly mistaken. The air raids had only increased the sense of unity.

'It's all right, Mother.' Letty was trying to comfort Beatrice by dabbing her forehead with her eau-de-Cologne-soaked handkerchief. 'It's all over now.'

'All over!' Beatrice was fairly close to hysteria. 'What happens if that bomb fell in Arlington Square. What happens if we find no home to go back to?'

Letty felt like pouring a whole bottle of Cologne over her mother's head. Instead she insisted patiently, 'Now just calm yourself down, and I'll go and buy you a nice cup of tea from the Salvation Army lady.'

'I don't want a cup of tea!' snapped Beatrice angrily. 'I just want to get out of this foul-smelling hole!'

'Beatrice.'

Beatrice's hysterical flow was suddenly broken by the appearance of a figure standing over her.

'Father!' Nicky yelled out excitedly, immediately springing to his feet. Letty was equally surprised. 'Father!' she asked, looking up at him. 'What are you doing here?' Beatrice was the only one not to react.

William was grave-faced. He addressed all three of them. 'We have some bad news.' There was a hoarseness in his voice as he spoke.

Letty's gaze switched from her father's face to his hand. He was holding a telegram. She immediately returned her look back to her father's eyes. 'Is it – Tom?' she asked quietly, but firmly. William lowered his eyes.

Beatrice gasped, and shook her head. 'Oh no! Not Tom!'

William handed the telegram to Letty, not Beatrice, who started to read it out calmly, without emotion, almost to herself: '*War Office regrets to inform you . . .*' Then she stopped. She didn't want to read any further. The worst had happened. Letty had always known it would – sooner or later.

Chapter 5

'Private 'Obbs! Atten-shun!'

Oliver woke with a start. 'Sir!' he responded mechanically. If it hadn't been for the searing pain in his leg, he would have sat up in his hospital bed and saluted. He had to content himself, however, with remaining flat on his back, a wire frame protecting his legs from the weight of the blankets. 'Vi!' The face he was focusing on was not that of an officer, or even his sergeant major. Bending down over him was his sister. 'You silly cow!' he snapped. 'You scared the bleedin' daylights out 'o me!'

The military hospital on Richmond Hill was the first place Oliver had been taken to on his arrival back from the Somme. It was a huge, airy building, formerly a stately home, which had been taken over by the Government during the first year of the war, and now converted into a hospital for Tommies who had been seriously wounded. The exterior was covered in a profusion of green shiny-leafed ivy, and the front and rear lawns were always kept neat and pleasant for the endless intake of patients who would spend their convalescence there, attempting to recover from their wounds and their memories. The interior, however, was a different story. Stark and functional, long narrow corridors presented a bleak vision of the world, especially to those patients being wheeled into the operating theatre. Some of them would stay in the hospital for weeks or months, others would be sent elsewhere for limb amputations or treatment for poison-gas fumes. The wards themselves were overcrowded, and hardly a day or night went by without the sound of men in pain groaning, weeping, or calling out from a nightmare the names of their wives, mothers, or sweethearts. But Vi, as ever, seemed blithely oblivious to the subtleties of the emotional climate around her.

'I 'ope you don't snore like that when you find yerself a wife!' she quipped, taking some apples and a packet of Woodbines from her shopping bag.

'Mum sent the apples,' said the young boy with her. 'The fags are from the old man.' Sam, Oliver's twelve-year-old brother and his favourite, had insisted on coming. He was a gangling, dirty-nosed kid but he would do anything for Oliver, the only one in the family who ever seemed to notice him.

Oliver grunted ungratefully, and turned his head on the pillow, away from Vi. Since returning from France with his leg wound, he had become very dispirited, finding it difficult to talk to people – even to his own family, and especially to Vi, who had visited him two or three times during the last month.

'I 'ope you're in a good mood,' persisted Vi. 'I've brought you a visitor.'

Oliver suddenly turned on her, eyes glaring. 'I told you I don't wanna see no one! What's the matter wiv you, Vi? Don't you listen to nuffin' I say?'

Vi was ignoring him, and beckoning to Letty who was peering through the glass-panelled door at the end of the ward. As soon as she saw Vi's signal, she nervously pushed the door open, and made her way towards Oliver's bed. She felt very self-conscious, and soon became aware of the soldier-patients watching her progress, and the sound of her own footsteps on the bare floorboards.

'Letty. I want you to meet my brother, Oliver.' Vi was at her most unctuous. 'Olly. This is my friend, Letty. We work together at the factory.'

Letty held out her hand, shyly. 'Pleased to meet you, Oliver.'

Oliver didn't even turn to look at her, merely mumbled a reply. ' 'Allo.'

Letty looked embarrassed, and quickly withdrew her hand. 'I – I'm sorry to hear you've had all this trouble.' When Oliver still didn't respond, she bit her lip nervously, then asked, 'I do hope you're feeling better?'

Oliver scowled, and pulled the covers up around his neck. 'You shouldna' come. I've told Vi time and again, this is no place for women. It smells of blood and ether.'

'I'm not afraid of blood or ether.' The defiant firmness of her reply surprised him. He turned swiftly to look at Letty. It was the first moment he had actually set eyes on her. She was standing beside the bed, looking as pretty as a picture, wearing her Sunday best, a yellow cotton dress and close-fitting felt hat to match. Her only jewellery was a tiny cat brooch which her elder brother had given her for her sixteenth birthday and, unlike Vi, she wore no make-up at all. But it was her eyes that immediately grabbed Oliver's attention. They were so blue! All of a sudden, he found himself smiling for the first time, and asked, 'What d'yer say your name was?'

'Letty.'

Oliver pulled his hand out from beneath the sheet, and held it out to her. 'Pleased to meet you, Letty.'

Realising Oliver was staring at her, Letty blushed shyly, and shook hands with him. 'Pleased ter meet you too, Oliver.'

Vi was getting impatient. 'I'm so thirsty, I can hardly spit two bleedin' hairs. Have they still got that tea-urn outside?'

'As far as I know,' replied Oliver who knew it wasn't tea

Vi was interested in, but a young doctor she'd been chatting up since her first visit.

In a flash, she was striding off down the ward, calling back, 'Keep an eye on him, Letty. If he gives you any cheek, give him a fourpenny one!'

Finding himself alone with Oliver and Letty, Sam was obviously feeling awkward. 'There's a penny on top of my locker, Sam,' said his brother. 'Why don't yer go wiv Vi and get yerself a rock cake?'

'Cor fanks, Olly!' Sam eagerly found the penny, and rushed off down the ward, tripping over his shoe laces as he went.

After he had gone, Letty couldn't help feel slightly embarrassed to be left alone with Oliver. 'He's a nice boy, your brother,' she said, finally breaking the silence.

Oliver smiled quickly in reply. 'Oh, he's not a bad kid, is Sam. Bit of a rough and tumble, but a heart o' gold.' He reached up with both hands to smooth back his cropped brown hair, which normally he would have greased down with Brylcreem. It was a good sign. This girl's presence had restored his vanity. 'Why don't you sit on the edge of the bed, Letty? I'm afraid they don't provide any chairs for visitors in this place.'

Letty seized the opportunity to stop being tongue-tied. 'Oh no. It's quite all right, thanks. I don't mind standing.' She suddenly found herself looking into Oliver's dark brown eyes, thinking to herself that he was a good-looking man. She particularly liked the two small moles he had on one cheek. But then she blushed suddenly, realising that he was looking at her too. He grinned, then stretched his hands back to the bedrail behind him in order to pull himself up into a more comfortable position. But the pain in his wounded leg immediately made him flinch.

Letty rushed to help. 'Don't move! Let me do it!' She

quickly put one arm under his back to support him, then straightened the pillows, and slowly eased him into a comfortable, upright position. 'You poor thing. Does your leg hurt very much?' Oliver bit his lip hard until the pain passed, then smiled dismissively. 'Nah, not really. Comes and goes.'

Letty decided to ask no more questions about his wound. Before they came to the hospital, Vi had warned her that Oliver was touchy about how he had received his injury, refusing to talk about it to anyone. But then he surprised her.

'Reckon I'm lucky to be alive after this packet, eh Letty? More than I can say for my mates. It 'appened when we was on foot patrol, y'see. It was this shell. Come up from nowhere behind us. Cut the whole lot of 'em down, 'cept me.' For a brief moment Oliver couldn't help re-living those horrific few moments. 'All eight of 'em.' He sunk his head back into the pillow, and stared at the ceiling. 'Reckon someone up there was lookin' after me that day.'

Letty didn't answer. She didn't know what to say. Ever since she'd heard that Tom had been killed in action in France, her mind had been overwhelmed by the obscenities of the war, and by the thought of those who had been consumed by it. For a brief moment, she looked around the ward. It was full of faces just like Tom's. Young men, who under normal conditions would be full of the prospects of life ahead. But what she saw were disillusioned young soldiers, some of them with terrible limb injuries, others with piercing coughs caused by the remains of poison gas still burning their lungs, and all of them, she knew instinctively, with images that would remain in their minds for the rest of their lives.

'I don't think you were lucky, Oliver,' said Letty suddenly. 'I think you were very brave.'

He snapped out of his distraction. 'Fanks, Letty,' he answered, with a grin. But as he spoke, a flash of anxiety crushed his smile. 'Edginton? Did Vi say your name was Edginton?'

Letty looked up, surprised. 'Yes.'

Oliver was suddenly ill at ease again. 'Edginton. Tom Edginton.'

'Yes!' Letty's eyes lit up eagerly. 'My brother, Tom. He was in the same regiment as you. Did you meet him? Did you know him?'

' 'Course I didn't know 'im!' Oliver found himself snapping back at her brusquely. He was running his fingers through his hair, straightening the sheet – anything, as long as he didn't have to look directly into Letty's eyes. 'There are 'undreds of blokes in my regiment – fousands! What makes yer fink I'd bump into your bruvver out of all that lot? He's just one bloke, I tell yer. One amongst fousands! It's stupid!'

There was a brief, embarrassing silence before Letty spoke. 'I'm sorry, Oliver. Of course it's stupid. It was just – well . . . I wasn't sure how you knew Tom's name.'

He was still edgy, still avoiding Letty's gaze. 'Vi. It was Vi told me about 'im. No. I've never met yer bruvver, never set eyes on 'im.' After a moment, he took a deep breath, and calmed down. Eventually, he turned to look at her. 'I'm sorry he copped it. I'm really sorry.'

Letty smiled weakly, but lowered her eyes. 'Thank you, Oliver.' She turned briefly to watch Vi at the end of the ward, chatting up her doctor. She couldn't get over how different Vi was from Oliver. Vi was such a strong character, so outgoing. Her brother was a complete contrast, a quiet man, really quite moody. Understandable, Letty thought, after all he had gone through. And yet, even though he didn't say much, in the few minutes they had been alone together,

Letty actually enjoyed being with him. She couldn't understand why, because they seemed to have little in common.

'D'yer know, I don't fink I've ever met anyone called Letty
before.'

Letty turned back, to find Oliver staring at her again. 'Oh,
it's not my real name. I was actually christened Elizabeth,
but my friends at school used to call me Betty. That sort of
became, well – Letty.'

Oliver was still staring at her. 'You've got blue eyes.' He
ignored her blush. 'Bright blue. Same colour as the sea – on
a fine day, of course.' Oliver brushed back his hair again with
one hand. 'Will yer come and visit me again next Sunday,
Letty?'

Letty fidgeted awkwardly with her handbag. 'I – I don't
know, Oliver. You see, I . . .'

'Of course, if yer don't wanna, I'll quite understand.'

Letty replied immediately. 'Oh no! No, it's not that.' She
turned around quickly to look for Vi. 'I – I think I'd better
go and see if I can find Vi. Visiting time's nearly over . . .'
As she spoke, Oliver suddenly gritted his teeth in pain again
and clutched his wounded leg beneath the bed-clothes. Letty
jumped to help him. 'What is it? Shall I call the nurse?'

'No! I'm all right, I tell yer, all right!' Oliver took a deep
breath and, when the pain finally passed, he sank back into
the pillow again and closed his eyes. 'What am I talkin'
about? Of course I'm not all right. I'm never gonna be all
right again. I'm gonna be in this bloody 'ospital for the rest
of me life!'

Quite impulsively, Letty sat on the edge of the bed and,
abandoning all sense of shyness, took Oliver's hand in both
hers, and squeezed it. 'That's not true,' she snapped
defiantly. 'You *are* going to get better! But you *must* make
the effort!'

This sudden show of determination took Oliver by

surprise. As his eyes sprang open, he found all the patients in the ward turning to look at him. 'Sorry,' he said, swallowing hard guiltily, 'I 'ad no right to take it out on you.'

But much to his delight, Letty was patting his hand reassuringly. 'You mustn't worry, Oliver. I'll do anything to help you. Anything at all.'

Oliver's eyes immediately brightened. 'D'you mean it, Letty? D'yer really mean it?'

'Of course I do!'

Oliver grinned, and pulled her closer. Then in a mischievous low voice, he said, 'Then come back and see me again next Sunday. Will yer, Letty – please?'

Letty dreaded Saturday nights at Number 97 Arlington Square. It was the night when her father usually came home late from his men's club in the West End, to be met by a furious Beatrice, waiting to pick a quarrel in the living-room. Tonight was no exception. About eleven-thirty, Letty, lying on her bed in the dark, heard her father coming in by the hall door, take off his topcoat and bowler hat, and slide his umbrella into the heavy oak stand. Within minutes of encountering his wife, the row was in full swing. Letty usually did her best not to listen, and in any case, it was normally nothing more than a distant raising of voices. Tonight, however, was different. The voices were much louder. Beatrice sounded shrill, almost hysterical, and William, clearly very angry, was shouting more than Letty had ever heard before. Unnerved by the commotion, Letty decided she had to investigate. She got out of bed, tiptoed quietly across to the door, and opened it just enough to listen. Shouts of "Dishonest!" from Beatrice, and "Liar!" from William were echoing up the well of the house. Even a spider on the staircase wall scurried back, as if in panic, to the sanctuary of its web behind a family portrait.

'Nicky!' Letty rushed out of her room. She'd spotted her young brother crouched on a stair at the top of the landing, listening to his parents battling it out below. 'If Mother catches you, you'll be for it!' She quickly grabbed him by the hand, and yanked him into her own room. Then she closed the door behind them, and turned on the light.

'Why do Mother and Father have to fight like that?' he asked. 'Do they hate each other?'

'Of course they don't!' Letty insisted, keeping her voice to a hush. 'People often quarrel with each other, but it doesn't mean anything. They'll have forgotten all about it by the morning.'

Nicky yawned, and rubbed his eyes wearily. '*They* might. But *I* won't.' As he spoke, a door slammed downstairs. 'Something's happened!' he said, immediately pressing his ear against the door. The next moment, they could hear someone rushing heavily up the stairs.

'It's Father!' gasped Letty, anxiously pulling Nicky back. 'Don't let him hear us!'

She had hardly spoken, when the door burst open and William was standing before them. 'Letty! Nicky, what are you doing in here? Get back to your room at once, please!' Nicky didn't have to be asked twice. He rushed past his father as fast as he could. He had never seen him so red-faced with anger before. 'Nicky!'

William's firm voice stopped the boy in his tracks. 'Yes, Father?'

'I want you . . .' William swallowed hard before continuing. What he had to say was clearly not easy for him. 'I want you to be a good boy. I don't only mean for now, I mean – for always. Do you understand?'

'Yes, Father.' Nicky blinked nervously, standing in the hall in pyjamas that were much too big for him.

William went to the boy, and kissed him gently on the forehead. 'Goodnight, son.'

After the boy had left the room, William turned to look at Letty standing by her bed, clutching the brass rail with one hand. Her eyes were lowered impassively and, as William approached her, his shadow fell across her face. She knew what her father was going to say. She had been expecting it for some time.

'Letty, you're a young woman now. I think you're old enough to understand.' Letty still didn't look at him. 'Sit down, my dear.'

Letty sat on the edge of her bed, and William joined her. The small clock on the mantelpiece above the fireplace struck one, then continued ticking remorselessly in the background.

William gently took hold of his daughter's hands, and started with difficulty. 'Your mother and I can't live with each other any more, Letty. We've decided to go our own separate ways.' Letty's eyes remained lowered, and she didn't reply. 'Do you understand what I'm trying to tell you?'

'Yes, Father. I understand.' For the first time, Letty raised her eyes to look at her father. Her response was formal and without emotion.

'You see, my dear, your mother and I don't love each other. We haven't done so for a very long time.'

'*Who do* you love, Father?'

Letty's question took William by surprise. Now it was his turn to lower his eyes, uneasily. 'Yes. There *is* someone else, Letty. Someone who cares for me, whom I can talk to.'

Again, her reply was quick and sharp. 'Mother hasn't had the chance to talk to you, has she, Father? After all, she hasn't seen much of you for the last few months.'

William was devastated by his daughter's response. It was so shrewd, but so lacking in sympathy. And yet Beatrice had treated Letty appallingly over the years! He was at a loss. 'Don't resent me, Letty,' he pleaded after a moment's silence. 'I promise you, I'd have done anything to prevent what has happened. But when two people drift apart, life can become intolerable.'

Intolerable for whom? Letty asked herself. Although she loved her father dearly, how could she forget all the misery he had heaped upon the family over these last agonising months? Night after night he had left them alone, whilst he wandered off into the arms of his mistress. Night after night Letty had seen the feeling of hopelessness in her mother's eyes, and suffered the consequences. Oh yes, Beatrice was a difficult woman, but she had feelings just like anyone else and in her own muddled way had tried to look after her family. In Letty's mind, her father was a weak man. Whenever she, Nicky or Tom had been bullied by Beatrice, William had hardly ever taken their part – not because he didn't want to, but because he just didn't want to know, like an ostrich burying its head in the sand. Oh, if only he had stood up to Mother, thought Letty. If only he could have been more like a father, more like a husband, how different things might have been! They might have been more of a *family*.

'I don't resent you, Father.' With one finger, Letty removed a stray hair curl which had fallen down across one of her eyes. Then she said, colourlessly, 'I'll never resent you.' But she knew she was lying.

William leaned closer and kissed her gently on the forehead. 'Take care of your mother, dear. She's going to need you so much.' Letty did not react. Her eyes were lowered again. William rose, but stood in front of her for a brief moment. 'But if you're ever in trouble, I want you to promise that you'll come and see me. D'you understand, Letty?'

When she nodded, William turned, and made his way to the door. But he paused briefly, and turned back to look at Letty, who was still where he had left her, perched on the edge of the bed, hands folded in her lap, eyes lowered. William smiled sadly at her. 'You know, Letty, when you were a little girl, I used to think you were growing up far too shy and weak to be able to cope with the problems we all have to face up to. But I was wrong. You're different. Goodnight, my dear. God bless you.'

Letty just sat there, staring at the door. Something inside her was telling her to cry. But no tears would come. In the Square outside, two cats were howling and screeching at each other. Alone in the dark, Letty listened to them. It reminded her of other nights, when the howling and screeching had been the angry shouts of human voices. It was some time before she went to sleep. She had so much to think about.

Chapter 6

Even though it was early October, the weather was unusually warm, and there were still plenty of unseasonal buttercups and daisies poking their heads through the grass. Every tree and hedge seemed to be turning a rich shade of brown and, whenever there was even a slight puff of wind, a cluster of dead leaves would gently float down. People everywhere had taken to the parks or, if they could, the countryside, doing their best to keep the war out of their minds.

For Letty, the past few weeks had been so eventful it seemed the summer had just sneaked away without her noticing. If the departure of her father from Number 97 Arlington Square had been a distressing experience for her, it had been a devastating one for her mother. Beatrice was now virtually a recluse. She hardly left the sanctuary of her bedroom during the day and most times took her meals there. Letty knew the break-up of her parents' marriage was now inevitable, but she nonetheless understood her mother's bitterness and despair. Yet Beatrice spurned sympathy, and anything Letty did to try and comfort her was resented. However, during these last days of autumn, Letty had someone else on her mind, someone she could talk to, someone who was beginning to give her life a new sense of meaning.

'She loves me, she loves me not. She loves me, she loves me not . . .' Oliver Hobbs was plucking petals from a daisy which Letty had just picked for him from one of the lawns at the back of the hospital. He hated being pushed around in a wheelchair, even by Letty. But the wound in his leg was healing, and he didn't want to jeopardise his chances of walking again. *'She loves me!'* He pulled out the final petal and threw it into the air. 'Is it true, Letty? Do you?'

'Don't be so silly, Oliver,' replied Letty shyly, 'of course I love you.'

She had to use all her strength to hold on to the chair as they made their way down a slope towards a huge oak tree which overlooked a shaded footpath alongside the Thames. The tree had been their favourite meeting place every Sunday afternoon since Letty had first started visiting Oliver. She loved it: it had so many inhabitants – two very musical blackbirds, one very fat pigeon, a skittish grey squirrel who darted in and out of the branches, a cluster of sparrows and a pair of robins who fought each other for every scrap of bread that Letty brought them.

The moment the wheelchair came to a halt, Oliver took off his uniform cap and undid the top button of his tunic. He took a deep breath of fresh air, and looked up at the sky to feel the warm autumn sun on his pallid cheeks. 'Y'know, I can't believe my luck. What am I doin' 'ere wiv a real good-looker, who says she loves me?'

Letty smiled, and sat on a bench beside Oliver. 'That's not luck. It's fate.'

Oliver turned to look at her. 'I never thought I'd look forward to seein' anyone so much, Letty. I couldna' got well without you comin' to see me every week like this.'

Letty reached for his hand and held it. '*I* couldn't have got through these weeks if it hadn't been for you.'

For a moment, there was silence. Both of them were staring out at the small boats bobbing up and down on the river. One of them had some home-made red sails, which fluttered gently in the breeze. They cut a wonderful contrast against the cloudless blue sky. From a far distant street somewhere, came the sound of a barrel-organ playing. It was one of Oliver's favourite tunes, and he was soon gently singing the words:

> You are my honey, honey-suckle,
> I am the bee,
> I'd like to sip the honey sweet
> From those red lips you see . . .

He stopped suddenly to say, 'The man who gets you, Letty, is gonna be a real winner. I wish to Gawd it was me.'

'Is there any reason why it shouldn't be?'

Oliver pulled his hand away. 'Don't make fun of me, Letty.'

'Make fun of you? Oh Oliver, how can you say such a thing? All I meant was, I'd be so proud to spend the rest of my life with a man like you.'

'How can you say that? You've only known me a few weeks.'

'Time has nothing to do with it,' replied Letty, taking the pin out of her hat. 'If two people love each other, they should – well, try and make a go of it.'

Oliver couldn't believe his ears. This slip of a girl was virtually proposing to him! And there was nothing in the world he wanted more. This feeling of love came so strangely to him. It was unlike anything he had ever experienced. Every Sunday afternoon since they'd first met, he had waited in agony to see Letty's face peering through the glass panel of the door at the end of his ward. She was always the first visitor to arrive and, as the doors opened, she was like an eager squirrel, scurrying along the ward to see him.

'You're not sayin' you'd actually *marry* a bloke like me?' Oliver asked incredulously.

Letty took off her hat and placed it on the bench beside her. 'Well, of course, if you don't want to—.' She was half grinning, teasing him.

Oliver's hand unconsciously felt for his wounded leg. 'You'd really wanna spend the rest of yer life wiv a cripple?'

Letty suddenly turned on him, her lips pursed with anger. 'Oliver Hobbs! If you dare say something like that to me again, I'll push you and your wheelchair straight into that river! Your wound is healing and you'll be out of hospital any day now.'

'Maybe so,' Oliver mumbled sourly. 'But what are we gonna live on? They're gonna throw me out the Army 'cos of this, and I'd never be able to get a job 'til I can walk prop'ly.'

'*I've* got a job, haven't I?' Letty's face was all screwed up with impatience. 'I know it's not much, but it could keep us going until you're fit and well again.'

Now it was Oliver's turn to get angry. 'I'm not 'avin' no wife of mine support *me*!'

Oliver's suddenly raised voice startled a military nurse, who was just passing with another soldier-patient. Letty exchanged an embarrassed smile with them both, and was relieved when they finally disappeared along the footpath. For a moment, there was silence again, but for the pigeon, which fluttered down from the tree and plonked itself in front of Oliver, demanding food vocally. Letty took out her usual bag of bread pieces, and gave a handful to Oliver. Soon every inhabitant of the tree was parading before them, squawking and fighting over every scrap. Letty watched and started to giggle. Then Oliver joined in, and soon they both found themselves roaring with laughter at the great performance being played out before them which lasted until all the bread scraps had finally been devoured.

Beneath the laughter Oliver was a little ashamed at the way he had snapped at Letty, so he took a deep breath and wheeled nearer her. For a moment, however, he couldn't speak. Incredibly, he realised this was the first time he had actually seen her without a hat. Her hair looked so soft and shiny in the mid-afternoon sun. And her eyes! Even looking at her from a side view, Oliver could still see the glistening blue depths which could so easily melt him. He was madly in love with this girl, but he just didn't know what to say or do about it. 'Listen to me, Letty,' he said eventually, his voice now soft and reasonable. 'Of course I'd like to marry yer. I'd like to marry you more than anythin' else in the whole world. But I might be on crutches for years. It wouldn't be fair on yer.' He indicated the wheels of his chair and said, 'Don't you understand? I'd never have got this far if it hadn't been for you.'

Once again, that defiant look flashed back into Letty's eyes. 'You're wrong, Olly! What you've done, you've done through your own willpower. It'll always be like that – always! Remember this, nobody gives you anything for free in this world. If you want to do something badly enough, you have to do it because you *want* to. Believe me, Olly, when you walk out of this hospital, it'll be on your own two feet!'

As Letty spoke, a first small puff of white cloud appeared in the sky and briefly passed across the sun. At the same time, a mischievous slight breeze twisted along the footpath, scattering dead leaves in twirling clusters out into the river. Letty felt chilled. She had always hated autumn. To her it smelt of bonfires and the end of summer.

'Come closer, Letty.' Oliver was holding a buttercup which he had just pulled out of the grass beside his chair.

Letty looked suspicious. 'Why? What are you up to?'

'Don't ask questions. Come on – lean yer 'ead back.'

Letty dutifully obeyed, allowing Oliver to hold the flower beneath her chin. Immediately, he found what he was looking for – a bright yellow reflection. 'Y'see!' he said excitedly. 'They say if you 'old a buttercup under someone's chin, yer can tell if they like butter.'

Letty laughed out loud. 'Well, you won't find out much from me. I haven't had so much as a taste of butter since the war started.'

'Out of my way!' Without warning, Oliver suddenly grabbed the arms of his chair and, with great effort, raised himself up from the seat.

Letty rose quickly in panic. 'Oliver! What are you doing?'

'I'm gonna stand up! I've 'ad enough of this bleedin' thing!'

'No, Olly! It's too soon! You know what the doctor said . . .' She tried to restrain him, but he was already wobbling on his feet.

'To 'ell wiv the doctor! You're not pushin' me back into that 'ospital again . . .' As he spoke, he lost his balance, and fell with a thud to the ground, sprawled out flat on his back.

Letty yelled, and dropped to her knees to help him. 'Olly! Oh, Olly, what have you done?' She put her arms beneath his back and tried to support him. Gradually she was able to lever him up. 'Are you all right? Are you hurt?'

To her surprise, he was grinning at her. 'Come on, Letty,' he whispered with a twinkle in his eyes. 'Give us a kiss.'

'Oliver!' Letty was shocked. But before she could say another word, he had pulled her close, and smothered her with a kiss.

'Shall I tell yer something, Letty Edginton?' Oliver was still grinning at her, but this time he was speaking like a man in love. 'You gotta mind of yer own, you know that, don't yer? I can see it's gonna cost me a fortune to keep you in butter.'

Beatrice Edginton got off the Number 38 tram at the Angel, Islington. She hadn't left Arlington Square very much since William had walked out on her, but when she did, it was always to the same place. Upper Street was a busy shopping area, which so far hadn't suffered any damage from the Kaiser's Zeppelins. Soon after she was married, Beatrice had spent a great deal of William's money on clothes in Upper Street. Most people thought Mrs Edginton had impeccable taste. She never bought any garment that didn't suit her perfectly. That, however, was a long time ago. These days, Beatrice couldn't care less how she looked. In fact the hat she was wearing was dusty, her chiffon dress looked as though it needed to be ironed and her velvet cape had several stains on it.

The place she was making for was beyond the Angel, in the direction of Highbury Corner. On her way, she passed Collins Music Hall on Islington Green, but, with its large posters and photographs displaying the current bill-toppers, she refused even to dignify it with a glance. Sordid entertainment, strictly for the working classes, Beatrice had always maintained.

By the time she had reached her final destination a thin layer of grey fog was settling on the road: November was promising to be a cold month. Her stopping place was beneath a gas lamp, just a few yards along from the police station. Although there were plenty of people passing back and forth, none of them even noticed Beatrice. She had paid many visits over the past weeks to this lamp. From here, she could get a good view of the shop on the other side of the road. It was quite an insignificant-looking little establishment. In fact, it's only distinguishing feature was the sign of the three large brass balls hanging over the front entrance.

* * *

84

Amy Lyall had first met William Edginton when he was playing in a fund-raising cricket match for Disabled Soldiers, in Finsbury Park. Amy was helping to serve refreshments at the time but, although she had stopped to talk for a few minutes to the gentle, mild-mannered William, she never expected to find him calling on her just a few days later. However, the meeting clearly raised her morale enormously, for it came in the wake of her divorce from Harry Lyall, an Islington pawnbroker. The marriage had only lasted two years, and fell apart because Lyall was a womaniser. Amy herself had been devastated by the divorce, but when William came along, she had gradually realised that it was possible to love again. And there was no doubt about the fact that William was in love with her. It was a strange match. Amy was not so very much older than Letty, and her association with William had caused many Islington tongues to wag over the past few months. There was no denying that she was a strikingly beautiful young woman. Some people thought she came from an Italian or Spanish family, for she had rich black hair and flashing dark eyes to match. However, she was a Londoner, born and bred, and her exotic good looks were deceptive, for beneath it all she was vulnerable and very sweet-natured.

The pawn shop in Upper Street had been Amy's saviour. Lyall virtually handed the business over to her as part of the divorce settlement, and since then it had thrived as never before. She ran the shop single-handed, for William had his own business as a gunsmith in the Aldgate. At times she found people's bad fortune very distressing, but as time went on, she became something of a confessor to anyone who wanted to confide in her. Now the shop was full of curiosities, endless articles, from trinkets to second-hand clothes, umbrellas to kitchen utensils. And every one of them was carefully numbered and reserved, all awaiting eventual reclaim by their owners who by then might have returned to better times.

Amy was in the back-parlour when the bell rang over the front door. When she came out, a middle-aged woman was standing by the door, hesitating before approaching the counter. 'Can I help you, madam?' Amy asked with a polite smile.

For a moment, Beatrice didn't answer. She just stared. 'Do you have something to pawn?'

Beatrice finally approached the counter. 'Yes. I have something to pawn.' She put her velvet purse down on the counter, pulled off the glove on her left hand and removed her wedding ring. 'How much will you give me for this?' she asked, handing the ring over.

Amy took the ring, and inspected it closely through a jeweller's eye-glass. 'It's a well-made ring. Eighteen carat,' she said. 'Are you sure you want to part with it?'

Beatrice answered with no expression on her face at all. 'Quite sure.'

Amy sighed, weighed the ring on her scales, then looked up some figures in her gold-market catalogue. 'How long would you like to leave it?'

'As long as necessary.'

Amy was puzzled. But after a moment's thought suggested, 'How about three pounds?'

Beatrice smiled. 'Oh that's too much. It isn't worth it.'

By now Amy was really startled – and curious. 'Well, I like to offer as fair a price as possible. Let's say three pounds, shall we?'

'As you wish. I'm sure you'll put it to better use than me.'

For one brief moment the two women's eyes met. But Amy felt an unnatural tinge of embarrassment, and quickly returned to business. 'One moment please, madam.' She moved off to the privacy of her desk behind the counter, looked up a number from her cash book, and scribbled it on to a tie-on pawn ticket. 'What name is it please?' she called. But as she spoke, the bell rang out over the shop's front door.

When Amy returned to the counter, Beatrice had gone.

Chapter 7

Sam Hobbs was picking his nose. He knew he shouldn't, but since his mum and dad rarely seemed to notice him, he was never told to stop. In fact, much of the time Sam was either picking his nose or biting his finger nails, usually in the scruffy back yard of the small terraced house in Upper Holloway where he was born. Summer or winter, he could be found out in the yard, sitting on an old beer crate talking to the neighbours' cats. He was a solitary boy, shy and uncommunicative, so different from his older sister and his three brothers, two of whom were now away, serving at the Front. But today was a special day because Oliver was inside the house, introducing Letty to his parents. And, as Sam was sitting right outside the back parlour window, he could hear every word.

'Get married? At your age?' Oliver's father, Ernie Hobbs, was a massive man, with huge biceps tattooed with cats and dogs. He was not used to mincing his words. Like his own father before him, and his grandfather, he'd gone straight out to work as a builder's navvy when he was twelve years old. 'Yer 'aven't got a farvin' to yer name,' he went on. 'You'd be in the poor 'ouse in no time!'

Oliver looked browbeaten, staring in silence down at his shoes, hands clasped together, with both thumbs aimlessly circling each other. Ever since he was a kid, he had been warned never to answer his father back. Ernie's word was law in the Hobbs' household, and that was that. Letty, however, felt differently. Sitting upright at the parlour-table, sipping tea from a cup with a chipped saucer, she felt the urge to reply, to force Oliver to assert his independence. But by the time she actually spoke, all she could say was, 'Oh, I'm sure we'll manage somehow, Mr Hobbs.'

Ernie grunted, and spat out a loose bit of tobacco from his tongue. Then he got up and replaced his 'baccy tin on the dresser behind him.

For one awful moment, Letty felt she had gone too far, and she blushed a deep crimson. The atmosphere in the tiny parlour was so claustrophobic, with its faded floral wall-paper and cold lino floor. And to make matters worse, the fanlight window in the wall above was closed, trapping the smoke from Ernie's pipe. It mingled with the smell of Lifebuoy soap: Ernie Hobbs was a meticulously clean man who insisted on changing into a clean shirt every evening.

'Letty's right.' The soft voice that broke what seemed to Letty to be an endless silence belonged to Olly's mother, Annie, a pale-faced woman, with expressionless eyes and coarsely cropped hair. Letty, however, had already noticed her smile, which was as glowing as the hot embers of the black-polished coke stove she sat in front of. 'Olly'll get a job sooner or later,' Annie said reassuringly and, turning her head towards him, she repeated what she had always maintained. 'Got a will of yer own, 'aven't yer, son?' Her eyes did not look straight at Oliver, because she couldn't see him. Annie Hobbs was blind, and although she had been warned, Letty still found it unsettling.

Oliver, who was sitting opposite Letty at the table, didn't answer at first. It hadn't been his idea to bring his girlfriend to the family home. He was ashamed of the pokey little place; it smelt of carbolic and stale beer. To Oliver his home was a hovel, where he and his four brothers had always been forced to share one room, sleeping on two old mattresses on the floor. He had cringed at the thought of bringing Letty here; she had been used to so much better. 'I'd never let no wife an' kids of mine starve.' He eventually sniffed indignantly as he took a gulp of tea, and dripped some of it on to the clean white table-cloth. 'As long as I've got a good pair of 'ands, I'd take care of 'em!'

Letty looked at Oliver with admiration and pride. Over the past few weeks she had watched him regain his morale and confidence, and he was able to use his crutches less and less. And now he'd had the courage to answer his father back.

Ernie fingered his moustache. It was a bad sign, usually meaning that he was irritated. 'And what about yer own muvver and farver?' he growled, glaring straight at Letty. 'What do they say about you gettin' mixed up wiv someone like Olly?'

Letty hesitated briefly before replying. 'My father has always said it's up to me who I take for a husband, Mr Hobbs.'

'What about yer muvver?'

'My mother?' Letty hesitated again, but this time lowered her eyes awkwardly. 'Well, as a matter of fact, I haven't actually mentioned it to her yet.'

Ernie looked at Letty suspiciously. His instinct told him he was on to something. Sitting in his own armchair on the other side of the stove, he asked, 'How old are you young lady?'

'Wos that gotta do wiv it?' snapped Oliver irritably.

'You 'old yer tongue!' bellowed Ernie, now fingering the thick-buckled belt on his trousers, as though he would use it on Oliver like he had when his children were little.

Letty quickly volunteered her answer. 'I'm eighteen, Mr Hobbs.'

'Eighteen? Then you're under-age.'

Oliver was getting more and more angry. For years he'd given way to his father, but this time he was going to say just what he felt. 'You 'eard what Letty said, Dad. 'Er old man says she can marry who she wants. There's no problem, I tell yer!'

'Why don't you two use yer common sense!' Ernie, hackles now raised, continued, 'Can't yer see you're chalk and cheese? You're from diff'rent worlds!'

'What yer talkin' about?' Oliver was glaring at his father. 'She's a girl, an' I'm a feller, an' we wanna get married. What diff'rence does it make where we come from?'

Ernie thumped his fist on the arm of his chair. 'What diff'rence!' he yelled. 'Money's the diff'rence! People like us 'ave ter work for their livin'!'

The knuckles on Oliver's hands were turning white as he gripped the support of one of his Army-issue crutches. 'And what about Letty?' he yelled back. 'She slaves 'er guts out day after day in that munitions factory!'

'Not 'cos she needs the money – that's for sure!'

Using his crutches, Oliver suddenly levered himself up from his chair. 'That's bleedin' nonsense, Dad – and you know it!'

Ernie was having none of this. He leapt to his feet, and pointed a menacing finger straight at Oliver's face. 'You swear like that once more in front of yer muvver, and I'll cuff yer!'

Father and son were now eyeball to eyeball, looking as if they were about to fight. Letty gazed at them, appalled and terrified.

'Give us a puff, Ern.' It was Annie's gentle voice that broke the tension. Although she couldn't actually see her husband, she reached out her hand towards him. Ernie was too busy glaring at Oliver to hear what she said, so she raised her voice

91

just enough to make sure he did hear. 'Ern. I'm dyin' for a smoke, mate.'

Ernie finally withdrew from his battle position, and handed his pipe over to Annie, who took a deep puff from it, and exhaled a huge cloud of grey tobacco smoke. 'Ah! 'as better! Nothin' smells as good as a full pipe of 'baccy.' She quickly took another puff, then handed the pipe back to Ernie. She wiped her mouth on the back of her hand, and turning towards Letty with a warm smile said, 'Would yer mind takin' me out to the lav' please, Letty?'

Letty looked up with a surprised start. 'Er – no, of course not, Mrs –'

'I'll take yer!' interrupted Ernie suddenly.

'I asked Letty,' insisted Annie, who was not only blind, but also an invalid and confined to a wheelchair. 'Anyway, I want her to 'ave a look at my garden.'

Ernie grunted as he eased himself down into his armchair again. 'Garden! Junk 'eap more like!'

'It may be a junk 'eap to you Ern 'Obbs, but it's a garden ter me.' Then she turned to Letty and smiled again. 'Thank you, dearie. Let's go.'

As she rose from the table, Letty flicked an awkward glance at Oliver. Then she positioned herself behind Annie's antiquated wheelchair, and pushed it out of the room.

In the back yard outside, the lavatory was hardly bigger than a cupboard. In the summer it was full of bluebottles, and in the winter it was freezing cold. Annie didn't really want to use it, of course. It was merely an excuse to get to talk to Letty on her own. As Letty squeezed the wheelchair through the tight fit of the back-yard door, she could already hear Oliver and his father shouting again in the parlour.

'Sling yer 'ook, Sam!' said Annie as she and Letty emerged into the yard.

His mother's voice was enough to send young Sam scuttling

off back into the house but before he went he managed a shy, endearing smile at Letty, who smiled back. She felt quite sorry for the poor kid. There seemed to be no place where he was welcome – except the street outside.

'I got tulips in that old tub,' said Annie, looking towards the back wall where the remains of the family's previous tin bath, now full of black London earth, was perched on two rows of bricks. 'Course it's not the right time o' year for 'em, but it won't be all that long before they start poppin' their 'eads out again for me.' There was a sharp nip in the air, and Letty took off her coat and wrapped it around Annie's shoulders. 'Don't you worry about me, dearie,' said Annie, looking up at Letty, trying to form her own picture of her. 'I'm a tough old cabbage. I don't feel the cold.'

Letty pulled the coat tightly around Annie's shoulders. 'Neither do I.' She tried hard not to let Annie feel her shivering.

Annie turned her head towards the old tin tub again. 'I loves tulips. Sometimes when I'm 'ere on my own in the springtime, I comes out just to feel them. They stand up ever so proud and firm – real show-offs. Mind you, I don't know what colour they all are, but I can guess. Red, yeller and pink. They're my favourite – the pink.' She smiled to herself, and leaned her head to one side. 'I talk to 'em, y'know. And they talk back – well, sometimes. I tell yer, I get more sense out of them tulips than I get out of me own family.'

As she, too, gazed in the direction of the flowers Letty wondered to herself why Annie was telling her all this. All she knew was that she liked the woman. In fact she'd liked her the moment she'd first stepped into Annie's parlour.

'Y'know Letty, you mustn't take too much notice of my Ern,' Annie went on. 'He means well.'

Letty tucked her coat snugly around Annie's shoulders. 'I know he does, Mrs Hobbs.' Although they were so different,

Letty felt an affinity with Oliver's mother. She liked her dignity and simplicity, her quiet, gentle nature. Annie looked much older than her fifty-seven years, and Letty could understand why. Even though she had been crippled since falling from a ladder twenty years ago, and blinded by a severe bout of sugar diabetes, Annie had tried to care for her family as best she could. She allowed Ernie to peel the potatoes, but she did the washing for the entire family, and that included the mangling and ironing. But what made Annie so special in Letty's mind was her obvious shrewdness.

'Yer know why they fight like that, don't yer? Olly and 'is dad, I mean.' Annie's sightless eyes surveyed her garden in the darkness of her private world. ''E's Ern's favourite, y'see. 'E finks I don't know, but I do. They're so alike both of 'em – obstinate ter the last!'

Letty thought about this for a moment before answering. Yes. What Annie was saying made sense. Oliver and his father were clearly very close. Maybe the reason Ernie was kicking up so much fuss was because he didn't want Oliver to leave home. 'I'm sure you're both fond of all your children, Mrs Hobbs.'

'If you're goin' ter marry my Olly, don't yer fink it's about time yer started callin' me "Mum"?'

Letty was taken completely by surprise. After what had happened in the parlour a few minutes ago, the last thing she expected was to be considered a future daughter-in-law by either of Oliver's parents. Before she had time to say anything, Letty suddenly felt Annie reaching up to clasp her hand which was resting on the back of the wheelchair.

'Will yer 'ave kids, Letty?'

Letty felt the warmth seeping through from Annie's hand into her own. 'Of course I will – Mum.'

'Not too many though. I 'ad five. *That* was too many. But I wouldn't swap none of 'em. Even though they've been little perishers in their time. There's nothin' like a family of yer own, Letty my girl. One of these days you'll know what I mean. Plenty of heartbreaks waitin' for yer – but it's worth it. But I want yer to remember somethin'.' Letty bent her head forward closer. 'Never let yer man think he's not the gaffer. That's the trouble wiv men – they got too much pride. Olly's a good boy, but he's got pride too.' Annie was now squeezing Letty's hand so tight that her fingers were turning white. 'As for my Ern,' she whispered. 'Don't you go worryin' yerself about 'im. Whatever 'e says, you're one of us now – you're an 'Obbs. An' I tell yer, no one's more 'appy about that than me.'

With her other hand, Letty hugged Annie and kissed her on the cheek. Then she looked out at her future mother-in-law's kingdom. Somehow it didn't look like a junk-heap to her either.

It was some months now since William Edginton had left Beatrice for the emotional peace he shared with Amy Lyall in her pawn shop. These days, Number 97 Arlington Square was beginning to look decidedly shabby. The day after William moved out, Mrs Simmons, the housekeeper, gave in her notice. She had only stayed this past year because she respected what she called 'the Master of the house'. To her, Beatrice was a tyrant who had only herself to blame for the breakdown in her marriage. Within a week, Sylvie the parlour-maid suddenly packed her bags and left. It was bound to have happened sooner or later, for Beatrice was clearly taking out all her frustrations on the poor girl. The result of these staff defections meant that Beatrice was left to cope on her own, and it was a disaster. Layers of dust were forming on every piece of furniture, and the front door step and path were hardly ever swept. Young Nicky, of course, was no help. Like his mother, he wouldn't have known how to wash up a plate or boil an egg if he tried, so the order of the day, most days, was chaos. Beatrice's only hope was Letty. Each evening she waited for her to come home from the munitions factory so that she could cook supper and do the household chores that Beatrice would never dream of tackling herself. As long as Letty was around, Beatrice found no need to employ further staff, for William was providing the minimum of financial support, at least until Beatrice had agreed to a divorce, which so far she was firmly resisting. Somehow, though, it had never occurred to Beatrice that Letty might not always be around.

'Marry my daughter? Young man, have you taken leave of your senses?' Beatrice wasn't prepared for this meeting. She couldn't believe that it was actually happening. And yet there they were, standing before her in her own living-room, Letty and this man she had brought home with her. What *could* Letty see in him, she wondered. Just look at him in that cheap, ill-fitting suit straight out of a pawn shop. He couldn't even stand upright without leaning heavily on a walking stick. A cripple! Imagine the very idea! Even the man's name had a rebellious sound to it. Oliver Hobbs! How *could* anyone in their right mind want to marry someone with a name like Hobbs!

But Oliver wasn't going to be put off. He straightened up, took a deep breath, and replied firmly, 'I love Letty, Mrs Edginton. An' she loves me. That's all I care about.'

Beatrice tried not to panic. As Oliver spoke, she was already making her way to her armchair in front of the fireplace. 'Marriage needs a great deal more than love, Mr Hobbs – that I can assure you.' And she meant what she said. Ever since William had left her, she had spent hour upon hour alone in her bedroom, trying to assess the years she had lived with him. Nothing made any sense to her. William had clearly never loved her, that was perfectly obvious. What she had never taken the trouble to find out, however, was why. 'May I ask you how you would intend to support my daughter?'

Letty was not going to let her mother intimidate Oliver. She took hold of his hand, and held it tightly by her side. 'As soon as he's well again, Olly's going to get a job on the underground. He can make a very good living as a ticket collector.'

Beatrice clasped the arms of her chair. 'A ticket collector? On the – underground?'

Letty squeezed Oliver's hand tightly. 'It's a good, sound job, mother! Isn't it, Olly? She turned to look up into his face. Her eyes were glowing with eagerness. 'You have to know a lot about fares and routes and things . . .'

Beatrice suddenly lost control. 'For God's sake, will you stop this! You're talking utter nonsense, Letty, and you know it! It would be absurd for two people like you to get married. Anyone could see that. You're from different social backgrounds. If you marry someone like this, you'll spend the rest of your life in a pokey little room somewhere in the East End.'

Letty stared straight at her mother in defiance. 'I'd be proud to spend the rest of my life in a pokey little room anywhere,' she lashed back, with more force and determination than even she had thought possible, 'as long as it was with someone I love!'

'Love! Love! *Love*!' snorted Beatrice, quickly rising from her chair to pace the room. 'That's all anyone can talk about. They never think about what the word means, about how it can break you into little pieces and throw you to the wind!' She suddenly swung round, her back towards the window, leaving her outline a silhouette against the morning light. 'Young man. I want you to know that I utterly refuse your request to marry my daughter.'

Letty immediately snapped back. 'Why, mother? Why?'

Oliver turned to go. 'I've 'ad enough of this.'

'No, Olly!' Letty quickly blocked his exit and linked arms with him. 'Don't let her bully you. That's just what she wants!'

Beatrice was now convinced she had Oliver on the defensive. 'Go back to your own people, *Mr* Hobbs.' Her voice was quiet and confident. 'Everyone should stick to their own kind.'

Oliver, who was already half-way to the door, stopped, and turned slowly. Although the light streaming through the window was shining straight into his eyes, he could clearly see the outline of Beatrice's silhouette. It immediately reminded him of the last time he had seen such an image, in the trenches out in France, during one of those endless dawn raids by Jerry. This bloke was suddenly standing on top of the sandbags, with fixed bayonet pointing straight down at him. Without a moment's hesitation, Oliver had fired his rifle at him, and the figure had just collapsed with a thump into the trench beside him. He'd turned out to be a kid of no more than seventeen, typical Jerry, blond hair, blue eyes, a couple of teenage pimples on one cheek. Oliver had poked cautiously at him with his rifle. He was stone dead, and as he lay there, just as real and vulnerable as anyone else.

'Yer know, Mrs Edginton, it's a funny thing,' Oliver was talking to Beatrice's silhouette, pointing his walking stick at her. 'You oughta meet my ole man. You 'an 'im'd get on like an 'ouse on fire. Yer see, he finks exactly the same way as you about all this. 'E reckons workin'-class people should stick ter their own kind, too.'

Beatrice's outline moved slightly. 'Thank God we share something in common.'

Oliver smiled. 'That's right. Fact is, my ole man don't

really know any uvver kind. He prefers it that way. In fact, as far as 'e's concerned, there ain't any uvver kind – 'cept 'is own. 'E don't believe we're all made of the same flesh an' blood.'

Without another word, Oliver turned and left the room. Letty was about to follow him, when Beatrice quickly moved away from the window and into the light. 'Letty,' she pleaded. 'Don't leave me, child – *please!*'

Letty stopped briefly, but spoke with her back still turned towards Beatrice. 'Mother. Oliver and I are going to get married.'

Chapter 8

Anyone searching for the Church of St Barnabas in Islington usually had a hard time locating it. Tucked away in a back street off the Hornsey Road, it was usually concealed from view by overgrown oak and elm trees, especially during the summer months. Most of the building looked in need of repair, with chunks of large masonry slabs missing from the façade and small steeple. But its charm was endearing, especially the narrow portico which was always kept spotlessly clean by the same two lady volunteers, one of whom worked in a local fish-and-chip shop.

When Letty first agreed to marry Oliver, it was on the understanding that they wait until the summer, when she could save up enough money for both of them to 'get started'. To Letty, getting started meant being utterly independent of other people, and not getting into debt. She chose St Barnabas' Church for her wedding because it was situated just fifteen minutes' walk from where her close friends, Tilly and Bill Brooks lived. Letty had first met Tilly at the munitions factory, where they worked on the same bench. Tilly was a rough diamond, who took no nonsense from anybody, but she had a heart of gold and a wonderful sense of humour; she was full of laughter and jokes that were at times, to say the least, bawdy. Although she came from an East End barrow-boy family herself, she had felt great sympathy for the way Letty was initially teased mercilessly at work, and it had been thanks to Tilly's threats – sometimes half joking, at other times deadly serious – to bash up the other girls that Letty was finally accepted as one of the gang.

Although it was still early August, the weather had been somewhat indifferent of late, and as Letty set out from Tilly and Bill's small terraced house in Leslie Street, just off the Caledonian Road, lumpy grey clouds were hanging down from the sky, threatening a damp wedding. But by the time bride and groom reached the church, there were, in Letty's words, 'enough patches of blue in the sky to make a pair of sailor's trousers'. In fact, by the time the ceremony was over, there were no clouds to be seen anywhere, and what followed was a veritable heat wave.

Ever since Letty had moved in with Tilly and Bill, after leaving home during the autumn of the previous year, the only money she had was the paltry earnings she was making at her new job, stuffing hairs into brushes in a paint-brush factory in Camden Road. Much to Oliver's disapproval, however, she had since managed to get an evening job too, as an office-cleaner in the City. It didn't pay much, but it did help her save up for her wedding dress. It wasn't a real wedding dress, white with veils and that sort of thing, but instead a neat, little cotton dress in one of Letty's favourite colours – pale yellow. Her pride and joy though was her hat, a kind of bucket shape, with a bluebird fixed to the side of it for good luck. The night before, Tilly had given Letty a home-perm, and her hair was held together with masses of small, tight curls. Tilly had also provided the posy Letty was carrying; all of the flowers in it came from the few beds in Bill's back yard in Leslie Street: one or two roses, some daisies, anemones, and even a few buttercups.

To Letty's great delight, Oliver had, for the first time in his life, a brand new suit. He hadn't paid for it himself, for he was still unemployed after several long spells in hospital having sporadic operations on his wounded leg. It was his mother, Annie, who had provided the cash. She had saved up just enough for such an occasion, taking sixpence each week from the three shillings Ernie provided for food and household expenses. The suit itself was double-breasted and navy-blue, and it had to be said that Oliver looked very handsome and dashing in it. But his new starched collar was clearly too tight; he pulled and tugged at it every few minutes. And Oliver had learnt a great deal about bull-shine during his square-bashing days in the Army: you could have seen your face reflected in his shoes. The moment Letty joined her boy at the altar, she stared at him with such pride, as she realised he had obstinately discarded his walking stick for the duration of the ceremony.

St Barnabas' was clearly too big for the number of wedding guests, and those attending hardly filled the first two pews. Beatrice Edginton had refused to have anything to do with the occasion and, to Letty's deep sadness and anger, her young brother Nicky was also forbidden to attend. Therefore, Letty's side consisted only of Tilly Brooks, two girls from the paint-brush factory with their boyfriends, and Old Smudge from Arlington Square. Letty had naturally sent an invitation to her father, but when he indicated that he wanted to bring Amy Lyall with him, she quickly withdrew it. William had been hurt by Letty's refusal to accept Amy, so he'd reluctantly decided not to attend his daughter's wedding without her. Oliver's father also stubbornly refused to attend the wedding, so, apart from his best man Bill Brooks, Oliver's pews consisted of his mother, who had been pushed to the church in her wheelchair by Vi; young Sam, who had been kicking an old tin can in the street right up to a few minutes before the ceremony; Mr and Mrs Potts from the newspaper shop where Oliver used to do his early morning round, and two of his favourite nurses from the

102

military hospital at Richmond. At the back of the church, there was also a sprinkling of people who had just wandered in from the street to pass the time of day. Letty was disappointed that Oliver's three elder brothers, Gus, Lou and Albert, two of whom were still in the Army themselves, had decided to ignore the wedding. But she was aware that ever since Oliver had been disabled from the Army, all his brothers, with the exception of young Sam, had grown more distant from him. The three elder Hobbs siblings were a proud, tough bunch, who always stuck together as a team. To their minds Oliver's wound was self-inflicted, caused by his own carelessness on the battlefield. Letty also knew that they resented her presence and, maybe because of the posh way she spoke, they felt embarrassed in her company. She had no choice but to accept their feelings but, even so, she hoped that one day they would come to accept her.

The wedding ceremony itself was quite short, not much more than twenty minutes or so. But whilst the vicar was reading a long passage from the Bible, Letty's mind kept wandering back over her life so far. She was happy, so deliriously happy. After all that had happened, she couldn't understand how she could suddenly be so lucky. Her only real sadness was that Tom couldn't be there to see her being married to Oliver. She knew he would have approved of the wonderful boy who, in a few minutes' time, would be her husband.

When it came to the time for Bill Brooks to pass the wedding ring to Oliver there was a great deal of sniffing from Tilly, who later pretended she had had a bad attack of catarrh. And young Sam got a hard whack on the back of the head from Vi, who took the opportunity to reprimand him for picking his nose all through the ceremony. At the end of the service, Letty and Oliver exchanged a kiss. It was the part Letty liked best but, as they embraced, she was amazed to see that Oliver's eyes were filled with tears. It made her love him all the more.

And so, despite the opposition of both Beatrice Edginton and Ernie Hobbs, Letty and Oliver were married. After signing the Register, they filed out of St Barnabas' arm-in-arm, followed by their small band of relations and loyal friends. There was no organist to play them out with the 'Wedding March'. Letty had already decided that the fee of two shillings and sixpence was far too much, and money that could be put to a far more practical use.

Within a few minutes, the shouts and laughter and confetti-throwing outside the church gradually disappeared, as bride and groom, and their guests, made their way to a get-together at Tilly and Bill's place. Inside the church, all was quiet again. The afternoon sun was streaming through a small oval window high above the altar, leaving deep shadows in some of the darker recesses on one side of the aisle. When silence was finally achieved, something stirred in one of the dark corners behind a stone column at the rear of the pews. After a moment or so, the echoed clip-clop sound of a woman's high heeled shoes was heard moving on the stone floor towards a side door half-way down the aisle. The door opened and closed quietly, and St Barnabas' was now fully at rest.

The residents of Leslie Street were only too aware that they were going to get very little sleep that night. Although blackout restrictions were still in force, nobody seemed to take much notice of them any more, for over the last months there had been no sign of the dreaded Zeppelins or fighter bombers. The summer sun had only just set, so it was not yet dark. However, the knees-up in the front-room of Number 22 was in full swing, and the shouts and laughter were exuberant.

The loudest voice of all was, of course, Vi Hobbs's. Sipping from a glass of her favourite port and lemon, she shrieked at every joke the men told. Nobody could get away from her, because Tilly and Bill's room was minute, with hardly enough space for people to sit. For Oliver, his sister's presence was almost as bad as being trapped in the trenches. It was even worse when she started to sing. 'If I Were A Tulip'. Not least because Vi had a truly terrible voice, a kind of half-baked, quivering soprano that left everyone stunned into silence when she'd finished.

'That was wonderful Vi. Really wonderful.' It was left to Letty to relieve the atmosphere of total disbelief. 'You never told me you could sing like that.'

Vi fluttered her eyes winsomely. 'Well, I only get the chance to sing on 'igh days and 'olidays,' she purred. 'Let's face it, my bruvver don't get married every day of the week, do 'e?'

Oliver tugged at his braces, and downed the last gulp from his glass of brown ale. 'Wiv a voice like that, fank Gord I don't!'

Everyone roared with laughter, but Vi looked hurt. Oliver was just like her other brothers, she thought, always teasing, always coarse. It never occurred to any of them that she had feelings. The best response was to sulk. So she very haughtily sat down on the settee, and tried to look vulnerable. But it was no coincidence that she chose to sit beside the young male guest whom she had been talking to after the service.

Letty started to help Tilly clear some of the dirty plates which littered the room. To her it seemed none of them had stopped eating since they got back from the church. Despite the fact that there still wasn't much food in the shops, Tilly had prepared a wonderful spread for the wedding party: sausage rolls, brawn sandwiches, pigs' trotters, winkles and whelks, rock cakes, and her speciality, bread pudding. Bill took care of the booze. He'd chatted up the landlord of his local and got most of the brown ale and stout at a discount. He got nothing off the spirits though and he had to charge Oliver full whack for the three bottles of black-market gin, two bottles of whisky, and Vi's port. Bill was an obliging and generous man. He'd do anything for anyone as long as they didn't take him for granted. He always resented the fact that because his eyesight wasn't good enough, he'd been unable to join Lord Kitchener's Army like the rest of his mates. But he worked hard at his job in the 'Cally' Road as foreman of a local food-packaging factory. He and Tilly had only been married a year themselves and because both of them were earning, they were able to rent Number 22, which was just right for setting up home. As a couple they were well-matched, and proving themselves to be loyal friends to Letty and Oliver.

After refilling Oliver's glass and his own, Bill perched on the arm of the chair Oliver had virtually taken over for the evening. 'So mate, 'ow much longer d'yer reckon we're gonna 'ave to put up wiv this war?'

Oliver took a gulp of brown, which left a rim of froth on his upper lip. 'All over by Christmas I say.'

'Christmas! You're jokin'!'

'Obvious, in't it?' Oliver wiped the froth away with the back of his hand. 'We in't 'ad no Zepps over for months now. We got Jerry on the run, I tell yer.' Then, lowering his voice so that he could not be overheard, he said confidently, 'Ever since we crossed the Somme, they nearly shit themselves. I tell yer, once we get our 'ands on Kaiser Bill, it'll be all over.'

Bill rubbed a hand through his greased blond hair. 'Well, I 'ope you're right. I'm sick of the bloody war. Let's get the lads back and get the Arsenal open again. I could do wiv some decent football, what say you, Oll?'

Oliver knew Bill meant no harm, but what he had said stuck in Oliver's gullet. All he could do was smile falsely and reply, 'Yeah – right.' Oliver's mind was on all those lads who wouldn't be coming home to watch or play football. He could suddenly see so many of their faces now, blokes he hardly knew, who'd shared the trenches with him, and ended up face down in some muddy French field with a bullet in their back. As he watched Letty pottering around the room with Tilly, he thought back to her brother, Tom, and that night they had tossed a coin to see who should go over the top. He had still not told Letty about that brief meeting, that let alone the fact that he'd let Tom go out instead of himself. He wasn't sure if he would ever be able to.

'Come on Vi! What yer mopin' around for?' Bill was suddenly on his feet. 'You 'aven't 'ad a tango wiv me all night!'

Vi screeched with laughter, as she allowed Bill to drag her up from the settee where she was making little headway with the young male guest. 'Don't be silly Bill! I can't do no tango. Not in this dress. It's too tight!'

'I know it is. Why d'yer fink I asked!'

Vi shrieked and everyone joined in her laughter. Tilly went straight to the piano and started playing a tango. It didn't sound too much like a tango, for she could only play music on the piano by ear. But at least it gave Vi and Bill the chance to give everyone a laugh, as long as they all made quite sure they kept their feet out of the way, for Vi was a big girl, and there was little space for dancing in the tiny front-room.

As the room vibrated, Oliver's eyes were firmly fixed on Letty, who was doubled up with laughter at Vi and Bill's antics. He couldn't believe how lucky he was to have someone like Letty as his wife – he a cripple, with no hope of supporting her in the way she'd been used to. Oh yes,

Letty was special all right. She wasn't like any other girl he'd known. She really loved and trusted him. Trusted him? Oliver suddenly felt the blood rising to his cheeks, and it wasn't just because of the booze. No. He felt overwhelming guilt. He knew how much Tom Edginton had meant to his sister, and yet he had been responsible for sending Tom to his death. Well, maybe not directly responsible – but as good as. How *could* he go on keeping this secret from his own wife? How could they start their lives together under such a cloud of deceit? As he watched Letty clapping her hands together in time to the tango, Oliver felt as though the whole of his guts was about to rip apart. He just wanted to be alone with her, to hug and hold her, to tell her what he'd done before it was too late. Quietly, he put down his glass, eased himself out of the armchair and grabbed hold of her hand. 'Letty,' he called closely into her ear. 'Come outside. I wanna talk to yer.'

Letty looked alarmed. 'Olly! What's wrong? Is it your leg? Are you in pain?'

'No! Course not!' He led her towards the door. 'I want a minute alone wiv me own wife, if yer don't mind!'

Still bashing out her version of the tango at the piano, Tilly yelled out, 'Ere, watch it you two! It ain't bedtime yet!'

Everyone roared with jeers and laughter as Oliver and Letty quickly slid out of the room.

Letty was blushing a deep red as they reached the passage outside. Oliver closed the door, then virtually pinned her against the wall. This was the moment. If he didn't tell her his secret now, he never would. 'Lett.' The words he had to say were on his lips. 'I've gotta tell yer somefin'.'

Letty stared at him, puzzled and anxious. But there was a long pause, and although Oliver was struggling hard, the words just wouldn't come. 'What is it dear?' Letty now looked concerned. 'Is something wrong?'

Oliver hesitated again, clearly in absolute torment. Then he looked into her eyes, and said finally, 'Give us a kiss, Mrs 'Obbs.'

'Olly!' Letty had no time to protest, for Oliver was already pressing his lips against hers.

'I've bin waitin ter do that ever since church this mornin'.' And he kissed her again, longer this time. 'You're the prettiest woman I've ever seen in my 'ole life. Yer know that, don't yer, Lett? I'm a lucky feller, that's the troof.'

Letty took a deep breath, and looked Oliver straight in the eyes. She could see such honesty there, such integrity. For the first time in her life, she had someone who cared for her. Oh, she had loved her Tom, and always would – and he'd loved her. But that was different. Oliver was not her brother. He was her husband, and she longed for the day when she could have his children. And yet, as they stood there in the narrow passage, with its faded floral wallpaper, the jollity of the wedding guests bellowing out from the front-room, Letty felt a moment of anxiety. Ever since she was born she had led a sheltered life. She had never been allowed even to look at a young man, let alone go out with him. Unlike Vi and some of the other girls at the factory, Letty had never slept with a man before. But tonight, she would be sharing the same bed with Oliver, and making love with him. Her nervousness suddenly gave way to a warmth which seeped throughout her entire body. She trusted Oliver. She loved him. That was all that mattered. 'I'm the lucky one,' she said, tenderly kissing him first on the forehead, then on each of his cheeks, and then his lips.

> You are my 'oney, 'oney-suckle,
> I am the bee . . .

Oliver started to sing the song that had become their own.

He and Letty had sung it together so many times when she took him for a stroll in the grounds of the hospital. Some of the other patients and nursing staff had thought they were mad.

> I'd like to sip the honey sweet,
> From those red lips you see . . .

Letty continued the song, but then stopped abruptly. 'We ought to get back, dear. It isn't sociable.'

Oliver refused to let her go. 'I'm sorry it weren't no fancy weddin', Letty. I promise I'll make it up to yer one day.'

Letty looked up with a start and stared him straight in the face. 'Oliver Hobbs! What *are* you talking about? It was a lovely wedding!'

For a brief moment, Oliver looked depressed. 'Oh no it wasn't,' he said, pulling her closer and hugging her around the waist. 'No organ playin' or church bells, no bridesmaids or weddin' cake, not even a 'orseshoe.'

'Who cares about wedding cakes!' snapped Letty firmly. 'We had far too much food as it was. Just look at that lovely bread pudding Tilly made us.' Letty had in fact tried to get Tilly some sugar and currants to make a cake, but since the Government had introduced rationing in February, it was impossible to get enough.

Oliver was still gloomy. 'And just look at that bit o' brass on yer finger. It in't worf a light!'

Letty sighed deeply, took hold of Oliver's shoulders, and shook him. 'Please stop saying such things!' She held up her hand and kissed her ring. 'I love my wedding ring. It's not how much it costs that matters, it's what it means. Olly dear, don't you understand? You could put a curtain ring on my finger, and it would mean just as much. Believe me, I have nothing to regret about today. Nothing.'

Oliver was watching her closely. Despite her assurances, he now knew her well enough to know that she did have misgivings about something. 'Nuffink, eh? Nuffink at all?'

'Well, I have to admit I'd have felt really happy if your dad could have come with your mum to the church this afternoon.'

Oliver smiled wryly, and shrugged his shoulders. He knew from the word go that his father would never turn up at his wedding. Ernie Hobbs was a law unto himself, thought Oliver. Not in a million years would he admit he was wrong, even if he knew he was. And yet, there was a moment, just a fleeting moment, when Oliver thought his old man was regretting his attitude. It had happened just as he was leaving home to go to the church. As he was hurrying out of the front door, Ernie had called to him from the scullery: 'Don't you keep that girl waitin'!'

It had only been a passing remark, but to Oliver it had meant a hell of a lot. And so it was difficult for him to be really dismissive in his reply to Letty. 'It's no good, girl. Yer can't put feelin's where there in't none.'

Now it was Letty's turn to look glum. 'I must say, I think it was unkind of Mother not to come. She never even had the decency to answer the invitation.' Letty had not heard from Beatrice since leaving home soon after bringing Oliver to meet her. Although Letty always knew what her mother's response would be, she had kept hoping that Beatrice would eventually feel the need at least to contact her. But it was her brother Nicky she felt really guilty about. Now left at home alone with his mother, Letty constantly worried about how the boy would manage to cope with Beatrice's moods and violent tempers. But Nicky had always been the strongest of the three Edginton children, and on each occasion Letty had gone to meet him outside his school, he'd appeared to be taking it all in his stride. On one occasion,

Letty had considered calling on her mother, but once she reached Arlington Square, she'd lost her nerve. Still she was concerned for Beatrice. 'Not lookin' 'erself these days,' Old Smudge had told her. 'Got a real stoop in 'er shoulders, and she don't seem ter bother ter comb 'er 'air any more.' Nonetheless, Letty thought that her mother might have made the effort to attend her own daughter's wedding, if only out of curiosity.

'Yer muvver *was* there, Lett.'

Letty looked up at Oliver with a jolt. She wasn't sure if she'd heard right. 'What?'

'I saw the old girl meself. She was hidin' at the back of the church when you arrived.'

'Olly! Is this true?'

'You can ask Bill. He saw 'er too. She was cryin' her eyeballs out when we left the church tergevver.'

Letty's eyes were already filling with tears. 'Oh Olly! Why didn't you tell me? We should have done something. I – I should have spoken to her!'

Oliver remained calm. He took her face gently in his hands and said, 'No, Lett. If yer ma wanted to speak to us, she'd 'ave done so. She did what *she* wanted ter do. We 'ave ter respect 'er fer that.' Oliver pulled his wife towards him and hugged her.

'Come on you two lovebirds! No more hanky-panky!' Bill Brooks was peering out of the front-room door. 'Time for that later!'

As Letty and Oliver returned to the party, there was a loud cheer. Vi had collapsed on to the settee, exhausted, and it was almost impossible to see across the room because nearly everybody seemed to be smoking.

Bill waited for Letty and Oliver to settle down together, then stood in the middle of what little space there was left in the middle of the room. 'Right then, ladies and gents!

112

Time to raise your glasses to the 'appy couple!' Everyone made a quick scramble to find their glass, and make sure there was something in it. 'I give you the toast. To two of the nicest people you could ever wish to know. The bride and groom, Gord bless 'em! Letty and Oliver 'Obbs!'

Everyone stood up and yelled, 'Letty and Oliver!' Then there was a chorus of 'For they are jolly good fellows', at the end of which everyone downed a good gulp of their drink. Then Tilly bawled out, 'Speech! Speech!' Immediately, everyone took up the chant.

'Come on Oll!' Bill was energetically trying to help Oliver to his feet. 'You've gotta say somethin' mate!'

Oliver was in a cold panic, struggling to pull away from Bill. 'No, Bill! I can't! I don't know how to make no speech, honest I don't!' In desperation, he quickly turned to Letty. 'Go on Lett! You know how to speak. *You* say somefin'!'

Letty was completely taken aback. 'No, Olly – I can't! It's not my place to make a speech. It's your job, not mine!

Sweat was pouring off Oliver's forehead, and he was practically pleading with her. 'It's no use, Lett. I can't do it. For Gord's sake, help me out!'

Unable to resist these pleas, Letty raised herself up to the accompaniment of loud cheers and applause from everyone in the room. For a moment her mouth went dry. She hadn't the faintest idea what to say – she had never made a public speech in her life. But then she suddenly remembered the time Beatrice took her and Nicky along to a talk her father gave to a Gunsmiths' Society in the City of London. So she took a deep breath, cleared her throat, and spoke, 'Ladies and gentlemen. Oliver and I . . .' She could hear her own voice, and it sounded terribly formal. 'We just wanted to say . . .' As she looked around, she realised that she was amongst friends, hers and Oliver's. From that moment on,

113

she smiled, and became her own self again. 'Oh, we just want to thank you all for coming to our wedding today. It was such a lovely service. I'll never forget it as long as I live.' And she thanked Tilly and Bill for all they'd done over the past months. Then she took another deep breath and continued, 'The fourth of August, 1918 is a day I'll remember all the days of my life. It's funny to think that it's exactly four years to the day that the war started.'

Everyone jeered as Vi yelled, 'Feels more like twenty-four bleedin' years!' But then they all shushed again for Letty. '. . . But I'll remember this day more than anything because of the way Olly got to the church – on his own *two* feet!' This nearly brought the ceiling down, and everyone cheered Oliver, who was trying to look inconspicuous in the corner.

Before Letty could say anything else, there was a knock on the street door outside. 'All right, I'll go!' called Tilly, who quickly picked her way over everyone's feet, and left the room.

'Like all of you,' continued Letty, now gaining confidence, 'Olly and I have got a lot of things we want to do in our future years. It can't be long now before this terrible war comes to an end. Every day, people seem to talk about nothing else but the armistice, and how soon it'll come. But when it *does* come, I hope Mr Lloyd George will see to it that this country becomes a fit place for our boys to live in again. I hope he makes sure that they all come back to decent jobs – because that's what they fought for, isn't it?' As she finished off, Letty fidgeted unconsciously with her wedding ring. 'Ladies and gentlemen, what I'm trying to say is that when we're living in the future, I hope none of us will ever be too busy to remember the past.'

At this everyone cheered and stamped their feet, until Tilly came rushing back into the room. She was clearly very excited. 'Letty! Letty! There's someone here to see you.' She opened the door and called gently to someone in the passage outside. 'Will you come in, please.'

There was a total hush. Everyone turned to look at the door, as a small, frail-looking woman came in. Her clothes were shabby, and her long, uncombed hair hung down her back almost to her waist. It was Beatrice Edginton. She looked awkward and self-conscious, as she stood there, unwittingly doing up a button which had become unfastened on her grubby-looking dress. 'I . . . I'm sorry if I'm butting in, Letty, but I . . .'

Letty ran straight to her, and threw her arms around her. 'Oh Mother! Of course you're not butting in.' Then she turned back apprehensively towards Oliver. 'Is she, Olly?'

Oliver stared in silence for a brief moment, then gradually eased himself up from his armchair. 'Course not,' he smiled supportively. 'You're very welcome, Mrs Edginton.'

'Thank you for coming, Mother.' Letty kissed her on the cheek, and smiled gratefully. 'I can't tell you how happy you've made me.'

Beatrice made a great effort to smile. But, as always, it didn't come easily.

'But where's Nicky?' asked Letty. 'Why didn't you bring him, too?'

Beatrice lowered her eyes guiltily. 'Nicky's gone to spend the night with his father. It's what he wanted.' Trying hard not to notice the embarrassed response to this from Letty, she swallowed hard and offered, 'All I wanted to say Letty is, well – if you and your – your husband don't have anywhere to stay until you have a place of your own, you're welcome to have your old room back, for as long as you like.'

Letty exchanged a quick, knowing glance with Oliver before answering. Both of them knew how much it had cost Beatrice to make such a gesture. 'Thanks all the same,

115

Mother, but we're going to stay on a bit longer with our friends here.'

Beatrice looked awkward again. 'Oh, that's all right then. I just thought I'd make sure.' She started to step backwards towards the door. 'Well, I'll be on my way then. Goodnight everyone. God bless you, Letty.' Then, taking a deep breath, she managed to force herself to say, 'You too, Oliver.'

Oliver immediately went over to Beatrice. 'Don't go – *Mum*. Why don't you stay on fer a bit? We'd like yer to, 'onest.' Then he called to everyone in the room. 'Wouldn't we?'

There was a chorus of 'Yeah!', and shouts of 'Come and sit down 'ere, Ma!' 'Over 'ere, Mrs Edginton!', 'What'll yer 'ave ter drink, gel?'

Beatrice was flustered and overwhelmed. 'No. No, I don't think so, thank you. I'd better be on my way.'

Oliver gave her a warm smile. 'Letty would like it,' he said, gently, kindly. 'So would I.'

The moment was too much for Beatrice, and her eyes filled with tears. It was too much for Letty, too. She threw her arms around her visitor, hugged her, and with a cry of 'Oh Mum!' burst into tears.

'Watch out!' yelled Bill. 'It's the bleedin' waterworks!'

The emotional tension was broken with this and within moments Beatrice was being introduced all round. To Letty's absolute astonishment she discovered that her mother had taken a recent liking to stout. It wasn't long before the party became a real knees-up, and Beatrice seemed to enjoy herself for the first time in many a long year. But when the celebrations moved into the early hours of the morning, everyone's energy started to flag a little. So it was left to Letty to persuade her mother to play the piano, something she also hadn't done in a long time. At first she resisted, protesting that she couldn't play anything without sheet music. But finally she admitted that there was one song that she might just remember without too much difficulty. 'Pray silence for our star of the evenin'!' yelled a now weary Bill Brooks. 'Ma Edginton!' Beatrice flicked one of her rather scolding looks at Bill for being so familiar, but quickly realised it was a term of welcome. Then she nervously took her place at Tilly's old joanna, and placed her fingers on the keyboard.

The pavements of Leslie Street outside were now deserted, and not even the slightest breeze was taming the humid August night. Suddenly, a gentle sound filtered out from the front room of Number 22. It was the tinkling of a piano, accompanied by a sweet, poignant voice singing words that seemed to rise up into the night air and drift off into the heavens . . .

> Just a song at twilight,
> When the lights are low,
> And the flickering shadows
> Softly come and go.
> Though the heart be weary,
> Sad the day and long,
> Still to us at twilight
> Comes Love's sweet song,
> Comes Love's Old Sweet Song.

Chapter 9

For the past twenty years or so, Reginald Henry Cotton had been trading as a mobile chandler in the Islington, Harringay and Tottenham districts of north London. His horse and green-and-gold-coloured shop on wheels were a familiar sight in the streets and whenever it appeared every kid in the neighbourhood turned out to follow it. The main attraction was, of course, Brunswick, Mr Cotton's old cart-horse. Brunswick had a gentle manner, and for a piece of sugar would allow you to stroke his nose for as long as you wanted. Tilly Brooks was one of many who rushed out of the house with a shovel and bucket when Mr Cotton's shop turned into Leslie Street, for Brunswick's droppings were perfect manure for Bill's roses in the back yard. The groceries in the shop itself were good value, especially the dried peas, which Mr Cotton sold by the pint; they made excellent home-made pease pudding. Mr Cotton himself was a dumpy little man who always insisted on dressing formally. Never once did anyone ever remember seeing him wear an alternative to his three-piece navy-blue suit and bowler hat. His gold watch and chain, which stretched across his waistcoat, had been in his family for nearly a hundred and fifty years and he was never seen without it. But, although Mr Cotton was quiet-mannered and soft-spoken, he was a shrewd businessman whose main source of income was the many properties he rented out.

Letty first met Mr Cotton when she went out to the mobile shop to buy some pumice powder for cleaning Tilly's front doorstep. Mr Cotton liked Letty, mainly because she was well-spoken and had impeccable manners. And so when she asked him about the possibility of renting a room somewhere, he promised to keep her in mind if and when one of his tenants decided to leave. However, despite Letty's weekly requests for news, it was three months from the asking before Mr Cotton finally had somewhere to offer.

Citizen Road in 1918 had a varied selection of residents. One or two of the houses were occupied by respectable lower-middle-class families, and the rest, rather neglected by their landlords, had rooms on each floor which were rented out to occupants of somewhat lesser means. But it was a pleasant enough neighbourhood, close to the busy Hornsey Road, and the flourishing shopping centre of Holloway. Its main disadvantage, however, was that the view from its rear rooms overlooked the track of the main London and North-Eastern Railway Company. It was such a room that Mr Cotton was offering Letty and Oliver.

'Of course, it's not Buckingham Palace, mind you. But with a coat of distemper here and there, I'd say you could turn this into a really nice place.'

Whilst Mr Cotton was giving his hard sell, Oliver was looking around. What he saw did not impress him. The room, on the first floor of the house, was a fair size all right, but it was in great need of repair and decoration. Half the wallpaper was hanging from the walls, the ceiling had damp patches, and the bare floorboards were badly stained and chipped. Its saving grace however was that it was bright and airy. This was due to the room's main feature, a huge arc-shaped window which overlooked the railway track. Oliver grunted and wiped his finger across his nose. 'Don't like this pong.'

Mr Cotton had an immediate explanation. 'Ah! That's the damp, you see. Hasn't been lived in since the old lady died. Still, a nice coal fire in the evenings'll soon put that right.'

Oliver particularly hated the stark, grubby furniture. He tried sitting on the settee, but quickly got up again when a twanging spring stuck in his backside.

But Letty felt differently. The moment she entered the room her eyes widened, and she felt her heart thumping excitedly. Of course it was a dump, she thought, but just think what you could do with it. Some nice new wallpaper, a coat of paint (which she could get at a discount from the factory where she worked), scrub that old kitchen-table, re-cover the settee, buy a new double bed in the Cally Road junk-yard – oh it could all look so wonderful! And her greatest joy of all was the window – *that* window! 'How often do the trains go by, Mr Cotton?' she asked, dreamily, staring down at the sparkling narrow railway lines at the end of the back yards.

Mr Cotton climbed the two steps to the window, and joined Letty there. 'Oh, no more than a couple each day at the most. Why, I'd be surprised if . . .'

He had no time to finish what he was going to say, for the room was suddenly shaking to the sound of a train, whistle screeching, roaring past on the track at high speed.

'Bleedin' 'ell!' With every object in the room vibrating as if in an earthquake, Oliver held on to the old kitchen-table with grim determination, for although he had finally discarded his crutches, he was still not too secure on his feet.

Mr Cotton had to shout to be heard above the noise, 'There used to be an old railway station just a bit further down the line there – not a very big one though. It hasn't been used since the war broke out. Somethin' to do with economy cuts, I heard.' The train finally disappeared into the distance, allowing Mr Cotton to lower his voice again. 'I promise you, Mrs Hobbs, you won't have no trouble with noise, not here. You see, the trains don't stop here any more.'

Letty was still in her dream-world, staring out of the window. 'Oh, I don't worry about the noise. I like the sound of trains. They give me a feeling of protection.'

Taken aback, Mr Cotton took off his bowler hat and scratched his head, quizzically. 'Well now – that's nice.'

Oliver, meanwhile, was looking more and more convinced that he hated the place. 'How much d'yer want fer this room then?' he asked.

Mr Cotton came back to him eagerly. 'Three and six. Have to do your own decoratin', of course.'

'Three and six!'

'It's a bargain for this area, I can tell you, Mr Hobbs. Don't forget there *is* a war on.' Even as he spoke, Mr Cotton could have bitten his tongue off. Of course there was a war on, and no one knew it more than Oliver who still limped heavily, and had had to be helped up the stairs. Mr Cotton suddenly found himself spluttering. 'Of course . . . er – if you're not . . . interested in the place . . .'

Letty came to the rescue. 'Mr Cotton, d'you think we could have a few minutes to have a look round on our own?'

Mr Cotton readily agreed, and left the room.

'Three and six!' exploded Oliver the moment the landlord was out of sight. 'It's 'ighway bleedin' robbery, I tell yer!'

'Come over to the window, dear,' called Letty. 'It's a lovely view.'

Oliver picked his way across the uneven floorboards, and when he reached the two steps leading up to the window, Letty was waiting there to help him. 'You call this a luvvly view?' he grumbled as he peered out through the window. 'We're practically on top of the railway line!'

Letty linked arms with him, leaned her head on his

shoulder, and sighed happily. 'Oh, but it's wonderful, Olly. Just think of all the places those trains go to up and down the country.'

'Yeah. Places you and me'll never get the chance ter see in our 'ole lifetime!'

Letty unlinked her arm, then put it around his waist. They were both now staring out of the huge window, the morning sun shining straight into their eyes. 'Stop being so pessimistic, Olly Hobbs! It costs nothing to dream, does it?'

No, it cost nothing to dream all right, thought Oliver. That was one thing he'd certainly learnt from Letty since they got married. Not only was she a perpetual optimist, but she was also more than anything else an incurable daydreamer. To Letty it seemed that the solution to the everyday problems of life lay in hopes and dreams. She refused to believe that anything was as bad as it appeared. She refused to believe that things could never get better. It was an odd characteristic for someone as practical as Letty. And although it worried Oliver, more often than not Letty's practical solution to their problems came from her daydreams. For Oliver, it could sometimes be maddening. 'This room's a dump, Letty,' he said finally. 'It in't worf the money!'

'We can clean it up, can't we? Bit of paint and carbolic, that's all we need. By the time I've finished with this place, it'll be fit for the King himself!'

Oliver pointed to the far corner of the room near the entrance door. 'I saw two large cockroaches goin' down those floorboards.'

'DDT! That'll take care of *them*!'

He shook his head in resignation. He knew he was fighting a losing battle. 'Letty. Are yer tellin' me, yer really *want* this place?'

'It's up to you, Oliver,' she said very formally. '*You* make the decisions, not me.'

Her words brought the first smile all morning to Oliver's face. He knew perfectly well who was making the decisions, but he loved Letty all the more for it. With a sudden urge, he pulled her to him, and kissed her forehead. She in turn kissed his chin, and they finished by hugging tightly, kissing each other fully on the lips.

For the next few minutes, they just stood there, staring out of the window again, voices low and intimate. They had so much to talk over: where they were going to be able to find three shillings and sixpence to pay for the rent each week, and how much would be left over for food and household expenses. Recently Oliver's morale had taken a turn for the worse. The London Underground had rejected his application for a job as a ticket collector, purely because the condition of his leg injury would be a hindrance to himself and to the passengers. And now, deep down, Oliver was convinced that nobody was going to offer a disabled man a job, and he had virtually given up looking for one. Letty, of course, would have none of this. She insisted Oliver keep on trying, and until he found something suitable, she was determined to get evening work, nearer to home this time. It would supplement her job at the paint-brush factory and give them enough to live on. For the first time, she dared to mention this scheme.

'No, Letty! No! No! *No!*' Oliver pulled away from her and leaned against the window with both hands, his head bowed low. 'I'm not gonna live off no wife of mine for the rest of my life,' he snapped. 'I won't do it!'

Letty was thunderstruck by Oliver's outburst. She had never known him to be like this before. She was furious with herself for her stupid lack of sensitivity. Only a few days before, Vi had warned her to be careful with Oliver, insisting he was as proud and obstinate as her father and other brothers. Letty had resented Vi's criticism of her husband

123

but what she hadn't taken into account was that Oliver's leg injury was affecting him not only physically, but also psychologically. 'All I was trying to say,' said Letty, desperately trying to be more tactful, 'was that when the war's over . . .'

Once again Oliver turned from her and flew into a fit of agonised rage. 'When the bloody war's over, fings are going to be exactly the same! Can't you understand that, Letty? Can't you get that into your thick noddle!'

For a brief moment, Letty was hurt. But she was determined not to show it. She and Oliver were having their first row, and it certainly wouldn't be their last one. But Letty knew she was in the wrong, and she had to put it right. So she took a deep breath and said, 'I was going to say, dear, that when the war's over, I wouldn't be surprised if they didn't open up that old railway station again. If they do, I'm sure you'll get a job there.' Oliver remained silent, as she added nervously, 'Just imagine it, Olly. It'll be like going to work in our own back yard.'

There was a pause, which seemed like a lifetime to Letty. Then Oliver turned slowly to look her straight in the face. 'Our own back yard?' he replied, almost quizzically.

Letty nodded her head. 'We can't go on living at Tilly and Bill's forever, dear. I want a home for you and me, Olly. A place we can call our own. A place we can invite our friends and relations back to tea and a chat. A home, Olly! Something both you and me have never really had. I want you and me to start building our future together, and if it has to be in a damp old barn of a place like this, then it's all right with me!'

At the end of Letty's speech, Oliver grinned. 'Cockroaches an' all?'

'Cockroaches and all!'

Oliver grinned wider. 'Then I reckon we've found our-selves an' 'ome – eh, Lett?'

Letty's face beamed with exhilaration, and she threw her arms around Oliver's neck and hugged him. 'Oh Olly . . . !'

The room started to shake again as another train, whistle shrieking, rumbled past at speed. However, it didn't stop at the old station just down the line, because the trains didn't stop there any more.

It was three weeks later before Letty and Oliver were able to move into their room in 'Cockroach House', as they called it, half-way down Citizen Road. On the day they did, Letty lived up to her word setting to work cleaning up the place. First of all it was the decorating. The old wallpaper was stripped off by thoroughly wetting the walls with water, and then scraping with a paint stripper which Bill Brooks had lent them. Oliver tried to help, but he was heavy-handed and left too many digs in the plaster. He did, however, turn out to be a skilful painter, whilst Letty's greatest talent proved to be wallpapering.

The next job was to scrub the old wooden kitchen table thoroughly, which Letty did early one morning before going off to work at the paint-brush factory. Oliver took a dim view of this, for he was trying to have a lie-in. Then she set about scrubbing the bare floorboards, using a strong carbolic. Each day, Oliver watched Letty's energy with utter astonish-ment, unable to believe that this same girl had come from Arlington Square. When the room was finally transformed, she took great pride in proclaiming, 'There you are, Olly. Now we've really got a home!' And Oliver felt he had.

But finding the means to pay the rent was not easy. After finally winning an endless battle with Oliver, Letty got an evening job, scrubbing floors at a local school, which she did in addition to her long hours at the paint-brush factory. Pakeman Street Juniors was in Holloway, nestling comfortably between Hornsey Road on one side and Roden Street on the other. In fact it was in a very convenient position for Letty; just a stone's throw from home. But she didn't get back from the factory until five in the evening, and her job at the school started at six, lasting until ten at night. During those four hours she was expected to clean out the headmaster's office and four classrooms, and scrub the vast area of the wood block floor in the main assembly hall, and the ground floor nursery hall. It was tiring work, but, because the school was trying to save money, Letty was the only cleaner they employed, so it gave her the chance to think a lot. Mainly she thought about Oliver, and the day when they might have their first child. She had already decided that she wanted at least three children, preferably two boys and one girl. But Oliver had told her he didn't want to have any kids, not until he could get a job and keep Letty at home to look after them.

During her evenings at the school, Letty hardly ever met anyone except the occasional teacher working late, or Mr Finch the caretaker. Sometimes Tilly would turn up, clutching a flask of hot tea and a piece of bread pudding, but most nights not a soul appeared and, as she scrubbed, she listened to the sound of bells coming from the Emmanuel Church in nearby Hornsey Road. One evening, however, she did have a visitor.

'I tell you it's not right, Letty.' Vi stood in the middle of the assembly hall, staring in horror at her sister-in-law who was down on her hands and knees. 'You can't keep this up for much longer – not two jobs in one day. You'll crack up.'

Letty waved a dismissive hand. She had already finished half the floor, which was glistening wet in the gaslight. 'Don't talk stupid, Vi. I'm not made of cardboard.' She wrung out her cloth, and said, 'I like being here after school hours. It gives me a chance to think.'

As usual, Vi was looking at her make-up in her handbag mirror as she talked. 'If yer ask me, you're spoilin' that lazy bruvver of mine.'

This angered Letty. Vi was always getting at Oliver, and she had no business to. She snapped back. 'Don't you talk about my Olly like that. He does what he can, and that's a great deal more than some people!'

Vi was taken aback by her outburst. 'All I was sayin' is it's bad for him if you're the one earnin', and he 'as to stop at 'ome.'

Letty continued her scrubbing. 'As a matter of fact, we've worked things out quite nicely. Olly peels the potatoes and lays the table, and I get the meal ready as soon as I get home.'

Vi sighed. In the short time Letty and Oliver had been married, she hadn't been allowed one single word in criticism of her brother; Letty just wouldn't tolerate it. 'Well, just remember what I've said. I know Oliver. You mark my words, once he starts to feel he's not a man any more, he'll turn against you.'

Letty knew exactly what Vi meant, but she tried not to show it. 'You're wrong, Vi,' she replied, keeping her head down as she scrubbed. 'Once that old railway station at the back of us opens up again, things are going to be different, you'll see. Olly'll have a job of his own, and a wife and family to take care of.'

Vi nearly dropped her mirror in shock. 'A family! You don't mean you're goin' to 'ave kids?'

'Well, of course we are – eventually! Don't you want to have children when you get married?'

Vi shuddered, 'You must be jokin'! I hate the little brats! It even give me a turn comin' into this place.' She shuddered again. 'No! I'll never 'ave no kids of me own!'

Letty chuckled to herself, 'Well, of course you've got to find yourself a husband first.'

As Letty spoke, Vi suddenly went all coy. 'As a matter of fact, Letty – I wanted to talk to you about that. There's somethin' I wanna tell yer.'

'Oh yes. Who is it this time, Vi? Who's the latest?'

Vi surprised Letty by crouching down beside her, and in a hushed voice said, 'No, Letty, you don't understand. I'm in love. I mean it this time, Letty – honest and true.'

Letty turned with a start to find Vi staring straight at her with a very peculiar look in her eyes. She immediately changed her attitude. 'Oh, Vi! I didn't mean to . . . I'm so happy for you! Who is he?'

Vi went on to describe the new man in her life. He was Frank O'Malley, a Liverpool Irishman, who worked at Holloway tube station in the booking office. They had apparently met on the spiral staircase at the station when Vi was making her way down to the platform and the high heel of her shoe had broken off. Frank had helped her and then asked Vi out for a drink at the local pub later that evening. They had been going steady ever since, and that was over three weeks now. Letty was delighted to know that Vi had at last found someone regular and asked if there was any prospect of them getting married. Vi admitted that she'd love to but, as Frank was a Roman Catholic and she was Church of England, there would probably be a few problems to work out. Letty declared that the first thing Vi should do was to bring Frank over to tea next Sunday afternoon at Citizen Road, because she and Oliver would love to meet him. On that score, however, Vi had reservations.

'I'm afraid it's not as easy as that,' Vi said anxiously. 'Oh, I know *you'd* like him, but I'm not so sure about Oliver.'

'Don't be silly, Vi! If he's your young man, and you like him, then so will Oliver.'

Vi bit her lip, and pulled a face. 'You see, well – Frank doesn't approve of war.'

'D'you know anyone who does?'

Vi bent down to take hold of Letty's hands, 'That's not quite what I mean, Letty. The fact is Frank's done time inside. He's a pacifist – a conscientious objector.'

Chapter 10

Sunday afternoons were always Letty's favourite time of the week. After dinner, which was always on the dot at one o'clock, she had her first real chance to put her feet up and have an hour's rest on the settee with Oliver. This week, however, she had foregone the monthly luxury of scrag end of beef in favour of sausages. She and Oliver were having company for tea, and she needed an extra shilling to buy some winkles and whelks from the Winkle Man, who always called about two o'clock on Sunday afternoons.

By the time Vi arrived with Frank O'Malley, Letty had laid the table beautifully, using the blue and yellow table-cloth her mother-in-law had given her for a wedding present. Young Sam was also there. It was Letty's idea that he join them for tea on Sunday afternoons, so that she could be sure the poor kid had at least one decent meal a week. He'd arrived, as always, over an hour early, and had immediately been given his favourite job, setting out the winkle needles at the side of each plate. Considering there was a ration on, the table looked well-stocked, with a large plate of thinly sliced bread and margarine, a bowl of lettuce and cucumber, which came from Bill Brooks' back garden, and a raspberry jelly Letty had found in the cupboard when they moved in.

Vi and Frank arrived just before four o'clock, and after brief introductions and a ten-minute chin-wag, everyone settled down at the tea-table. O'Malley turned out to be quite a pleasant-spoken little man, slightly older than Vi, who was a good twelve inches taller than him. He seemed more of a 'scouse' than an Irishman, and though she quite liked him, at times, Letty had difficulty following what he said. Oliver being Oliver, however, decided on sight that he didn't care for O'Malley, his main reason being that the man was wearing brown shoes with a black suit, which didn't seem at all right to him. He also disliked their visitor's nasty habit of occasionally spitting into his handkerchief and saying, 'God rest his soul!'. What *did* it mean, thought Oliver? Letty had already decided not to mention anything to her husband about O'Malley's time inside as a conscientious objector, and all through tea she did everything in her power to keep the conversation off the subject. O'Malley, however, had other ideas.

'Anyway, the way I look at it is this,' he said, chewing on one rather tough winkle, and doing his best to prise another out of its shell with a needle, 'if only Asquith had played his cards right, there'd have been no need for this war. I tell youse, the whole thing was nothing but a political cover-up.'

Vi replied with her mouth full of a whelk sandwich. 'Don't be so daft, Frank! What were we supposed ter do – sit down and wait for Kaiser Bill to march down White'all?'

O'Malley dipped the next winkle into some vinegar on his plate, then popped it into his mouth. 'I tell youse, the Liberals needed this war. It was the only way they could get rid of unemployment.'

'Well, I don't believe it,' insisted Vi, washing down the last of her sandwich with a gulp of tea. 'Everyone knows that if we hadn't stopped the Boche, they'd have taken over the whole o' Europe.'

Letty was desperate to change the conversation. 'What about some lettuce and cucumber, Sam. It's lovely in a sandwich.'

'No, fanks,' replied Oliver's young brother, hardly able to speak because his mouth was so crammed with food. It was the first time he had refused anything, but he had eaten so much cold apple pudding left over from Letty and Oliver's Sunday dinner, and now he was half-way through the jelly.

To Letty's consternation, however, O'Malley was still more interested in what he was saying than what he was eating. 'Yer know, Vi, yer real German people are human bein's just like the rest of us. We shoulda appealed direct to them, not the politicians. What do you say, Oliver?'

This was the moment Letty had dreaded. Oliver's face was grim and tense as he replied dourly without looking up from his plate, 'I say the only good German's a dead one.'

The fractured silence that followed was broken only by the sound of Sam slurping over his raspberry jelly, until Frank said incredulously. 'You don't mean that – do yer, Oliver?'

Oliver sat up in his chair, and stared straight back at O'Malley. 'Of course I mean it. I mean every word.'

Everyone else had seen the danger signals except Frank. 'Now I find that very interestin',' he persisted. 'I mean, how does a man like you justify the takin' of human life?'

'Ask the Boche. It was *their* idea in the first place – not ours!'

'Come now, Oliver. Thousands of yer pals have been slaughtered out there in France, y'know. Like scared rabbits shot in a field.'

This was where Letty took umbrage. She swung a quick glare at O'Malley and snapped, 'I hope you're not suggesting that my Oliver's scared, Mr O'Malley?'

'Oh come now,' he said with a sickly, condescending smile on his face, 'What has Oliver got out of this war? Nothin' but a gammy leg, and no decent job ter come home to. Is that all the thanks he gets fer riskin' his life?'

Oliver's temper was rising. 'I was proud to fight for my

country, mate. Most *men* are, yer know!'

'Hah!' snorted O'Malley. 'The next thing you'll be tellin' me is you don't even regret goin' into the Army!'

'If I 'ad two goods legs ter stand on, I'd take on the Army as a career any day!'

'Holy Mother of God!' O'Malley's eyes bulged, 'I don't believe what I've just heard!' He found it obscene that anyone should actually *want* to be in the Army – *any* Army. He came from a good Roman Catholic family. His father was from Cork in Southern Ireland, and his mother was a tough Liverpool girl. She had to be tough, because she had given birth to ten children – six boys and four girls. Frank was the fourth to be born, and was very close to all his family. But when war broke out, he was the only son who'd refused to volunteer for 'Kitchener's Army'. In fact he'd been so opposed to the war that he took part in a violent demonstration outside Liverpool's City Hall that resulted in his arrest, and a three-month spell as a prisoner in Strangeways Gaol, Manchester. When he was released, he'd found himself a virtual outcast of society, including his own family. And his objections took on a tragic significance, when two of his brothers were killed whilst serving on active duty.

Oliver was now not only fed up with listening to O'Malley, but he was downright suspicious of him. 'Why the 'ell aren't you doin' *your* bit anyway?'

O'Malley continued eating his winkles. 'I don't believe in this war, Oliver. So I see no reason why I should take any part in it.'

'A bloody conchy!' Oliver sprung up from his seat, knocking his chair over behind him.

'No, Olly!' Letty immediately went to him.

Vi got very agitated, too, and spilt tea on the tablecloth as she slammed down her cup into the saucer. 'You just shut your gab, Olly! Just because somebody don't believe in war.'

133

Letty immediately sprang to Oliver's defence. 'Nobody believes in war, Vi. We'd be poor creatures if we did.'

'Can I 'ave some more jelly please, Lett?' Sam seemed to be about the only one who was completely oblivious to the conversation. Without being conscious of what she was doing, Letty started sploshing helping after helping into his bowl. By the time she had finished it was full to the brim.

Considering he was the one who had started the rumpus, O'Malley looked as though he was quite enjoying all the fuss. 'Tell me this, Letty. If yer don't believe in somethin', then why don't youse condemn it?'

Letty had managed to get Oliver to help her clear the finished winkle shells and plates from the table. But she called back, 'Because I cherish my freedom, Mr O'Malley. If you take that away, what do you have left?'

O'Malley swung round on his chair. 'Exactly *my* sentiments! That's why I'm a socialist.' Then he launched into a long speech about the right of the individual to say what he wants at any time, and how, in his opinion, big business was responsible for starting the war.

Oliver greeted O'Malley's tirade with a stony silence, busying himself helping Letty, who managed to keep the peace just long enough for Oliver to go back to the table and have a cigarette, something he always did when he was disturbed. But it was an uneasy truce, for it was clear that Oliver deeply resented sitting at the same table as 'a conchy'.

It was a pity, for in many respects it turned out that both men had much in common; a mania for watching football matches, and a passionate respect for the royal family. However, they did disagree on one particular point of topical interest. Unlike O'Malley, Oliver had no time for the recently formed Women's Movement, and thought a woman's place was in the home. O'Malley, on the other hand, forecast the day when women would even take their place in Parliament.

It wasn't until the tea-table had been completely cleared that trouble erupted again. Letty had gone downstairs with her jug to the tap in the back yard, to collect some water for the washing-up. Sam was in the street outside, making friends with a stray cat, leaving Vi to play a round of cards with the men.

Oliver, however, was not really concentrating on the game. Despite Letty's pleas that he should be civil for his sister's sake, he was still obsessed with the fact that Vi's gentleman friend was a conchy. 'Tell me somethin', Mr O'Malley,' he said suddenly. 'If you was a married man wiv kids, would you still refuse to fight if you saw the Boche marchin' down the street where you and yer missus lived?'

O'Malley looked up briefly from his hand of cards and replied acidly, 'As long as they let me go about me business, it wouldn't bother me.'

Oliver came back sharply. 'You'd bother all right if they took away yer freedom!'

'Freedom!' As O'Malley spoke, the room started to vibrate and rumble as a train went rushing past, whistle shrieking, forcing him to shout, 'You call *this* freedom! Is this what you fought for, Oliver? Look at it!' He stood up, threw his cards on the table, and looked around the room. 'Just look at this place?' he yelled. 'Is this what you call a soldier's reward from a grateful government? A one-room dump at the side of a railway track!'

By the time Letty returned, she was horrified to find Frank O'Malley lying flat on his back across the table, with Oliver's hands around his throat apparently trying to throttle him. Vi was screaming hysterically and punching Oliver repeatedly on the back with her fists. It was a scene of utter pandemonium, only brought to an end when Letty managed to persuade Oliver to release Frank. Within moments, Vi had virtually dragged him out of the room, vowing never to

135

set foot in Letty and Oliver's place again.

After it was all over, Letty did her best to calm Oliver down. But much to his amazement, Letty did not launch an attack on him for his awful behaviour; she suddenly burst into uncontrollable laughter, saying she hadn't enjoyed herself so much in years.

In the street outside, however, it was a different picture. Vi was furious with O'Malley for not defending himself. But, as he dabbed his swollen eye with his handkerchief, he insisted that being a pacifist meant no response to physical violence. And to emphasise his point, he asked Vi to pray with him for Oliver's misguided ways. Raising his bowler hat and spitting into his handkerchief, he took a quick glance up to the Almighty and called, 'God rest his soul!'

The first colours of autumn were beginning to appear in Arlington Square. The leaves on the big chestnut tree in the corner near Old Smudge's hut were just tinged with a golden brown, enough to show that within the next few weeks, they would be scattered all over the path. Letty didn't care for autumn. To her it smelt of bonfires and summer's end. But there was no denying it did have a certain beauty and when the first early morning frost appeared, it was Nature's way of warning everyone around the Square that it was time to start preparing for winter.

Letty's reason for coming back to Arlington Square was that she hadn't heard from her mother for nearly three weeks. The last time they had met was when Beatrice had come to have a cup of tea with her and Oliver at Citizen Road. It had been a brief meeting, for although Beatrice had made her peace with Oliver, she could still not truly forgive him for taking Letty away from her. Letty had been disturbed to see her mother looking much older and she was also aware that Beatrice was bluffing about the way she was

136

living. It was, of course, her own fault that no money was coming in, because she still solidly refused even to discuss a divorce with William. Under the circumstances, she'd had no alternative but to send Nicky away to a private school in Wiltshire, for which William had agreed to pay the fees. Letty had no idea what her mother was now living on, for she had been a wild spender in her time and, to Letty's knowledge, had no savings.

Carrying two large shopping bags, Letty entered Number 97. As her mother wasn't at home, she let herself in, using the personal key she had kept. It proved a distressing experience. The house was almost completely deserted except for Beatrice's own room on the first floor. Apart from a few pots and pans in the kitchen, there was practically no furniture anywhere, and the curtains were laden with dust and grime. The only exception was Beatrice's beloved upright piano, which had been dragged into the middle of the vast sitting-room, and left there like a desert island. As she toured the house, Letty became more and more depressed. Her room was stripped bare, one of the window panes broken, and there were dust marks on the walls where some of Letty's own paintings and photographs had been hanging. Tom's room was in the same state, and Letty paused there briefly, crouched on the bare floorboards, where she had a little weep all to herself.

Finding it too upsetting to stay in the house for long, she left quickly and made her way slowly towards Old Smudge's hut in the Square's gardens. She hadn't been there since before she was married, and she felt a mixture of sadness and excitement at this belated return. It was, after all, in these same gardens that she'd seen Tom for the last time – over there on that bench. As she passed it, she could still hear his voice whispering to her, 'Whatever happens, we'll always be friends, won't we, Letty?' It seemed a lifetime away.

137

'Don't see 'er much these days, Miss Letty.' Old Smudge sounded a bit croaky on the chest as he chatted with Letty. 'Mrs Edginton seems to go off every mornin', much the same time as I get 'ere.'

Letty was puzzled. 'Have you any idea where she goes?' Old Smudge had always been the eyes and ears of the Square.

'Not my place ter know, Miss. Mrs Edginton in't the sort o' person yer ask questions. The one thing I *'ave* noticed though is, she's lookin' very tired these days. Sometimes, when I'm lockin' up these gates soon after sunset, I sees 'er makin' 'er way along the Square like some ole lady twice 'er age. By the time she reaches Number 97, she looks fair ready ter drop. Fing 'as puzzles me though, is the furniture. All sorts o' people 'ave been turnin' up at the 'ouse for weeks now. They always comes out carryin' bits and pieces. I seen all sorts o' fings go – settees, chairs, a great big polished table, little beds, big beds, lots o' carpets. I tells yer Miss Letty, I can't make 'ead nor tails of it all.'

Unfortunately, Letty could. Now she knew where her mother was getting the money to live on. But how long would it last? And how long would it be before Beatrice would have to move out of Arlington Square? After bidding an affectionate farewell to Smudge, Letty made her way on foot to Upper Street via the New North Road, where she caught a Number 38 tram to the Nags Head, Holloway and found a front seat on the top deck. At least life was a little easier for *her* these days, she reflected, as she bounced towards her destination. Owing to a lack of orders at the paint-brush factory, she was now only working mornings. However, it had meant a cut in her weekly earnings, and if hadn't been for her evening job cleaning at the local school, she knew she would have had to cut down on some of their outgoings. Still, she reflected, she was managing.

*   *   *

Two weeks later Letty crossed the wide Holloway Road and headed towards Pakeman Street School. Today was a half-term holiday, so she was taking the opportunity to do her cleaning job during the day. She'd decided to do the ground floor first, so after collecting her materials, she filled the bucket with water from the outside tap, and set to work. As she scrubbed away her mind was, as usual on other things. First it was her mother. What was she up to, thought Letty? She still hadn't managed to talk to her: every time she'd gone round to Arlington Square she'd been out. She wrung her cloth and decided there and then she must call on her the following evening.

'Excuse me, lady. Would you like a sweet?'

Letty looked round with a start. Standing behind her was a small girl, probably aged about five or six years, a pretty little thing, with blonde curly hair, blue eyes, clean and tidy in a neat fawn-coloured cotton dress. She was holding out a bag of sweets, urging Letty to take one.

Letty's face lit up. She quickly wiped her hands on her apron, and replied, 'Thank you, dear. Thank you very much. Are you sure you can spare it?'

'Oh yes. They're barley sugars. My mum bought them for me in Charlie's shop across the road. There aren't any left though. He only got a few on the ration.' She shook the bag at Letty. 'Please take one, lady.'

Letty smiled as she popped one into her mouth. 'What's your name?' she asked.

'Rosie,' she replied, a barley sugar in her own mouth.

'Pleased to know you, Rosie. Do you go to this school.'

Rosie shook her head energetically. 'No. But my bruvver does. We live down Mayton Street. My mum works in Stagnells the baker's. I don't have a dad – not any more. He got killed in the war.'

Letty's face crumpled. But before she could say anything,

Rosie turned and ran off, calling back, 'Bye lady!'

For a moment, Letty just knelt there, leaning back on her heels. She could hardly believe the simplicity of her encounter with Rosie. It was so quick, and yet so direct and to the point. Rosie was just one of so many, thought Letty. Children all over the country were now without fathers. It was some moments before Letty realised that she was still sucking the barley sugar she'd been given. The meeting had given her a strange feeling inside. When she one day had a child, if it was a girl she hoped it would be like Rosie.

Letty carried on with her scrubbing. In no time at all her mind was racing again, especially as there was one other major problem she had to face up to, something that had been keeping her awake night after night for weeks. Money.

'Mornin', Mrs Hobbs.'

Letty found herself swinging around with a start. This time, instead of a child she saw a man. He was standing over her and raising his bowler hat.

'Been meanin' to catch up with you for the last couple of weeks, Mrs Hobbs. You and your husband seem to have been out quite a lot lately.'

It was Mr Cotton. He was the last man in the whole world she wanted to see just now. 'Oh – hallo, Mr Cotton,' she answered, nervously. Then she wiped her hands on her apron, and stood up. 'Yes, we have been rather busy, I suppose.'

'Good! I'm glad to hear it. So I take it Mr Hobbs is now actively employed?'

Letty took a deep breath, and held back her shoulders. 'No. Not yet. But any day now. They say there's a good chance the old railway station is going to open up again soon. Did you know?'

Mr Cotton looked at her expressionlessly. 'No. As a matter of fact I didn't.' He tried a faint smile, but it looked insincere. 'Mrs Hobbs, I take it you *did* receive the note I sent you?'

'Yes, I did, Mr Cotton.' She answered immediately, trying to sound as confident and businesslike as possible. 'And we *will* be paying the rent just as soon as we can. You see, we've had quite a lot of unexpected expenses just lately, and—'

Mr Cotton did not allow her to continue. 'Mrs Hobbs. I have to tell you that it is not my policy to allow tenants to become overdue with their rent for more than a month at a time.'

'Oh I do understand, Mr Cotton, and I promise we *will* be settling with you any minute now.' Letty was desperately playing for time. But she knew very well there was absolutely no hope of her paying the rent in the foreseeable future. How could she tell him that now the paint-brush factory had closed down, she no longer had a day job? How could she explain that the only wages coming in were from her part-time work here at the school?

Mr Cotton smiled again, which brought a reciprocal, hopeful smile from Letty. 'Mrs Hobbs. I want you to know that I'm a reasonable man, and it's only right that I should show my appreciation for all the hard work you and your husband have done to transform that room of – mine.'

Letty clasped her hands together in relief and eagerness. 'Oh, thank you, Mr Cotton! Thank you! I can't tell you how grateful we are . . .'

'Good!' Mr Cotton pulled out the gold pocket watch from his waistcoat, and looked at it. 'Then shall we say – seven days?'

Letty's face crumpled again. '*Seven* days!'

'All back-payment by Friday of next week. If not . . . well, I'm afraid I shall have to ask you and your husband to vacate the premises.' He raised his hat again. 'Mornin' Mrs Hobbs.'

Letty watched him go in absolute disbelief. In the period of just a few short moments, she had seen her world start to collapse.

141

Chapter 11

Amy Lyall and William Edginton had been living together above the pawn shop in Upper Street for the best part of a year now. It hadn't been an easy time: both their families had virtually disassociated themselves from them. Amy missed seeing her parents, who were devout, practising Methodists, and had deeply disapproved of her liaison with a married man who was so much older than she. For William, too, it was particularly distressing to have to fight for contact with either Letty or Nicky. And there seemed little way forward with Beatrice categorically refusing to consider a divorce. Despite all this, however, Amy and William were growing more devoted to each other day by day. He found her ways so kind, and kindness was something he had never seemed to have in his marriage to Beatrice. And in William, Amy found a man whom she could talk to, and so love.

Letty had not seen her father since he left Arlington Square. She still hadn't forgiven him for not attending her wedding, even though he had sent a message of congratulation, together with a five-pound note. It was, therefore, no easy decision for her to visit him at the pawn shop. She arrived there later than she had planned, for on the way she had stopped by at the doctor's to ask for some medicine for a recurring stomach upset. By the time she got to the pawn shop it was already late morning. She hadn't been inside such a place before, and for some reason it gave her the same feeling she always had when she visited a cemetery.

'Yes, miss? Can I help you?'

Amy Lyall was different from what Letty had imagined. Somehow, she'd expected her to look like a Soho tart, with a provocative neckline and lashings of make-up. What she saw, however, was an attractive young girl, inclined to be a little on the dumpy side, but with striking black hair and dark eyes to match. Yet behind the sweetest smile there lurked the face of someone who had had her share of suffering. 'I'm looking for Mr Edginton,' Letty asked, awkwardly, and coldly, 'Mr William Edginton.'

Amy smiled courteously. 'Do you have an appointment, miss?' she asked pleasantly. 'Mr Edginton doesn't actually have anything to do with the shop himself. Did you have something to pawn?'

Letty tried to avoid eye-contact with Amy, and replied brusquely, 'My name's Letty Hobbs. I'm Mr Edginton's daughter.'

Amy's smile froze, and for a brief moment, there was a rigid silence between the two women. But just as Amy seemed about to speak, William himself appeared at the door of the back-parlour. 'Letty! My dear child!' He almost ran from behind the counter to greet her.

Letty showed no emotion or warmth, and turned one cheek for him to kiss her formally. 'Hallo, Father.'

It was an uneasy reunion. William thought his daughter was looking tired and strained, but when he asked how she was Letty insisted she'd been perfectly well except for a brief bout of sickness. Although it had been a long time since they'd actually met, William admitted that several times he had stood outside the paint-brush factory where Letty used to work, just to catch a glimpse of her, without ever having the nerve to approach her. Letty thought her father was looking extremely well, and much younger than his age,

143

probably because he'd shaved off his moustache. But when William attributed his good health and happiness to Amy, Letty quickly changed the subject. After quick introductions, Amy herself decided that William and Letty should be left alone, so she told them to go into the back-parlour to talk, whilst she went off to make a pot of tea. Alone with Letty, William talked about his sadness at not being able to attend the wedding, but he insisted he was far more devoted to Amy than ever he had been to Letty's mother, and wherever he went, Amy would always accompany him.

Letty decided she should broach the subject of her mother. 'I feel so sorry for her,' she said, lowering her eyes. 'Now that Nicky's not at home any more, she must be very lonely.'

William looked depressed. 'I know that, Letty. But there's nothing I can do about it.'

'She's got rid of most of the furniture from Number 97.'

'Yes, I know that, too,' replied William, smoking the remainder of a cigar he'd left in the ash-tray when Letty arrived. 'She wrote me a fairly abusive letter about what belonged to whom. So I wrote back and told her she could do what she wanted with it all. I want none of it.'

'I have a feeling she's sold it.'

'Good. Then at least she's got something to be going on with.'

Letty looked up sharply. 'It's not enough for her to live on.'

William took another deep puff of his cigar, 'Look here, Letty. I've done everything in my power to help your mother. I told her she could divorce me and claim an allowance. But she won't hear of it. For some reason, she's determined to cope on her own. I've heard she's leaving Number 97, and moving into a two-roomed flat in Bedford Terrace.'

'So that's it!' This is what Letty had suspected. But she couldn't understand why her mother hadn't told her. 'Where *is* Bedford Terrace?'

William scratched his head, then shook it. 'Not too sure. Up towards Hornsey Rise somewhere, I think. Sounds like an odd sort of area for her to go to. God knows why she's doing it.'

'Mother's a proud woman, father. You must know that by now.'

William knew only too well. During some of his more despondent moments alone, his mind often cast back to those times before the war when Beatrice had stubbornly refused to go out to a business dinner with him unless she had a new dress, or a new piece of jewellery. How many times had she humiliated him in public by drawing attention to the way he wore his hair, or his tie, or even the brand of cigars he smoked. Proud – yes, and vain! That was Beatrice. Maybe she couldn't help herself. Now, however, thought William, she would simply *have* to. He carefully stubbed out his cigar in the ash-tray and said, 'Letty, what can I do? If your mother won't accept an allowance from me, how can she live? Money is impossible to come by these days.'

Letty looked anxious. 'I know that, Father. As a matter of fact, that's why I've come to see you.'

'Letty!' William immediately knew something was wrong. In fact he had sensed it the moment he'd laid eyes on her. She was always such a secretive child. If ever she was in trouble, she invariably kept it from everybody. In some ways, she was just as proud and independent as her mother. 'What is it, my dear? Are you in trouble?'

'The night you left home,' continued Letty, 'you said that if ever I *was* in trouble, I was to come and see you.'

William leaned across from his chair, took hold of Letty's hands, and said gently, 'My dear child . . .'

Letty, however, was resisting sentimentality. Her approach was businesslike to the point of being brusque. 'I need money, father. And I need it desperately.' Then she went on to tell him how Oliver hadn't been able to work since he came out of hospital, and how the landlord had given them a week to find the rent or get out of the room in Citizen Road.

Without saying a word, William went to his desk on the other side of the room, opened the flap, and sat down in front of it. 'This is a cheque for twenty pounds,' he called, busily scribbling as he talked. 'If you take it to my bank in the City Road, they'll cash it for you immediately.'

'No, Father! That's not what I came for! All I need is enough cash to see us through until I can find another full-time job.'

'Then let me help you.'

'No, Father! I want to do this *my* way.' She opened her handbag, and brought out something wrapped in a handkerchief. 'I've brought something to pawn.'

William sprang up, 'Letty! Don't be absurd!'

Letty was adamant. 'Look, Father. I've never been to a pawn shop before, so if you want to help me, please take this. And, if you don't mind, I'd prefer you to tell Mrs Lyall as little about this as possible.'

William reluctantly took the handkerchief, and unravelled it. Inside was a small but delicate piece of jewellery, a brooch in the shape of a heart, embedded with an array of different sized precious stones, mainly blue sapphires, Letty's favourite colour. William was clearly shocked. 'Letty! This is the brooch your mother and I bought you for your sixteenth birthday.'

'Yes. So you know how much it's worth.'

William immediately wrapped up the handkerchief again. 'No, Letty! You can't part with it. I won't let you.'

Letty stared her father out with a look of grim determination. 'Father! A roof over my head is far more important to me than something to pin on my dress! Besides, it'll only be a temporary measure. As soon as Oliver's well enough to find a job, he'll buy the brooch back for me again. You've no idea how important that'll be for him. Not only for the money, but . . . well, for all sorts of reasons. Look, if you won't help me, there are plenty of other pawn shops around, you know.'

For a brief moment, William thought of the last time he had talked with his daughter back in her bedroom in Arlington Square; she'd been just a teenage girl then, with all the high emotions and arrogance of any other girl her age. But now, she was someone's wife. How she had changed, he realised. In such a short time she had taken on her shoulders the burdens of day-to-day survival. God! What a proud, stubborn woman she had turned out to be. Just like her mother. Whoever this Oliver was, William sincerely hoped he realised what he'd taken on with Letty. 'Give me the brooch,' he said. Letty gave him the handkerchief, and he started to unravel it again. 'I'll get Amy to take a look at it . . .'

Hardly had he spoken, when a loud explosion from the street outside caused everything in the room to shake.

'My God!' gasped Letty, who for the past few minutes had been looking strained. Now sweat was appearing on her forehead. 'What's that?'

The first sound was quickly followed by more, and people could be heard shouting and yelling in the street outside.

William was already at the parlour door. 'It sounds like the Maroon Warning Signal.'

'An air raid?' Letty clutched her forehead. Her cheeks had suddenly turned as white as a sheet. 'It can't be!'

William rushed out to where Amy was already standing in the open shop doorway. In Upper Street outside, groups of people were gathering everywhere, waving newspapers, whistling, hooting. There was an air of jubilant hysteria. 'It's over!' someone shouted. Then the cobbler next door cheered out loud, 'Down with Kaiser Bill! May 'e rot in 'ell!' Only the flower lady from across the road was calm enough to tell them that the war was over. Overjoyed, William and Amy turned and hugged each other. Then they rushed back into the shop, with William calling, 'Letty! Letty, my dear – it's over!'

William reached the parlour first. The door was open, but for a fleeting moment, there was no sign of anyone. Suddenly, however, William saw her. 'Oh my God! Letty!' Then he called to Amy to come quick. As she entered, William was crouched on the floor beside a white-faced Letty, sweat now pouring down her cheeks. As he helped her to her feet, and eased her into a chair, William was desperate with worry. 'What is it, my dear? What's wrong?'

Letty clutched her forehead, and tried to recover. Her colour had still not returned. 'It's – all right, Father. There's nothing to worry about. There's something I should have told you.'

William stopped fussing over her, and for one brief moment was even irritated. If Letty was ill, why hadn't she told him so? After all he was always the one she came to, not her mother. And Letty was usually the one who knew when her father was unwell. In fact, where care and attention was concerned, she had always been more of a wife to William than Beatrice. 'What's happened, Letty?' William said, his eyes burning with anxiety.

Amy used her own handkerchief to wipe his daughter's forehead. But as she took a closer look, she didn't seem at all worried. In fact, the moment Letty had walked into the shop, Amy had shrewdly guessed what was ailing her.

Oliver was at home peeling the potatoes when he heard the distant sound of the Maroon Warning Signal, followed by the pealing of church bells. Letty wasn't back yet from doing the shopping and, although he knew she liked to chin-wag with neighbours on the way, she had been gone rather longer than usual. So he decided to go outside and investigate.

Citizen Road was full of people cheering and flag waving, and Oliver soon discovered why. Near the junction with Hornsey Road, an upright piano had been carried out on to the pavement and was accompanying a huge crowd of jubilant revellers doing a mass 'Knees up Muvver Brown!'. A fat lady in a man's flat cap and overalls grabbed hold of Oliver and tried to get him to dance with her, but when she realised he was disabled, quickly apologised with a 'Sorry, mate!' and let him go.

He had not brought his walking stick with him, so he paused briefly to sit on the ledge of a front-garden wall. After a moment or so he was joined by a red-faced teenager named Robbie, who worked in the Dairy Yard just round the corner in Isledon Road. 'So that's that then, eh mate?' enthused the youngster, breathless after an endless knees-up with the crowd. 'That'll teach Jerry to try and put one over us!'

Oliver smiled and agreed.

Robbie started clapping his hands in time to the hokey-cokey, and had to shout to be heard. 'Pity *I* never got a chance to have a go though. Coupla more years and I'd 'ave been out there wiv the rest of 'em!'

Gord forbid, thought Oliver as the lad rushed off to re-join the merry-making. Too many kids not much older than Robbie had been left out there on those blood-stained fields as it was. And even though the war was now finally over, look how it had left Oliver, and thousands like him. What was there to celebrate, he thought? The bloody, soddin' war had left him a cripple for the rest of his life. It was more than possible he'd never work again. He quickly took a half-finished dog-end of fag from behind his ear, and lit it. The

149

spontaneous street party was beginning to get him down. He was getting anxious to know what had happened to Letty. Why couldn't she be with him *now* when he needed her most?

Just a few yards away in Tollington Road, Letty was getting out of a motor cab. After thanking the driver, and paying him with the money her father had given her for the fare, she started to pick her way through the revellers now filling every main road and side street. As she went, she waved up at the people leaning out of top-floor windows everywhere, armed with anything they could lay their hands on: Union Jack flags, bits of bunting, hastily scribbled cardboard notices such as, 'It's Over!' and 'Bring The Boys Home!'. Letty laughed and shouted with the rest; she looked and felt so much better than she had at Amy Lyall's pawn shop a short while before. As she turned into Citizen Road, the overjoyed locals grabbed hold of her and tried to get her to dance. Letty laughed with them, but hurried on her way. It was only when she was making her way to the gate of Number 48 that she suddenly heard Oliver shouting to her.

'Letty!'

Turning with a start to see Oliver marooned on the opposite side of the road, shouting and waving at her, she couldn't help thinking how lost and vulnerable he looked amongst the surging crowd. 'Olly!' She rushed back to the road, and as she fought her way through the masses, Oliver was trying to do the same. Finally they met in the middle of the road.

'Letty!' Oliver's face was quivering with pain and anxiety, as he grabbed her by the shoulders and shook them hard. 'Where've yer been? Why've yer done this to me?'

Letty tried hard to explain her absence, but Oliver was too distressed to listen. Finally she managed to speak. 'I'm all right, Olly dear – truly I am!' But she had to shout to be heard above the singing crowds. 'I'm sorry I'm late. I couldn't help it. I didn't feel well. I had to see a doctor.'

Her words made Oliver even more anxious. 'Doctor? What is it, Letty? What's wrong wiv yer? Tell me!'

For the first time, Letty smiled. 'There's nothing wrong with me, dear. I promise you – there's nothing wrong. It's wonderful. Everything's absolutely wonderful!'

Oliver shook her hard, and yelled at her. 'Tell me!'

A group of children suddenly appeared and formed a circle around them to sing, 'Knees up Muvver Brown! Yer drawers are fallin' down!'

'You're going to be a father, Olly!' shouted Letty in total exhilaration. 'We're going to have a baby!'

As Letty threw her arms around Oliver and hugged him, his blood seemed to burst in his veins. 'A baby?' he said, at first quietly to himself, then louder for the whole world to hear, 'Christ! We're gonna 'ave a baby!' he yelled. And he hugged Letty so hard, she could hardly breathe.

The children who were milling around them didn't really hear what he said. But whatever it was it excited them enough to sing even louder:

> Knees up Muvver Brown,
> Yer drawers are fallin' down,
> Under the table you must go,
> Ee-aye-ee-aye-ee-aye-o,
> If I catch yer bendin',
> I'll saw yer legs right orf,
> So – knees up, knees up
> Don't get the breeze up
> Knees up Muvver Brown!

Chapter 12

There was hardly a chimneypot along Bedford Terrace that wasn't billowing out thick palls of choking black smoke. And as there was no breeze blowing that late November Saturday afternoon, the smoke just curled its way silently up into the atmosphere to form a thin layer of fog. It waited for dusk to appear before it lowered itself seductively on to the cold, wintry streets.

Letty had decided that she wanted Oliver to be with her when she visited her mother for the first time in her new home at 17 Bedford Terrace. Although it wasn't too far from Citizen Road, they had to take a Number 14 omnibus from The Nags Head, Holloway, to half-way up Hornsey Road, where they got off at the junction with Andover Road. From there, it would normally have taken anyone with good strong legs no more than five minutes to get to Bedford Terrace, but Letty was unfamiliar with this part of London, and Oliver was still using his walking stick, so it took three times longer. The first thing she noticed was that Holloway was a very different area from Arlington Square. This became even more apparent when they turned the corner at The Bedford Arms, and got their first glimpse of the terrace. All the houses were the same shape and size, and built on two floors. In one or two of the doorways women neighbours, wearing either coat aprons or jumble-sale clothes, stood gossiping about their landlords, husbands and neighbours. Further down, a bunch of scruffy kids were shouting and wrestling in the middle of the road, which, Letty thought, wouldn't be much to her mother's liking!

To her dismay, Number 17 itself looked the most dilapidated house on the terrace. Paint was peeling off the front door and around all the windows, and the coping-stone wall and wooden fence were badly chipped and broken. There was no front garden, merely a stone recess only big enough to take a lidless, rusty dustbin. Letty felt a deep, sinking feeling inside as she took hold of the iron knocker on the front door and banged it hard, once. For a full minute or so, there was no response. So Oliver tried, literally thumping the knocker on the door.

After a moment, the door opened and a disgruntled middle-aged woman appeared, with straight, uncombed hair and ruddy cheeks riddled with broken veins. 'What d'er want?' she growled.

'We're looking for Mrs Edginton.' Letty tried smiling sweetly, but it didn't help much.

'Edginton's upstairs. Two knocks fer upstairs,' she growled irritably, then without another word, slammed the door. Letty pulled a face at Oliver, and just as she banged the knocker twice on the door, she heard the woman inside yelling, 'Edginton! Fer you!'

Almost simultaneously, one of the two upstairs windows was flung wide open, and Beatrice's head peered down. 'Who is it?'

Letty looked up, and called back. 'It's me, Mother – Letty. Me and Oliver.'

Beatrice was clearly shocked. 'Letty! What are you doing here?' The top half of her body was leaning out precariously. 'Wait a minute!' she yelled. 'I'll get the key.' She disappeared inside for a moment, then quickly reappeared to throw the key down on to the pavement. Letty picked it up, then very cagily opened the door.

Letty came into the passage first, closely followed by Oliver. They closed the door behind them as quietly as they could, then made their way to the stairs at the back. The first thing Oliver noticed was that the place stunk of stale beer, cats, boiled greens and damp. The wallpaper was peeling, holes everywhere needed plastering, and the lino on the staircase was worn right down to the treads.

'Why didn't you let me know you were coming?' Beatrice was waiting on the landing as Letty and Oliver climbed the stairs. And when she heard Mrs Wolf, her downstairs neighbour, closing her parlour door she called out pointedly in a loud voice, 'I wish people would mind their own business!'

A few minutes later, Letty and Oliver were sitting with Beatrice in her parlour. Letty was shocked by the size of the room and its lack of home comforts. All it contained in the way of furniture was a kitchen-table and two chairs, a small sofa, Beatrice's piano and an armchair, all of which came from Arlington Square. The only real additions to her old furniture were a second-hand gas cooker tucked away in a corner, and surprisingly a sewing machine, with a wind-up handle gramophone player and horn sitting on top of it. Oliver thought the room was a bit on the cold side and when he looked he saw there were only two or three lumps of coal burning in the tiny black grate beneath the mantelpiece. The saving grace, however, was that Beatrice clearly did not have to sleep here, for she had her bed in a small annexe on the other side of a heavily curtained archway.

'It's very nice, Mother,' said Letty, looking around the room disconsolately. It seemed such a drastic change of lifestyle for a woman who had been used to so much more. 'How long have you been here now?'

Beatrice was pouring boiling water from a blackened tin kettle into her best china teapot. 'A couple of weeks, I suppose. Actually it was the day after they signed the Armistice.'

Oliver was sitting as close to the fire as he could, trying to warm his hands by what little there was of a flame. 'You should've let us know, Mum. Lett and me could've come up and helped.'

'Not at all,' Beatrice answered confidently. 'I manage perfectly well. And in any case, you and Letty have quite enough to do in your own place, Oliver.'

'Not 'arf as much as we're gonna 'ave this time next year!'

Beatrice turned and stared, 'What d'you mean?'

'As a matter of fact, Mother, that's really why we came to see you.' Letty got up from her chair at the table, and took her mother's arm. 'Come over here for a moment. We want to tell you something.' Letty went with her to the small double sofa, and they both sat down. 'We're going to have a baby, Mother. Oliver and I.'

Oliver grinned cheekily. 'There yer go, Mum. You're gonna be a granma!'

'Isn't it wonderful, Mother?' Letty was leaning back on the sofa, with her hand around Beatrice's shoulder. 'When the doctor told me, I could hardly believe it. It's due next year, a couple of weeks after my birthday.'

Beatrice was in a state of shock. 'Your birthday? When is that? April, isn't it?'

Letty exchanged a pointed glance with Oliver. 'July, Mother. July the eighth.'

For a brief moment, Beatrice seemed unable to say anything. Her mind was racing. Most of all, she was thinking about how old being a grandmother would make her seem. All of a sudden she felt her life ebbing away from her. Finally, she pulled out a handkerchief from her sleeve, and dabbed her nose with it. Then she asked acidly, 'Have you told your father?'

Letty smiled awkwardly. 'As a matter of fact, I was with him just after I found out. He's sent me to his own doctor.'

Beatrice's response became ice-cold. 'Really?' She went back to the table to pour some tea. 'Do you take milk, Oliver?'

Letty exchanged a look with Oliver, got up and went to Beatrice. 'Mother. I want to talk to you. Let's go into your bedroom for a moment.'

Left on his own, Oliver thought this might be a marvellous opportunity to have a quick snooze, but just as he was about to do so, something caught his eye on the floor beside his chair. It was a copy of the *Racing Gazette*.

There was barely enough space to move in Beatrice's bedroom, so Letty sat on the bed whilst her mother sat at her dressing-table. It felt like an odd place for them to talk, for at Arlington Square, Letty had rarely been allowed into her mother's bedroom. For Beatrice, it was the one place she regarded as completely private: her own personal sanctuary. The irony was that there was now no one to disturb her anyway.

'Mother. Why won't you divorce Father?' This was the most direct question Letty had ever asked her mother, and she expected a gale-force reply.

But Beatrice only half turned to look at Letty. Before replying, she took a comb from the dressing-table, and started to comb her hair. She no longer wore it in a tight bun, but let it hang down her back to her waist. 'Your father and I took each other for better or for worse,' she said calmly and without emotion. 'I don't care what he does with his life now, but I for one will never break that vow.'

'But why not, Mother? What's the point in hanging on to

something that doesn't exist any more. Why ruin both your lives for the sake of principles and bitterness?'

Beatrice put down her comb, got up from the dressing-table, and peered out of the window into the drab back yard. For one brief moment, Letty thought she looked quite beautiful standing there, the fading afternoon light just picking out her pale features and slight figure. 'My life was ruined a long time ago,' she said, rubbing one of the window panes with her hand so that she could see out more clearly. 'If only I'd known how much your father has always hated me.'

'I don't believe that, Mother. Father is just as sad about what has happened as you.' Letty got up and went to her. 'He did love you. I know he did,' she lied. 'Even when I last saw him, only a couple of weeks ago, he told me how there isn't a woman in the whole world who has such beautiful hair as you.' Letty felt she had to do something to cheer her mother up. Her father clearly had no feelings left for Beatrice and Letty could never forgive him for it. It was true that Beatrice only had herself to blame for the break-up of her marriage, but Letty knew she had paid for her mistakes in the most traumatic way. Her morale was low, her living standards reduced to little more than a slum and, worst of all, she clearly felt rejected. All Letty's instincts told her to take her mother's part for it was her mother who needed her most.

Beatrice merely smiled faintly as Letty stroked her hair affectionately and pressed her again, 'Why not agree to a divorce, then you won't have to live in a place like this?'

'I'm earning for myself now.' Beatrice had the most defiant look on her face that Letty had ever seen. 'I don't have to rely on *anyone* any more.'

After Letty and Oliver had left Bedford Terrace, they could talk of nothing else but Beatrice's determination to fend for

157

herself. Oliver was wary of the neighbourhood the 'old girl' had chosen to live in. As he pointed out, it was not much more than a spit and hop away from the notorious Playford Road, one of the most dangerous areas in London. He was also curious about the copy of the *Racing Gazette* he had found. Could it be that the old girl had taken to gambling? But for Letty, the most astonishing part was what her mother had finally revealed to her: that she had found herself a job, hand-sewing in a clothing factory in Hackney. Letty found it incredible to believe that her mother was capable of looking after herself, yet she couldn't help but admire the way Beatrice had faced up so determinedly to the change in her life. In fact it occurred to her that her mother had never really had any true feeling at all for William Edginton. After all, she'd never seen any evidence of affection in her parents' marriage, even before the days of Amy Lyall.

Back in Bedford Terrace the evening fog was gradually starting to engulf the bleak back street, bringing with it an unwelcome premature darkness. Although the war had now been over for two weeks, the lamplighter had still not returned to ignite the street lamps.

Inside Number 17, Beatrice Edginton lit the gas mantle which hung down from the ceiling in the middle of the room. It was a precarious evening ritual, for she could only reach it by standing on a chair. As soon as it built up into a bright glow, she adjusted it, then went to the windows and drew the curtains. For a moment, she turned and cast her eyes around her new home, finally allowing them to come to rest on the large ornamental mirror hanging on the wall above the fireplace. After no more than a second's thought, she made her way over there to look at her reflection. What she saw was an old woman – much older than her years. Her mind was reflecting on so many things, tiny incidents in her life that would have meant nothing to anyone except her. Like the time when William wiped his cheek after she had kissed him, or even that moment on their wedding night when William saw her naked for the first time, but made no comment on how lovely she was. But whilst she continued to gaze into the mirror, it was Letty's voice that kept whirling over and over again through her mind. 'What's the point in hanging on to something that doesn't exist any more?' and 'Father is just as sad about what has happened, as you. Even when I saw him only a couple of weeks ago, he told me how there isn't a woman in the whole world who has such beautiful hair as you.' Beatrice leaned her head back and shook it, so that her hair swirled back and forth behind her. Then she reached for a huge pair of paper scissors on the mantelpiece. Without stopping for one moment to think what she was doing, she gathered together all her hair in a bunch and started to hack away at it.

The last train of the day roared past the back yards of Citizen Road at three minutes past midnight. Letty knew it was on time because, even though she and Oliver were always in bed by then, she was usually wide-awake. She could never get to sleep before the early hours and lying in bed at night was such a perfect time to sort out all the troubles of the world. Oliver, of course, was no help, because he just fell asleep the moment his head touched the pillow, and he snored like a pig.

Tonight, however, was different. Letty had more practical things on her mind, and she was sitting up at the kitchen-table, carefully counting out a pile of coins. ' . . . penny farthing, penny ha'penny, three farthings . . . twopence . . .'

She was driving Oliver mad. His snoring suddenly came to a stop, and with a tired, disgruntled groan, he peered over the top of the bedclothes. 'What the 'ell you up to, Lett? Don't you know what time it is?'

159

Letty carried on with her counting. '... sixpence ha'penny, sixpence three farthings ... Go back to sleep, dear. I'm just trying to see if we've got enough money to have sausages for dinner tomorrow.'

Oliver couldn't believe what he was hearing, and in the middle of the bleedin' night! 'What do we want sausages for? We've got 'taters and carrots, in't we?'

Letty turned with an indignant start. 'Olly, you've got to have meat sometimes. You're a man. You need building up.'

Oliver eased himself up in bed: even though Letty had the gas mantle turned down low, it was still too bright for Oliver at this time of night. 'Always workin' fings out. Always puttin' pennies away fer somefin' or uvver.'

Letty finished counting the coins, and put them back into her purse. 'It's the only way. If I put a little aside from my wage packet each week, it stops us from getting into debt.' As she spoke, she crossed her fingers. There was so much she was keeping from Oliver, and she hated it. But what could she do? By pawning her brooch she had only just had enough time to prevent Mr Cotton from evicting them. But the money wouldn't last forever. If she didn't find a full-time job soon, they'd be in real trouble, and Oliver would inevitably blame himself.

Oliver, however, was no man's fool. In the short time that he and Letty had been married, he knew exactly when Letty was worrying about something, and even when she was keeping something from him. In a curious sort of way, both of them were getting to know each other more than they realised. Oliver edged out of bed, sorted out a dog-end for himself from an old tobacco tin he kept to hand, and quickly lit up. He also took something else from the tin – a ticket – which he slipped into the top pocket of his flannel vest. Whilst Letty turned off the gaslight over the mantelpiece, he made his way up the two steps to the big arch-window.

There was a heavy frost outside, and a lot of condensation had formed on the glass inside. He rubbed one of the panes, and peered out. After a moment, Letty joined him. Although she'd turned the gasmantle off, the room was flooded in a bright white light from the full winter's moon. Letty put her arm around Oliver's waist, and he put his arm around her shoulders.

As she shivered and leaned on Oliver's shoulder Letty said, 'Wouldn't like to be out there tonight. It's freezing!'

The railway lines outside were glistening in the frosty moonlight. Letty, dreaming again, thought the lines looked as though they'd been touched by a magic wand. Any moment now she expected them to rise up into the sky and form a delicate web of criss-cross patterns.

Oliver's mind was on more practical matters. 'Where d'yer get the money from, Lett? You lost yer job at the brush factory some time ago now. Where d'yer get the money from to pay the rent?'

Letty turned her head away guiltily. 'Don't be silly, dear.' She quickly took out a handkerchief from the pocket of her nightdress, and blew her nose, quite unnecessarily.

Oliver refused to let her dismiss the matter, so he gently pulled her back to face him. 'What did yer 'ave ter 'ock?'

There was a brief moment of silence between them, before Letty finally decided to own up, but in as light-hearted a way as she could. 'Oh it was nothing much. Just some old brooch Mother and Father gave me for one of my birthdays. That silly cupid's heart thing. I never really liked it all that much.'

Oliver watched her closely for a moment, then kissed her on the lips. 'Don't keep things from me, Lett – will yer?'

Letty smiled, and shook her head. 'Come on. Let's get back to bed.'

'No, wait a minute. I gotta present for yer.' Oliver dug into the top pocket of his vest, took out the ticket, and gave it to her. 'I bought it fer a tanner from Fred Williams over at The Globe. He says he knows at least two uvver people who've been lucky.' He watched Letty looking at the ticket without having the slightest idea what it was. 'It's a sweepstake ticket. The draw takes place in January,' he said eagerly. 'First prize 'undred quid! Fink of it, Lett! Just fink what we could do wiv 'undred quid!'

Letty roared with laughter. 'You artful devil! Don't tell me I've married a gambler!'

Oliver laughed with her. '*Me* a gambler? What about yer old woman? I saw that *Racin' Gazette* under 'er chair. I bet she puts a bob or two on the 'orses.'

Although Letty dismissed that idea, she did remember that her father had once taken Beatrice to Ascot. 'Anyway, I'm surprised at you, Olly. I think it's all such a terrible waste of money.'

Letty had not stopped to think what she was saying.

'Well fer Christ's sake – it's only a tanner!' Oliver yelled and moved quickly away from her. 'OK so I know it's *your* money. But I'll pay yer back. I swear ter God I'll pay yer back every last farvin' of it!' He cupped his head despondently in his hands. 'I know I shouldn'a spent the money. It was a bloody silly thing ter do. You're the breadwinner in this place, not me. Here we are, wiv a kid on the way, and I go and throw money down the drain. Jesus Christ!'

Letty hurried to put her arm around his shoulder. 'Oh, Olly,' she said gently. 'How many times do I have to tell you? What I earn is not *my* money – it's *ours*! If you want to spend sixpence on a sweepstake ticket, you've got every right to do so!'

Olly broke away from her again. 'It's bloody madness! What are we doin' 'avin' a kid, when we don't 'ave a brass farvin' to our name? I 'ad no right ter do this to yer, Lett.

Letty felt her stomach churning. How could she have been

162

so stupid, so insensitive, she thought? What was it Vi had said to her about Oliver? 'Once he starts to feel he's not a man any more, he'll turn against you.' How true those words were. Letty felt that whatever happened, she should never allow Oliver to feel that he wasn't living up to his part of their relationship. He had to have faith that things *would* change sooner or later. After taking a deep breath, she cautiously put her arms around him, whispering, 'Thank you for giving me such a lovely present, dear.'

Oliver covered his eyes with one hand. 'Don't make fun of me, Lett. I can't take it.'

'Why would I want to do that, Olly? I love you too much.' She gently pulled his hand away from his eyes, and leaned her head on his shoulder again so that they could both look out of the window again. 'Just look at that railway line down there. Oh Olly, d'you know what I want to do when we win that hundred pounds? I want you and me to go for a trip on one of those trains.' Letty was determined to enthuse. 'We could go to . . . Bournemouth! Or Ramsgate! We might even go to Brighton. Mother and Father once took us all. The beach stretches for miles, and there are two piers, and lots of places to get a nice cup of tea . . .'

'Dreams, Letty. Nuffink but dreams.'

'Dreams cost nothing to buy, Olly.'

As if on cue, they turned to look at each other. In so short a time, they had established this bond between them. Oliver's eyes searched every feature of Letty's face – her nose, slightly bending at the tip, her dimpled chin, thin lips, clear complexion – and those blue eyes!

Letty loved all of Olly, every single bit, but – and it made her giggle – what she loved most were his ears. There was something about them that set off his personality. Large – yes. But not *too* large – just right, in fact. As Letty raised her hand and removed some of the greased hair from his eyes, she couldn't help feeling how strange it was that this man, who had once clearly had such inordinate physical strength, could be so sensitive and vulnerable.

Oliver kissed her on the nose, then said, 'Let's get some kip, girl.'

They made their way back to bed and snuggled up together. Oliver immediately complained that Letty's feet were cold, so she told him to warm them up for her. It was some time before she promised to shut up and go to sleep but, after kissing him goodnight, she finally turned over to one side, and he the other.

Although Letty's eyes were closed, she still did not sleep. Her mind was racing once more; she started dreaming to herself and, without realising it, was talking out loud again. 'They still say they're going to open up the old railway station any minute,' she whispered. 'Oh, wouldn't it be wonderful! After all, they've got to have somewhere to bring the hospital trains to. Since the war ended, there must be thousands of our boys waiting to get back from the Front.' Oliver didn't answer, so she assumed he had fallen asleep. 'If they did decide to use that train station for the troops, then they'd have to open it up again for good. Surely that would prove that the Branch Line is worth keeping up.' As she lay there, she tried to imagine what it would be like if the train station did open again. Olly could get a job there as a porter or a ticket-collector, and he could come home for his meals every day, regular as clock-work. 'Thing is, though,' she said to herself, 'I don't know what I'd do if I saw a train actually standing out there at that old platform. I mean, I've got so used to seeing them just rush past the window.' She sighed and turned on her back to stare at the ceiling. 'You're right, Olly. Dreams. Nothing but dreams! But, we should think positive. If you want something to happen badly enough, it'll happen. And when it does, you mark my words, Olly, the world is going to seem a much better place for you and me to live in . . .'

To Letty's consternation, Oliver suddenly sat up in bed and turned on her angrily. 'Stop it, Letty! Stop it! I don't wanna 'ear anuvver word about the bloody trains!'

Taken aback, she turned towards him. 'Olly! What is it? What's the matter?'

'I'll tell you what's the matter. I'm sick to death of you moonin' on about that bloody train station! It's never gonna open up again – never, never, *never*!'

Letty watched in desperation as Oliver suddenly threw off the bedclothes and got out of bed. She did likewise, followed him to the window, pleading with him. 'You mustn't lose hope, Olly. You *mustn't*! We've got so much to look forward to – you, me, and our kids . . .'

Once again Oliver swung round on her angrily. 'I don't want no kids, Letty! I never want 'em!'

Letty was now horrified. 'Oliver Hobbs! How can you say such a thing?'

'Kids need money, Letty. Money! That's somefin' I don't 'ave, and never will 'ave! Why can't you understand that? *Why*?' To her dismay he covered his face with his hands, and started to sob.

She quickly threw her arms around him, and held him close. 'Oh Olly, my dear. What have I done to you . . . ?'

'I can't take much more of this, Lett. I can't! If only I could be like you. If only I 'ad your guts! There's no way we can get outa this mess, Letty. No way . . .'

For a few moments, the two of them just stood there. She'd known only too well that this moment had to come sooner or later, for Oliver had been in despair for so long now, so she held him tighter and tighter, willing him to find the strength he lacked. As far as Letty was concerned, whatever happened, they would always be together. That was *her* strength, what helped her carry on, and she knew it would see them through these dark days. She willed it to be so and it would be so.

As they stood clasped together, the eerie silence of night was gradually broken by a distant, mesmeric sound. At first it was only a hum, but as it gathered momentum it was enough to cause Letty to turn her head towards the window. 'What's that?' she asked, quietly, almost to herself.

Then Oliver looked up, wiped his nose on his finger, and also looked towards the window. 'What?'

'Listen!' Letty's eyes were piercing out through the moon-shine. She *could* hear something approaching.

The sound grew closer and closer, and within seconds both their faces were pressed against the frosty windows, peering out to the railway lines below. It was only when they heard the shriek of an engine whistle that they realised what was happening. Yes! It was a train all right. But this time there was something different about it.

'It's slowin' down!' Oliver was desperately trying to rub clean the inside of one of the window panes, and ignored Letty's cry of disbelief. 'It's stoppin', I tell yer!'

The train was indeed slowing down with a deafening screech of brakes, and when it drew parallel with the back yards of Citizen Road Letty and Oliver could even see the faces of the passengers lit up inside the carriages.

Letty was jumping up and down excitedly. 'It's full of troops . . . and nurses! It's a hospital train and it's stopping at the old station!'

Just a few yards down the line the train and its long haul of carriages halted alongside the platform, which was in sore need of repair. As it did so the old station burst into life as men and women, carrying oil lamps, seemed to appear from nowhere, descending on the train with stretchers and chairs, to collect some of the more badly injured passengers.

'It's open again!' yelled Letty, almost delirious with joy. Then she clasped her hands together, and prayed. 'Oh thank you, God, thank you!' She threw her arms around Oliver, and hugged him. 'It's all right now, Olly. Everything's going to be all right. Now we can really look forward to having our kids!' As she spoke the whistle of the hospital train shrieked loud and clear. It was obvious that the back yards of Citizen Road were never going to be quite the same again.

Ronald Ernest Hobbs was born on 20th July 1919. He weighed nearly eight pounds at birth, and cried an awful lot every night. Oliver thought he had a pug-shaped face, more like a bulldog's than a baby's. But Letty did not agree. In fact she was absolutely convinced that the newcomer was a carbon copy of his father.

Chapter 13

Although Europe was no longer at war, the 1920s turned out to be a bleak and sombre time for the thousands of British troops who had returned home from the battlefields. What they came back to was unemployment, long dole queues, food shortages and above all a soul-destroying lack of morale. Nobody had any faith in the politicians. Even though Parliament was dissolved two weeks after the signing of the Armistice, the Coalition Government, led by David Lloyd George, seemed completely incapable of coping with the material and psychological aftermath of one of the bloodiest wars in living memory. There was also a sense of bitterness and division between ordinary people and those who, although they may have suffered with them during the war, seemed so much better off after it. Whilst the bright young things flapped their way through the Charleston in London's ballrooms, in working districts throughout the country the soup queues never dwindled.

Fortunately, however, Oliver at last got himself a job, collecting tickets from local passengers on the three trains a day that stopped at the re-opened railway station behind Citizen Road. It didn't pay much, but at least it restored his independence, giving him the chance to feel he was helping to put money aside for the first new addition to the family. Sadly, the job was short-lived, for the London and North-Eastern Railway Company decided that the old station was not, after all, a viable permanent proposition. So, once again it was closed down, this time for good. Luckily, Oliver's gloom did not last too long for, quite unexpectedly, his application for another job as a ticket-collector at the Finsbury Park Underground Station was accepted. Overnight, his life seemed to change, for he was at last a full-time, permanent wage-earner. Furthermore, he was given his own uniform and cap, which he wore, as smartly as if he were still in the Army. The job itself was in three daily shifts – or 'turns', as Oliver called them, early, middle, and late. Despite the fact that his wounded leg obstinately refused to heal properly, he always insisted on walking the half-mile or so to work. First turn commenced at five o'clock in the morning so it was a solitary figure whose noisy footsteps echoed along the silent, deserted pavements of Isledon and Seven Sisters Road.

For Letty, the years after the end of the war were some of the happiest she had ever known. Giving birth to Ronnie had not been easy but she revelled in the joy and pride of being a wife *and* mother. Although there was now no need to keep on a full-time day job, she insisted on carrying on with her cleaning job at Pakeman Street School, even though it sometimes meant taking little Ronnie along with her. One of her favourite pastimes was going to meet Oliver at the end of a middle turn, which usually meant around seven o'clock in the evening. Sometimes during the summer months, she took a flask of hot tea and some sandwiches, and they all three went for a stroll in Finsbury Park. Letty was in her seventh heaven, watching baby Ronnie throw scraps of bread to the ducks at the edge of the lake, or just simply strolling arm-in-arm with Oliver through the rhododendron gardens. And just sometimes she would remember back to the boating trips she and Tom had had on the lake years before.

There was a long gap before any more additions were made to the family. But on 31st January 1928 Edward Richard Hobbs arrived, seven pounds at birth, with a voracious appetite and, much to everyone's despair, a determination to make monotonous humming sounds in his cot – morning, noon and night! Letty's constant anxiety, however, was the condition of Oliver's old leg injury. Night after night she lay awake, listening to him groaning in pain in his sleep. By the beginning of 1930 he had been in hospital for seven operations, but the wound remained inflamed most of the time and stubbornly refused to heal. By the middle of April, Letty became even more concerned, when Oliver showed her several ugly-looking ulcers which had formed on the injured leg.

Things finally came to a climax one Thursday afternoon when Oliver didn't return home after an appointment with an orthopaedic specialist at the Roehampton Ex-Servicemen's Hospital. Worried out of her mind, Letty went down to Finsbury Park to see if he'd gone straight on to work. She was surprised to find Mr Pearson, the station master, on duty at the ticket-barrier. Oliver was supposed to be there on middle turn, but there was no sign of him.

' 'Allo, Mrs Hobbs. What you doin' here?' As he caught sight of Letty, Pearson continued to collect tickets from the passengers filling past him. 'I thought you'd be at the 'ospital wiv Olly?'

'He wouldn't let me go with him, Mr Pearson. He hasn't been home yet, so I thought he must've come straight back here.'

'Sorry, Mrs 'Obbs. 'Aven't seen Oliver all day. All tickets now, please!'

Letty turned around to look up at the small station clock on the wall above them. It was four o'clock and Olly's hospital appointment had been for nine o'clock that morning.

Pearson dropped a pile of used tickets into his collection box, and stopped briefly to talk with Letty. 'I don't know if I should mention it or not, Mrs 'Obbs, but – well, on my way to work a coupla hours ago, I thought I saw your Olly going into the park.'

Letty's mind immediately rushed to all sorts of conclusions. Oliver was the most punctual man in the world. The one thing she could be quite certain about was that he would sooner die than be late for his job. Something was wrong. She recognised all the symptoms. Within a few minutes, she was turning through the main gates of Finsbury Park. She knew exactly where she was making for. By the time she reached the children's playground, her stomach was churning and churning, for she was now positive that something must have upset Oliver at the hospital. Suddenly, her destination was in view. It was the railway bridge just alongside the football pitch. Letty knew that was where he'd be. It was the place he always came to when he was depressed or needed to think. Already she could see a solitary figure standing half-way along the bridge, arms resting on the iron railing, peering down to the line below.

'Oliver!' Letty called gently. 'Olly, dear.'

Oliver turned slowly, and looked at her. A cigarette was drooping from his lips. He didn't answer.

Letty walked quickly to him. 'Olly, dear. What are you doing here? You should be at work.'

Oliver turned slowly; he threw down his fag, and stamped on it. 'Go 'ome, Lett. I'm not goin' in ter work today. And I'm not gonna start answerin' yer questions! Get back 'ome to the kids!'

'They're perfectly all right. Ron's looking after little Eddie.' She moved a pace towards her husband. 'What did he say, Olly?' she said, carefully. 'What did the specialist tell you?'

'Nuffin'!'

Letty foolishly put a hand on his arm. He quickly shrugged it off. Then she waited a moment before questioning him. 'What did he say about the ulcers on your leg? Did he tell you why . . . why it's turned black below your knee?'

Oliver snapped back. 'It's gangrene!' Then he swung around to look at her. 'Are yer satisfied now?'

Letty looked at him with a mixture of anxiety and confusion. 'Gangrene?'

'It means that my bloody leg is rottin' away! It means . . .' Gradually his voice was cracking with emotion. '. . . it means . . . it's gotta come off! They wanna amputate me leg – just below the knee-cap, they said. But I'm tellin' yer right now I won't let 'em do it. I won't!'

For a brief second, Letty closed her eyes and took a deep breath. She quickly composed herself, and said calmly, 'Are you sure you've got it right, Olly dear? You know how you get things muddled up at times.'

'For Chrissake!' – he was so worked up, he was grinding his teeth – 'Yer don't 'ave ter be told twice when someone tells yer, yer bloody leg's gotta come off!' As soon as he had spoken, he moved away to stand in the middle of the footbridge, staring in total apathy up at the sky.

Letty did not know what to say or do next. So much was going through her mind, she could hardly think straight. All these years she'd tried to look on the bright side, convincing herself that one day Oliver's leg *would* heal. And now it was clear it wouldn't. She had no answers this time.

Eventually, she went to him again. 'How – how soon does he want to do it?'

'Termorrer mornin'.'

Letty's face crunched up in agony. 'Tomorrow! So soon?'

' 'E says there's a danger the poison'll get into me blood.

172

If they wait any longer chances are I'll, I'll . . . I'm not gonna do it, Lett. I'm not goin' through wiv this – not for no one!'

Letty put a comforting arm around him then said, 'Olly. You *must* go through with it.'

Although Oliver wasn't actually crying, he was bursting with tension and fear. 'Yeah – that's right. I thought *you'd* say that! It's easy for you to talk standin' there on two good feet!' The moment he spoke, he realised what he had said. He immediately felt so ashamed that he threw his arms around Letty, and broke down.

'Oh Christ, Lett! What am I gonna do?'

Letty held on to him tight. It no longer felt strange to have him crying in her arms. It had happened so many times before. Why shouldn't he if he felt the need to? And, my God, thought Letty, if anyone had the right to cry it was Oliver. How much had he gone through over the years? Night after night, sitting up on the edge of the bed, trying to rub away the pain that had engulfed his limb. Letty felt she wanted to cry too. In fact she hadn't wanted to cry so badly since her brother was killed during the war. But, for some strange reason, the tears wouldn't come. Her mind, despite itself, was running on to the future, and how she was going to get Oliver through these coming nightmares.

Oliver snuggled his head on to Letty's shoulder, and his cap fell to the ground. Neither of them bothered to pick it up.

'It's the end of my life, Lett,' he whispered in a quiet sob. 'I've got nuffin' to live for now. Nuffin' . . .'

There was a split-second pause. Then, as Letty gradually took in what had just been said, she felt the blood rushing through her veins. She suddenly took hold of him, held him at arm's length and said firmly, 'Oliver Hobbs! Don't ever let me hear you talk like that! You've got a hell of a lot to

173

live for, and don't you ever forget it! There's me, and the kids, and all our future years together.' From her coat pocket, she took out a handkerchief and started to dab Oliver's tears. 'Shall I tell you something, Olly? I was talking to Mr Cotton the other day. He says he might have a little house he could rent us in a couple of months' time. Oh, it won't cost us much. But at least the kids wouldn't have to sleep on the floor any more. Think of it, Olly.' She held his face up, and looked into his reddened eyes. 'A house of our very own!'

Oliver's voice was barely audible. 'Pearson told me that if I 'ave to go into 'ospital any more times, 'e wasn't sure 'e could let me 'old on to me job.'

Letty stooped down and picked up Oliver's cap. 'That's the last thing we're going to worry about,' she said dismissively. 'You'll soon find another job. You're a good, honest worker, Olly, and you work damn hard. Anyone would jump at the chance of employing someone like you.'

Oliver stared at her. There was a trace of an ironic smile on his face. 'Someone like me? A cripple wiv one leg?'

'Yes, Olly. You're worth more on one leg than most people are on two.' With one finger she removed a few strands of his greased hair that had flopped across his eyes. 'Listen to me, dear. We're going to get through this *together*, you and I. We've got be strong, Olly! And d'you know why? Because we've got so many things to look forward to, that's why.' She drew close to him, and with the tips of her fingers from one hand, touched him delicately, affectionately on his lips. In reply, he kissed her fingers. 'It's not the end of your life, my dear Olly,' she said quietly. 'It's just the start of it.'

Letty plonked Oliver's hat on his head, and put her arm through his. Then the two of them slowly walked off the bridge, and made their way back home to Citizen Road.

*　　*　　*

174

That night, before Oliver went into hospital, was the longest Letty could remember. Early in the evening she went to the sweetshop in Hornsey Road to buy him some of his favourite treacle toffees to take into hospital. It wasn't really much of a treat, she thought, but at least he could have something to nibble at when the operation was all over. She took the long way round because she needed time to think. Who should she let know about Oliver's operation? What was life going to be like for them all from now on. For a start she would have to find a full-time job again, and someone to baby-sit just until Oliver was able to do it himself. Maybe her mother? Or Vi? No, not Vi. Oliver would never allow it; he just couldn't get on with his sister. Anyway, Vi had enough on her plate, being married to that Frank O'Malley, with three kids of her own and probably more on the way now she'd been converted to a Roman Catholic. So much to think about, so much to plan.

Whilst Letty was out, Oliver washed himself down in their aluminium bath and thought a lot too. Hard as he tried, he just couldn't get out of his mind what it was going to be like to come to after the op and find a gap where his leg should be. For a start, he'd never be able to kick a football around with his kids, or run after them in the street. And never be able to take on anyone who tried to pick on him in the pub. He also dreaded the thought of his father seeing him hobbling around on one leg. He just bet himself the old git would take the piss! So would his elder brothers. But most of all, it was Letty he worried about. It just wasn't right! What would she feel like sharing the bed at night with him? Right then and there he decided that whatever happened, he would always make sure that Letty never actually had to see what was left of his leg. In fact, the only honourable thing for him to do would be to leave Letty and the kids. They had a right to a life of their own, without having to cater for a

175

cripple day after day. There was no other way.

They didn't say much to each other when Letty got back, and when the time came for bed, without saying a word they both knew the other didn't want to turn in as normal. Neither had any sleep: they sat up through the night on the settee, drinking cocoa. The only sounds were from Ronnie and little Eddie turning restlessly in their bed on the floor behind the settee. Occasionally Letty or Oliver would check on them, and Oliver hoped bleakly to himself that they would never have to go through what he was going through now.

By the time daylight finally filtered through the big arch-window, Letty was already packing Oliver's little suitcase for him. It was the suitcase she had bought for him years ago, after the war, when he started going into hospital to have his operations. Although it was getting a little worn by now, it still had very strong locks on it, and had been well worth the two shillings and sixpence she had paid for it. Letty had decided she would not think about Oliver's operation now, not until it was all over. For the time being she had to think of practical things. First she packed his cotton pyjamas. Oliver hated the things and never wore them at home: he much preferred his flannel button-up vest and long under-pants. Then in went some handkerchiefs, his football pools coupon, the treacle toffees, and a clean pair of socks. Letty suddenly stopped what she was doing. She was holding the pair of socks in her hand. For a brief moment, the whole reality of what was about to happen came into focus. She decided not to pack them.

At the Roehampton Military Hospital, Oliver was checked into his ward by a bright-faced young nurse, and Letty waited for him to change into his pyjamas. Letty spoke briefly to the Ward Sister who told her that the operation would not be taking place until around about eight o'clock that evening, since they would have to do various tests first. She could spend half-an-hour with Oliver, but after that it was best that she went home and not return to the hospital until after the operation, preferably the following morning.

Letty hated seeing Oliver in a hospital bed again. He looked so lost, so uncomfortable in the clean pair of pyjamas she had ironed for him the evening before. For the first few minutes of their half-hour together, neither said a word. Letty sat in a chair beside the bed, holding Oliver's hand, squeezing it every so often to show that she was sharing his thoughts, and rubbing this thumb with hers to show that he was not going to go through his ordeal without her support.

'I don't want yer comin' up 'ere, Lett.' As he spoke, Oliver's head was leaning back on his pillow, and he was staring aimlessly up at the ceiling. 'I don't want yer comin' up 'ere 'til – 'til I get out. That is – *if* I get out.'

Letty squeezed his hand hard, and turned on him sharply. 'Don't you dare talk like that, Olly! Don't you ever let me hear you talk like that! You'd better get out! Me and the kids can't manage without you, so just remember that! And if you think you'll keep me away, well I'm telling you right now, you haven't a chance.' She was deliberately being firm and practical with him. It was the only way to give him strength. It was *her* way. 'Of course, if you don't want to see me – .'

Oliver raised his head up from the pillow, and looked at her. Nothing Letty said could disguise how she was feeling, and he knew it. It was that look in those blue eyes of hers, the anxiety, the fear. Although she was a tower of strength in practically everything she did, Letty – *his* Letty was as near to breaking point as he was. 'I wanna see yer, Lett. Yer know I do.' Once again they stared into each other's eyes in silence, then gradually exchanged a gentle smile.

A few minutes later, a nurse arrived to offer Oliver a cup of tea. Without betraying any sign of emotion, Letty kissed

Oliver on the lips, and with an almost formal, 'Bye, bye, dear. See you later,' she calmly walked out of the hospital grounds, and almost immediately caught the Number 14 bus. She was just in time, for within a few minutes, a chilly wind arose, bringing with it a skyful of fluttering white snowflakes.

Chapter 14

The following morning, Citizen Road was covered by a good two inches of snow, and Letty had to walk with caution to the Hornsey Road bus stop. But even though it was only six o'clock, and not yet light, there was already a thaw setting in. She had to wait a good twenty minutes for the first bus of the day to appear, and when it did, it seemed to travel at no more than a snail's pace; the journey to Roehampton seemed to take forever. All along the way, people were busily shovelling snow away from their pavements, leaving heaps of dirty slush in the kerbside gutters. Just occasionally, she closed her eyes, hoping to catch up on some of the sleep she hadn't got during the night, but her mind was pulsating with too much anxiety.

Finally inside the hospital building itself, the heat from the cast-iron radiators was a welcome relief, but as she hurriedly made her way up the stone steps to Oliver's ward, she felt as though her legs were going to give way beneath her. The stench of ether, iodine and carbolic everywhere made it even worse. When she eventually reached the ward gates, she peered through first to see if she could see Oliver inside. But there was no sign of him. She took a deep breath, and entered.

'The operation was quite satisfactory, Mrs Hobbs.' A different Ward Sister from the one Letty had talked to the previous evening greeted her. She couldn't place her accent – she thought she might have come from Devon or Cornwall – and although the sister seemed to have a permanently strict expression on her face, she treated Letty with care and sympathy. 'He's still a bit groggy after the operation. But I think it'll do him good to see you – just for a few minutes though.' She turned to go, then briefly stopped again. 'It's a difficult time, Mrs Hobbs,' she said, almost in a whisper. 'He'll need all the love you can give him.'

Letty nodded that she understood, then quietly followed the red and white of Sister's military nursing uniform into the ward. As they went, she tried to avoid looking at the other patients, most of whom seemed about the same age as Oliver. By the time she reached the end of the ward, Letty's heart was in her mouth with trepidation. This was the moment she had been dreading most of all: she would see for the first time that awful space in the bed where Oliver's leg should be.

'Remember now, just a few minutes.' Sister's hand was on the curtain screen surrounding Oliver's bed in the far corner at the end of the ward. 'Here we are, Private Hobbs.' Sister kept her voice low, as she pulled back the curtain to allow Letty to enter. 'Look who's come to see you.'

Letty took a deep breath, broke into a broad, forced smile, and entered. 'Hallo, dear,' she said softly. 'How you feeling?'

Oliver didn't answer. His face was turned towards the wall.

Sister drew the curtain behind Letty, and left them.

For a brief moment, Letty stood near the end of the bed. She forced herself to look at Oliver's face first and then she decided to do it quickly, and without thought. But when the moment came, the impact was less than she'd expected: Oliver's right limb was concealed beneath the sheets by a wire frame. Letty went and sat in the chair beside the bed.

'I must say, they're taking good care of you here, aren't they, dear?' Her voice was not much more than a whisper. 'You've got a lovely view from the window. Not that you want to be out there in this weather though. It's freezing!'

Oliver still didn't answer. His face remained turned away from her, but his eyes were wide open.

'You're going to be all right, Olly. Sister says the doctors are very pleased with you.'

''Alf a man.' His voice was groggy, only just audible. 'That's all that's left of me now. 'Alf a bloody man!'

Letty felt as though her insides were being torn apart. But she willed herself to be strong. 'Half a man's better than no man at all, Olly.' Her voice was quiet, but firm, as she bent over him and kissed him on the forehead. 'Come on now, dear. You know what they say: Every cloud has a silver lining. It's all over, Olly. All you've got to do now is to hurry up and get yourself better. I miss you. So do the kids. They want to know when their pop's coming home again.'

Oliver's face crumpled. 'I don't wan'em ter see me like this, Lett. Not ever.' As he reached up with one hand to dab at the tears that were gradually trickling down on to his pillow, Letty took hold of his other hand, and held it firmly. 'I've never heard such nonsense!' she scolded. 'Ron and Eddie are proud of their pop. So am I! You'll always be my handsome soldier boy.' Letty meant what she said. Letty still thought Oliver one of the most attractive men she had ever seen. As he lay there looking forlorn, she had already decided that when he was fit again, they must go in for another child – just one more.

'Ow'm I gonna get 'round on one bloody leg?' asked Oliver, trying to lick his dry lips. 'I'll be a stone round yer neck for the rest of me life.'

Letty quickly became very practical. 'Not at all. Sister was telling me they make the most wonderful artificial legs these days. In a few months from now, you'll be right back to normal again. We'll do it together, Olly – you *and* me. But we've got to be sensible. We've got to make a pact. No more secrets. From now on we share all our problems together. That's what you made me promise that night the train stopped for us, and that's what we'll do now. Is that a bargain?'

Oliver, with tears still falling back on to his pillow, looked up at her almost like a child. 'Yeah – bargain.' As he lay there, he felt crushed with guilt. How could he make a bargain that he knew he was never going to be able to keep? How could he deceive the one person he loved more than anybody in the world? And yet, his instinct kept telling him over and over again that he just *couldn't* tell her about his meeting in the wartime trenches with her brother Tom.

'Right then. I'll tell you what we're going to do first.' Letty stood up straight, and took hold of the bed-clothes. To Oliver's horror, she pulled them back. 'Don't upset yourself, dear. I just want to see what they've done to you, that's all.'

Oliver was pleading. 'No, Lett! Please don't look at me!'

For a brief moment, Letty stood there, just looking at the heavily bandaged stump which had once formed part of Oliver's leg. Whatever she felt inside, outwardly she showed no emotion, no fear, no distaste: there was no expression on her face whatsoever. Then she calmly replaced the covers, and tidied them.

As Oliver turned his face away again, Letty bent low over him and said quietly, 'Olly, dear. Will you do me a favour, please? From now on, will you let *me* be your other leg? I promise, I'll be as firm as a rock.' She leaned across and urged, 'we've both got to be strong, haven't we? It won't be long before you're back in our own home again. We'll soon be having some of our sing-songs together. Hey – Olly, what's your favourite?'

182

Oliver just shook his head.

'Well I bet *I* know.' She drew closer, so that she was whispering in his ear. 'Remember that song we used to sing together – soon after we were married? How does it go now?' Quietly, she began:

> You are my honey, honey-suckle
> I am the bee,
> I'd like to sip the honey sweet
> From those red lips you see . . .

Although hardly audible, Oliver gradually managed to join in with her, singing:

> I love you dearly, dearly
> And I want you to love me,
> You are my honey, honey-suckle
> I am the bee.

On the other side of the curtains which were drawn around Oliver's bed, the Ward Sister had stopped to listen to Letty and Oliver singing quietly together. It made her day.

There was no snow around on the morning that Oliver finally left Roehampton Hospital almost two months later. In fact it was so warm, Letty had to buy him a second-hand Panama straw hat, just in case he caught sunstroke: after nearly ten weeks locked up in a hospital ward, Oliver wanted to make quite sure he didn't have to go back. Needless to say, Letty had visited him every single day, including Saturdays and Sundays. She was always the first visitor to arrive, and practically ran down the ward to Oliver's bed. After a week and a half, the other patients had started timing her. Although at first Oliver hadn't wanted any other visitors, he was pleasantly surprised when, one Sunday afternoon,

Beatrice Edginton turned up, bringing with her a half-bottle of whisky, which she knew was her son-in-law's favourite tipple. She didn't stay long, though: she'd got herself an office cleaning job at the Archway, and had to be up at crack of dawn most mornings. A frequent visitor was, of course, Oliver's young brother, Sam, who was now a strapping twenty-six-year-old and spent most of his time looking for navvying work on building sites. It was Sam who usually filled Oliver in with all the gossip about the rest of the family. Vi and Frank turned up once in the entire ten weeks. The excuse was that Vi was too exhausted by looking after their three kids, and hinted that another one was on the way. But in truth Oliver was relieved that she didn't come again. Even though he was, to his surprise, getting to like Frank O'Malley, his inability to get on with Vi increased every time he saw her. It puzzled Letty. The other regular visitors were Tilly and Bill Brooks, who never came empty-handed.

Whilst he was in hospital, Oliver had made plans as to how he was going to cope when he got out. Encouraged by Letty, he'd worked hard at mastering the use of his crutches, though he longed for the day when he would be strong enough to be fitted for an artificial limb. But the reality of the situation surfaced on the day Oliver returned to Citizen Road. The first hurdle was getting up the stairs and, even though he bitterly resisted the idea, he finally had to agree to be carried up by Sam and Bill Brooks. His greatest surprise, however, was the kids, for neither Ron nor Eddie seemed to take any notice of his disability. In fact, they discovered a lovely bed-time game when Oliver wiggled his leg at them, sending them into fits of laughter and in time, Letty found a wonderful use for the old woollen stump socks with which the hospital had issued Oliver. She washed and unwound them, then knitted them into blankets. 'Waste not, want not,' she insisted.

And so started Oliver's long period of convalescence and rehabilitation with the world at large. It wasn't easy. But, thanks partly to Letty's bullying, and partly to his own obstinacy and determination, each day brought him a little more strength and confidence. Soon he had mastered the art of getting up and down the stairs using only one crutch. And it wasn't long after that that he was hobbling his way along the streets in the evenings to Pakeman Street School, where to Letty's delight he was waiting to meet her after she finished her spell of cleaning. But the only snag in his life was a major one. Once again he was no longer the bread-winner, and it was a constant anxiety to him that Letty was slaving her guts out each day at two jobs. From six-thirty in the morning until five in the evening she was serving bread and cakes at 'Stagnells', the baker's in Seven Sisters Road, and from six to ten every evening she was scrubbing floors at the school. It was a pulverising daily routine for her, and Oliver didn't know how much longer she would be able to keep it up. He longed for the day when he would have an artificial leg, and be able to find a job of his own.

Neither Letty nor Oliver had seen anything of Annie and Ernie Hobbs since before the operation. All their children, except Sam, had now left home, and were married with kids of their own. However, Letty was always puzzled why Olly's three older brothers never kept in contact with him, despite the fact that they all lived in various parts of the same borough of Islington. In fact, ever since Letty had married, she had had to come to terms with quite a lot of unusual things in the Hobbs' family life. None of them seemed to think it was strange for members of the same family not to meet up once they moved away from home. It wasn't exactly that they didn't get on with each other, just that they preferred to 'keep themselves to themselves'. It was a kind of unspoken, rather callous attitude to family life, but although Letty didn't approve she had no alternative but to accept such behaviour. She and Oliver did meet up with two of the brothers and their wives once or twice, usually out shopping, or in a local pub, but, despite Letty's efforts to start a conversation, the Hobbs' brothers showed little desire to renew their family ties. For obvious reasons, however, Letty did understand that old Annie could never have made the journey to the hospital at Roehampton. But she felt bitter that her father-in-law, Ernie, had never made the effort. After all, Oliver *was* his own son, and the very least he could have done was to have written or something. But Oliver dismissed these irritations of Letty's. Over the years he had come not to expect anything from the 'old git', as he always called him. In any case, Olly explained, Ernie had never learnt how to read or write, and he'd have only taken the piss out of Oliver with his one leg. Nonetheless, Letty was still not happy about what she saw as her father-in-law's callousness, but decided to obey Oliver's instructions not to make contact with him.

It was therefore something of a surprise when, on 8th July – Letty's birthday and over three weeks after Oliver had returned home, Elsie Layton, their ground-floor neighbour, called up the stairs to tell the Hobbs they had a gentleman-caller. Oliver nearly fell off his chair when he saw Letty bring Ernie into the room. The 'old git' was certainly looking a good bit older than his sixty-four years, for his hair was as white as snow beneath his flat cap, and he had developed a stoop which seemed to make him shorter than his six foot one inches. He wasn't wearing a jacket, but he still looked neat and tidy, with a clean white shirt, red polka-dot choker round his neck, and his usual braces and belt. Letty was polite, but very straight-faced, and, even though she begrudged it, she offered her father-in-law a chair and a cup of tea.

'No – fanks all the same, Lett.' Ernie stood there gawkily, shuffling from one foot to the other. 'Gotta get back. The missus in't feelin' up ter much. Touch o' the flu, I reckon. She wants yer ter 'ave these.' Ernie held out something in a paper bag. ' 'Appy berfday, Lett. Annie remembered – not me. They're Osbornes. She says yer like 'em. Our Sam said so. Is that right?'

Letty took the packet of biscuits, which were indeed her favourite. She held them in her hand as though they were made of gold. 'Oh yes, Dad. I like them very much.' She had to stand on tip-toe to kiss him on the lips: the Hobbs family always thought that kissing on the cheeks was la-de-dah.

During this exchange, Ernie had deliberately avoided casting a glance towards Oliver's leg. Whilst Letty busied herself making tea, it occurred to her that Ernie was going to leave without even mentioning it. But eventually he turned to Oliver, who was sitting in his usual easy-chair by the stove, and said, matter-of-factly, ' 'Ow's fings then, son?'

Oliver nearly decided not to answer. But a quick glare from Letty soon changed his mind. 'OK, fanks.'

Ernie rubbed the stubble on his chin nervously, then ventured a few paces towards Oliver. He stood in silence, looking down directly at the space where his son's leg should have been and at the trouser-leg which was held up with a huge safety-pin. Then Ernie took a deep, uneven breath. 'Yer've 'ad a rough time all right.' As he spoke, his voice cracked, and to Letty's consternation he quite suddenly broke down. Oliver watched in absolute astonishment as Letty rushed to comfort him. In all the years he had been living at home, Oliver had never seen his father cry and it was shattering. He, too, reached out to his weeping father, and embraced him.

It was some minutes after he'd recovered that Ernie

revealed the main reason for his visit. Annie was not suffering from the flu at all. The doctor had told him she had an ailment called dropsy, and that her body was swelling up with fluid. By the look of her, Ernie didn't think she'd last much longer.

Within an hour, Letty and Oliver were at old Annie's bedside. Once they saw her, there was no doubt in their minds that it was only a matter of time.

Chapter 15

Annie Hobbs died peacefully in her sleep at ten minutes past three on the afternoon of 10th July 1930. The old lady died as she wished, in her own bed, and with Ernie at her side. By the end, her legs were swollen to almost double their size. It wasn't difficult to accept that it was a happy release.

Apart from Ernie, the only person with Annie when she died was Letty. The moment she knew her mother-in-law was ill, she'd spent as much time with her as she could. In those last forty-eight hours, the two had developed a closeness that Letty knew she'd never forget. 'Let no 'arm come to yer, Lett gel,' were the last words Annie whispered into Letty's ears. 'Gord in 'eaven bless yer.'

After Annie died, it was Letty who laid her out. It was the first time she had ever laid eyes on a dead person, but to her surprise she wasn't at all frightened.

Vi arrived only after her mother had passed on. But she refused to enter the bedroom, becoming hysterical at the thought. So for five minutes, she stayed on the landing outside, praying for her mother's soul, crossing herself frequently.

Annie's funeral was a sparse and uneventful affair, except for one fleeting moment, which made Letty and Oliver smile: the well-groomed black horse pulling the old lady's hearse suddenly met a companion horse en route from the church, and they exchanged snorted greetings. Old Annie would have liked that. She was buried in Finchley Cemetery, with all her family around her graveside. Strangely though, none of them shed any tears. Except Ernie.

Saturday afternoons were Letty's favourite time of the week, for Sam always took Oliver to watch a local school football team playing in Finsbury Park, giving her the chance to go shopping in the Holloway Road with Ron and Eddie. The day always ended up with high tea, and usually Sam stayed the night, sleeping on the landing covered by one of Letty's home-knitted blankets.

Over the past year and a half, Sam had grown to worship Letty and Oliver: they had almost taken the place of his own parents, and to him, Oliver was a hero. If anyone had ever dared to raise even a finger to his brother, he would have leapt to his defence, and made short work of it too. Sam had a strong, muscular build, and a hard punch in his right hand, which he'd used against opponents in both street and pub in his time – for although Sam had always been a shy and sensitive kid, he had had to learn to stand up for himself.

The trouble had always been that he was the youngest. His arrival had been, to say the least, unexpected, and with three brothers and a sister before him, Ernie and Annie Hobbs had run out of energy to take enough care of him. From a very early age, Sam knew that the only person who could really look after him was himself. But when Letty came along, his whole life had changed. She actually took the time and trouble to talk to him, to ask him what *he* thought. Oliver had been astonished by Sam's transformation from a tough streetfighter to someone who wanted to find out about things. Now, each day, everyone was discovering something new and surprising about Sam. But the biggest surprise came during the tea-time one Saturday afternoon, when Sam announced that he wouldn't be able to stay the night because

190

he'd asked a girlfriend to go out to the pictures with him.

' 'Onestly Lett, you'd really like 'er. 'Er name's Peggy. She lives up near the Angel. Her mum and dad run a newspaper shop in Offord Road. That's where I first met 'er – when I went in to buy some fags.' Sam looked eagerly, first at Letty then at Oliver. It was almost as though he was trying to sell Peggy to them. 'She's a good-looker. Lovely eyes. Knows what she's talkin' about, too.'

Letty found herself chuckling affectionately at him. 'Sam, I think it's wonderful! She sounds absolutely lovely, doesn't she Olly?'

'Yeah. Dinky-dink. You crafty bugger, Sam. How long's this been goin' on then?'

Sam became self-conscious and flushed slightly. ' 'Bout six munffs.'

Oliver nearly choked. 'Six munffs! Blimey, yer oughta be married by now!'

All three of them laughed, but Letty was determined that Sam wasn't to think they were making fun of him. 'Why don't you bring her round to tea one Sunday?' she asked. 'We'd love to meet her. Wouldn't we Olly?'

'Course! Bring 'er over!'

Sam's eyes lit up like beacons. 'D'yer mean it, Lett? D'yer mean it, Oll? Could I really bring 'er over? Honest? Ter-morrer's Sunday. How about termorrer afternoon? Course, if it's too early . . .'

'Oh no! Not at all, Sam. Bring her along. I can soon make a cake or something.' Letty exchanged a quick look with Oliver, who merely grinned back at her.

Sam was overjoyed. He leapt up from the tea-table with a 'Oh fanks, Lett! Fanks, Oll! Wait 'til I tell Peggs! She won't 'arf be pleased!', then with great excitement, rushed to the door, grabbing his flat cap as he went. 'Mustn't be late,' he called back before leaving. 'I said I'd meet 'er outside the

'Olloway Empire at seven. They got this new pianist for some 'orror film that's on. It'll scare the daylights out of 'er – I 'ope!'

Letty and Oliver roared with laughter as Sam slammed the door, and they heard him rushing down the stairs. For the next hour they could talk of nothing else. Letty was overjoyed that Sam had at last found a girl he liked, and immediately started making plans as to how she and Oliver could help the boy to find a job, so that he could marry and settle down. Sam had had a raw deal in life; this was his chance to prove that he was worth so much more than his parents had ever been able to give him.

Sunday afternoon couldn't come soon enough for Sam. He couldn't wait to introduce his 'Peggs' to Letty and Oliver, and to get their blessing. Needless to say, Letty had done everything she could to make sure that Peggs felt at home. The tea-table was neatly laid with a clean white table-cloth, the best Prince Albert china tea-set was used, and there were even a few marigolds in a small glass vase. Letty had prepared thinly-cut cheese and pickle sandwiches, a tomato and lettuce salad, a fruit cake which she'd made with some of the raisins and sultanas left over from Christmas, and a strawberry jelly mould with tinned pears. Sam couldn't have been more proud of the home he was showing off to his special girl.

Peggy Taylor was quite brassy-looking, with grey-green eyes and curly blonde hair. Although she was only just twenty, she looked older than her years, and in some ways her features were not dissimilar to Letty's, for she had the same shape face, mouth and lips. Oliver took to her at once, and thought she was a 'real good-looker'. Letty, however, wasn't quite so sure.

'Mum and Dad are hopin' to sell the shop eventually.

Sellin' newspapers an' tobacco seven days a week is very tirin' work.' Peggy sipped her tea, then delicately wiped her lips on one of the yellow paper table napkins Letty had provided. 'They're hopin' to move out near my Auntie Nellie in Walthamstow. There are some lovely places out that way.'

'So I've heard.' Letty smiled weakly, and offered Peggy a slice of fruit cake. To her irritation, Peggy smiled back, shaking her head politely.

Sam was sitting at Peggy's side, and he was hanging on her every word. 'Tell Lett and Oll about yer Aunt Nellie, Peggs,' he spluttered eagerly, his mouth chewing on a huge piece of Letty's cake. 'You know – about the dress.'

Peggy lowered her eyes shyly, and coloured slightly. 'Oh, they don't want to hear about that, Sam.'

'Course they do!' Sam turned to Letty with great enthusiasm. 'When Peggs gets married, her Aunt Nellie's gonna let her use her own weddin' dress. Cost a fortune up West.'

'Really?' Letty turned to Peggy. She was impressed – or looked as though she was. 'How wonderful.'

'So when's the big day then?' asked Oliver, mischievously.

Peggy quickly sipped her tea again, trying hard to disguise her blushes.

'Yer never know – eh, Peggs?' Sam leaned across, and plonked a kiss on Peggy's blushing cheek. Letty couldn't help noticing that Peggy immediately wiped her cheek on her paper napkin.

'Leave the poor girl alone you two!' Letty was quick to relieve Peggy's embarrassment, and started re-filling everyone's cups with tea from her huge brown china tea-pot. 'She'll get married sooner or later – *when* she finds the right man.'

Everyone laughed at that, and dug into the strawberry jelly and tinned pears.

Sharing the washing-up with Peggy, Letty thought the girl was actually more intelligent than she had at first imagined, and was really quite nice. But something worried her: it was to do with the fact that she hardly once talked about Sam, how they met, or how they got on together. In fact, ever since they first arrived, Letty had been troubled that it was Sam who had done all the fussing around, without getting anything in return. Somehow, the relationship didn't seem to be mutual. They were two very different people.

After Peggy and Sam had left, Letty hardly discussed them with Oliver. But she thought a lot. And what she thought was that Peggy was not a natural choice of partner for the easy-going Sam.

Sam and Peggy had decided to walk back to Peggy's place above the newspaper shop in Offord Road. On the way, Peggy told Sam how much she liked Letty and Oliver, that they were so warm-hearted and genuine. Sam was thrilled to hear her talk like this, and after he had said goodnight to her outside the shop, he walked home again, elated, convinced that, before too long, Peggy would become part of the Hobbs family.

A few months later, Peggy told Sam that she didn't want to marry him, for she had fallen in love with someone else. The lad was clearly devastated and, watching him trail miserably round the house, Letty thought her heart would break for him. But, deep down, she'd always known it would end like this.

It was almost six months before Oliver was fitted for an artificial leg, and another three and a half months before he had the chance to try it on. At the Roehampton Hospital, he was given two or three days' instruction on how to use it. Learning was laborious and sometimes quite painful, but gradually he became confident enough to go into the outside world, albeit with the back-up support of his walking stick. But the 'leg' itself was cumbersomely made in hard leather and steel joints, and he complained to the hospital many times that the balance of the artificial leg did not match the weight of his other, real leg. He fell over twice, because he hadn't learnt how to master the art of lifting his 'dummy' foot as he walked, instead of dragging it. Thankfully both falls occurred at home, and all he received was a bruise on the bottom.

His daily practices became a source of great fascination to the kids, especially little Eddie, who sometimes walked alongside him, impersonating his limp. For a time he had to rely on Letty to help him lace up the leg, which seemed to take forever. Then there were the thick shoulder straps that held the artificial 'leg' on to his body. This was another crude device that, by the end of the day, left sore marks on the top of the shoulders. For weeks Oliver persevered with his exercises, despite the huge blisters that formed where the hard leather cut into his flesh. But, with Letty's constant encouragement and his own determination, he made it.

His day of triumph came when, for the first time, he walked down the stairs and on to the pavement outside – without his walking-stick.

'Now take it easy, dear. Don't rush it.' Letty followed closely behind Oliver, as he carefully manoeuvred first his artificial 'leg' down one stair, then his real leg.

'Put yer weight on me, Oll,' pleaded Sam, who tried to wedge himself at the side of Oliver as the perilous descent began. 'I don't want yer fallin' arse over tip!'

Oliver ignored Sam's pleas, and declined his offer of a supporting arm. He was determined to do this on his own, without anyone's help or interference. Slowly but surely, he edged his way down the stairs, clutching the banister, thumping the heel of each foot down cautiously until it had settled firmly on the slippery lino.

'Ye're doin' great, Oll! Mind 'ow yer go, mate!' The ground floor neighbours, Sid and Elsie Layton were watching Oliver anxiously from the hall downstairs, ready to rush up and grab him if he lost his balance. But Oliver held himself as firm as a rock, and by the time he finally reached the last stair, he got a loud 'Hooray!' from Sid, Elsie, and Sam – and an enormous sigh of relief from Letty.

To his embarrassment, and secret pleasure, it seemed like the whole street was waiting for him outside, cheering and applauding, patting him on the back with calls of 'Good old Olly!' and 'Well done, mate'. Oliver's moment of triumph was an exhilarating experience for everyone who witnessed it.

Within three weeks Oliver was walking with such apparent ease that strangers were unaware that he even had a disability.

For Letty and Oliver Hobbs and their family 1931 turned out to be an eventful year in more ways than one. Throughout the country ordinary families everywhere were in trouble. Unemployment was at its worst since the end of the war, and nearly seven million people, including Sam and his three married brothers, had joined the dole queues. Letty held on with grim determination to both her jobs, at Stagnells the baker's, and at Pakeman Street School. As before, Letty's money was all that was coming in and, after the triumph of his recovery from the operation, Oliver started to sink into another of his deep depressions. They were still living from hand to mouth each day, and it was too much for Oliver to accept now that he was walking perfectly well on his new 'leg', and more than capable of doing a full-time job. To Ollie, that cloud with its silver lining, as Letty called it, seemed further away than ever. But one morning in June, the postman brought him an unexpected letter.

Dear Mr Hobbs,

Under the agreement recently signed between ourselves and the United Kingdom Limbless Ex-Servicemen's Association, we are happy to inform you that we are able to re-instate you as an employee of the London Passenger Transport Board. Will you please report to the station master, Manor House Underground Station (Piccadilly Line Extension), on Friday 12th June at 10 a.m. bringing this letter with you. He will then advise you with regard to preliminary medical examination.

Yours faithfully, G. Rawson.

Divisional Superintendent,

London Passenger Transport Board (Underground).

Letty never knew how Oliver was able to contain himself until the morning of the twelfth. His excitement at the prospect of getting work again was so intense that he hardly slept a wink until after his interview with the station master. In fact, the night before, he bullshined his shoes – both of the pair – making quite sure they looked every bit as good as when he was in the Army. Within three weeks, wearing his new staff uniform and cap, Oliver was back at the Underground ticket-barrier again.

Manor House was a mile further down the Seven Sisters Road from his old job at Finsbury Park, but he still insisted on walking there for every 'turn'. The station itself was brand new, on an extension of the Piccadilly Line, which had only recently been opened by the Prince of Wales. Oliver was the proudest man alive, standing there in his own ticket collector's box at the top of the escalator, shouting 'All tickets now, please!' with more conviction than ever before.

1931 was a difficult year for many, but for once in their lives, things were easier for Letty and Oliver. With Oliver now the real breadwinner, they were determined to save a little each week for the time when they would be able to afford to move into something bigger than the room in Citizen Road. The chance came earlier than they expected. Near the end of August, in the same week that Prime Minister Ramsay MacDonald's Labour Party resigned from office, and a new National Government was formed, Mr Cotton accompanied the Hobbs family to Number 13 Roden Street. Standing in the little passageway of their new home, he solemnly clutched a small brown envelope.

'There we are Letty. There we are Oliver' – after being their landlord and friend for over twelve years, Mr Cotton was happy to be on first-name terms with them – 'I am happy to inform you that this house is now at your disposal. Mark my words, thirteen is going to be a lucky number for the Hobbs family. You'd better take the front door keys before I forget them!' He offered the envelope to Letty.

Letty refused it with a polite nod of the head. 'It's for Oliver,' she said primly.

Oliver took the keys. 'Fanks a lot, Reg. Much obliged.' He slowly opened the envelope and for a moment stared at the keys in the palm of his hand, as though they were alive.

As the front door closed, Eddie, closely pursued by Ron, rushed laughing and shouting out into the back garden at the far end of the passage. Letty and Oliver let them go, then made their way together into their new home.

Mr Cotton had told them about the place only two weeks before. The house had become vacant because the old people who'd been living there were wanting something smaller and what he suggested was a swap. Letty had loved Number 13 on first sight. It wasn't a bit like Mr Cotton had described. It was much better. Furthermore, Roden Street led right into Pakeman Street School where Letty worked in the evenings. In fact, the terraced house itself was only a few doors away from the school, just one house from the corner of Annette Road. From the moment they first stood outside its front door, both Letty and Oliver had felt a warm glow about the place. The only snag, however, was the rent. Fifteen shillings a week was really more than they could afford. But, surprisingly, it was Oliver who had insisted they could manage it. Furthermore, he was determined that Letty should give up her job at Stagnells the moment they moved in.

'I don't know how we're going to afford to buy all the furniture we need,' said Letty, as they strolled around the house. Almost reverently they walked into their new front-room, in darkness because the wooden shutters were still drawn. Letty quickly found the way to unlatch them. 'You know what would look nice in here,' she said, flooding the room with sunlight 'A three-piece suite. We might pick one up second-hand at that junk shop in the Cally.'

'I'm not 'avin' no second 'and junk in *my* 'ouse! We'll wait 'til we've saved up enuff ter buy new.' Olly strode proprietorially towards the window.

Letty was impressed, but, then again, she always knew that once Oliver had a whole house of his own he'd be firm about just how he wanted it.

They next moved into the back-parlour. It wasn't very big, but it did include a lovely oak dresser which almost covered one wall, and two cupboards, one used as a pantry, the other for storage. But Letty was most excited about the clothes-rack on the ceiling, which could be lowered down by rope on a pulley; she'd missed it when they'd first looked round the house. 'Now I can really get my drying done on rainy days!' she told Oliver.

But Oliver didn't really hear her, for he had already left

through another parlour door into the scullery. 'Come an' 'ave a butchers at this, Lett: I can get a barf' in private now!'

Their oval-shaped aluminium bath was one of the few things they knew they could bring with them from Citizen Road, and the scullery was just about big enough to take it. There was a white-washed stone copper in the corner, helpful for heating up water on Friday bath nights, and as Letty gazed through the scullery window at their little back garden, she wondered about the neighbours whose windows overlooked them. By the back wall of the garden Ron and Eddie had discovered a ramshackle tool shed, and were clearly already turning it into their headquarters.

A few minutes later, Oliver was following Letty up the stairs. She warned him to take them carefully, but today he quite literally chased her. Their immediate job was to make up the beds in the two rooms on the first floor. Until then the boys would still have to sleep on their mattress on the floor, but in Letty and Oliver's room overlooking the street, there was a double brass bedstead, which the furniture cart had delivered earlier in the morning. It was Letty's pride and joy, the first bed she and Oliver had actually owned, even though it was only second-hand from the Caledonian Road Furniture Market.

Although Oliver had managed to climb up the first stairs with perfect ease, it was a little more tricky getting up the narrow winding staircase to the attic. The room itself was tiny, and they had to bend their heads because of the sloping ceilings, but built into one of the slopes was a small, high window that was just big enough to offer a spectacular view. Laid out before them were all London's rooftops.

'Look, Olly!' Letty had to stand on tiptoe: 'St Paul's Cathedral! D'you see? Over there!' She was pointing frantically.

Oliver finally picked out the grey dome and gold cross. 'Oh

yeah. That's it, is it? Looks like a river down there.'

'Well of course it's a river! That's the Thames.'

They stood there, peering out at the great city sprawled out before them. Letty also thought she could just make out Tower Bridge, along the river beyond St Paul's, but she wasn't quite sure. All she knew was that London Town had never looked so beautiful, with the different shapes and sizes of all the buildings, many old, some new, and the way the sky dipped in and out of their rooftops, the summer sun glistening in their windows.

As they stood there, Oliver slipped his arm around her waist. ' 'Appy now, gel?'

'Oh Olly,' she responded, putting her arm around his waist. 'I've never been so happy in my entire life. Mr Cotton's right. Number 13 *is* going to be lucky for us. I can feel it in my bones.'

'It'd better be – wiv the cash we're gonna 'ave to find ter pay for it.'

Letty squeezed him around the waist reassuringly. 'Oh we'll manage, you'll see. We could always sub-let this top floor. Mr Cotton said he wouldn't mind. Needs a bit of a paint first though. And I know exactly who we could get as lodger.'

'Who?'

'Your brother Sam.'

Oliver was laughing. 'There yer go again! Makin' plans fer someone before they've even 'ad time ter breave!' But only the next minute he was distracted by the shouts of Ron and Eddie as they yelled up from the garden below. 'If I come down there, yer'll get it,' he growled.

The kids roared with laughter, and rushed back inside their shed, with Ron shouting up to his father, 'Can't catch me, Pop! Can't catch me!'

Letty tensed. Luckily, Oliver didn't appear to take in

Ron's jibes. At least, she hoped he hadn't. 'Little devils,' she said hastily. 'Still, it is a lovely garden, isn't it, dear?'

'Garden? Junk-'eap, yer mean.'

'Don't you worry, I'll soon get it into shape. After all, look how your mum brightened up her little back yard. I think I'll buy a few packets of poppy seeds from Woolworth's. Oh Olly. We're so lucky to have a house of our own. We've come such a long way since we got married.'

'A long way? I wonder.' There was a note of sourness in his voice. 'When I look at this country, I sometimes wonder if it's the same place I fought for. Dole queues, people with no roof over their 'eads – scrappin' around fer any bit o'grub they can lay their 'ands on. I tell yer, I'll never trust anuvver politician again as long as I live. Promises! That's what we live on! This country's in a real mess, Lett!'

'I love you, Olly.'

Taken completely by surprise, all he could reply was 'Huh?'

'I've loved you since the first day I met you.' She was looking at him, 'You know that, don't you?'

Oliver hesitated a moment, then smiled. 'You've got such blue eyes.'

Three weeks before they had celebrated their thirteenth wedding anniversary, and now here they were, entering the next phase of their life in Roden Street, thought Letty. Whatever had drawn them together, had kept them together. It wasn't just sex, or even the fact that they genuinely liked each other. They just never wanted to be apart. Without needing to say a word, they kissed.

Letty laid her head on Oliver's shoulder. 'Olly,' she whispered into his ear. 'I'd like to have another child. Just one more. Maybe a girl this time.'

Holding Letty close to him, her head buried into his shoulder, Oliver stared out of the window. 'No more kids,

Lett. Not now. Not the way things are.' He sighed forlornly. 'I'm beyond all that now.'

Letty suddenly raised her head and looked at him scoldingly. 'That's nonsense, Olly! And you know it! Number 13's *our* new start. I want this house to be a part of us – of you and me and the kids. We're a team, you and I. We're living *for* each other as well as with each other.' She drew closer again, and they kissed once more.

And so the chimneypots and rooftops of Roden Street welcomed the new residents in number 13. For the sparrows and pigeons who cooed and twittered, and nested there, it was just a day like any other. But for the Hobbs family, it was the end of one era, and the beginning of a new.

When Michael Francis Hobbs arrived, it was a hot October day. He weighed seven pounds six ounces at birth, and annoyed the midwife who delivered him, because he was inconsiderate enough to be born during her lunch-hour. For the first few weeks, Michael kept his parents awake practically every night. On one occasion, Oliver threatened to take the baby to the window and 'frow the little bugger out'. Letty made quite sure the window remained closed.

Chapter 16

'In this grave hour, perhaps the most fateful in our history, I send to every household of my people, both at home and overseas, this message, spoken with the same depth of feeling for each one of you as if I were able to cross your threshold and speak to you myself.

For the second time in the lives of most of us – we are at war.'

Grim-faced around the wireless set in the back-parlour of Number 13 Letty, Oliver and the boys listened to King George VI's solemn address to the nation, broadcast direct from his study at Buckingham Palace. Although the King's words meant little to Eddie and his young brother, Mick, Ron, now nineteen years old, understood. His mother understood even better: she had been dreading the coming of this second war. The first bloody conflict had claimed the life of her brother and left her husband permanently disabled. And now she was expected to hand over her own son to the war-machine. Oliver felt the same way. After his own experiences in the mud and slaughter of the battlefield trenches, he felt sick in his stomach at the thought of Ron being called up.

The declaration of war on Germany by England had seemed more and more inevitable as Adolf Hitler and his so-called National Socialist Party gradually seized power in

Germany during 1933 and 1934. It seemed that everyone, with the exception of Britain's misguided Neville Chamberlain, knew that Hitler had no intention of honouring any international treaties. If only Prime Minister Chamberlain had listened to Oliver, or Frank O'Malley, or Sam Hobbs, or indeed any respectable darts-player in the local pubs up and down the country, Hitler would have been given a black-eye before he'd ever had the chance to march into Poland.

> 'The task will be hard. There may be dark days ahead and war can no longer be confined to the battlefield. But we can only do the right as we see the right, and reverently commit our cause to God . . .'

All those listening knew it was an agonising experience for the King, too. After being hauled on to the throne after the abdication of his brother in 1936, it was a gargantuan effort for the poor man to make public speeches whilst inflicted with the burden of a speech impediment.

> 'If one and all we keep resolutely faithful to it, ready for whatever service or sacrifice it may demand, then, with God's help, we shall prevail.
>
> May He bless and keep us all.'

The King's grave broadcast came to an end, and the small group around the wireless set got up from their seats to stand in silence for the playing of the National Anthem.

Letty then switched off the wireless set, and for a few moments, no one said anything. They just sat down again with their thoughts, until the silence was finally broken by Letty.

'I never thought I'd live to see the day when all this would start again.'

'Won't last long, Mum,' replied Ron. 'Once Hitler sees we mean business, he'll soon get the hell out of Poland.' Over the past few years, Ron had grown to look more and more like his father. He was the same height, and his hair was only a couple of shades lighter. But he had a more cherubic shape to his face, and, unlike Oliver, his skin was clear, without any moles. 'All over in a month, I say.'

Oliver took an unfinished dog-end from behind his ear, and lit up. 'One munf, one year. It's still enuff time for people ter get killed.'

Ron flicked through the pages of the *Daily Sketch*, which was full of photographs of members of the new war cabinet arriving at 10 Downing Street. 'Someone's got to stop them, Pop. If Hitler gets his way, the Nazis'll take over the whole world. I tell you, I can't wait to get *my* call-up papers.'

Letty swung round with an agonised start. 'Ron! Don't say such things!'

'Don't upset yer mum, Ron,' pleaded Oliver's brother, Sam, now in his mid-thirties and himself eligible for military service. 'She don't wanna see you in khaki after what 'appened to yer dad.'

'Who said anything about khaki?' sniffed Ron, without looking up from his newspaper to acknowledge his uncle's plea. 'I want to get in the Navy.' Ron always found it difficult to communicate with his Uncle Sam. For some reason, he had always deeply resented his father's younger brother moving in with the family seven years ago. To Ron, Sam was an interloper, taking attention away from himself. Whether this was true or not, Ron managed to ignore the fact that, over the years, Uncle Sam had been a wonderful help to the family. He had been almost like a second father to the kids, helping out with all the things that Oliver couldn't do.

'Dunno wot yer wanna go in the Navy for.' Oliver was indignant at Ron's suggestion. 'Wot's wrong wiv the foot-sloggers?'

'Don't *you* start Olly!' snapped Letty. 'I don't want Ron to go in the army or the navy! In any case he's only just turned nineteen. They can't call him up 'til he's twenty.'

'Mum! Where's Poland?' Young Mick was attempting to share his eldest brother's newspaper. Although he was only six, he was fascinated by bad news of any sort.

Letty was quickly on her feet again. 'Never mind about Poland! Get yourself to bed. You too, Eddie.'

Neither lad argued with their mother, not when she used that tone of voice. Over the years Letty had made it clear that, although she loved her kids, she was determined to maintain their respect, both for herself and for Oliver. All three boys were treated equally. There were no favourites, although Oliver did have a special, sneaking affection for Ron, his eldest son. But Letty made sure that, if any of her kids were in the wrong, she told them so, and they had to take the consequences.

After their usual cat's-lick wash in the scullery, Letty tucked up Eddie and Mick together, in the same bedroom that they shared with Ron and Uncle Sam. She sat on the side of the bed for a few moments and, as she waited for them to fall asleep, her mind started racing again. War! What would it mean for the family? Would the Germans start bombing London again? Dear god, she asked, why is it all necessary? Why can't people talk instead of fight? Why can't someone talk some sense into that Hitler and his gang? She agonised over what they might all have to put up with in the next few years, and sighed deeply. These recent times had been so good for her and Olly. They had the kids, a good roof over their heads, and even though they still didn't have much money, there was always food in their stomachs. But now that there was war again, everything could change so quickly. Already the Government was talking about evacuating children from all the big towns. What would happen if they sent Eddie and Mick away? No! Letty had made up her mind. She would *never* allow anyone to take her boys away from her and Olly. Their place was here, in Number 13, in their own home.

'Don't upset yourself, Lett. Fing's'll turn out all right.'

Letty turned quickly from the window, to see that Sam had entered the room quietly. 'Oh Sam,' she sighed. 'It's all so horrible. I can't bear the thought of going through another war all over again.'

Sam sat on the edge of the kids' bed, his voice a whisper, 'Ron's probably right, y'know. It could all be over in a munf or so.'

'It could. But it won't. *I* know it. So does everyone else.'

Sam was looking down at his nephews, 'Whatever 'appens, I won't let no 'arm come to you an' Olly – nor these two.' He turned to her with a reassuring look. 'You can rely on me, Lett.'

Letty smiled back gratefully. 'I know that, Sam. Thank you.'

She left the room, but paused on the landing outside to peer upstairs to the top floor. Their lodger, old Miss Florrie, had clearly fallen asleep again in her easy-chair by the stove, for Letty could hear her snoring. Letty reflected how she had always hoped that those two top rooms and the attic above would have been used by Sam when he got married. Poor Sam! To her intense sadness, her brother-in-law had never so much as looked at another girl since Peggy had left him for another, and probably never would. And yet when Sam had said a few minutes ago, 'You can rely on me, Lett', she had known only too well that, apart from Olly, he was the one person in the world who truly meant it. Shaking her head sadly, she turned to go back downstairs to Oliver.

Needless to say, the war was lasting longer than the 'month' that Ron had forecast. For the next *few* months, the country lived out a war of nerves. Although the skies above London remained ominously silent, German bombers had already started devastating large towns and villages along the east and south coasts.

Whilst Hitler's armies rampaged across Europe, the residents of Roden Street prepared for the inevitable aerial onslaught. Most of the children at Pakeman Street School were among the first to be evacuated, mainly to country districts outside the capital. A few teachers continued at the school, so for a time Eddie and Mick found themselves in half-empty classrooms. However, once the Luftwaffe broke through the British coastal defences, they all knew it was only a matter of time before the Dornier bomber planes and Messerschmitt fighter aircraft would be able to reach the heart of London itself. Letty agonised over whether she had the right to subject Eddie and Mick to the danger of air raids. One evening, when Oliver had been drinking too much brown ale, she had had a terrible row with him about whether they should be evacuated or not. In the end he told her point blank that if one Jerry bomb fell on Islington, Eddie and Mick would have to pack their bags. But Letty still held out, ignoring everyone who told her she was holding on to the kids for her own selfish reasons. And so, whilst they watched and waited for the first sign of an air raid, life in Number 13 Roden Street carried on as usual, until one humid August Sunday evening.

The Hobbs family were up the Cally, at number 22 Leslie Street, having high tea with the Brooks family. It was a

209

Sunday evening ritual that had been going on for years. Last time it had been Letty and Oliver's turn to entertain Tilly, Bill, and their kids at Roden Street; this Sunday they were all back at the terraced house in Leslie Street. These get-togethers were the highlight of both families' week, for it gave the adults a chance to have a good old chin-wag, leaving the kids to do whatever they wanted in the back garden. Tilly and Bill had two boys and two girls. Their eldest son, Jeff, a marvellous cook, was training to be a chef at a hotel up West. But his great hobby was motor-cycling, and most Saturday afternoons he was on the road, whatever the weather. Like Sam Hobbs, he had recently been turned down for National Service on medical grounds. Jeff's brother, Fred, was already in the Army, square-bashing at a camp 'somewhere in England'. Pauline Brooks was grow-ing into a very attractive eleven-year-old, who had flashing dark eyes, and an idea she resembled one of the heroines in the popular novels she read avidly. Her sister, Rita, just a few years younger, was the mischievous one, who always loved bullying Eddie and Mick when they came to tea. High tea itself was an excuse for exchanging all the gossip of the week, culminating in the weekly 'battle of the celery tops', which usually involved the adults being pelted across the table with the uneaten tops of celery sticks, left over from tea-time. Once that indulgence was over, the kids were speedily despatched either to bed or to a sofa in the next room, to await going-home time while their elders settled down to their weekly chin-wag. Inevitably, the subject was the war. For the past few weeks the news bulletins on the BBC Home Service had been getting gloomier each day. First, it was the evacuation of the British Expeditionary Force from Dunkirk, then the capitulation of France, and now, the real possibility of air raids on London itself.

'They'll never get 'ere, mate!' Bill assured both Oliver and

Sam, as he filled them each a glass of bitter. 'By the time any of their bombers get past the coast, our planes'll blow 'em outa the sky!'

'*Our* planes?' asked Tilly indignantly. 'We 'ain't bleedin' got none!'

'Don't you believe it. Old Churchill's got somethin' up 'is sleeve, you mark my words.'

Letty looked doubtful. 'They did reach Croydon the other night, Bill. There was quite a lot of damage at the airport.'

Bill shook his head. 'Nah! That was just one Jerry tryin' to commit suicide. I 'eard the ack-ack brought 'im down in some park over there.'

Jeff Brooks opened some packets of crisps and offered them around. 'Aunt Letty's right, Dad. We can't shoot down every Jerry that comes over. They're bound to get through sooner or later.'

Letty was getting more depressed every minute. She wasn't sure whether it was the conversation, or the black-market gin she and Tilly were drinking.

'Oy, Sam,' asked Tilly, who was smoking one of Bill's players. ' 'Ave yer finished diggin' out that shelter in your back yard yet?

'More or less, Till,' replied Sam, after taking down a gulp of bitter. 'I'm gonna start gettin' the thing fitted up termorrer.'

Bill exhaled circles of smoke from his fag. 'Rarver you than me, mate. We've got a Morrison inside one ourselves. Them Anderson shelters need too much work for my likin'.'

'Yeah, and they're bleedin' cold!' added Tilly.

Letty took a crisp and crunched it as she talked. 'Still, the kids enjoyed helping Sam do it. They think an air-raid shelter in the back garden's a great adventure.'

'What about your Ron?' Tilly asked mischievously. 'Did 'e do any diggin'?'

Letty was immediately defensive. 'Oh yes. He helped whenever he had any free time. He's been on late turn a lot just lately.' Letty, of course, was lying. She knew that Ron, who worked in the Booking Office at Manor House Underground Station with his father, actually worked less time than Oliver. Furthermore, Ron was able to use his bicycle to get to the station, whereas Oliver usually had to walk.

Tilly and Bill exchanged a sly look with each other across the room. They didn't dislike Ron, but they didn't admire the way he always seemed to be giving his parents so many problems. 'Actually, I've seen 'im a coupla times lately,' said Tilly. 'He uses that pub in 'Olloway Road, don't 'e? Corner of Windsor Road.' She turned to Oliver and added mischievously, 'Olly. Is that your sister Vi's girl 'e's always knockin' around wiv? Wot's 'er name – Rose?'

Oliver turned with a start. 'Wot's that?' For the past half hour or so he'd been sitting happily in a chair by the open window, twirling his thumbs aimlessly around each other, as was his usual habit. But suddenly, he was glaring sharply at Tilly. 'Rosie's 'is cousin.'

'Yes, I know, Oll.' Tilly was already beginning to regret she'd mentioned it. 'They seem to get on very well tergevver, don't they?'

Oliver quickly turned his glare towards Letty. 'Lett! D'you know about this?'

Letty was prone to flushes when she was anxious, and she was having one now. 'There's no harm, dear. After all, Rosie's only his cousin. If they want to meet for a drink sometimes, I don't think we should –'

Oliver's voice was raised in anger. 'It's that bleedin' sister of mine again! I told yer she was a bloody trouble-maker!'

Letty was embarrassed. 'Olly, dear. Watch your language.'

'I told yer, Lett! I told yer I don't want *any* of my family mixin' wiv Vi an' 'er bunch. Give that woman a chance,

212

an' she'll stab yer in the bleedin' back!'

In the brief, tense silence that followed, Letty tried to fathom out why Oliver was so intensely hostile to his sister. Although he had never had any real liking for her, his loathing seemed to have come to a head a couple of years ago when Vi had called at Roden Street one afternoon, whilst Letty was out shopping. Vi had clearly said something that had upset and angered Oliver, but Letty had never been able to find out exactly what it was. Anyway, she hadn't been seen since, and because Oliver had warned Letty never to meet with his sister again, Letty had resisted the temptation to call on Vi. Even so, she was still curious why Ron had never mentioned that he had been meeting Rosie.

Bill Brooks saved the evening. 'Blimey! It's like a bleedin' wake 'round 'ere! Come on you lot!' Without waiting to be asked, he started to sing 'Let the Rest of the World Go by', pushing Tilly towards their old upright piano.

Sam was next to join in; it was his favourite song. With Tilly now in full spate at the piano, everyone quickly followed their lead. Eventually even Oliver was belting out the words at the top of his voice. They'd finished the last verse of 'For Me and My Gel', and launched into 'When Irish Eyes Are Smiling', when the wail of the air-raid siren, echoing across the streets from the rooftop of the 'Cally' Road police station, brought them to a sudden halt. For a moment, everyone just stared at each other in silence, waiting for it to stop. When it finally did, an air of confused disbelief hung in the quietened room.

'Take no notice.' Bill was the first to speak. 'It's only anuvver false alarm.'

'Better put up the blackout.' Jeff closed the window, then drew the covers across the cotton-net curtains, which Bill had lined with strips of sticky paper tape.

Letty stood up. 'We'd better be getting home,' she said

briskly. 'Thank you Till and Bill for a lovely evening. Our turn next time.'

By now, Oliver was reluctant to leave. He was quite merry on his three pints of bitter, and was just beginning to enjoy the sing-song. 'Wot's the rush?' he said, slurring his words after downing the last drop from his glass. 'There's nuffin' goin' on out there.'

'Oll's right,' said Tilly, getting up from the piano stool. 'Come on, Lett. Why don't you and me go and make us all a cuppa?'

Letty still looked uneasy. 'Well, another ten minutes then.'

She and Tilly had hardly reached the door when it happened. All hell seemed to break loose outside. The streets echoed to the sound of ack-ack fire, and in the far distance they could hear one explosion after another.

'Bloody 'ell!' Oliver was out of his seat in a flash. Bill had quickly turned off the light, and drawn back the blackout curtain and everyone crowded round to peer out of the window. Above them, the night sky was criss-crossed with searchlight beams, and shells were burst into gleaming white puffs of smoke in and out of them.

Within seconds, Pauline and Rita, still in their nighties and rubbing their eyes, rushed bewildered into the room. Close behind them followed Eddie and Mick, both wide awake, and for the moment at least, thoroughly enjoying all the excitement.

Letty insisted that she, Oliver, and Sam get the kids back home to Roden Street as soon as possible. Tilly and Bill didn't like the idea of them going out in the middle of an air raid, but they had come to know that when Letty made up her mind to do something, there was no stopping her. So reluctantly, they bid all the Hobbs goodnight. Once they were on their own, the Brooks family crowded into the safety of their Morrison shelter in Jeff's ground-floor bedroom. As they crouched, listening to the constant sound of aircraft buzzing overhead, and the deafening barrage of ack-ack guns and exploding bombs, Tilly prayed to herself that Letty, Oliver and family would get home safely.

In the night outside, Oliver swung his artificial leg at a frenetic pace as he led the others down the Caledonian Road towards The Nag's Head and Holloway. Letty was determined to show no fear, but clutched Oliver's arm whilst Sam hurried on behind with Mick on his back. Eddie refused to walk alongside his parents, marching ahead as though he were a soldier defying the enemy. Above them, the skies were lit up for as far as the eye could see, and the red glow from buildings on fire could be seen coming from the direction of Kings Cross behind them. People rushed to and fro along the Cally, anxious to get home before the bombing got any closer. All the way, the terraced houses were vibrating to the thunderous sound of gunfire and explosions, and the tinkling of shrapnel as it fell to the rooftops and pavements all around.

It took them just twenty-five minutes to walk the mile and a half back to Roden Street. When they finally got there, the air raid was in full swing, and the first thing Oliver did was to make sure his family all took cover under the parlour-table.

The raid lasted throughout the night, until the early hours. Fortunately, on this occasion no bombs reached Roden Street or its neighbours. Elsewhere, the Hobbs knew that others were not so lucky.

Chapter 17

Putting up the Anderson shelter in the back garden of Number 13 was a job and a half for Sam. Not only did he have to dig out an area eight feet square by six feet deep, but he also had to work out how the ruddy structure fitted together. However, at least he'd had his two 'helpers', Eddie and Mick, to join him in the digging part of the operation, and when it came to erecting the curved aluminium roof and walls of the shelter, he was not short of suggestions and advice from Letty and Oliver, and even from old Ma Florrie upstairs. When the structure was finally fitted together and secure, Eddie and Mick helped to shift the earth they had dug out of the hole back on to the roof of the shelter. After the 'topping up' was complete, Letty looked out at what was left of her poor garden, and sighed despondently. But she quickly decided that the best thing to do was to buy some more seeds from Woolworth's, and scatter them all over the soil on top of the shelter. After a couple of days drying out with a paraffin stove, the Anderson was ready for occupation. It was only big enough to take two bunks fitted to the walls, so Eddie and Mick were assigned the top one, and Miss Florrie the lower. As for Letty, her sleeping accommodation during raids consisted of a deck chair, and one of her own blankets knitted from the wool of some of Oliver's old stump socks. Oliver himself stubbornly preferred to sleep through any air raid in the comfort of his own bed whilst Sam spent most nights sleeping on the floor in the scullery, waking every so often to check that all was well outside.

By the first week in September, nightly air-raids on London were a fact of life. With Pakeman Street School now closed down, Letty was under increasing pressure from everyone to evacuate Eddie and Mick. Night after night she lay awake turning it over in her mind, her instincts telling her to keep her boys with her, her reason telling her she should send them away. Then one night, the decision was made for her.

Oliver was on late turn at Manor House ticket-barrier and, as usual when there was an air raid, Letty had left the boys with Sam and gone down to make sure Oliver was all right. This time, she'd been met not only with Oliver's exasperation at her putting herself at risk to check up on him, but also with the news that everything was arranged – the boys were being evacuated.

'The kids are goin' on Tuesday, Lett. And that's final!' Oliver could only talk to Letty in between batches of passengers who were streaming up the escalator. 'It's too dangerous to let 'em 'ang 'round the streets wiv Jerry frowin' all 'e's got at us. It's not fair on them, an' it's not fair on us.'

Letty's face was fraught, 'I wish you'd have talked it over with me first, Olly. Why did you have to arrange it all behind my back?'

'Because you'd have tried to stop me, that's why.' For the time being there were no more passengers, so Oliver turned back to talk to her. 'We've gotta think of Eddie and Mick now, Lett. London's just too dangerous for them. If I could get you to go wiv 'em, I'd send you too.'

Letty scoffed at the idea. She would never leave Oliver alone in London, not for a million pounds. But she did understand he was concerned for her safety: tonight the journey to Manor House on the number 653 trolleybus had been a hazardous one, and all along the Seven Sisters Road tiny bits of shrapnel from ack-ack shells had been raining down on to the metal roof of the bus.

'Olly, if we send the kids away, we won't even know who they're going to. I'm not so worried about Eddie, but you know what young Mick's like. He'll get homesick so quick.'

'E'll have ter get used to it. The kids've gotta go, Lett. That's all there is to it. I mean, what're yer gonna do when Ron gets his callin'-up papers? They're not going to let us 'ang on to 'im, now are they?'

'Ron won't be called up now, I know he won't. He was twenty nearly two months ago, and they still haven't sent for him.'

Oliver sighed. 'Don't kid yerself, Lett.'

Letty was trying to convince herself more than Oliver. For some weeks now, Ron had been on her mind constantly. The boy had always been very secretive, but just lately he had become surly and uncommunicative. 'I still say he won't go. He'd fail his medical anyway with his weak eyes. You know, Olly, I wouldn't be surprised if he needs glasses.'

Oliver laughed out loud. 'So now we give in to 'Itler cos our Ron needs glasses!'

Letty hated Oliver laughing at her. He was being so insensitive at a time when all their children were about to be taken away from them. Distress and anger were mixed in her voice as she replied, 'I don't want the kids to leave us, Olly. I love them too much.'

'You're not the only one, Lett. Do remember that, won't yer.' As he spoke, another batch of passengers surged up the stairs from a train that had just deposited them on the platform below. 'Tickets please! All tickets now, please!' Only as the last passenger disappeared did Oliver turn back to Letty again. This time he was more sympathetic. 'Lett.

If this country's goin' to win this war, it's goin' to need every man it can get. You're gonna 'ave ter be strong. Ron's not a kid any more. He's a man.'

Letty raised her head, misery written all over her face. 'He may be a man to you, Olly, but he's still my son.'

Oliver said nothing and, realising it was useless to carry on arguing, Letty turned to go. A quarter of an hour later, she was making her way back home on foot to Roden Street. She had tried waiting for a bus, but when none appeared after ten minutes or so, she imagined they had probably stopped running because of the air raid. As she hurried down the Seven Sisters Road, she could hear the constant buzzing of planes in the sky above, although there were too many clouds around to be able to see them. Her route along the main road ran parallel with the outer boundary of Finsbury Park, from which barrage balloons were being operated, but most of the silver monsters had already been winched, high above the clouds, so that they, too, were completely invisible from the ground, Letty had never really understood what the great wind-bags were supposed to achieve, and she walked past the Park without a second glance. Twenty minutes later she had reached the junction of Hornsey Road. As she passed the Eaglet on the corner, it was quite obvious from the noise inside that none of the drinkers were interested in the air raid. Letty shivered; every time she passed the pub, she recalled that during the first war, it had been the first building to fall to the Kaiser's Zeppelins.

By the time Letty got safely home, old Florrie and the kids were tucked up in their bunks in the Anderson shelter. Sam was nowhere around, but Letty found a note from him saying that he was on standby duty at the ARP post in the school playground. Letty decided that tonight she would wait up for Oliver – they still had so much to discuss so she went up to the bedroom – and changed into her slippers.

219

When she'd done so, she heard the sound of the attic window flapping in the breeze. Florrie was very absent-minded, and this wasn't the first time she'd gone down to the shelter without closing all her windows. Not for the first time, Letty went up to do it for her.

Because of the blackout Letty could not switch on a light as she climbed the narrow attic staircase. She found Florrie's room in total darkness, except for a red glow reflected on the sloping ceilings. As she reached the window, Letty understood why. She could see the whole sky before her, with low clouds illuminated by the glow of fires which were burning for as far as the eye could see. And in the middle of that glow was a transformation of Letty's favourite view, the proud and defiant silhouette of St Paul's Cathedral, surrounded by the crackling, fiercely burning flames of a city at war. She knew, in her heart of hearts, that Ollie was right – the boys would have to go.

The following Monday evening, Letty packed a small suitcase each for Eddie and Mick, and labelled them carefully. Their gas-mask cases were also labelled, but Letty had doubts that Eddie's would still be there by the time he and Mick joined their foster parents. She had washed and ironed most of their shirts and underclothes over the weekend, and had packed their essentials plus some comics for Eddie, and some writing pads for Mick. It was a job she hated doing, and everything she put into the cases upset her. She still didn't know where they were to be evacuated to: that was a closely guarded secret until they were actually at their destination. All Letty knew was that she was dreading every single minute up until the time she was to see her boys off at Marylebone Station.

For the present moment, at least, neither Eddie nor Mick had really taken in what was happening to them. In some curious way, they felt they were just going away for a short holiday, and would be back home with Mum, Pop and Uncle Sam within a week or so. Soon after tea, Eddie had virtually closed himself off from the world, settling down to read some of his comics. Fingers in ears, elbows propped on the parlour-table, humming tunelessly, he was oblivious to everything and everyone around him. Ron had finished his early turn at work, and had withdrawn to the temporary sanctuary of his bedroom to read a book about the Navy, and Sam sat in his usual chair at the table reading the paper. But Mick had more important things to do. Not content with listening to the six o'clock news on the wireless, he was now engrossed in the nine o'clock news. Tonight's broadcast was full of reports about the Germans' brutal occupation of France, Belgium and Holland, and of Mr Churchill's warnings about the threat of a Nazi invasion of the British Isles. Mick listened with awed fascination, waiting excitedly for his favourite programme, 'Into Battle', a round-up of that day's events in the war.

'Come on you two – bed!' Letty had held out for as long as possible, knowing that this was the last night the kids would be with her for a long time.

Crouched on the floor, his ear next to the wireless, Mick groaned loudly. 'But Mum, I'm still listening to the news.'

Letty switched the set off. 'No, Mick! You're far too young to be listening to things like that. It'll give you nightmares.'

'What about the murder play? You all listen to it. Why can't I?'

Letty had no reply to that. It was true that she listened to murder plays, for they were her favourite, and the more gruesome and horrific they were, the more she liked them. Futhermore, whenever there was a 'H' certificate horror film on at the any of the local picture houses, Letty always dragged Oliver and Sam along to see it. But such things were not, however, for kids of Mick's age. 'Bed!' she snapped, without even having to raise her voice.

Even Eddie heard their mother this time, and knew she meant business. He closed his comic quickly, and took it with him out to the scullery, where he and Mick started their wash.

Sam watched her pottering around as she despatched her sons to bed, her mind already racing ahead to Marylebone Station and the morning. He knew only too well what she was going through. The kids were the whole world to Letty. For the first time in her life she wasn't going to be able to be with them, to protect them. 'Don't worry about 'em, Lett,' Sam said, carefully. 'You and Oll are doin' the right thing, believe me.'

'I'm not at all convinced about that.' Her reply was edged with a touch of bitterness.

'Fings are gettin' worse, gel – there's no mistakin' it. Specially now we're gettin' these raids every day as well as the night.' He knew the war was getting uglier by the day, and from the way Churchill had been talking, there was now a real possibility that Field-Marshal Goering and his Luftwaffe had every intention of bombing the daylights out of London as a softening-up process before the invasion. 'Anyway – who knows?' he continued, casually browsing through the newspaper. 'P'raps they'll enjoy themselves so much, they won't wanna come 'ome.'

Letty flared with anger. 'Sam Hobbs! How can you say *my* kids'll be happier with someone else!'

Sam quickly put down his paper. 'That's *not* what I said, Lett. What I meant was, the kids of terday 'ave a way of – well, adjustin' to fings. Even if it means they 'ave ter be away from you and Oll, it's safer for 'em ter be outa London.'

'How would you know about kids? You've never had any of your own!' Letty suddenly stopped dead in her tracks, and looked straight across at Sam. She couldn't believe what she had just said to him! 'Oh God, Sam!' she gasped, going to him. 'I'm so sorry! How could I say such a thing to you of all people!'

'It's all right, Lett.' With great dignity, Sam put his paper down on the table, and rose from his seat. 'It's not my place ter interfere.'

He made a move to leave the room. But Letty quickly took hold of his arm, and stopped him. 'No, Sam. Please don't go. I had no right at all to talk to you like that. You may not have kids of your own, but my God, I don't know what ours would have done without you. You're like a second father to them.'

Sam smiled back reassuringly at her. 'No, Lett. They've only got one farvver. And 'e's a real good'un.'

'I'm home!' Oliver's voice called from the passageway outside, as he shut the street door. He took off his cap, then his uniform jacket, which he hung up on a hook in the passageway near the back-garden door. Letty could never understand how he could bear to wear that jacket all day – it seemed to weigh a ton, mainly because the pockets were lined with leather, to take the coins from excess fares.

Hearing their dad was home, the boys rushed out to the scullery yelling, 'Night, Pop! Night! Mum says we can sleep in our own bed tonight!'

'Only if there's no air-raid. And there's not much chance of that.' He exchanged a glance with Letty. 'Hey! 'Ang on a minute you two! Wot yer lookin' so guilty for? You been at my sugar ration agin, 'ave yer?'

'Oh no, Pop.' Eddie immediately looked guilty. 'We had spam and mash for tea.'

'Spam and mash?' gasped Oliver, over-acting. 'Wot d'yer fink we are – bleedin' dookes or somefin'! You just remember, there's a war on. We've all gotta cut down on our food.'

Mick was in a daring mood. 'Mum says you've got a sweet

tooth, so *you* take all *our* sugar rations.'

Oliver tried to look indignant. 'Oh she says that, do she? Well, I'll be 'avin' a word wiv your mum about that! Go on then – off yer go!' He kissed them both goodnight, then stopped to watch them rushing up the stairs to their bedroom. Knowing that they wouldn't be there tomorrow gave him a sinking feeling in his stomach.

A few minutes later, Letty was watching him eat his cheese sandwich and pickled onion. Sam opened a quart bottle of brown, and poured a pint glass each for him and his brother. Ever since rationing had been introduced in February, everyone seemed to be living on either cheese, spam, fish and chips, or even whale-meat. Two weeks ago Oliver had complained that Letty was giving most of his sugar ration to the kids, so the next Monday morning she had decided to give him his three-quarters of a pound allowance all to himself. Needless to say, it was gone by Wednesday.

But sugar was the last thing on Letty's mind tonight. No matter how hard she tried to disguise her feelings, she was miserable, and feared she was going to cry at any moment. 'The kids're not bein' locked up in the clinker, y'know, Lett,' said Oliver, aware of the gathering tears in her eyes as he crunched a huge pickled onion. 'Anyway, who knows – we might be seein' 'em sooner than we fink.'

Letty looked up suddenly. For the first time since Oliver got home, she took notice of something he'd said. 'What d'you mean?'

'What I mean is, Station Master's given me my 'oliday dates at last. We can take a week at the end of October.'

'Oh Olly!' Letty leapt up from her seat, and hugged and kissed him. 'We can take Eddie and Mick. The school said we could always collect them for holidays.'

Sam downed a gulp of brown. 'Gonna be a bit nippy end of October, in't it?'

'Who cares!' Suddenly, Letty was happy, already beginning to make plans. 'If we can get a booking on the Orange Luxury Coach, I don't see why we shouldn't rent that bungalow Tilly and Bill told us about down in Hayling Island, near Portsmouth. Be a bit difficult, mind you, with all those mines and barbed wire on the beaches. But we can all go for lovely walks.' Once again she threw her arms around Olly's neck, and kissed him on his vinegary lips. 'Oh Olly, the kids'll be absolutely thrilled!'

'Well don't get too excited. You'd better find out 'ow much we've got saved up first.'

Being the tallest of the three, Sam was elected to reach up to the family money-box on top of the dresser.

'How long have we got now?' Letty asked busily. 'Five or six weeks at the most. Let me see now, I could probably get in a few hours scrubbing the school hall. The Home Guard leave it in a terrible mess after they've finished training there.'

'Feels a bit light to me.' Sam was holding the box in his hand.

Letty stopped dead. 'It can't be.' She quickly grabbed it from Sam. It wasn't locked, and she opened it immediately. There was absolute silence. The look on Letty's face told all. There were only a few penny coins and some threepenny bits inside. 'It can't be,' she said, looking up incredulously at Oliver. 'I've been putting away five shillings from your wages every Friday for the past six months. Last time I looked at it, there must have been at least fifteen pounds in it.'

Oliver, stone-faced, said nothing.

For the next ten minutes all three of them sat there, trying to puzzle out what had happened to the hard-earned savings. To Letty and Sam it was a complete mystery.

'Why the bleedin' 'ell didn't yer keep the box locked,'

snapped Oliver, tight-lipped, eyes glaring at Letty.

'Don't be silly, Olly! Why would I want to keep the box locked in our own house? Nobody from outside ever comes in this room unless one of us are here, not even old Florrie upstairs, and she's as straight as a die.'

Sam, feeling awkward, felt he had to look Letty straight in the eyes. 'I swear ter God, Lett, I know nuffin' about this, 'onest I don't.'

Letty was horrified by such a suggestion. 'Sam! How could you say such a thing. You're part of this family. We'd all trust you with our lives. And in any case, there were a lot of your own savings in that box.'

Oliver was grinding his teeth with anger. 'You're absolutely sure yer didn't take it out of 'ere and put it somewhere else?'

Letty clutched her head anxiously. She was deeply depressed. 'Of course not. I *always* put our holiday money in the box, regular as clockwork every Friday pay-day. I just don't understand this.'

Without saying a word, Oliver got up from the table, went to the door, opened it, and shouted up the stairs. 'Ron! Ron, are you in? Are you up there?'

Letty exchanged a quick glance with Sam. She looked bewildered. 'Olly? What are you doing?'

A bedroom door opened on the first floor, and Ron's voice shouted back down the stairs. 'What d'yer want? I'm busy!'

'I don't care if yer are bloody busy! Get yer arse down 'ere and quick!'

Letty watched thunderstruck as Ron, in his pyjamas, rushed down the stairs. 'What's up then?' he growled irritably. 'What d'you want?'

Oliver stood back, and with an angry flick of the thumb gestured towards the parlour. 'Inside!'

Letty immediately panicked. 'Oliver!'

Oliver turned quickly and pointed a menacing finger at her. 'Keep out of this, Lett!' He also waited for Sam to leave, then stomped back into the parlour, and slammed the door behind him.

Letty, left outside in the passage, knew full well that it would be unwise to defy Oliver.

'Right! What've yer done wiv it?' The moment the door slammed, Oliver launched straight into a shouting match with Ron.

'What're you talkin' about?' Ron's voice was defiant, but cautious.

'You know bloody well what I'm talkin' about, yer feevin' little bugger! What've yer done wiv yer muvver's 'oliday money?'

'*I* haven't got her money!'

'You bleedin' 'ave, yer lyin' sod!'

Thoroughly distraught at the door outside, Letty could hear Oliver slam down the empty cash-box on to the table.

'This box was full of yer muvver's hard-earnt savin's. You put it back, or by Gord I'll cuff yer!'

'I tell you, I don't know what's happened to the money!' Ron's voice was getting more and more shrill, a sure sign he was nervous. 'Why do I always have to get blamed every time something goes wrong in this house! Why don't you ask my dear little brothers? They spend more time in this room than I do.'

'Your bruvvers've got nuffin' ter do wiv this and yer know it!'

'Oh no! Of course they haven't. Eddie and Mick never do anything wrong, do they? Butter wouldn't melt in their little mouths!'

Oliver was suddenly shouting at him. 'Yer little git! Why don't yer start growin' up!'

Ron yelled out. 'No, Pop! Leave me alone!'

Hearing this was more than Letty could take. She burst into the room to find Oliver holding on to Ron's pyjama collar, and on the verge of cuffing the boy round the face with the back of his hand. 'Olly – no!' Letty rushed to Ron's aid, and placed herself between him and his father.

Oliver was raging mad with her. 'I told yer ter leave this ter me!'

'*Why*, Olly?' Letty was shielding Ron with her back. 'Why are you picking on Ron? How d'yer know *he* took the money?'

Oliver came back at her immediately, but it was Ron he was glaring at. 'Because it's not the first time.' On hearing this, Ron turned to the door and tried to leave. But Oliver was there before him, and blocked his exit. 'What've yer done wiv it, Ron?' he growled. 'I wanna know!'

'For the last time, I haven't taken the bloody money!' Although utterly defiant, Ron now looked really scared of his father.

Oliver was brandishing his clenched fist at the boy. 'You swear in front of yer mother, and by gord, even on one leg – I'll do yer one!'

Again Letty tried to intervene. 'What are you saying, Olly? Tell me!'

But Oliver wouldn't tell her. How *could* he bring himself to tell her that this wasn't the only time their own son had stolen money. The first occasion had been when he left school and got his first job, in a silk screen factory just around the corner. One day, the manager had called on Oliver when Letty was out, to tell him that he was giving Ron the sack because he had stolen a few shillings from a workmate. And then, only a few months ago, it had happened again, in the job on the underground that Oliver himself had got for the boy. He would never have known about it if the station master at Manor House hadn't told him that Ron had been caught 'fiddlin' the books' in the booking office. Luckily, on this occasion, the matter had been overlooked because Ron had paid the money back. But it was Oliver who got the warning and the reprimand. He'd been told that if Ron was caught doing such a thing again, both their jobs could be on the line. All this Oliver had kept from Letty, in the hope that the boy had now reformed once and for all. But to steal from his own mother, from his own family – *that* Oliver could never forgive.

Ron was now prepared to say anything, to release all his pent-up anger and bitterness. 'Prove it!' he snarled. 'Go on! Just try and prove that I took your lousy money!'

Oliver looked more hurt than angry, and gathering himself together, tried to speak calmly. 'Why d'yer 'ave ter keep lyin', son? Yer're not a kid any more. Yer're a man.'

'You wouldn't recognise a man if you saw one,' the boy snapped back. 'You haven't the brains!'

For the first time, Letty was outraged. 'Ron!' she gasped, angrily.

Suddenly, Sam appeared from the scullery, where he had deliberately kept clear of Oliver's confrontation with the boy. 'That's enough now, Ron! That's no way ter talk ter yer farvver!'

Ron immediately turned on his uncle. 'You keep out of this! *You're* not my father – I hope!'

'Ron!' Letty was horrified.

Sam rushed across the room, grabbed hold of the boy's shoulder with one hand, and held his other clenched fist close to Ron's face. 'Wot d'you say?'

Ron grinned. 'That's it, mate. All brawn and no brains!'

'No, Sam! *Please!*' Only Letty's intervention prevented Sam from pummelling his fist into the boy's face.

Sam paused a moment, then lowered his fist, and released the boy. 'Now you listen to me, sonny Jim,' he said to Ron firmly. 'I may only be a builder's navvy to you, but I know

229

what's right an' wrong in this world, an' that's more than you can say. But I'll tell yer this. Your old man on 'is one leg is worth ten o' you on both yours. So you listen ter what he says – see!' Having said his piece, he pulled Ron away from the door and opened it. As he was going out, he stopped, and turned. 'I'm goin' round the boozer. At least the air's worf breevin' round there!'

There was silence whilst Letty, Oliver, and Ron waited to hear Sam close the street door as he left the house. In those few moments, all Letty could think about was the small boy who used to kick an old tin can around the streets, back in the first war. It seemed so unfair that Sam should have to be the one who was constantly being hurt. And what had happened to Ron? When he was young, he had been such a loving boy, but now, quite suddenly, he was completely changed, and Letty just couldn't understand why. What on earth had gone wrong? Exhausted, she lowered herself down wearily into a chair at the table. 'That was a wicked thing to say to your uncle, Ron.' Looking straight up at him she added pointedly, 'And totally untrue.'

'So where d'yer 'ear all that filth from then, eh?' demanded Oliver, far from giving up the fight. 'Yer cousin Rosie? Or was it that mouff-an'-trousers muvver of 'ers?'

Ron's eyes glistened with anger. 'You leave Rosie out of this!'

'Why? Are yer so 'ard up for a gel that yer 'ave to go out wiv yer own cousin? If you're so fond of yer Aunt Vi and 'er family, I wonder yer don't go and live wiv 'em.'

Ron grinned back icily. 'Thanks, Pop. That's not a bad idea.'

Chastened, Oliver forced himself to calm down. 'Look son. If yer tell me you only borrowed the money, and mean ter pay it back, I'll try ter understand. But I want to know wot yer've down wiv it.'

Ron crossed his arms defiantly. 'I spent it all. And if you want to know what on – yes – I took Rosie on a day trip to Southend. We had a damn good time.'

Letty wanted to cry, but somehow she just couldn't. All she could do was to cover her face with one hand and mumble to herself, 'Oh God!'

Even Oliver was lost for words. When Ron was a child, he had been Oliver's pride and joy. Whether it was because this son was so physically like him or not, Oliver had seen his own future image reflected in the little boy. And yet, what he had seen and heard tonight made him think that he didn't even recognise the lad any more. 'Yer've gotta pay it back, son. Yer know that, don't yer? Yer've gotta pay back every single penny.'

Ron lowered his eyes. For one brief moment, it looked as though he was distressed. 'I'll do my best – in time. But I can't pay back fifteen quid just like that.'

'You'll just have to do some overtime.'

'Overtime! You've got to be jokin'!' Suddenly his mood changed again. 'I've had enough of that bloody tube station. It may be all right for you to spend the rest of your life propped up at a freezin' cold ticket-barrier. But it's not for me, Pop. Oh no. Not for me!'

Letty looked up from the table her eyes glaring. 'And what's so wrong with earning your living at a ticket-barrier may I ask?' She stood up and pointed her finger at him. 'Let me tell you something, my son. No one's more proud of your father than I am. And d'you know why? Because, despite the fact that he's only got one leg of his own – he *stands* there!' Ron tried to interrupt her, but she raised her voice before he could speak. 'Just you remember that your father has never failed to support his family, to keep a roof over our heads, and provide food for us. It takes guts to survive all that, Ron – something *you* just don't have!' She went to the door, opened it, and stood aside to let him pass. 'Now for God's sake get out of here, before I really say something I regret!'

Ron strolled casually to the door, stopped briefly, and turned. 'Oh, by the way, I forgot to mention. I didn't bother to wait for my call-up papers, so I volunteered.' He glanced wryly at his father, 'For the Navy, I'm glad to say. Luckily, I got through my medical OK. With a bit of luck, I should be on my way any day now. Can't be soon enough for me, I can tell you. Anyway, I thought you'd like to know.' He turned and went, leaving Letty to close the door behind him.

A few minutes later, the wail of the nightly air-raid siren echoed across the rooftops of Roden Street and its neighbours. Clutching her hot-water bottle and a vacuum flask of hot cocoa, old Florrie grumbled her way down the stairs, cursing Hitler with every foul word she could think of. Just behind her came Eddie and Mick, still half-asleep, prepared to spend their last night with their mother in the stark comfort of the Anderson shelter.

The raid turned out to be long, noisy, and, as always, frightening. Not many people in London slept much that night. Especially Letty.

Chapter 18

Beatrice hated railway stations. To her they were places where people were either sad or happy, and extremes of emotion embarrassed her. She couldn't bear the noise and the smell of the steam engines, or even the bumpy, ugly railway lines they ran on. In fact it had always been a mystery to her why Letty and Oliver had ever gone to live in that house overlooking the railway line, in Citizen Road. But she had offered to accompany her daughter to Marylebone Station, to see Eddie and Mick evacuated to the country, for to her surprise she had grown fond of her grandchildren – although she was careful not to show it too often. On the whole she preferred Mick; he took the most notice of her when he and Eddie came to visit her at Bedford Terrace on Sunday mornings. But she liked Eddie, too; he made her laugh when he tap-danced for her, much to the fury of her downstairs neighbour, old 'Mother Wolf'.

Beatrice Edginton was now in her early seventies, and people who'd known her over the years thought she had shrunk. She couldn't have been more than five feet three at the best of times, but now she seemed even smaller. After over twenty years, she still hadn't given William a divorce, and having to fend for herself had taken its toll. She was a stooped old woman: the expensive wardrobe of clothes gone, replaced by cheap off-the-peg coats and dresses which had to last until there was no way to repair them any longer.

Having lived in a rough area for so long, Beatrice had also lost her precise, haughty tones: it was only when exchanging words with old Mother Wolf that the Arlington Square style of speech returned most conveniently.

The journey from Pakeman Street School to Marylebone Station had been by a specially chartered charabanc, and had not been to Beatrice's liking. For a start there were hordes of excited evacuees shouting in her ears, and some of the parents looked as though they were only too delighted to be getting rid of them. Letty was no help. She hardly spoke a word all the way to the station, clearly dreading the approaching separation.

By the time they reached the station, the 'Evacuee Express' was jammed with children of all shapes and sizes. Special police constables wearing tin helmets and carrying gas-mask cases over their shoulders, were on duty everywhere, and sweet-smiling WVS ladies were scattered at intervals all along the platform, handing out an orange and a paper-thin bar of Nestlé's Plain Chocolate to each child.

'Now, don't forget what I told you, Eddie.' Letty was helping Mick up into a carriage that was already chock-full. 'You and Mick are not to lean out of the train window, d'you hear?'

'Yes, Mum.' Eddie had already fought another boy for a seat, and won.

Beatrice was holding her handkerchief over her mouth as protection from the puffs of white steam that were hissing under the wheels and swirling up around her ankles. 'I wish you'd stop fussing, Letty,' she grumbled. 'They're not goin' to China, you know!' With that, she let out an almighty sneeze, which produced a chorus of 'Bless yer!' from the gang of excited kids on board the train.

Pandemonium was mounting all along the length of the platform as harassed schoolteachers and officials from the

London County Council ran from one carriage to another. Groups of parents were talking with each other: cursing Hitler; cursing the lack of organisation; cursing their kids; in fact cursing anything they could think of.

Suddenly a porter blew his train whistle, immediately throwing Letty into a panic. 'Eddie! Eddie, listen to me. If Mick wants to go to the lavatory on the journey, you're to wait outside for him. All right?'

Eddie was already peeling his orange with his teeth. 'Yes, Mum!'

Looking miserable, Mick had managed to squeeze his head above the open carriage window, from which Eddie and two other kids were leaning out. 'Mum, I don't want to be evacuated,' he called, his face crumpled up and close to tears. 'I want to stay here with you and Pop and Uncle.'

Using all her strength to hold back her own feelings, Letty replied briskly and practically. 'Don't be a silly boy now,' she said. 'As soon as the Germans stop dropping their bombs, we'll have you back home again.'

'I'm not scared of bombs, Mum,' replied Mick, quickly. 'Honest I'm not!'

Eddie pulled Mick's school cap over his eyes. 'Oh yes you are. You're scared stiff!'

'I'm not!'

They started to push and pull each other, thrusting the other two children away from the window.

'Stop that you two! I shall tell your father!' snapped Letty reaching through the open window to separate them. 'You're lucky Pop's on early turn this morning. He'd have walloped the pair of you! And blow your nose, Mick. I've told you a hundred times, you'll get sores on your lip'. Suddenly the roof vibrated with the voice of the station announcer, booming out that the Evacuee Express was about to leave, and doors should be closed immediately. Although no destination was given, most parents seemed to know that their children were on their way to 'somewhere in Hertfordshire'. As Beatrice said, it really wasn't too far from London, but for Letty, it seemed more like a million miles away.

'Eddie, don't forget now!' she panicked as train doors slammed all along the platform. 'As soon as you know which address you're going to, write and let me know. You've got the postcard and stamp I gave you, haven't you?'

'Yes, Mum.'

Beatrice suddenly produced two paperbags full of jelly-babies, which she'd managed to get on her ration coupons in Chapel Market. 'You can have these on the journey,' she yelled above the noise, pushing one bag at Eddie and the other at Mick. 'And don't eat them all at once!'

Both kids yelled, 'Thanks, Gran!' and as they did so, the train guard waved his flag and blew the departing whistle.

'Oh God!' gasped Letty. 'It's not time already, is it?'

Close to tears herself, Beatrice took a firm grip of Letty's arm. 'Don't Letty!' But Letty pulled away from her and reached towards the carriage.

There was a great swell of cheers from all the kids as the train whistle screeched and spurt of white steam gushed up from the engine funnel, scattering terrified sparrows and pigeons into every direction.

Through the window Letty could see that Mick was now in tears. 'I don't want to go! Mum, I don't want to go!'

'It'll be all right, boy! It'll be all right!' Letty repeated on the verge of weeping. As she spoke, the train guard sounded his whistle again, and the train very slowly started to move. 'We'll soon be together again.'

The excited roar of cheers, laughter, and whistles was deafening. Everyone was waving – kids, parents, porters, a group of sailors on another platform, even the Special Constables.

'Be'ave yourself, you two, or I'll . . .' Beatrice couldn't say anything else and, too small to reach up to the carriage window, she just waved her handkerchief.

As the train moved a little faster, Letty quickly hugged Eddie and kissed him firmly on the lips. 'Be a good boy, son!' she spluttered desperately. Then she grabbed hold of Mick, held his face in her hands, and kissed him briskly, first on the forehead and then on his wet cheeks.

'Bye, Mum!' Bye, Gran!' yelled Eddie, cheerfully. Then, as the train gathered speed, and Letty tried to keep up with it, Eddie called back, 'Don't drink too much whisky from that bottle under your bed, Gran! Hooray!'

Hiding a smile, Beatrice pretended to be outraged and, shaking her fist at the departing train, she yelled back, 'You cheeky little—! Give us back my jelly-babies!'

Letty finally had to come to a halt, for as the train moved faster and faster, she was beginning to bump into groups of other parents. As the train wound its way clear of the platform and into the tunnel all Letty saw through the blur of her tears was a sea of excited, cheering faces, leaning and waving out of the windows. And she thought she could make out Mick, just disappearing into the tunnel, his chubby cheeks awash with tears, calling, 'I don't want to go! I don't want to go . . . !'

Apart from a porter pushing his empty trolley back towards the ticket-barrier, Letty and Beatrice were the last two people to leave the platform. Once they were quite sure the train had gone for good, they waited for everyone else to go before they moved off themselves. Beatrice linked arms with Letty, and guided her weeping daughter carefully out of the station.

Within the hour, Letty arrived home at Number 13, having kissed her mother goodbye at the end of the street. She put the key in the door, opened it, and went in. To her surprise, Oliver was home from his early morning turn, waiting for her in the passageway. Neither said a word as they held each other tight.

Half an hour later Beatrice also returned home. After removing her hatpin, and taking off her outdoor clothes, she went straight through the curtained archway into her bedroom. She knelt on the floor and reached for the bottle of whisky hidden there. She took it back to her sitting-room, and poured herself a glass, adding a little fresh water from the pail she kept in the corner. Then she settled back in her chair, to reflect on a morning she hadn't cared for one little bit.

It must have been almost a month later that, quite by chance, Letty met Vi O'Malley outside the Marlborough Cinema in the Holloway Road. In the old days, when Islington was a fashionable place to live, the Marlborough had been a popular theatre for staged melodramas. Letty had heard that Mr Tod Slaughter once appeared there and she only wished she could have seen him in his famous Sweeney Todd role; for there was nothing she liked better than a bloodthirsty story. That afternoon she'd interrupted her shopping to have a look at what was on offer at the Marlborough that week.

''Allo, Letty. Long time no see.'

Letty stopped looking at the photograph displays in the cinema foyer, and turned with a start. 'Vi! What are you doing 'round here? I thought you lived up near the Archway somewhere.'

Vi stiffened slightly, and straightened up her shoulders. 'Actually, it's 'Ighgate,' she said rather haughtily. She hadn't aged or changed a bit. Her hips were a touch wider, and there were a few wisps of grey hair just showing beneath her feathered hat, but nothing more. 'We've come down ter meet our Daddy outside the Gaumont, 'aven't we, Do-Do? There's a new Alice Faye-Don Ameche film on there.'

'Oh, I see.' Letty turned to look at Do-Do. She was a pale-faced little girl, about eight years old, but quite tall for her age, with fair hair combed into two pigtails. Her black school uniform hat, jacket and skirt looked very smart. On the jacket pocket there was a blue motif with the letters 'SJ' emblazoned on it. Letty thought Do-Do seemed an intelligent child, with features more like Vi's than her father's. 'This must be Doreen,' she said, smiling at the girl. 'I haven't seen you since you were a little baby.'

Vi glowed with pride, obviously doting on her youngest daughter. 'Do-Do. Say 'allo to your Aunty Letty.' She looked even prouder as the child did so.

For a few minutes they stood there, talking over what they'd been doing since they last met. Most of Vi's conversation concentrated on her family and the posh house they lived in on the corner of Grovedale Road, which in actual fact wasn't in Highgate at all, but Upper Holloway. She carried on about how brainy Doreen was, and confided that she was the most highly regarded pupil in her class at St Joseph's Convent School or 'Holy Joe's' as Letty usually knew it. According to Vi, her other daughter, Rosie, now eighteen, was also brilliant and had turned out to be a wonderful ballroom dancer. And as for Frank, well, there was no stopping him now, because he'd recently been appointed station master at Holloway Road Tube Station. Knowing how Oliver felt about his sister, Letty decided not to talk too much about the Hobbs family, or life in Number 13. She couldn't help wondering how much Vi might have heard from Ron before he went into the Navy. Needless to say, when Vi heard that Eddie and Mick had been evacuated, she insisted that she'd never let her Doreen be taken away from her. 'As long as Our Holy Mother Mary's there,' she said, gazing up to heaven and crossing herself several times, 'no 'arm will ever come to the O'Malleys.'

Letty didn't mind a bit when Vi told her she'd aged since they last met: that was fairly obvious. But she had to smile when Vi suggested that Letty should start using make-up, something she'd never done in her entire life, and didn't intend to start now. But she could see that Vi still used just as much as ever. These days she still shaped her lips into a bright cupid's bow, her cheeks heavily powdered and rouged, and her eyes positively bulging with mascara. 'I'm very particular about my complexion,' Vi said demurely gazing at her reflection in the box-office window. Letty agreed with her, wondering, as she had done years ago, why Vi needed to use so much make-up when she had such a lovely skin.

Aware that the afternoon was drawing rapidly to a close, Letty tried to tell Vi that she had to get home to get Oliver's tea.

'And 'ow *is* my dear bruvver?' Vi interrupted cuttingly. 'Just as grumpy as ever, is 'e?'

Letty sprang to Oliver's defence. 'Olly's not grumpy, Vi,' she said firmly. 'He's just set in his ways, that's all.'

'Well, I fink you're marvellous the way yer cope wiv both 'im and 'is bruvver.' She allowed a slight pause, whilst she took a sly glance at Letty. '*E's* still wiv yer, is 'e? My bruvver Sam?'

'Of course, Vi. Sam's part of the family. He's like a second father to the kids.'

'Oh really?' Vi exercised her shoulders, as she always did when she knew she was being mischievous. 'An' 'ow does your Olly feel about that?'

'What d'you mean by that, Vi?' Letty loathed the suggestiveness of her sister-in-law's remark, and wasn't afraid to show it. She narrowed her eyes furiously.

240

'Nothing, Letty. But you've got to admit, to some people it *is* a bit – well – peculiar, you livin' under the same roof wiv yer 'usband *and* 'is bruvver.'

Letty bristled with anger. So Oliver was right about his sister. She *must* have been the one who'd been poisoning Ron's ears with her talk. There was no doubt about it, Vi was a trouble-maker. 'There's nothing peculiar about your brother Sam or anyone else living with us, Vi. We're the first family he's ever had in this world. We're the first people who've shown that we care for him – *all* of us – Oliver, the kids and me!'

At last Letty's outrage started to impinge on Vi. She had never seen her like this before. What's happened to her, she thought? She was so different before she got married. All right, she'd had a mind of her own in the munitions factory days, but not like this! Vi decided the best thing to do was to change the subject quickly. 'You mustn't take offence, Letty. I'm not suggestin' anythin' – yer know I'm not. Goodness, yer know how fond I've always been of yer. I do 'ope we can all get tergevver again some time, just like the old days, eh? You and Olly must come up to 'Ighgate an' see all of us.' She lowered her voice and leaned closer to Letty. 'Frank knows where 'e can get some black-market brandy.'

Letty tried her best to sound friendly. But it was an effort. 'Thanks, Vi. Let's wait and see. You'll have to excuse me now. I have to get going.'

Once again Vi stopped her. 'Oh, by the way. I 'eard from your Ron the uvver day. 'E's such a nice boy. My Rosie finks the world of 'im.'

Letty turned slowly. 'You've had a letter from Ron?' She wasn't sure whether Vi was being mischievous again.

'Why yes. 'E's trainin' on some ship up in Scapa Flow or somewhere. 'Aven't *you* 'eard from 'im then?'

Letty hesitated for a moment. 'Yes. Yes, of course we've

heard from him. As a matter of fact, we've heard lots of times.'

Vi shook her head anxiously. 'I must say, if I was you and Olly, I'd be very worried about a son of mine goin' off to fight in the war. I mean, every day yer 'ear about ships bein' sunk by Jerry, don't yer?' Letty let her continue without interruption. 'Still, as long as yer 'ave faith, that's all that matters. I tell yer Letty, when I married Frank an' became a Catholic, it changed my 'ole life. It taught me that yer 'usband an' kids are the most important fing in the 'ole wide world.'

'You don't have to change your religion to know that, Vi.'

Letty quickly said her farewells to Vi and Doreen and made her way back home along the Holloway Road. After going a few yards, she took a quick glance over her shoulder to watch the two of them walking off, hand-in-hand towards the Gaumont; Vi was hobbling along on her painful high-heeled shoes and Doreen, tagged along at her side, her eyes fixed skywards on two glistening barrage balloons.

Just as Letty was turning into Bovay Place at the far end of Roden Street, the late afternoon echoed to the triple wail of air-raid warning sirens from the Cally, Holloway Road, and Hornsey Road police stations.

Within the hour, a German Messerschmitt fighter plane broke through the ack-ack barrage protecting central London and machine-gunned the silver balloons, which immediately exploded into two enormous, glowing balls of fire.

Chapter 19

The little village of Wareham was on the map of Hertfordshire, but only just. In fact, if you'd been driving up from London, you might have passed through without realising it was a village. It had its own village stores, sub-post-office, church, and petrol pump, but most of its one hundred-and-thirty-seven residents lived in houses outside the village itself: Wareham was a rural community, and so on all the fringes of the main wheatfields there were small pockets of nineteenth-century farmworkers' cottages. Around the village green there were also several timber-framed houses, some of them thatched, belonging mostly to retired people who had moved out from Hertford, about twelve miles away. It wasn't easy to get to the village at the best of times, for Wareham Railway Station was on a branch line, and since there was a war on, there were only services to Hertford on three days a week.

But when Eddie and Mick had arrived at Wareham, they found that what there was of the village opened its arms to them and all the other twenty-five London evacuees its parish council had agreed to take. Mrs Fisher in the village stores chose twin nine-year-old girls from Shoreditch, and greeted them with as much love and affection as if they were her own children – of which she already had two boys and a girl. Eric, a cheeky eleven-year-old from Bethnal Green, with whom Eddie had made pals on the train, found himself made welcome to life with a childless farmworker and his wife, who were clearly anxious to spoil him thoroughly. Eddie and Mick had experienced a funny feeling in their stomachs as they waved goodbye to their other travelling pals. Nice as people were to them, Wareham didn't look anything like their familiar haunts back home, and Mick was already missing Mum and Pop, Uncle Sam and everyone in Roden Street.

Together with ten other boys, Eddie and Mick had been the last to reach their new home, with the Meacham family, which most villagers considered to be the finest house in the area. But as they got out of the small charabanc, they stared in wonder at the place, which, to Mick, looked more like a museum than a home. Wareham Hall stood in ten acres of magnificent cultivated grounds, set off by spectacular gardens and regularly cut lawns, which rolled down the River Rib just by the rhododendron bushes. The house itself was Elizabethan, set on three floors, with a faded red-tile roof and old beams – pockmarked with woodworm – which were exposed on both the inside and outside walls.

On their arrival, the boys were lined up by Mrs Meacham who, wearing black rubber gloves, inspected their hair for lice. From that moment on, Eddie and Mick referred to her as the 'old goat', mainly because that's what she looked like to them, with a few grey hairs sprouting from her chin, and a white headscarf tied in such a way that it looked as though she had goat's ears. The 'old goat' was not amused by Eddie and Mick's constant giggling, so they were amongst the first to be taken to the bath tub, where a manservant made quite sure they scrubbed themselves down thoroughly in steaming hot water, heavily laced with Dettol antiseptic, and a huge bar of carbolic soap. Once that was over, they were introduced to their 'dormitory officer', Roger Meacham, the Meachams' thirty-two-year-old son who had been rejected from military service because of poor eyesight. After supper, which consisted of three cracker biscuits, a piece of cheddar cheese and a glass of powdered milk, they were given a quick run-down of the house regulations by Roger who, in Eddie's mind, spoke as though someone were holding a bad smell under his nose:

'Bed at eight-thirty, no talking after lights-out, rise at seven, wash and dress, breakfast at eight, and ready to march in single file to school by eight-thirty! Any questions?'

Yes, Eddie had a question. *What about some more grub?* But he didn't actually ask it.

And so Eddie and Mick Hobbs started their days in Wareham Hall.

On their first morning, they'd been inspected by the head of their household, Colonel Meacham, who had apparently delighted the parish council by agreeing to house twelve evacuees. His only condition had been that they were to be all boys for, as an ex-military man himself, the Colonel considered that girls would be less given to obey orders.

'Name?' demanded the Colonel, as he bent down to stare menacingly into Mick's terrified face.

'Mick, sir.'

'Surname! Surname!' The Colonel's red cheeks puckered impatiently, and his bearded chin jutted out firmly from a well-worn face.

'Hobbs, sir. Michael Francis Hobbs.' Then he quickly grabbed hold of his brother's hand at the side of him. 'This is my brother, Eddie.'

'Is it now?' The Colonel flicked his piercing brown eyes from Mick to Eddie. 'Your name Hobbs?'

Eddie sniffed, and wiped his running nose with his finger. 'That's right.' Then after a resentful pause, he added, 'Sir.'

'From now on, you and your brother will be known as Hobbs one and two. Do you understand?'

Eddie and Mick replied in unison. 'Yes, sir.'

The Colonel stood upright again. He was a tall, thickly-set man, who had apparently once been the scourge of his regiment during colonial service in India. These days he spent most of his retirement riding horses from his own stables, and always wore a riding cap, jacket and breeches. Mick, however, never took his eyes off the Colonel's constant companion, a horse-whip which he frequently flicked against the side of his leg.

During that first week, Eddie and Mick felt as though they were being enrolled into the Army.

Most of the house was treated like a military headquarters, so the only room that Eddie, Mick, and the other kids were allowed to see was their own living quarters, which was converted out of an unheated 1920s wash-house. Built as an annexe to the main house, it contained twelve camp beds, six of them lined up on each side of the room: previously the furnishings had consisted only of the wash-basin and bath. Lavatories, if they could be called such, were situated under canvas in a secluded corner at the far end of the garden. In reality, they were portable Elsan buckets, which the boys were quickly instructed to empty themselves each day, into the main septic tank.

Eddie in particular didn't take too kindly to the Hall's military discipline, and when he and the other boys treated the front lawns like a football pitch, he got himself into real trouble.

'Hobbs Two!' The Colonel's voice bellowed out from the far side of the lawn, and at double quick-time he was upon them, eyes glaring, horse-whip tapping angrily against the side of his leg. 'If I catch any of you boys behaving like London guttersnipes again, I'll have you out of your beds at dawn, with no breakfast. Understood?'

'But, sir,' replied Eddie, the only boy with the cheek to

answer back, 'we were only playing football.'

The ball was confiscated, and never seen again. For Eddie, that was the most unforgivable thing anyone could ever do to him. For both boys each day seemed to drag by, and only Eddie had the resilience and good humour to cope with the situation. But for Mick it was a different story. Each evening after lights out, he lay in his bed beneath one of the four dormitory windows. From outside, he could hear a barn owl hooting in the distance. For a short while, he would stay awake and listen to it. But his mind was really on other things. He could hear old Miss Florrie snoring in her bunk in the Anderson shelter back home. And he could see his mum trying to settle down for the night in her deck chair. It all seemed such a long way away, but as the tears trickled down his cheeks and on to the pillow, each night he wished he were there.

Even after a month of life in Wareham Hall, things seemed no better for the evacuees. Admittedly, life wasn't completely bleak. Eddie and Mick grew fond of the two full-time gardeners, both of them too old to be otherwise involved in the war effort. Mick's favourite was a small, plump old lady named Maisie, who irritated George, her male counterpart, by being quicker and better at digging than he. The friendliness of the old couple was a small glimmer of light on a grim horizon. But one Thursday morning there was a real ray of excitement. It was Mick's birthday, and Mr Hawthorne the village postman, brought him not only birthday cards, but also several small parcels. He had a packet of pencils from Auntie Till and Uncle Bill, a *Film Fun* annual from Uncle Sam and a postal order for a pound from Mum and Pop. But the greatest excitement came when he opened a small cardboard box containing a plain sponge cake made specially for him by his mother. As the Colonel and Roger had forbidden any eating in the dormitories other than regulation food,

247

Mick decided that he and Eddie would have to find a safer place to celebrate.

That night, in the garden outside, Mick's owl was hooting as usual as he and Eddie, wearing only their new striped pyjamas that Letty had bought them, slipped out through the dormitory back door. Quietly, they made their way down to the lavatories at the bottom of the garden. Luckily, there was a full moon out and they could find their way about in the dark quite easily. It wasn't as bitterly cold as it had been earlier in the week, but there was a thin film of mist over the river, and it was very damp underfoot. Just as they were passing the 'old goat's' vegetable bed, Eddie suddenly slipped on the grass, and fell backwards. As he picked himself up, he found the seat of his pyjamas was covered in horse manure.

'Cor! What a pong!' snorted Mick, holding his nose. 'I hope they don't give us *that* for dinner t'morrow!' And both of them started to giggle helplessly.

Eddie picked up the cabbage he had just fallen on, and gave it a good kick into the nearby river, where it landed with a loud plop. 'That'll teach 'em to nick my football!'

Covering their mouths to suppress the giggles, they rushed off down the garden.

They heaved a sigh of relief when they reached the shelter of the canvas enclosure. There was no partition between each of the portable Elsans, so they were able to sit down on one each, and share out the cake. Eddie produced a small tin of cough sweets that their mother had sent them a few days ago. They were the best substitute he'd found for proper sweets and, as usual, he ate too many of them at once, forcing him to make a rude noise into the Elsan. They both roared with laughter at the echoing noise, falling hysterically against the canvas walls.

Suddenly, Mick thought he heard a movement outside,

and they both sat still, as quiet as mice. Hearing nothing more, they continued with their party, savouring every morsel. Then Eddie broke wind for a second time, once again sending them into fits.

'Stop it Eddie!' snorted Mick, mouth full of cake, choking with laughter. 'It's a terrible pong!'

At that moment the canvas door awning was pulled aside, to reveal the beam of a torchlight aimed straight at Eddie, then Mick. A tall, dark shape stood before them.

'So this is how you disobey my orders, is it?' It was the Colonel's voice.

'I'm sorry, sir,' replied Mick timidly. Everyone in the house had to be addressed formally. 'We didn't mean to do anything wrong. Honest we didn't.'

'Give me the box!'

Mick put the remainder of his cake back into the box, and held on to it. 'But it's mine, sir. My mum sent it to me.'

Eddie, too, stood up defiantly. 'You don't understand, sir! It's the tenth of October. It's my brother's birthday!'

The dark shape moved forward quickly, and angrily snatched the cake box away from Mick. 'I shall be waiting to see you both when you return from school tomorrow afternoon. Now get back to the house!'

The Colonel's dark shadow waited for them to obey, then moved on a few paces to the bank of the river. There he reached into the cardboard box and took out what was left of Letty's cake. In one swift movement he threw the remains into the water, where they disintegrated into tiny pieces.

One night a couple of weeks later, Letty lay awake later than usual. She was thinking of Mick, wondering what sort of birthday he'd had away from the family for the first time, and how miserable she felt about that. But there were many other things on her mind too. First of all, she thought about her chance meeting with Vi, and the malicious way she had talked. How could anyone think like that! And yet, obnoxious as it sounded, Letty was aware that people *did* talk. When Sam first moved in with them, the neighbours had talked: Alice and Ted next door; old Polly Myers who lived opposite; Mr Mitchinson the caretaker of the school and his wife – and who knows how many more. It was all just hints, nothing more, but Letty knew the tongues had been wagging. The clock in the Emmanuel Church tower in Hornsey Road suddenly broke her thoughts, sounding one o'clock in the morning. Oliver continued to snore loudly, and Letty eased herself quietly out of bed, and went to the window. The room was chilly; Oliver wouldn't light the gas-fire, insisting that they shouldn't waste the 'juice'. But Letty was always grateful for Olly's caution – it had never let her down yet.

For once, there was no air raid that night, and as she pushed back the thick blackout curtain she thanked the Lord that she was able to sleep in her own bed with Olly. Old Florrie, however, had decided to go down to the shelter, for she was fed up with having her nights interrupted. Letty yawned, and looked down at the deserted pavement of Roden Street outside. There was certainly an autumn chill in the air, and a thin film of mist was floating around the chimneypots on the other side of the street. Once again, her mind started racing. This time it was Ron. What a heart-breaking time it had been when they'd discovered he'd stolen the family savings. But after all, Ron was part of the family, and the money was as much his as anyone else's. She wanted to tell the boy that whatever he did, she and his father would always love him. But the tragedy was, she had never had the chance because the next day he had just packed his things, and moved in with Vi and Frank. And then, within a week he was in the Navy and they hadn't heard from him since.

Letty felt an aching feeling in her stomach.

'Ain't yer ever gonna get any sleep, Lett? Wos up now then?'

Letty hadn't realised that Oliver had stopped snoring, and was sitting up in bed. 'Nothing's up dear,' she whispered. 'I'm just not tired yet, that's all.'

Oliver groaned, and flopped his head back on to the pillow. 'Puttin' the world ter rights agin!'

'Olly. Tell me, do you believe in God?'

Oliver merely groaned again.

Letty turned and looked across at him. 'No, but do you? Living near a church makes me feel much closer to God. Doesn't it you?'

' 'Ow can yer believe in somefin' yer can't see?'

'Get away with you! I remember what you were like when we got married. You cried like a baby when they sang 'Onward Christian Soldiers'.

'Hymns is diff'rent. I like a good sing-song.'

Letty didn't believe a word he said. In his own way Oliver was more religious than most of the Bible-punchers she knew. What's more, he had always been a marvellous father to his kids, even though he insisted he wasn't. Every Sunday morning before they were evacuated, Oliver had taken Eddie and Mick up to the West End to feed the seagulls over the bridge in St James's Park. On the bus there and back, he would spin them the most dreadful yarns. The kids absolutely adored Pop's terrible tales. But most of all, Letty thought, they adored being *with* him. The sad thing was Oliver refused to believe just how much he meant to them.

With a heavy sigh, Letty made her way back to bed. Just as she got there, however, Oliver suddenly cringed with pain. 'Olly! What is it, dear? What's wrong?'

Oliver rolled from one side to another. 'This bleedin' leg! That's wos wrong! I've got 'an ulcer comin' on it.'

'Oh no, not another one.' Letty quickly turned on the light and pulled back the sheet and blankets.

Oliver panicked and pulled the sheet up again. 'Don't turn on the light! You've still got the bloody curtain back. I don't want Polly ter see all I've got!' He was referring to Polly Myers, the old girl who lived on the top floor opposite, who spent most of her time with her bosom on her windowsill, straining to look into everyone's front-parlour or bedroom.

Letty turned off the light saying, 'To hell with Polly! Let's have a look at you.' She reached for the torch on her bedside cabinet and took a look at what the doctors had left of Oliver's leg. In the torchlight, she could see two large sores there, turning into vicious looking ulcers. 'Oh Olly, dear – it *is* inflamed.'

'It's that bleedin' Limb Fittin' Centre agin! They keep sendin' me these replacement legs that don't fit! Every one I get rubs me raw!'

Letty tried to soothe him, and gently kissed his forehead. 'It's not fair, dear. It's just not fair the way they treat you First War veterans. Why should they give all the new equipment to the young ones? I'll put some Lyon's ointment on it for you in the morning.'

When Oliver's pain subsided, he settled back beneath the sheet. It was at times like these that Letty felt so helpless. She couldn't bear him being in pain, and he'd had so much of it over the years. Whenever she could, she helped him to unlace his artificial leg, usually when he was sitting on his bedside chair. But it was a tough and delicate job for her to pull off the clumsy contraption, because there was always the risk that she would burst one of his blisters. Letty's side of the bed was quite cold now, but she couldn't have a hot-water bottle because the last time she'd filled it with boiling-hot water, and it had burnt Oliver's back-side. Although there was silence between them for a few minutes, neither was asleep. Then, as usual, Letty suddenly started to sing very softly. After the first line of 'You are my honey, honey-suckle', Oliver joined in. It was like this every night whenever they couldn't get to sleep; they just snuggled up close and sang songs quietly together. The neighbours must have heard them, poor old Sam too, but no one had ever complained.

Eventually, the song came to an end. 'Olly,' she whispered.

'Go ter sleep, Lett.'

'I do hope young Mick had a lovely birthday. D'you think that colonel or whatever he is – d'you think he gave him a party?'

'Ow should I know?'

Letty started to worry again. 'It's funny we've heard nothing from them except that postcard Eddie sent. And Mick hasn't even written to thank me for his cake. It's so unlike him. He loves writing letters.' She raised her head, now, to talk to him. 'Olly, I'm not sure I like the idea of this retired colonel they've gone to.'

Oliver yawned. He was beginning to get grumpy. 'They're perfectly all right, Lett. The colonel's got a wife, ain't he?'

Letty immediately sat upright. 'A colonel's wife is no substitute for a mother!' she said haughtily.

Oliver sighed, and turned over. As the moon had now disappeared outside, all he could see of her was a silhouette. 'Lett. We've got one night wivvout an air raid. Can't we get some kip?'

Letty carried on talking, knowing she was pushing her luck. 'I saw your sister Violet the other day.' She'd been wanting to tell Olly and she couldn't keep it to herself any longer. There was absolutely no reaction from him until, dangerously she ventured, 'Don't you think we should ask them all over to tea some time?'

Oliver reached behind him to grab the brass headrail of the bed and eased himself upright. 'I've told you before, Lett,' he said slowly. 'I'm not 'avin' that woman in my 'ouse. And that's final!'

'But why, Olly? Why d'you have to be so bitter? What did Vi say to you that day she came over. Please tell me, dear. Was it something about me? Or about Sam? We *should* talk about these things, you know.'

' 'Ow many times 'ave I gotta tell yer? I don't wanna discuss that woman – not now – not never! So once an' fer all, Lett, pack it up will yer?'

They both sat looking into the dark, saying nothing. It was Letty who finally broke the quiet again. 'Olly. Vi's had a letter from our Ron.'

'That's up to 'im,' he snapped, non-commitally.

'We can hardly blame him, Olly. Not after all the fuss we made about that money-box.'

Oliver came back quickly. 'We lost our 'oliday because of 'im. 'E's a bloody daylight robber!'

'He's also our son, Olly.'

'No son 'fieves from 'is own. I don't know 'ow we produced somefin' like 'im. 'E's not a bit like the uvver two.'

In the dark, Letty reached for his hand, and held it. 'Then maybe it's *our* fault. We shouldn't blame Ron. He's our son. We've done something wrong – somewhere.' She leaned closer.

Oliver was unrepentant, and unforgiving. 'If 'e wants ter go and live wiv his aunt – then let 'im. 'E's the one that's done wrong, Lett – not us.'

Letty turned towards him. 'Ron's our son, Olly. If he committed murder, even if it was wrong, it'd be our duty to stick by him.' Then she leaned closer, her voice almost to a whisper. 'He's your favourite, Olly – you know he is. You've always loved him, and whatever happens, you always will.

It's our duty to stick by him and we've got to make it up with him, Olly. Because if anything should ever happen to him, we'd never forgive ourselves.'

There was a moment of silence, then Oliver took her hand, and gently kissed it. Almost as he did so, the silence of the night was shattered by the triple wail of the air-raid warning sirens.

'Oh no!' Letty was out of bed in a flash.

'Not again!' He threw off the sheet and blanket, and struggled to get out of bed. 'I've only just got my bleedin' leg off!'

The sirens echoed across the streets. Lights went on behind blackout curtains everywhere and in the distance the first hum of airplanes could be heard approaching fast, closely chased by searchlight beams and the constant barrage of anti-aircraft fire. Within minutes, Roden Street was alive again with the flickering of small hand-torches, and from every house a steady stream of tired families scurried down into the protection of their garden 'dug-outs'.

' 'Itler! May yer die of constipation!' If he had heard old Miss Florrie's angry yell, the Fuehrer might well have thought twice about sending his bombers over in the middle of the night to disturb her kip yet again.

Letty and Florrie settled into the Anderson shelter for what was left of the night, Florrie snuffling unhealthily in the stifling atmosphere: not only was there a constant smell of damp, and condensation running down the aluminium walls, but also the small paraffin lamp seemed to eat up any fresh air that still remained. Letty didn't want to lie down in Eddie and Mick's empty bunk, so she took her usual place in her deck chair. Florrie was tucked up like an eskimo in her lower bunk. She had two cardigans on over her nightie, a heavy winter overcoat, a woollen scarf tied around her head, and two pairs of her late mother's old bedsocks. She looked like a refugee from the frozen wastes of Canada.

Sharing a shelter with Florrie was a nerve-racking business and every time a bomb dropped, or an ack-ack gun fired, the old girl let out a piercing yell. To make matters worse she suffered from indigestion, a problem she didn't try to hide. 'You mustn't be scared, Florrie, dear,' said Letty, reassuringly, after the umpteenth bomb screeched down from the sky, and exploded what seemed to be just a few streets away. 'You're quite safe down here.'

Florrie retorted indignantly, 'Scared? Who said I was scared? I just object ter bein' pulled outa me bleedin' bed in the middle of the night. I fought yer only got shoved down a 'ole in the ground *after* they carry yer out in yer box!'

As usual Oliver and Sam had refused to go down with them. Needless to say, Letty never stopped worrying about them, especially tonight, for the air raid was clearly a severe one. Sam popped his head through the entrance blanket just once, to tell Letty that there was a dirty big fire burning over Tottenham way. The night sky, he informed them, was absolutely jammed with searchlights, and planes – ours and theirs – darting in and out of the barrage balloons. He assured her that he and his brother were quite safe; they were having a bit of a booze-up with their mates, Eric and Bert, from across the road. 'You crafty bleeders!' snapped old Florrie, enviously. 'What about us? Yer don't fink of uvver people, do yer?'

Letty leaned her head back and closed her eyes. Her only comfort was to know that Eddie and Mick were at least safe, and being looked after.

'Oh my Gord!' Florrie suddenly sat up in her bunk. 'I knew there was somefin'. I forgot to give yer the bleedin' letter! It come wiv the post this mornin'. I took it up upstairs by mistake, wiv me new rashun book. If yer pass me me 'andbag, Mrs H, I'll give it yer. I've got an idea it's from your Mick.'

'Mick!' Letty was up in a flash. Yes! It was from Mick. She'd know that large, undisciplined scrawl anywhere. Much to Florrie's displeasure, she turned up the oil-lamp. She could almost hear Mick's voice as she read:

> Wareham rotten Hall. 16th Oct 1940
> Dear Mum and Pop,
> I'm writing to tell you that Eddie and me aren't living together any more. That old rat the colonel came in the other day and said that me and Eddie was nothing more than common London scruffs all because we used the lavatory upstairs instead of the one at the end of the garden. Anyway on Saturday morning he sent Eddie to some farm on his estate and he sent me to live with some people who work for him in a garage. It was all because I wrote a letter to you and because the old rat found it and tore it up because he wont let any of us write any letters to our mums and dads. Anyway when I shouted at him he hit me and Eddie round the face and sent us to bed. The next day I told Eddie I was going to walk home to London but he said it was too far so I changed my mind. Please Mum and Pop could you bring us home because we dont like being evakuated.

Letty came out of her state of shock for a brief moment to try and steady herself, but after taking a deep agonised breath, she continued reading.

> Anyway when we go to church on Sundays, Roger (that's the old rat's son) hits us on the back of our leg with his horse whip. Please Mum and Pop we dont care if we're killed by the bombs as long as we can be at home with you.
> From your everloving son Mick.
> P.S. Down with Hitler!
> P.P.S. God save the King!

Letty finished reading the letter, and covered her eyes with one hand. She couldn't hear the bombs dropping and ack-ack fire that was going on outside. Her mind was too busy concentrating on just one thing: how soon could she get down to Wareham Hall?

Chapter 20

Before they were evacuated, the last time Eddie and Mick had been to church was when they were baptised. Their mum had always told them how God was a good man, and that the church was His house. Eddie said that was all very well, but there were lots of churches around, so why did God need so many places to live in?

Neither boy was thinking very much about God when they joined the other evacuees and local congregation in Wareham Village Church for the Sunday morning service. There was November snow outside, and everyone was wrapped up in warm coats, scarves and hats. But even so, the church wasn't heated and when the vicar started reading out loud from the Bible his breath steamed out in short bursts. The children who were in the charge of the Meacham family sat in line in one pew on the left-hand side of the aisle. The Colonel, his wife, and son Roger, all sat in the front pew just ahead – in the same position the Meacham family had occupied for generations, much to the displeasure of some of the villagers, who had very little rapport with the present Meacham generation. Eddie and Mick sat on the end of the kids' row, which gave them a chance to catch up on all the news. Ever since the Colonel had separated them, Sundays in church had become the only time they met for he insisted that though they no longer lived at the Hall they should still assemble there on Sundays to join the other evacuees on the march to and from church. And if he'd thought separating the Hobbs boys had been a punishment, he'd have been surprised by the glowing reports each gave of their new foster parents – saints compared to him.

Once the service was over, the Meachams took their customary farewell of the vicar on the church steps outside. Their 'house guests' did likewise, making quite sure they doffed their school caps as they shook hands. Then it was time for assembly, in which the kids were formed up into a single file for the march back to Wareham Hall. The journey was to be a cold one, for few of them had topcoats, and all of them shivered in their short trousers. They were accompanied, as always, by the Colonel and his son, still wearing formal Sunday overcoats and bowler hats, and both riding their own horses which had been tethered outside the Church. The Colonel, his horse-whip at hand, led the march, like a regimental commander leading his troops to battle. Roger trotted along at the rear with Mrs Meacham, who was also riding a horse. As the bizarre procession passed them by along the country lane, the departing congregation from the church could only look on in bewilderment.

Light snowflakes were floating down from thick, dark grey clouds as the procession wound its way along the quiet country lane. On each side, leafless trees were painted white with the previous fall of snow. The church was about a mile from Wareham Hall, and it was not until they had covered about half that distance that the Colonel suddenly caught sight of an obstruction ahead. There were three figure standing in the middle of the lane, all of them holding up their hands to stop his party.

'What's going on there?' he called.

The three figures, a woman and two men, walked briskly towards the Colonel. 'Your name Meacham?' It was the woman who was yelling at him.

Eddie and Mick immediately broke ranks, and rushed forward. 'Mum! Pop! Uncle!' They leapt up into the arms of Letty, Oliver, and Sam, who hugged and kissed them.

'Get back into line, you two!' The Colonel flicked his horse-whip furiously against the side of his leg. 'At the double now!'

'Stay where you are, Eddie! You too, Mick!' Glaring fiercely, Letty grabbed both boys, and held on to them.

Looking at her, the Colonel decided it was safer to remain on the saddle. 'Madam! You are interrupting my Sunday morning church parade. Who are you?'

'Hobbs is my name! *Mrs* Hobbs to you!' Letty stood aside to let the Colonel see Oliver and Sam, who were standing right behind her. 'And this gentleman here is my husband. And this is my brother-in-law. We've all come up specially on the train from London. You've heard of London, haven't you, Colonel? That place where all the scruffs come from?'

Oliver was embarrassed, and reproached her in a low voice. 'Take it easy now, Lett!'

Riveted, the other evacuees suddenly forgot the cold and abandoned their single file to get a closer look at Eddie and Mick's mum.

Letty pushed Eddie and Mick back to Oliver, then joined the other children. 'Just look at them, the poor little mites! They're absolutely blue with the cold!' Then she swung her anger back up at the Colonel. 'So this is how you treat kids from the Blitz, is it? Just wait 'til I tell the authorities back home.'

The Colonel sat back in his saddle, '*I* am the authority in this village. And being cold never did *me* any harm at their age.'

'Is that so?' She pointed one finger menacingly up at him. 'And just *who* gave you the authority to separate my kids without informing their parents?'

Without being invited, the Colonel's son was foolish enough to join in the conversation. 'Your two children were separated, madam, because we all considered they abused the hospitality we offered them.'

Letty was in full-throttle and more than ready to take on such a remark. 'Well now, you must be the famous Roger – the old rat's son! The one who likes hitting defenceless kids with a horse-whip!'

'Stop it now, Lett!' Oliver made himself heard.

Mrs Meacham, too, could bear to hear no more. She pulled at the reins of her horse, and rode off, calling behind her, 'I'll have your children's clothes and ration books sent to the station.'

Letty shouted after her. 'Tuck your drawers in, girl! You don't wanna get them caught in your stirrup!'

Letty's jibe brought howls of laughter and cheers from all the kids, but Oliver shrank with embarrassment. He loathed seeing his own wife behaving like any mouth-an'-trousers up at Chapel Market. He had never seen her like this before, and he hoped he never would again.

'Let's move on, Father,' suggested Roger. 'We're wasting our time.'

Letty lashed out again. 'One more word from you, young man, and I'll have your bleedin' guts for garters!'

'Lett!' Oliver was now flaming angry, and grabbed hold of her arm. But she shrugged if off only just in time, for suddenly, Roger lashed his whip on to his horse's rump and tried to charge the animal straight at Letty.

'Oh no yer don't!' It was the first time, Sam had said a word. He darted forward, grabbed hold of Roger's foot, and pulled him off his horse. To loud cheers the shaken Roger was sprawled out on the ground, with Sam's clenched fist held up menacingly in front of his face. 'Try somefin' like

262

that, mate, and it'll be the last fing yer'll ever do!' Roger made no attempt to protest.

The Colonel, now red with outrage, was looking down at Letty from his saddle with real disgust and loathing. To him, she was the kind of lower-class person he most hated. What did someone like her know about courtesy, or manners, or discipline in the home? 'The trouble with you people is you have a chip on your shoulder,' he sniped. 'You always think your children are so precious.'

'Tell me, Colonel – or whatever you are' – Letty was staring him out – 'I'd like to ask you if you'd allow that son of yours to live in the same conditions as these poor little mites? We've just been to see this marvellous accommodation you've so unselfishly donated to them. It's nothing but Army barracks with a slops bucket for a lavatory at the end of the garden!'

'All children need discipline, Mrs Hobbs. No matter who they are or where they come from.'

Oliver tried to contribute his own calm protest. 'I have ter say, I do agree with the wife, sir. You 'ad no right to separate our boys. Not wivout notifyin' us first.'

'No right?' Letty glared at him in amazement. 'What this man has done is inhuman. I wouldn't treat animals the way he's treated these kids.'

There was a moment's silence as Oliver gazed at his wife tight-lipped. Then, head bowed, hands in pockets, he slowly walked away from her. Whether it was a hangover from his army days or not, he still felt it was insubordinate to speak in such a way to an officer: he just couldn't stand any more of this awful argy-bargy.

'Mrs Hobbs,' said the Colonel, turning back to Letty with surprising restraint, 'it may interest you to know that there are families like mine all over the country, who have sacrificed their own home-life to care for these evacuees.'

'Evacuees?' Letty wasn't shouting this time. 'They may be just evacuees to you, but to all of us who have to part with them they're our flesh and blood. Thank God not all people are like you and your lot. We never wanted to get rid of our kids, but we had no alternative. You think you're doing us a favour by taking them in. Well, let me ask you something. D'you really think we like the idea of our kids being looked after by complete strangers? Well we don't! We want to watch them grow up at home – where they belong. God knows how much longer this war's going on, but I tell you this much. I'd sooner my Eddie and Mick took their chances in the dug-out with us, than have to rely on the charity of the likes of you!'

As soon as Letty had finished speaking, the Colonel decided he had nothing more to say, and moved his horse on. Oliver and Sam, with Eddie and Mick, stood out of the way for him to pass, gazing at the reduced procession which followed him, with Roger bringing up the rear.

As they all moved off down the lane, Letty called to them just once more. 'Don't worry kids! You won't be at Wareham Hall much longer!'

Some of them glanced back, grateful, and one or two waved their caps in the air before disappearing out of sight.

Sam was already striding ahead with Eddie and Mick, as Letty rejoined Oliver. 'Oh Olly, I'm so happy!' She linked arms with him as they walked. 'The Hobbs family are all together again. And from now on, nobody's going to part us!'

To Letty's surprise, Oliver suddenly stopped and pulled her arm away. 'Right! Then yer're satisfied, are yer?'

'Olly, dear! What's wrong?'

His face was bursting with suppressed anger. 'Wrong? Why should there be anyfin' wrong? I mean – you've 'ad *your* say, ain't yer? Lett. If yer can't see what's wrong, then

I just don't know yer! I'm sick an' tired of playin' second fiddle to yer! Every time I open me mouff, I get squashed!'

Letty was horrified. 'Olly, how can you say such a thing! You were a wonderful support to me just now. I could never have dealt with that man without you here behind me.'

'That's it, Lett. That's just it! Me *behind* yer. Sometimes I wonder who wears the trousers in our 'ouse – you or me!'

On hearing their father's voice raised in anger, Eddie and Mick stopped walking and turned back to see what was going on, but Sam deliberately kept them on the move, pushing them gently down the lane.

Letty was close to tears. 'Olly, I don't know what you're saying. I'd never do anything to hurt you, you know that.'

'Then don't try an' make a bloody fool of me in public!' He was now shouting at her. 'I just won't 'ave it, Lett!' He strode a few paces away from her then swung round, pointing an outstretched finger at her, 'An' I won't 'ave you usin' that kind o' language d'yer 'ear? You're not a Billin'sgate fish porter, Lett – yer're me wife! If yer ever let me down in front o' people like that again, as God be me judge – I'll walk out on yer!'

He strode off towards Sam and the boys, leaving Letty numb and shocked in the middle of the lane. Oliver had never talked to her like that before. It was a few moments before she pulled herself together, and started to walk on slowly. As she went, her bewilderment gradually turned to understanding, and she felt herself cringing with guilt. Of course Olly was right, she said to herself. What sort of a person had she become? Was it really necessary to be so coarse and vulgar when trying to make a point, even if it was when trying to defend your own kids? Her ability to stand up for the kids was not why Oliver loved her. He loved her because she was a wife, a mother – and a woman. It was *his* job to do the fighting. A long time ago, when Olly'd had his leg amputated in hospital, she'd asked him to let her be his other leg, to support him. But now she felt she had abused that offer. It was one thing to support him; it was quite another thing to take over from him.

Letty found herself walking faster and faster to re-join the others. For once in her life, she had learnt a lesson about Olly that she was not likely to forget.

Jeff Brooks was a motor-cycle fanatic. It wasn't that he rode too fast, or that he took undue risks, but he did spend hours of his time off cleaning and polishing the monster he owned. His mother, Tilly, hated the thing, and was fed up with seeing it taken to bits on the pavement outside Number 22 Leslie Street every time she came home from shopping. The bike itself was a Triumph 500 and although it was quite a heavy machine, it was pretty good on petrol, which was just as well, considering it was rationed and hard to get. However, in between training as a hotel chef Jeff worked on essential war services as an electrician in a fighter aircraft factory out in Hertfordshire, so he was granted supplementary weekly ration coupons which he was only too happy to use.

It was a lovely sunny Saturday afternoon when Jeff called at 13 Roden Street. Nearly all the snow had gone, but it was very cold, and on the pavement outside the school gates a snowman built by the kids obstinately refused to melt. Letty always loved to get a visit from Jeff, even though it was usually only for a quick cup of tea and a chat. She couldn't make cakes as well as him, mind you, but he had tasted her suet pudding and thought it pretty good. Letty had known Jeff since the day he was born. He'd grown into a handsome boy, and so warm-hearted and considerate. The girls adored him, and Letty was waiting for the day he made somebody a first-class husband. However, she was not prepared for the

266

depressing news he was bringing her.

'We're moving, Aunty Lett. Dad's got a job as store fore-man out at de Havilland's, where I work. It's good money, and they provide a house – at least 'til the war's over.'

Letty's heart sank. She'd known the job was on the cards, but somehow she had tried to put it from her mind. Tilly Brooks was her dearest and most loyal friend. If ever she had a problem that she couldn't discuss with Oliver, it was always Tilly to whom she would turn. And Tilly did the same with her. Back and forward they travelled between Roden and Leslie Streets, consuming many a cup of tea in between heartfelt baring of the souls. Tilly had been a marvellous comfort to Letty after Oliver had gone for her over her outburst against Colonel Meacham. Although it had happened three weeks ago, Olly had sulked most of that time, and only spoken to Letty when it was necessary. It had been a miserable time for her, and if it hadn't been for Tilly's advice to 'talk it out wiv 'im – like 'usband and wife', things would have got worse. But she did take Tilly's advice, and when she finally got Oliver to speak to her, she'd found that he felt just as guilty about the whole episode as she did.

'I'm very pleased for you all, Jeff.' Letty didn't sound in the least convincing. 'But there's no use denying – I shall miss your mum.'

Jeff smiled reassuringly. 'She'll miss you too, Aunty Lett. We all will. But you'll have to come and visit us. There'll always be a spare room for you and Uncle Olly, and Uncle Sam can have my room.'

Sam was warming his rump by the fire in the oven stove. 'Get off! I can kip down anywhere. Put me in the barf if yer like!'

They all laughed. But Sam was clearly just as sad to see the Brooks family leave London as Letty. Bill had become a close mate, and up until a few years ago, they used to play football together in Bill's firm's team. Today Oliver was working middle turn, but Letty knew that when he got home, he'd be upset to hear the news.

'How soon will you be moving then?' asked Letty, biting her lip anxiously.

Jeff took a gulp of his tea, and wiped his lips with one finger. 'End of next week. Just between you and me, Aunty Lett, they're working on a new secret fighter plane at the factory. They're trying to get all the people they need settled in before Christmas.'

'Oh, I see.' She was horrified. So soon!

Jeff could see the look of hopelessness in Letty's eyes. He took her hand, and held it affectionately. 'I hope you won't let us down at Christmas, Aunty. We're not all that far away, you know. We expect you to come over to us, just the same as usual. I've already made the Christmas pud!'

Letty put a brave face on it. After all, there was nothing else she could do. 'Tell your mum, if she needs any help with the packing, I'll come up.'

Jeff only had just enough time to thank her when Eddie and Mick came bursting in to the room. The sight of Jeff's motor-bike parked outside had been enough to set them off. They both adored Jeff. To them he was more of a brother than Ron, mainly because he would let them tease him, and he would wrestle with them. When they visited Leslie Street, they would watch in awed fascination as he prepared all the ingredients for one of his cakes. But their greatest excitement of all was to see his bike roar to a halt at the kerbside outside their house.

'Give us a ride, Jeff! Go on!' Eddie, who had clearly recovered from his ordeal at Wareham Hall, was pestering again.

'Don't ask me,' laughed Jeff. 'Speak to your mum.'

Letty felt the same way about motor-bikes as Tilly, but the

last thing she wanted to do was be a spoilsport. 'You don't really want to take him, Jeff, do you?'

'Quarter-of-an-hour round Finsbury Park, Aunty.' Jeff was already putting on his heavy bike gloves.

'Me too!' Mick jumped up and down excitedly, but that was where Letty drew the line. Mick was still too young to ride pillion. As it was, she didn't rest until Eddie was safely home again.

The following week, in between frequent daytime air raids, Letty spent a great deal of her time travelling back and forth to Leslie Street. She and Tilly spoke very little whilst they packed suitcases, tea-chests, cardboard boxes, and carrier bags. Both knew that if they *did*, they would probably burst into tears. It came as something of an anticlimax when on the day the Brooks family moved to Hertfordshire, the Hobbs family stood outside Number 22 Leslie Street, to bid them a fond, muted farewell.

As the removal van wound its way out into the dear old Cally Road, Letty watched it go with a feeling of utter despair. She knew that for both the Hobbs and Brooks families Sunday tea-times would never be the same again.

Chapter 21

During the last three months of 1940 the Luftwaffe's aerial onslaught on London and the main provincial cities gathered momentum. Although the Battle of Britain was over by the end of October, the wanton destruction of Coventry in November shocked the nation. The ruthless attack was carried out by relays of bombers flying over the city from dusk until dawn, and the loss of life was horrific. Within a few days, however, the Royal Air Force had taken decisive reprisals against German cities, including Berlin itself, much to the jubilation of Mick, who listened regularly to every BBC news bulletin carrying reports of the raids.

To everyone's surprise, there was a Christmas lull in the nightly assaults on London. For the first time in months, people felt it was safe enough to have family parties and get-togethers without the fear that they would have to rush down into the shelter at the first sound of the air-raid siren. Even old Florrie became bold enough to go and stay with some of her relations up at Tottenham, and on Christmas and Boxing nights, the front-rooms of Roden Street and its neighbours resounded to the tinkling of old joannas, and home-made choirs belting out chorus after chorus of 'O Come all ye Faithful'. Never had the words taken on such a poignant significance.

For the Hobbs family, however, it was to be the first Christmas they had spent outside London. The journey to

Tilly and Bill's new place in Hertfordshire involved taking a train from the British Railways station at Finsbury Park. Because of the air raids, the trains weren't too frequent and usually took twice as long as they needed because they stopped at every station. Nonetheless, on Christmas Eve it was a great excitement for Eddie and Mick, as they set out with Mum, Pop, Uncle Sam, and 'little Gran', as the boys called Letty's mother. Gazing enraptured from the train window, the two youngest Hobbs saw all sorts of wonderful places and things they'd only heard about before, including 'Ally Pally', with its huge glass roof, glistening in the icy sunlight.

Letty thoroughly enjoyed the journey, too, catching up on knitting a blanket out of another of Olly's old socks. From time to time she casually looked up to peer out at the hundreds of little houses and back gardens spread out along the side of the track, a happy reminder of their days in Citizen Road. It all looked like a beautiful Christmas card, she thought, with everything barely visible after the recent heavy falls of snow.

An hour after they'd left Finsbury Park, their train finally puffed its way into Hatfield Station, where Jeff Brooks was waiting to meet them. It was a half-hour walk through the snow from the station, for there were only two buses a day. Nobody grumbled, except Gran, and Oliver took the whole thing in his stride as usual, marching off yards ahead of everybody, with Jeff shouting directions from behind.

Tilly and Bill's new home at Number 16 Green Lanes was a semi-detached little house in a long, straight lane, bordered on one side by the endless terrace of little houses, and on the other side, by a vast stretch of open wheatfields. Inside, all the rooms were small, though cosy. But what the house lacked in space, Tilly and Bill certainly made up for in warmth and friendliness. It all looked so welcoming and

Christmassy, for Pauline and Rita had spent all week pasting together paper-chains, and Bill had been down to the woods at the end of the road to dig up a pine tree, which somehow had been fitted into the small front-parlour. By the time the Hobbs descended upon them in the afternoon, the kettle was boiling, tea brewed, and the table in the tiny back-parlour positively bulging with all sorts of Christmas goodies – lettuce and tomato salad, spam and fish-paste sandwiches and, of course, a selection of Jeff's cakes. It was hard to believe there was a war on!

It was a miracle that the two families managed to cram themselves into that tiny house. But everyone mucked in, and nobody cared very much where they slept. Everyone that is, except Gran. She was given Jeff's small room, just in case she decided to throw a scene, and wanted to be on her own. Even then she grumbled how lumpy the bed was. Letty and Oliver had Pauline and Rita's room, leaving Sam, Jeff, Eddie, and Mick to sleep on the floor in the front-parlour. Pauline and Rita didn't mind sleeping in the back-parlour, relishing all the excitement of having their favourite company for Christmas and of sleeping in a strange room.

Christmas morning saw all the men going off for their traditional pre-dinner booze-up at the local pub. Bill had already found his favourite, The Fiddle, but it was a good mile's walk from Green Lanes. As always Tilly and Letty stayed at home, to deal with a rather tough old chicken that was determined to take as long as it could to cook. It also gave the two women a chance to catch up on all the local gossip, and have a couple of black-market gin and tonics as they did so.

Christmas evening was party-time, as was Boxing Day. It was standing-room only in the tiny front-parlour, and once again Tilly was put on 'old joanna' duty and in between a great deal of brown ale for the men, gin and tonics for the women, and Tizer for the kids, Green Lanes was treated to a rousing chorus of 'Good King Wenceslas'.

At the end, amidst cheers and applause from everyone, Letty had to raise her voice to be heard. 'Well done, everyone! That was really lovely!' She fanned herself in the stifling room and, seeing her, Jeff opened the door to let some air in.

But his father immediately lit up another fag. 'If we took this lot out on the streets, I bet we'd make a packet,' he joked. 'What say you, Oll, mate?'

Oliver was already half-cut, and very red-faced. 'Done! As long as I'm Treasurer!'

Tilly roared with laughter. She'd also had a few. 'Olly Hobbs! Yer bleedin' old Scrooge!'

Letty was sharing the piano chair with Tilly. 'Oh, Till,' she said, putting her arm around her mate's shoulder. 'Won't it be lovely when this war's over. No more bombs, sleep safe in our beds at night.'

'It won't last much longer,' said Sam, who was going round giving brown ale re-fills. 'Yer mark my words. It'll be all over in forty-one.'

'Ow d'yer make that out then, Sam?' asked Bill.

'Well, just look at it. 'Itler's gettin' desp'rate, in't 'e? That's why 'e's bin tryin' ter bomb the daylights out of us. But we're closin' in on 'im, in't we? Yer've only gotta see what our troops are doin' to 'im in Norf Africa. We've already marched inter Libya.'

'I don't like it.'

Everyone turned to look at Gran, who had already consumed an acceptable amount of gin and tonic. 'What was that, Mother?' asked Letty.

'I said I don't like it.' She was slurring her words badly. 'We haven't had a single air raid since before Christmas. I tell you, Hitler's up to something – just you wait and see.'

Bill rubbed his chin thoughtfully. 'I agree wiv Mrs Edginton; Jerry's not done yet. Not by a long chalk.'

Tilly joined in with the brief moment of anxiety. 'If they keep on droppin' their bleedin' bombs, there'll be nuffin' left of poor ole' London Town.'

Letty knew exactly what Tilly meant. Only a few days before Christmas, she had gone up to Mitford Road to find out if Millie, the girl she used to work with at Stagnells was safe. Letty had heard that the road had been badly damaged by a land mine which the Germans had dropped by parachute. When she'd got there, she'd not been prepared for what she saw. Mitford Road had been part of a modest, working-class district, consisting of a long terrace of tall, narrow houses on either side. But all Letty had seen was sky – a long gap of open, blue sky, which was where the houses should have been. Apart from a few obstinate walls that refused to give in, both sides of the road were flat, the buildings completely obliterated by the intense explosion that had overwhelmed them. Letty had stared in wonder at the scene before her. Hordes of people were scrambling over the wreckage of their homes, tearing with their bare hands at the smoking rubble, desperately trying to help the army of rescue-workers dig out their families and friends. Children who had lost their parents were crying, dogs barking, whistles blowing – everyone was shouting frantically. And everywhere, there were reminders of the time of year, the season of goodwill – remains of Christmas parcels that would never be opened, scattered all over the debris, a Christmas tree complete with tinsel poking through the rubble, and paper chains that had once adorned parlour walls providing the only flashes of bright colour amongst the relentless piles of bricks and mortar. But the most poignant sight of all was when Letty had stopped in front of what was originally a fish-and-chip shop, which had taken the full blast of the deadly bomb. On top of the collapsed shop wall, someone had propped a piece of cardboard on which was scribbled: *Business As Usual. Frying Tonight*. Letty had felt as though her heart would break.

She was suddenly shaken from her thoughts by a loud wail from Gran. 'Mother!' Letty leapt up from the piano chair, and rushed across to her. 'What is it? Are you ill?'

Gran was holding an empty glass. 'I'm getting old. I shan't be with you for much longer.' And with that, she started sniffling, weeping large alcoholic tears, her shoulders shuddering with sobs.

Crowding round her, everyone except Oliver tried to assure her that she still had many years left on earth and Bill, convinced Gran's agony was caused more by the gin than old age, quickly filled up the old girl's glass again. Putting her arm around her, Tilly told Gran that she guaranteed nobody would ever take her for being past seventy. In a flash the old girl came back at her. 'Seventy!' she snapped. 'Who said I'd reached seventy?' This rejoinder brought the house down, and Tilly and Letty thankfully took the opportunity to go off and make the bubble-and-squeak.

Tilly's kitchenette was a tiny area, partitioned off from the back-parlour, so most of the preparation for meals had to be done on the parlour-table. Bubble-and-squeak was a favourite of both families, and more vegetables had been cooked than needed at the two-o'clock dinner, so that they could all be mashed together for the evening 'squeak'. Tilly took care of the potatoes, leaving Letty to deal with the brussels sprouts, carrots, and greens. A lump of lard was quickly heated in the frying pan, and within a few minutes, Number 16 was filled with an enticing aroma. Whilst all this was going on, Letty sliced some cold left-over chicken and Tilly cut some bread, buttered it, and opened a tin of spam. In between sips of gin and tonic, they got going with the job of putting the world to rights.

Letty was deliriously happy to be with her old mate again. In fact there was only one thing that prevented this from being a really perfect Christmas for her. 'I was hoping Ron might've got some leave,' she said, wistfully to Tilly. 'I know he'd have had a lovely time with us all.'

Tilly snorted indignantly. She had no time for the way Ron had treated Letty and Oliver. 'I dunno why yer bovver about 'im, Lett. 'E ain't even written to yer. It makes me bleedin' blood boil, when I fink 'ow Olly used ter idolise that boy.'

'He still does, Till. And whatever happens, he always will.' Letty knew only too well how much Oliver missed Ron. He was, after all, their eldest boy, and no matter how much he'd hurt them, they could never *really* stop loving him. From the next room, Letty could hear Oliver singing out loud to himself one of his favourite songs, 'Red Sails in the Sunset'. It was a good, strong voice, and even more confident after a couple of pints of brown. But what she really heard was what Olly was feeling inside: the anxiety, and fears for Ron's safety ever since the boy had left home. If only they could have had a letter, just to tell them that he was in no danger. But they knew nothing other than what Vi had told Letty that afternoon in the Holloway Road.

The small varnished clock on the mantelpiece over the grate struck once for half-past eight, and Tilly pulled up a chair to sit with Letty for a moment at the table. 'At least someone's enjoyin' themself,' she said, taking a swig from what was left of her glass of gin. ''E sings a bleedin' good song, y'know – old Olly.'

Letty chuckled. 'Yes. I knew once they got Mother tipsy she'd play the piano for him.'

Tilly hesitated for a moment. She was aimlessly following

the floral pattern on the tablecloth with her finger. 'Shall I tell yer somefin' I've never told yer before, Lett. When I first met your Oll, I never fought you two coulda made a go of it.'

Letty looked up with a start. Her lips were still moist from the sip of gin she had just taken. 'Whatever do you mean, Till?'

'Oh, I've got nuffin' against Oll, believe me. Salt o' the earf 'e is. But – well, you take me and ole Brooksy. We're just a coupla bleedin' ole barrer boys really. We fink alike, do alike, and breeve alike. Mind you, sometimes I could brain 'im, specially when 'e takes me for a bleedin' waitress!' She accidentally knocked over the salt-cellar and quickly picked up a pinch of the spilt salt, and threw it over her left shoulder. 'But you and Oll – chalk and bleedin' cheese, really. And yet, sometimes I look at you both, and ye're like a coupla young lovers! Every time yer sit down, ye're always 'oldin' 'ands.'

Letty laughed, and blushed slightly: even though she was no longer a young woman, she could still blush. 'Olly's a good husband to me, Till. I've no complaints.'

'None at all?'

'Oh, he has his moments, just like anyone else really. I have to admit, he is a bit moody at times. But then, so am I.'

From the frying pan a smell of burning wafted in and Tilly leapt up and rushed into the kitchenette to stir it. In those few seconds Letty thought about what Tilly had said. Yes, she and Oliver were chalk and cheese. But in a funny way that was one of the reasons why they were so fond of each other. The struggle to survive over the years had only drawn them closer and closer together.

Tilly came back from dealing with the squeak. 'Y'know, Lett, yer've never told me exactly 'ow Oll caught 'is packet in the war? In fact, I've never 'eard yer say anyfin' about 'is time in the trenches.'

277

Letty lowered her eyes, and self-consciously did up the top button of her blue cardigan. 'Olly never talks about it.'

Tilly was puzzled. 'Yer mean – *you* don't know wot 'appened?'

'Olly often talks about *this* war, Till. But he won't say anything at all about the last one. It's as though he wants to cut his mind off from it completely.'

'Well, in a way, I suppose yer can't blame 'im. 'E must've gone through 'ell, poor sod.'

'Yes.' Letty agreed. 'But I think something happened out there, Till. Something that Olly wants to keep to himself and doesn't want me to know about. I tried to ask him about it once, but he only got angry and told me he didn't want his wife and kids to know about all the blood and guts he saw in the trenches. But there's something more than that, I know there is. All I can hope is that one day he'll share it. It's no good keeping secrets that upset you.'

A short time later, everyone was tucking in to spam, cold chicken, and a well-crisped bubble and squeak, followed by re-heated slices of Jeff's Christmas pud, all washed down by a glass of brown for the men and a cup of 'Camp' coffee for the women. As soon as the meal was over, it was time for more Christmas-night frivolities with Tilly back hammering away at the piano, and everyone competing with each other for the loudest voice of all.

It was past eleven o'clock when the door bell rang. Not surprisingly nobody heard it the first time, but eventually the insistent ringing caught Jeff's ears and he sneaked out to see who it could be.

'Ron!' Letty was first to leap up from the sofa, and rush across to throw her arms around the young sailor who was standing there, wearing the uniform of an Ordinary Seaman. 'Oh God! My boy! Oh Ron!' She was hugging and kissing and holding on to him.

278

There was a split-second silence in the room, until Eddie and Mick both rushed forward, and with loud squeals of delight, leapt into his arms. For a moment, Tilly and Bill didn't know how to react, and Gran was too busy trying to focus on what all the fuss was about. Sam kept absolutely quiet, and deliberately avoided Ron's look.

It was left to Bill to break the ice. ' 'Allo, Ron,' he said briskly, shaking hands. 'Ow's the Navy then?'

'It's fine, Bill, thanks.' Ron used Eddie and Mick's excitement to cover up his nervousness.

'How long have you got, son? Where are you based? How did you know where to find us?' Letty had so many questions, she didn't know where to start.

Ron pushed his cap to the back of his head, which accentuated his high forehead even more. 'I went home first. When I found you weren't there I asked Alice and Ted next door. They told me where you'd gone. It's taken me a hell of a time to get here. I hitched a lift from Barnet.' Realising that everyone was looking at him, he suddenly felt self-conscious. 'I've only got five or six days.'

Tilly's reaction to Ron was very cool. She smiled as best she could, but shook hands rather than give him a welcoming kiss.

But Letty was brimming with pride. 'Let me look at you,' she said, standing back to admire Ron in his uniform. 'You've got much too thin. I always thought the Navy was supposed to feed their men. What d'you think, Olly? Don't you think Ron's got thinner?' There was silence in the room, and no reply from Oliver. Letty turned back to him, and asked again. 'Olly, dear?'

Without looking up at Ron, Oliver said dourly, 'I presume you'll be stayin' at yer Aunt Vi's?'

Ron looked embarrassed, 'No, Pop. If it's all the same to you and Mum, I'd like to come back home with you.'

Oliver's eyes suddenly flashed up at him. 'Ome? Which 'ome are yer talkin' about?'

Letty was horrified and there was a ripple of embarrassment around the room, as Ron turned quickly to Tilly. 'I'm sorry, Aunty Till. I shouldn't've come. Cheerio, Mum.' He turned, and rushed out.

'No, Ron!' Letty yelled after him frantically. She rushed out into the passage, just as he was about to leave. 'No, son! You can't go! I won't let you! It's Christmas. You've got a right to be here. I *want* you with us!'

'It's no good, Mum. Pop's right. I've made a lot of mistakes, and I can't expect you to put up with them. All I know is, that for the past few weeks, I've been thinking about you both an awful lot.'

Letty's eyes were filling with tears. 'For God's sake, son, we're your parents. We love you.'

'I know,' replied Ron, eyes lowered. 'But I don't deserve it.' He bent down, and kissed her gently on the cheek. 'G'bye, Mum.'

Despite Letty's pleas, Ron put on his duffel coat, picked up his kitbag and suitcase, and left the house. It was bitterly cold outside, and the snow that had fallen the day before had now turned to ice, glistening like diamonds in the moonlight. Ron's feet crunched on it as he made his way down Green Lanes, towards the main London Road which stretched alongside the front of the de Havilland Aircraft factory. The blackout curtains were up at the windows of each house he passed, but everywhere he could hear the sound of people enjoying the last half-hour of Christmas night, singing and cheering. It all made him more miserable than he'd ever felt in his life, and he did his best to shut off the sounds, and get to the main road as quickly as possible. However, by the time he got as far as the pillar box half-way down the lane, he heard someone calling to him. He turned, and saw a figure striding out at speed towards him. It was Oliver. Still in shirt and braces, and wearing no coat, he totally ignored the perils of the ice beneath his artificial leg. Ron walked back a few paces to meet him, and finally they stopped. For a moment, neither of them said anything. They just stared into each other's eyes.

As he spoke, the warm steam from Oliver's breath rushed out into the ice-cold night air, and disappeared into the moonlight. 'Yer muvver's right,' he said, gently. Even his eyes were glistening with the cold. 'Yer are gettin' *much* too 'fin.'

Ron's face crumpled. He immediately dropped his kitbag to the ground and said, his voice cracking with emotion, 'Merry Christmas, Pop!'

For a brief moment, the two of them just stood there and hugged each other. Then Ron took off his duffel coat, draped it around his father's shoulders, picked up his gear and led them both back to Number 16.

The next few days were some of the happiest Letty had ever known, for there was nothing in this world she'd wanted more than to see her family together again. Ron and his pop seemed to get on better than they had ever done before and, after a while, even Tilly forgave the boy for the way he had treated her pals. The strain still showed between Ron and his Uncle Sam however, and Ron seemed to have very little time for Eddie and Mick. Despite their obvious affection for him, he continued to treat them as though they were somehow privileged that they were not old enough to go to war: there was a resentment there that none of them understood. Nonetheless, those days for the Hobbs and the Brooks were idyllic. There were walks to the woods at the end of the lane, a Boxing-Day morning visit to a local school's football match, and long sessions at the Fiddle, where Ron never had to put his hand into his pocket once for a drink. In fact, even though he hadn't seen any active duty so far, he was treated like a hero by both the missus of the pub, and her customers. Ron's involvement with his Aunt Vi and her family was never once mentioned. As far as Letty was concerned, that was all in the past. Just now there was only one thing she was dreading – the day Ron's leave was to come to an end. Ron had said little about what he had been doing since he was called up, or where he might be sent on his return. All she knew was that he had been training to be a signaller up at the Scapa Flow Naval Depot, where the Germans had torpedoed the great British warship *The Royal Oak* during the first months of the war. It was only too obvious to Letty that sooner or later Ron would be posted to a ship on active service, where she imagined a signaller would be needed most. Not until the last day of their Christmas holiday in Green Lanes did Ron confide to his father the possibility that he might be posted to one of the Navy's biggest battle-cruisers – either the *King George V*, or the pride of the Navy itself – *HMS Hood*.

At the end of their Christmas break, all the Brooks family walked to Hatfield Station to say farewell to their friends. Much to the amusement of the male members of each family, Letty and Tilly cried themselves silly, vowing to meet again at the earliest possible opportunity. Bill Brooks kissed Gran on the cheek before helping her into the compartment, but as soon as she had sat herself down, she distastefully wiped that cheek with her handkerchief. By the time the train actually arrived, everyone was frozen stiff, and had said goodbye to each other at least half a dozen times.

Almost as soon as the train chugged out of the station Eddie fell asleep with his head resting on Pop's lap, and Mick did likewise by snuggling up to Letty. It was after nine o'clock at night, and pitch-dark outside, not even a moon.

It was dark inside, too, for no lights were allowed on trains during the hours of blackout. Gran sat by the far window, complaining about the lack of a corridor train and Ron sat next to his mother, facing his Uncle Sam in the seat opposite. They couldn't actually see each other's faces, and the only contact was the glow from the fags they were both smoking.

The old steam train chugged its way back towards London. For once it was a non-stop service, so the darkened stations en route were passed by, hardly noticed. Oliver and Eddie had fallen fast asleep in the seat by the window, opposite Gran, and all three were snoring as though in concert with the rumble of the train wheels. In fact, everyone in the compartment was asleep, except Letty. She was idly staring out at the dark countryside, occasionally looking down at Mick to cover his bare legs with her coat. Her mind was at peace. She could look out at the dark, cold void outside, and feel absolute joy at what these past few days had brought her. She savoured the presence of her family all around her, and it sent a warm glow through her blood. All she could hope and pray for now was that they would all be kept safe and sound, until the end of this horrible war.

It was as the train passed through Brookman's Park Station that Letty thought she could see something lit up in the distance. It looked as if the sky was a little brighter quite a way down the line – and she puzzled over it. It was not until she saw the words 'Wood Green' in the darkness of a passing station, that she sat bolt upright. What she had seen in the distance was now much closer. The sky beyond her side of the train was a dramatic bright red and the clouds themselves seemed as though they were on fire. In the middle of the great glow small puffs of smoke burst steadily all over the sky. Gradually, the train started to slow down, and Letty could see the tiny silhouettes of barrage balloons exploding over the City beyond. When the train brakes screeched to a halt, everyone in the compartment woke up with a start.

'Wos goin' on?' groaned Oliver wearily, pushing Eddie off his lap.

Letty was still clinging on to Mick, who was sitting up and rubbing his eyes. 'Oh God, Olly! Look at the sky over there. The whole place is on fire!'

Ron was at the window in a flash. 'There must be an air raid on. I didn't hear the siren.'

Gran woke up irritably, and straightened her hat, 'How can you hear the siren on a train?'

With the train now at a halt between stations, there was an unnatural silence. Ron had opened the window and was exchanging questions with passengers in the next compartment when from the distance came the rumble of anti-aircraft fire. Letty was starting to get nervous. 'Oh, I do hope we don't hang around here too long. I don't like being on a train in an air raid.' She looked apprehensively at Oliver for reassurance.

Sam lit up a cigarette, then offered one to Oliver, and another to Ron. 'Don't worry, Lett. It looks as though they're 'avin' a go at the City or somefin'. It's not comin' our way.'

As he spoke the silence was broken by the screech of the train's whistle, followed immediately by the shrieks of people in the carriages at the far end.

'What *is* it, Ron?' begged Letty, anxiously grabbing hold of both Eddie and Mick. 'What's happening?'

'Down!' Ron was yelling at the top of his voice. 'Everybody down on the floor! Quick . . . !'

Without exception, they threw themselves on to the floor of the compartment. As they did so, the roar of an aircraft could be heard approaching just above them and with it, the rat-a-tat of its machine-gun. Letty, had thrown herself on top of the two kids, crying out, 'Oh God! No! Please God – keep us safe!' as the sound drew closer and closer, and the ricochet from the bullets made a pinging sound on the ground alongside the train.

'Keep down everyone!' Ron was yelling his head off.

Letty's heart was beating faster and faster; she could hear the aircraft and its machine-gun disappearing into the distance. Then, just for a split second, there was silence.

'They've gone!' spluttered Eddie from beneath the protection of his mother's body.

'No!' Ron had only enough time to say the word, before there was an almighty flash and bang from the distance. The train rocked, and despite the protecting strips of paper, the windows on Letty's side of the compartment shattered, splattering glass over everyone.

For a moment or two, no one dared move. Then gradually, voices were heard on the edge of the line outside, and everyone in the Hobbs' compartment felt it was safe to get up from the floor.

Letty's heart was still pounding fast. 'Is anyone hurt?' she asked frantically. Carefully shaking off the broken glass from their backs, it was soon clear they were all quite safe. But in the corner Oliver was raging at their having been subjected to such a cowardly attack from Jerry, muttering words beneath his breath that he had never used in front of Letty and the kids before. Gran was even more furious. Apart from the indignity of being pulled down on to the floor by Sam, she had also discovered that the feather on her hat had snapped in half.

A few minutes later, the guard came along the line to find out if anyone had been injured. When he was convinced that everyone was safe, he climbed back aboard, and used a green light in his lantern to signal the driver to move on.

By the time the train pulled into Finsbury Park Station, the air raid was in full swing, and the noise from anti-aircraft fire was deafening. A quick, reckless decision was taken by Letty, Oliver, and Sam, not to look for the nearest public shelter like the other passengers, but to make a dash for home. However, as there were no buses on the road, the journey down Isledon Road had to be on foot. Mick was lucky enough to get a piggy-back ride from Uncle Sam, but Eddie had to be content with being practically pulled along the road, grumbling all the way. Ron was given the job of looking after Gran, who protested that she'd rather go back to her own home for the night. But her protests were ignored, and she was made to walk faster than she'd ever done in her entire life. Underneath his decisive exteriors, Ron himself was more nervous than all the family put together. He hadn't seen an air raid since he'd joined the Navy. 'If this is what it's like at home,' he called ruefully, pulling his cap-strap firmly beneath his chin, 'I'd feel safer on board ship!'

The Christmas 'truce' was over. This was a night no one would ever forget. The date was 29th December 1940.

Chapter 22

During the first few months of 1941, the German bombardment of Britain's towns and cities continued at a frenetic pace. In May, hundreds of bombers flew over the capital night and day in an attempt to burn the city to the ground. The Houses of Parliament, Westminster Abbey, and the British Museum were severely damaged, and there was hardly a residential area in the whole of London that escaped the brutal, indiscriminate attacks.

Holloway received its share of bomb damage. Incendiary and high explosive bombs rained down on shops and schools, cinemas and houses, and those buildings that were not directly hit had their ceilings down and windows blown out. The greatest shock, however, came with the bombing of the local police station in Hornsey Road, in which many policemen were killed or injured. The following day the devastated building and its survivors received a visit from King George and Queen Elizabeth. Letty and Oliver took Eddie and Mick to see them arrive, and the welcome the royal couple got from the crowds who gathered along the bomb-scarred Seven Sisters Road was enough to assure all that London's spirit was far from broken. As the Queen started to move quite casually amongst the crowd, offering a few words of comfort and support to the line of police survivors, Oliver quickly took off his cap, and made Eddie and Mick do likewise. Then as the Queen passed by them,

Letty curtsied and Oliver and Mick bowed. Eddie also bowed, but he got a whack from his father later for poking at his nose whilst doing so. Letty was very taken by the lovely pastel blue colour of the Queen's two-piece costume and matching hat, and, as they walked back home to Roden Street, she wondered when she'd next see Tilly to tell her about it.

So far, Roden Street had escaped the worst of the bomb damage, and had got away with little more than tiles blown off the roof, a cracked chimneypot, a few shattered windows, and some plaster down from the ceilings. However, there was a scare one windy night in March, when an incendiary bomb from a 'Molotov breadbasket' exploded on the roof of nearby Pakeman Street School. Nobody really knew where the deadly thing got its name! It appeared to be some kind of canister full of small incendiary bombs, which for some reason, obscure to the inhabitants of the street, was named after the Russian foreign minister. However, thanks to quick action by Sam and the rest of the volunteer ARP neighbours on duty in the school playground, the fire was soon put out by the determined use of a collection of hand-operated stirrup pumps.

It was at the beginning of May, however, that Roden Street suffered its most terrifying experience of the war so far. During an endless night full of the sound of droves of planes, a German bomber indiscriminately dropped what was said to be a new weapon, an aerial torpedo. It landed directly on top of a line of shops in the Seven Sisters Road, completely devastating at least ten of them, and the same number of houses backing on to them in Mayton Street. Luckily, Letty was in the Anderson shelter with Eddie, Mick and old Florrie at the time, but the force of the explosion was so close, she immediately yelled out in terrified anguish, convinced that Number 13 had been hit. Oliver and

Sam, however, were quite safe, although the explosion was so violent, the pressure from it blew them off their feet in the passage. It was the closest shave Number 13 had ever had, for Mayton Street was situated just behind the houses on the opposite side of the road.

As soon as it was daylight, Oliver left for work as usual, to open up Manor House Underground Station by five o'clock. With the help of Eddie and Mick, Letty and Sam set about clearing up the mess caused by the bomb. Florrie's language was worse than a barrow-boy's when she saw the state her rooms upstairs were in: all her ceilings were down, windows blown out, and the attic walls were completely stripped of plaster. But although most of the tiles were off the roof, the chimneypot remained stubbornly upright against the crimson ball of the rising sun. 'Sling yer bleedin' 'ook!' yelled Florrie, to an inquiring pigeon who was cooing to her down the chimney, as she gazed, appalled, at what was left of her precious bedroom. In Letty's front-parlour downstairs the furniture had been saved from damage by the shutters which were carefully closed each evening. The windows themselves were blown to pieces, and Letty's lace curtains were bulging with broken glass. Bits of the window frames were left protruding like matchsticks, and the small front garden was littered with fallen gutters, bricks, masonry and shattered glass.

Not a single house in Roden Street escaped damage and for the whole day after the bomb had fallen, every resident was out on the pavement, sweeping, shovelling, pulling down bits of broken window, carrying out buckets of fallen plaster. The air was filled with the sound of glass being swept into the kerbs, and people chattering, cursing, or putting a brave face on it, sharing jokes on how they had coped the actual moment when the bomb fell. Neighbours were not strangers to each other in Roden Street that day.

289

They were all part of the same family.

Sam was up on the roof removing broken tiles when Vi Hobbs and little Doreen arrived. Letty didn't see them approaching from around the corner of Annette Road, for she was outside Number 11 next door, helping her neighbours, Alice and Ted, who were struggling to pull out their settee which was pitted with broken glass.

'Thank goodness you're safe, Letty!' Vi hadn't changed a bit in her appearance, for, despite the rationing, she wore just as much make-up and was as flamboyantly dressed as ever. What was beginning to change, Letty noticed immediately, was the way she spoke. Since she'd been living in fashionable Grovedale Road, she had clearly decided to assume a posher voice.

Letty waited until Alice and Ted's settee was safely on the kerb outside, then got her breath back. 'What are you going here, Vi?'

Vi turned her cheek for Letty to kiss. 'Don't be silly! What do you think I'm doing here? We nearly had a fit when we heard you'd had a bomb in the very next street. Didn't we Do-Do?'

Letty flicked away a curl of hair that had fallen into her eyes. 'Oh, thank goodness it's not as bad as it could have been. I think poor old Florrie on the top floor's got the worst of it.'

After introducing Vi and Doreen to Alice and Ted, Letty took them into the house for a cup of tea. As they entered the passage, there was the sound of a piano being played in the front-room. Letty explained that it was young Mick, who'd taught himself to play on an old upright that Olly had bought in a junk yard just off the Hornsey Road. He was playing 'La Golondrina', Letty and Olly's favourite. Vi immediately mentioned the fact that Doreen was learning to play the flute, and was, of course, already brilliant at it. Mick and Eddie were then introduced to their aunt, and young cousin. Vi hadn't seen the boys since they were tiny babies, and they had never met Doreen before. As she stood there in her school hat and uniform, Eddie and Mick both had the one thought: she was stuck-up and soppy. They weren't in the least impressed to be told that she went to the famous St Joseph's Convent at Highgate. Their only education was a daily visit from one of Pakeman Street School's teachers, who gave them English and Arithmetic lessons, using the slate on the back of their upright billiard table as a blackboard, and that was quite enough for them. But Letty and Vi thought it was a good idea to leave all three of them in the front-room to get to know each other. Before long, however Eddie had sneaked off to meet up with his pal, Kenny Waller, down the road, leaving poor old Mick to hold the fort with his cousin, whilst the two women talked next door.

To her surprise, Letty found Vi much more subdued than normal, not nearly as highly-strung as she had always been in the past. Over a cup of tea they talked about all sorts of things, mainly about Vi's other brothers, who kept themselves to themselves, and never made contact. As usual, Letty reflected on the old days, and told how Vi's father, when widowed, had often visited them in Roden Street for a cup of tea, a puff of his pipe and a chin-wag. Typically, however, Letty never mentioned how, each week, for years before he died, she had secretly bought her father-in-law an ounce of baccy for his pipe. 'Yer're a good gel, Lett,' had been Ernie's customary reply. 'My Annie never fergot yer and no more won't I.' Vi carefully avoided talking about her parents: the only time she had ever really been to see them during those last years was when they were each laid out for their funerals.

From the front room came the sound of some angry piano-playing from Mick. Clearly, the presence of his cousin watching critically over his shoulder was getting him down.

'Tell me something, Letty,' asked Vi, who had slipped into one of her probing moods. 'Haven't you ever wished you could've had a daughter?'

'A daughter?' Letty leaned her head back against her easy-chair, and smiled. 'Yes. It would have been nice to have had a daughter. Not so much for now, but for later, when I'm older.' Then she added, ruefully, 'I'd have liked someone to confide in.' But, changing the mood quickly, she got up and poured them another cup of tea. And when Vi pointed out how Eddie and Mick were chalk and cheese to each other – one playing the piano, the other mad on football, Letty was quick to spring to their defence. 'Oh, they're not so different. In fact they remind me an awful lot of Olly and Sam. Absolutely devoted to each other. Something tells me it's always going to be like that.'

For her part, Vi seemed very much at peace with the world these days and Letty found her much easier to talk to. The boasting was still there, but, to Letty's surprise, Vi had clearly become a good mother to her kids, idolising the very ground they walked on. In fact, having a family had trans-formed Vi's life, for over and over again she talked about how much Frank and the two girls meant to her. 'If anyone should ever try to take them away from me,' she said, her eyes clouding over, 'I wouldn't want to go on living.' At long last, Letty thought, Vi Hobbs had grown a heart and she was a different person.

'What the bleedin' 'ell are you doin' 'ere?' Oliver, back from his early morning turn at the station, entered the room quite suddenly, his abrupt greeting making the two women jump half out of their skins.

Letty got up from her chair immediately. 'Olly, dear. Isn't it good of Vi to come and see us? She heard about the bomb in Mayton Street.'

Vi remained seated, looking nervous. 'Hallo, Oll. Thank God you're safe.'

Oliver pulled off his cap, and threw it on to the table. ''Ow many times do I 'ave ter tell yer, I won't 'ave this woman in my 'ouse!'

Letty was crushed with embarrassment. 'Oliver!'

Vi calmly put down her cup and saucer, and got up from the easy-chair. 'I think you're being very childish, Oll. I was worried about you all. That's the only reason I came.'

Oliver was having none of it. 'Yeah! I know about yer reasons, Vi. I'm used to 'em.'

'Don't, Olly – please!' Letty, distraught, was standing between them both.

Oliver turned on Letty angrily. 'You keep out of this!'

'It's all right, Letty.' Vi's hackles were rising, and she straightened her shoulders. 'I know how to take care of myself.' Then she turned to Oliver, 'Look Oll. It's about time we made up for the past. I admit I've made a lot of mistakes in my time. But I'm getting older now. We all are. I want to put things right before it's too late. So why don't you stop being so obstinate, and let's all get together again.'

'Don't you bleedin' talk ter me about bein' obstinate! Yer're a schemin' cow! Yer always 'ave been!'

Letty found herself yelling in anguish at him. 'No, Olly! Don't! It's wrong to talk like that!'

Furious with his wife, Oliver turned back to the door and opened it. 'Out of 'ere, Lett! This is between 'er an' me!'

Vi grabbed hold of Letty's arm, and gave her a reassuring look, making it clear she thought it was better she did what Oliver said. Reluctantly Letty walked towards the door and as she left the room she was crying. 'Oh God! What's the matter with everybody?' she asked as she stumbled into the hall, leaving her husband and his sister to fight things out between them.

293

Oliver closed the door behind her, then turned on Vi immediately. 'Now you listen to me! I warned yer never to come here again be'ind my back! Why don't yer get back to yer own bleedin' family, and keep away from mine? 'Aven't yer done enuff damage?'

Vi's face was flushed with anger. 'I don't know what you're talkin' about?'

'D'you deny what you said – about Lett and Sam?'

'I was only sayin' what everyone else was thinkin'!'

'You insinuated. You tried to turn my Ron against his own uncle!'

The more worked up Vi got, the more she dropped her new way of speaking. 'All I said was that it was askin' fer trouble to 'ave Sam livin' under the same roof as 'is own bruvver's wife.' Vi had come to regret that afternoon when she'd called on Oliver, and poured poison into his ear about Sam being far too fond of Letty. She'd known exactly what she was doing. But what she didn't know was that Oliver would never forget what she said. Once something was said to upset him, it was there for the rest of his life. So many times since then Vi had thought about her words, and *why* she had said them. Guilt. That was her inevitable conclusion. She was ashamed that Letty and Oliver had been the only ones who had taken Sam in and looked after him. Jealousy. Vi had deeply resented the fact that anyone could actually love her brother; until she'd had a family of her own, love had been something that had always eluded her. Worst of all, she had been false to Letty, someone she had dared to call her friend. But, by sowing ugly seeds in Oliver's mind, she had betrayed that friendship, and she was now desperate to do something about it.

'Now you listen ter me, yer mischievous bitch!' Oliver was on the attack, his eyes bright with fury. 'I know wot yer up to. Yer tryin' to say that somefin's goin' on between the two of 'em.'

'No I am not!'

'Oh yes you bleedin' are! But I tell yer this much. I'd trust Lett wiv my life. Which is more than I'd ever say for you! Yes – and I trust Sam too! Yer've tried ter make trouble for that poor sod ever since Mum died. Yet you and yer ole man never offered ter take 'im in, did yer? Oh no! An' even when we took 'im on, you went 'round tellin' everyone we only did it fer the rent money. Sam! A poor bleedin' builder's navvy, who couldn't split a penny fer two 'a'pennies!'

'I never said anyfin' of the sort!'

'Oh yes yer bleedin' did! An' a lot more besides! Yer even tried ter make out that Eddie and Mick looked more like their Uncle Sam than their own farver!'

Vi snorted indignantly, and waved a dismissive hand at him. 'You've got a dirty mind!'

'No, Vi! *Yer* the one wiv the dirty mind! You wanna go back 'ome an' and wash yer bleedin' mouff out wiv carbolic!'

Vi snatched up her handbag from the table. 'I don't 'ave to stand 'ere and listen to your nasty little accusations! You've never liked me, and you never will.' She pushed past him, and opened the door. 'I came 'ere to try and put things right. But it's no good. And d'yer know why? Because you're too bloody stubborn and set in your ways.'

Letty, who had been listening in the passage outside, came forward. 'Don't go, Vi. Why can't we all talk this over like sensible people?'

'With your husband, the past is never the past,' said Vi, whose face was now drained of all colour. 'And there's no way he's ever going to forget it.' She bent forward, and kissed Letty on the cheek. 'Don't worry, Letty. All families have their problems. I reckon we're no exception.' She turned, went to the front-room to collect Doreen, and left the house.

Letty waited a moment, then rejoined Oliver, who had moved into the scullery. He was staring out into the back garden, one hand in his pocket, the other nervously smoking a Woodbine. Letty stood beside him, and stared out of the window, too. After a moment she put her arm around his waist, and leaned her head on his shoulder. Neither of them said a word.

In the street outside, Vi and Doreen hand-in-hand, made their way past the flurry of neighbours who were still clearing up debris from the bomb damage. Neither of them looked back.

At Number 13, Mick was playing the piano again. His performance sounded much more confident now that he could be left in peace to concentrate. The sweet sound of 'La Golondrina' fluttered up poignantly, like the swallow of its title, from the front-room, to the first floor, top floor, and finally to the roof. On the tiles up there someone heard Mick's music as they watched Vi and little Doreen hobble their way through the broken glass and fallen plaster until they finally disappeared around the corner into Herslet Road at the end of the street.

After they had gone, Sam Hobbs stubbed out the dog-end of his fag, and carried on working.

Eddie and Mick hated bath night: the whole thing was such an unnecessary exercise because, they were sure, they never got *really* dirty. And in any case, it was such a rigmarole. First the water had to be heated up in the stone copper in the scullery, then the hot water had to be transferred by bucket into the aluminium bath, and finally, the curtains drawn between the scullery and the back-parlour. But worst of all – was Oliver. He always insisted on bathing the kids himself, because he knew that they would never do the job properly otherwise. The trouble was, he was so heavy-handed, always smothering them with carbolic soap, which invariably got into their ears and mouths. Furthermore, he always used the flannel to clean out their eyes and by the time he'd finished, both lads would be yelling their heads off because their skin was so sore.

Ever since the day before, when he had had his bust-up with Vi, Oliver had been in a very dour mood. He went to work, and came home again, and spoke very little to anyone, including Letty. The most disturbing thing, however, was when he suddenly wouldn't allow Sam to do anything for him that he usually couldn't cope with himself, like climbing up on a chair to reach for something on top of the dresser. Eddie and Mick's bathtime, however, had always been Oliver's territory, and no one was ever allowed to interfere.

'That old bath is much too small now to take both the kids!' Letty was calling from the passage outside, only too conscious of all the water she would have to mop up from the scullery floor. 'We ought to look round for a new one.'

'Git off!' Oliver had lathered the boys' hair with soap, and was aggressively massaging Eddie's scalp with his fingertips. 'When I was their age, my old man used ter scrub me an' my bruvvers down in some ole beer-barrel.' Both boys screamed as he filled a bucket with cold water from the tap above the old stone sink, and poured it over their heads.

Eddie coughed and shivered. 'No, Pop! It's cold!' Then he called out desperately, 'Mum!'

Mick was spluttering, half-crying. 'Pop! I've got soap in my eyes! Mum!' he yelled out, as though he was being murdered. 'Save me!'

'Shut up , will yer!' Oliver continued pouring the water. 'Yer're like a coupla pansies!'

Letty was now listening with wry amusement through the curtain across the scullery door. 'Olly, be careful with that cold water! They're not in the Army. We don't want them catching colds!'

'They're not going ter! Stop fussin', will yer?'

The kids were still shivering and squawking as Sam, with a broad grin on his face, poked his head round the scullery door from the passage. 'Blimey! Wos goin' on out 'ere? It's like Finsbury Park lake!'

'Uncle!' Both boys yelled out in unison.

Oliver ignored them, and carried on scrubbing and massaging.

'The water's cold, Uncle!' spluttered Mick.

'Pop! You're hurting me!' Eddie was reeling beneath Oliver's heavy hands. 'Let Uncle do it, Pop – *please*!'

'Uncle!' both of them yelled, time and time again.

Letty could stand it no more. She stooped down under the curtain, and entered the scullery. 'Olly! For goodness sake – why do you have to be so rough! Why don't you let Sam do it?'

'Right! That's it then!' Oliver straightened up, and threw the flannel down angrily into the bath. 'If that's the way yer wan' it, then go right ahead! We'll go on then, Sam! What're yer waitin' for?'

Sam stood at the open passage door, silent, and bewildered.

Eddie and Mick were still shouting their heads off. 'Uncle! *Please* Uncle!' Then Mick started crying.

Oliver turned on them, eyes blazing with anger. 'Shut up, will yer – both ov yer! I'll cuff the bleedin' pair of yer!'

As Oliver raised his hand up at them, they ducked. Letty was there in a flash, anxiously placing herself between him and them. 'Olly – no! What's the matter with you?'

'You listen ter me, Lett!' Oliver was pointing a menacing finger straight at her face. 'You ever ask me ter do anyfin' fer these kids agin, an' I'll – I'll . . . !' He stopped what he was going to say, pushed her out of the way, and stalked off into the back-parlour. From there he shouted back at the top of his voice, 'Sometimes I wonder who my bleedin' kids belong to – me – or my bruvver!'

The boys, still in the bath, went suddenly quiet.

Letty paused a moment whilst she listened to Oliver open and slam the door, and thump his way up the stairs to their bedroom. Then she turned in horror to look at Sam. He was ash-white.

Chapter 23

St James's Park was a favourite of all the Hobbs family. Not only did it have views of Buckingham Palace on one side, but you could see Big Ben and Westminster Abbey in the distance on the other. There were seagulls, crows, starlings and all kinds of exotic birds like cranes and pelicans, as well as a single pink flamingo on the lake. And, probably most important of all, in the middle of the water there was Duck Island. Every shape and size of duck lived there, from mallard to mandarin, to Javanese penguin and Australian musk. The air above the lake was filled with angry quacking sounds, as the residents of the island fought a constant battle against winged intruders who stopped by on their way to pastures new.

Sunday morning was always the best time for the family's visit. When Oliver was not on early or middle turn, he and Letty would get the kids up early and after a quick breakfast, they would all clamber aboard a Number 38 tram which eventually dropped them off at Westminster Bridge. Once a year they made the same pilgrimage to Whitehall for the Armistice Day service, in which Oliver lifted the boys up one by one on to his shoulder, to get a glimpse of the King laying a wreath at the Cenotaph. Then it was into the Park, and always to the bridge across the lake.

• Each one of them, including Letty, took either a piece of bread or a scrap of bacon rind. Then they all lined up along the bridge rail, looked up into the sky above the lake, and held their hands up high. Almost immediately, the squealing of seagulls was deafening as the birds swooped down from every direction. Once all the food had gone, Eddie and Mick rushed off on their own to make the acquaintance of the ducks at the lakeside.

Letty relished the chance to have a few moments alone with Oliver. They stood together at the bridge; across the lake they could see Duck Island, and behind them in the distance, Birdcage Walk, where a long time ago King Charles I had walked across the Park on his way to his execution at Whitehall. Today, however, it was a different picture. The trees were just as lovely as ever, with the spring blossoms bursting out on every branch. The grass was growing fast after one of the coldest winters for years. And grey squirrels were scampering up and down the tree trunks for the first time after their winter hibernation. But even here the signs of war could not be disguised. A brick-built emergency air-raid shelter, displaying a large 'S' outside, was hidden amongst the bushes and in the sky above the silver windbag barrage balloons floated high above the tree-tops of nearby Green Park.

Letty sighed deeply with pleasure, and linked her arm through Oliver's. 'Oh, I do love this Park. You know, Olly, it reminds me of the sea. One day, I'd like you and me to live near the coast. After the kids have got married and left home.'

Oliver didn't feel the need to answer. He and Letty just stood there, watching Eddie and Mick chasing each other back and forth along the lakeside, scattering the waterfowl. Oliver hadn't mentioned his outburst when he was bathing the kids on Friday night. But then, he was always like that. He liked to think that if he lost his temper about anything, it would just be forgotten.

'Olly,' Letty spoke, 'Do you honestly believe Eddie and Mick are not your kids?'

Oliver turned with a start to look at her.

'Tell me.'

Oliver hesitated, then answered. 'Of course I don't.'

'Then why didn't you tell me? Why didn't you talk to me? We're husband and wife, Olly. If we can't talk to each other about things that are important to our marriage, then how can we solve them?'

Oliver sighed, and took off his cap. 'I don't know, Lett. Sometimes, I just can't see straight, that's all.' Oliver turned to look at her. Her glistening blue eyes were staring straight into him.

'Olly. Your brother Sam is one of the kindest men I know. But I don't love him in the way that I love you. And I do love you, Olly. You're my husband – the father of our kids – all *three* of them. Do you believe me?'

'Fer Chrissake, Lett – of course I believe yer!' Oliver was torn apart by a deep sense of shame. He had never really known how to express himself. He had always snapped first, and thought afterwards. 'It was Vi. That bleedin' bitch of a woman! She put a filthy idea in me mind – just like she did wiv Ron – just like she does wiv everyone!'

Letty took hold of his hand. She could feel one of the veins there throbbing with tension. 'If you give someone the chance to make mischief, they'll make it. But I still don't believe Vi said what she said out of mischief. I think she was just genuinely trying to warn you – to warn us, that people were talking. Let's face it, in a sense, we're to blame. After all, not every married couple have the husband's brother come to live with them. Whether we like it or not, Olly, people *do* talk. They just do.'

Olly put his cap on again, but casually, on the back of his head. Then he took out his fags and lit one. 'If fings 'ad bin diff'rent – I mean, wiv my leg an' all that – I wouldn't've fought twice about it. But it's the kids.' He blew out a puff of smoke and turned to watch Eddie and Mick, who were now crouched at the water's edge. 'I just feel I've never really bin a farver to 'em. Not like uvver farvers.'

Letty was looking at his face from the side, and she could see a little dry blood where he had cut one of his moles whilst shaving that morning. 'You know, Olly, when you had your leg off all those years ago, I told you that if you'd let me, I'd be your other leg for you. But there wasn't any need, because *you've* been the one that's supported *me*. Me, and your kids. Don't you ever forget that.'

Oliver drew on his fag again. 'If only I'd 'ad a education, fings might've bin diff'rent. I'd a known 'ow to fink straight.'

'Education's got nothing to do with it, Olly. It's how you feel that counts.' Letty turned to look at him. 'Let's make a new pact, shall we? Let's promise that unless we've got a really good reason to do so, we'll never keep secrets from each other. How about it, Olly? Agreed?'

Oliver hesitated. But he gradually smiled. 'Agreed.' As he kissed her, a passing group of young teenage boys jeered good-naturedly at them and whistled. Letty buried her head in Oliver's shoulder. Oliver held her, but was looking forlornly out at the lake. 'The fing is though, what do we do about Sam? 'E asked me last night if we wanted 'im to get out an' find a place of 'is own.'

Letty looked up with an anguished start. 'Oh, Olly. He didn't, did he?'

Oliver took a deep puff of his fag, and blew smoke out of his mouth, aggressively. 'If I 'ad two good legs, I'd kick meself! 'Ow could I treat Sam like that?' 'Im of all people!'

Letty hesitated. 'Do you want him to go Olly? Because if you do, I'll understand.'

Oliver turned to look at her. His expression was firm and

303

confident. 'No, Lett. I don't want him to go.'

Letty smiled, and kissed him. Then she noticed something up in the sky. It was a small patch of blue, just peeping through a gathering of snow-white clouds. ' "Just enough to make a pair of sailor's trousers", my old grandmother used to say.'

Oliver dropped his fag-end to the ground, stubbed it out with his artificial leg, and looked at her. 'You know somefin'? Yer've got blue eyes. Bright blue. Just like yer gran'muvver's patch up there.'

Letty smiled. There was so much love in her eyes, they almost melted Oliver. 'You told me that once before. A long time ago. Before we were married.'

He cupped her face in both his hands, and kissed her gently on the lips. 'Fank Christ I got somefin' right.'

The Saturday morning queue outside Lipton's General Food Shop in the Seven Sisters Road stretched almost to the pub on the corner of Herslet Road. Forty yards was a long queue, even for wartime, but the rush had been caused by rumours that the shop had acquired a consignment of currants and sultanas. Letty had got up bright and early to claim her place near the front. Oliver adored fruit-cake, and Letty was determined to bake him one for his birthday on 29th May. Most of Letty's neighbours were also in the queue. There was old Polly Myers and Mrs Downs from across the road in Roden Street, the school caretaker's wife, Mrs Mitchinson, and even a few men with shopping bags.

Most of the gossip, as usual, was about who had 'got it' the night before. Somebody talked about a land mine which came down by parachute and got caught up, without exploding, on the spire of a church in Camden Road. Then someone else said they'd heard rumours that poor old Collins Music Hall had been badly blasted by a bomb on

Essex Road up at Islington Green. There was also a lot of speculation about the big news story of the past week or so – the landing in Scotland of Hitler's deputy and so-called dearest friend, Rudolf Hess. Most people in the queue thought he had come to negotiate a secret armistice between Hitler and Churchill. One man, however, suggested that Hess had been forced to get out of Germany because he'd fallen foul of his friend Adolf, and had to save his own life. What to do with Hess was the real dilemma. Old Florrie, at the back of the queue, had the answer, which had everyone in fits of laughter, although her suggestion was not very ladylike.

By the time Lipton's doors opened at eight-thirty, the queue had turned into a social occasion, with people swapping stories about various air-raid incidents. When it was Letty's turn to collect her six ounces of mixed currants and sultanas, she handed over her ration book to a rather gormless counter girl, who tore out too many coupons and had to return one of them. But Letty was delighted to get at least one of the ingredients for Oliver's birthday cake, and left the shop with a great sense of achievement.

It was only when Letty got outside the shop that she knew something was wrong. Sam Hobbs was waiting for her. 'Sam! What are you doing here? What's up?'

Sam was grim-faced. 'Lett. We've just 'eard some news. Mick 'eard it on the wireless. They broke inter the programmes.'

Letty's eyes were filled with panic. 'Oh God, Sam! What is it?'

Sam paused before telling her. He could hardly bring himself to say what he had to. 'It's the *Hood*, Lett. Those bastards 'ave gone and sunk the *Hood*.'

At Number 13, Oliver was waiting for her when she got back, and she immediately threw herself into his arms. All she could say over and over again was, 'Is it true, Olly?' Oliver assured her that there was no doubt about the report he, Sam and Mick had heard twice on the wireless already. The Admiralty had issued a statement confirming the Germans' claim that, in an engagement somewhere on the high seas between Iceland and Greenland, their 'invincible' battleship the *Bismarck*, had sunk the Royal Navy's most modern battle cruiser, *HMS Hood*. Letty was crying, but Oliver remained remarkably calm. He told her that she would have to be brave, because virtually all the 1,300 crew had gone down with the ship, and it was obvious that Ron was amongst them. But Letty refused to accept that Ron was dead, and made every excuse in the world why he shouldn't be. She was convinced that there would be at least some survivors. Ron was a tough boy, she insisted. He'd know how to take care of himself in a disaster.

'What's goin' on? What's for dinner?' Eddie came rushing in, not expecting the greeting he received. It was strange, both for him and Mick. Ron had always been a difficult brother, and shown little or no interest in either of them. But both boys felt he was their big brother nonetheless and since Ron went back to service after his leave at Christmas, Mick had written to him every single day, treating him as a hero, and always signing off with patriotic slogans like 'All of Roden Street are proud of you, Ron! Long live Great Britain! God save the King!' When he heard what had happened, Eddie had to put a comforting arm around his weeping younger brother, and gently lead him out into the garden.

'Suppose he's not on the *Hood*?' This thought suddenly occurred to Letty, and for a brief moment gave her a glimmer of hope. 'After all, when we last saw him at Christmas, he said he'd either be going on the *KG5* or the *Hood*.'

Sam wanted to be optimistic, but couldn't bring himself

to raise Letty's hopes, only to have them dashed. 'Lett. When we was in the pub at Hatfield, 'e told me 'e was more likely ter be posted to the *Hood* than the *King George V*.' Even as he spoke the words, Sam felt like biting off his own tongue.

Letty was undaunted. 'But we're not a hundred per cent sure! Ron never actually told us and we haven't heard from him since he went away again.'

Oliver shook his head sombrely. 'The reason we in't 'eard from 'im, Lett, is because 'e's been on active service.'

'I won't believe it until I know for certain. We should 'phone up the Admiralty or something.'

'They won't tell yer, Lett,' said Sam. 'Not until they notify yer officially.'

Letty's glimmer of hope was now turning to anger. 'Well *someone* must know which ship he went on. Maybe he wrote to someone.' She stopped with a start. 'Vi and Frank.'

Oliver's response was immediate and firm. 'Keep away from 'er, Lett.'

'I don't have to go the house, Olly. I could ask Frank. He's station master at Holloway Road tube.'

'You're wastin' yer time, Lett!' Oliver took her by the shoulders, and shook her. 'Yer've gotta get it inter yer 'ead! Ron's gone down wiv that ship. And there's nuffin' in God's world we can do about it!'

'We'll see about that!' Letty pulled away from him, and rushed out of the room. Within a few minutes she was half walking, half running down Annette Road, which eventually led to the main Holloway Road.

Frank O'Malley was in the mess room at his station when Letty arrived. As he hadn't seen her for some years, it was something of a surprise, to say the least, when she was shown in by a cleaner. The moment he saw her, however, he knew at once why she had come. 'No, Letty, we haven't heard from Ron since before Christmas.' Frank was looking older than his forty-six years. His hair was greying quite visibly above the ears, and he had a weary look about him. But he had not lost his gentle, Liverpool-Irish brogue. 'All I know is that he told us the same as he told you. He was hoping to get a posting either on the *King George V*, or the *Hood*.'

Letty had noticed that Frank was very ill-at-ease. The fact that he couldn't look her straight in the eyes suggested that he knew more than he was prepared to say. And, even more worrying, he talked about the boy as though he were in the past. At one time, he raised his uniform cap, said, 'God rest his soul', and crossed himself twice. But he quickly covered up his tactlessness by assuring Letty that one should never give up hope. They sat talking for a good fifteen minutes, and Letty soon realised that there was more to Frank than she had ever given him credit for. He genuinely liked her boy, and was clearly distressed by the news he himself had just heard on the wireless. However, Letty decided there was nothing more she could get out of Frank, so after bidding him a tearful farewell, she left the dark and dingy atmosphere of the small tube station, and made her way home.

Outside, she decided to take the long way back along the winding Hornsey Road. As she walked, she couldn't really take in people or places. It seemed as though *she* were drowning, for elements of her life kept flashing before her. If it were true that Ron really had gone down with his ship, it was like history repeating itself; it felt so like when Tom had been taken from her all those years ago. She remembered the last time she ever saw her brother, in Arlington Square, when their mother had ordered him out of her house. 'Whatever happens, we'll always be friends, won't we, Letty? You, me – and Marguerite.' So many times, Letty had heard those words ringing in her ears. And Marguerite. The French girl Tom had loved. What of her? Did they ever meet again? A horn suddenly echoed out aggressively as a car passed by, missing her by inches. Letty's mind suddenly came into focus. She found herself standing in the middle of the road, which she had crossed without looking. As she continued on her way, it was difficult for her to understand why she was thinking of her brother, when it was her own son that was now being taken from her. Soon, she was overwhelmed by guilt. All the things she had wanted to say to Ron, but had never had the chance to do so. Yes, of course he had been a difficult boy. But then, she and Oliver should have made more effort to understand him. Then a heart-piercing thought suddenly struck her. She would never see Ron married. She would never be a grandmother to his children. She stopped walking, stood where she was in the middle of the pavement, and covered her face with her hands. There was no one around, so she could sob to herself quite freely. As she wept, she felt something brush against her leg. She took her hands away from her eyes, and saw a black cat gently twirling his tail around her leg. Letty took out her handkerchief from her dress pocket. 'What do you want?' she asked, and crouched down; in a flash, the cat leapt on to her lap, allowing her to stroke it. By the time she left it to go home, she was convinced that Ron had not gone to the bottom of the ocean in *HMS Hood*. After all weren't black cats lucky?

For the next few weeks, life seemed to have no meaning for Letty. Each night she continued to go down into the Anderson shelter with Eddie and Mick, but old Florrie's snores did not give her much chance to get a decent night's sleep. Not that she felt like sleep anyway. Sometimes, she would get up from her deck chair, and sneak through the house into the street outside. There, she would sit on the coping-stone, and just gaze down Roden Street, as though expecting that any minute Ron would appear round the corner and rush straight into her arms. But all she ever saw was the nightly gathering of the neighbourhood felines. If the air-raid siren had sounded, she would watch the criss-cross of searchlights frantically strobing the dark night sky, and once the sound of ack-ack fire drew closer, she would return to Eddie and Mick in the shelter. Oliver didn't get much sleep these nights either. To him, the fact that there had been no official notification from the Admiralty that the boy had gone down in the *Hood* clearly confirmed in his heart of hearts what he already knew – that his son had been lost at sea. Night after night in his bedroom, he would listen to Letty creeping in and out of the house downstairs. Often as not, he wouldn't take off his artificial leg, but just stand at the window and watch her sitting on the coping-stone outside. Sleep seemed to elude Sam too. Each night as he lay in his made-up bed on the scullery floor, he tried to work out in his mind why Ron had resented him so much. Sometimes he felt that perhaps Ron was right about him. Maybe he had been an intruder into Letty and Olly's marriage. For them all the nights seemed to get longer and longer.

Thursday 29th May was Oliver's birthday, but it turned out to be much less of an event than Letty had planned. She still baked his birthday fruit-cake, but very little of it was eaten. For tea, there was a dumpling stew made with some scrag ends of beef she had managed to get under the counter from Mr Dornier, the butcher in Hornsey Road. Again, nobody ate very much of it except Eddie, who had a voracious appetite, and usually ate about three pounds of boiled potatoes to himself at every meal. Since hearing about the tragedy at sea, the past few days had brought a cloud of deep gloom over Number 13. Nobody spoke much, and when they did it was only out of necessity.

One Saturday morning, Letty went round to get some vegetables from Woods' the grocers, in the Seven Sisters Road. It was quite a hot day, and for once she didn't wear a coat or hat. On the way, various neighbours said 'Good morning, Letty' or 'Hallo Hobbsy', but others were only too aware of how she was feeling, so they merely waved from their doorways.

On her way back, Letty was carrying two heavy bags full of potatoes, spring greens, carrots, onions, turnips, and a lettuce, and by the time she had got as far as the gates of Pakeman Street School, she had to put them down on the pavement for a moment to rest. Looking ahead of her, she could see a blurred image of someone, just turning the corner of Herslet Road at the far end of Roden Street. She blinked her eyes a couple of times, to try to clear them, and what appeared gradually was a figure – the figure of a man – a young man – he was wearing a uniform. Yes! It was definitely a sailor's uniform. And he was carrying a small suitcase, with a kitbag slung across his shoulder. Letty's eyes widened. Without even thinking twice, she left her two shopping bags on the pavement and rushed along the street, shouting, 'Ron! Ron!' People pulled back their curtains to look through their windows, others who were chatting in their front doorways with their neighbours, stopped and turned. Some of them yelled out, 'Welcome home, Ron! Gord bless yer!'. Some burst into cheers and applause, others had a quiet weep.

Moments later, Letty, half crying and half laughing, was hugging Ron close to her. As she did so his cap fell off his head, and one of the neighbours sent her little girl across to pick it up for him. 'Oh Ron!' Letty was almost choking with tears and excitement. 'Thank you God! Thank you, thank you!'

'I wasn't on the *Hood*, Mum,' explained Ron, the moment his mother was calm enough to listen to him. 'It was a toss up between me and a mate of mine. I got the *King George V*.' He thanked the little girl for picking up his hat, which he put on the back of his head. Then he collected his kitbag, and walked with Letty back to the house. As they went, all the neighbours were hanging out of their windows, and everywhere, people were standing at their front doors to watch and cheer.

Roden Street felt as though it had been given a new lease of life, and later, when Oliver heard his son's story of how he'd been saved by the toss of a coin, he felt for a moment as if he were reliving part of his past. A past he intended to carry to his grave.

Chapter 24

After over five years of a gruelling, bitter war, the British people were at last believing that the end of it all was in sight. In December 1941, the United States had entered the war against Japan, Germany, and Italy, which escalated the whole conflict into a global one. For the past three years, both the RAF and the US Air Force had been making daily bombing raids on Germany and her occupied territories, and in June 1944 the Allies invaded France. By November, American troops had landed in the Philippines. In Europe, Allied forces were battling their way towards the River Rhine. And in London, street lighting was gradually returning again, for the first time since the early months of the war.

However, ever since that historic broadcast by the King way back in September 1939, everything had been thrown at London and the rest of Britain – high explosive bombs, parachute land mines, aerial torpedoes, Butterfly bombs, 'Molotov breadbaskets', and during the summer of 1944, the pilotless V-1 flying-bomb.

The Hobbs' first experience of the V-1 came one evening in June '44, when Oliver and Sam were playing darts in the back yard with Eddie and Mick. Letty was only half watching them whilst knitting one of her blankets and sitting on the back wall gossiping to her neighbour and friend, Alice Cole. As usual, there was a lot of frustrated shouting from the kids, who constantly accused Pop of cheating, which he invariably did, by pretending that he'd scored a treble when he pulled out the dart. The sound that caused them all to look up at the sky was at first distant. But it was unlike anything they had heard before, like an aeroplane throbbing with engine trouble. When they eventually saw the sinister black machine approaching high above the houses at the end of the yard, Oliver immediately christened it a 'plane wiv its arse on fire'. And as the Germans' new pilotless flying-bomb roared overhead, with a red glow from its rear propulsion unit, the noise became quite deafening. But suddenly, the piercing sound of its engines cut out, and there followed a terrifying few moments of silence, then an almighty explosion from just a few streets away. Everyone in the back garden of Number 13 threw themselves to the ground as the familiar sound of windows being blown to pieces filled the air.

This was but the start of the V-1 bombardment of London. There were many more to follow. Mick's new school at Highbury Grove was an early casualty. Many of the pupils and several of the teachers were seriously injured when one of the deadly machines plummeted on to a block of flats on the opposite side of the road. Luckily for Mick, the explosion occurred during the lunch-hour, when he was several minutes' walk away from the school.

When the vicious campaign of V-1 attacks came to an end by September '44, the people of London breathed a sigh of relief that they could once again walk the streets in peace and safety, but it was only a matter of time before they were to experience the horror of the Germans' newest and most devastating weapon.

Gran Edginton hated Guy Fawkes' Night. She could never understand why people wanted their children to let off fireworks that scared other people, especially during wartime when there was too much of the real thing about anyway. But the war had brought one good thing: there were no bangers around, which was just as well, for this year Guy Fawkes' was a Sunday, a day of rest. Rest! Some hopes of that with all that racket coming from downstairs, thought Gran, as she scanned the pages of the *Greyhound Express* at Number 17 Bedford Terrace. 'Old Mother Wolf' had got her grandchildren in for the day, so there was not much chance of any peace for anyone else. What had really irritated Gran, however, was that Eddie and Mick hadn't turned up for their usual Sunday morning visit. She knew perfectly well why. It was Letty's doing. Just because Gran gave the kids biscuits and ginger beer when they came, they were stupid enough not to eat their Sunday dinner when they got home. Who's fault was that anyway! 'Well, if they can't find the time ter come and see their poor, lonely old grandmother,' she nattered to herself, putting on her one and only decent coat and her felt hat with a huge pin through it, 'I'll go down and see them!'

Gran had developed arthritis in the heel of her right foot, and she now needed a walking stick as support. But most of the time she wielded it like a weapon, such as when she was crossing a road and a car refused to stop for her. On the way down Hornsey Road, two small kids were chilled with terror when they dared to ask her, 'A penny for the guy, lady?' Raising her walking-stick, she poked it at the bundle of old clothes that was supposed to represent Guy Fawkes, asking grumpily, 'Call that a Guy? Looks more like 'Itler!' Which was precisely what it was, only Gran had missed the point and the children didn't dare explain it to her, simply leaving her to make her bad-tempered way onward.

'Letty! Letty, are you in there?' Gran had long ago found yet another use for her stick. She pushed it through the letter box of Number 13 Roden Street when nobody answered her knocks on the front door. 'Letty!' she bent down to yell. 'I know you're in there. It's no use trying to hide from me.'

When Letty eventually opened the door, she was very cross. 'Mother, will you stop that noise! Nobody's trying to hide. Now for goodness sake, come in!'

Mick was in the front parlour conducting the London Symphony Orchestra to a gramophone record of the Tchaikovsky Piano Concerto in B Flat minor. But he called a halt in the performance when Letty told him to come and talk to his Gran. Eddie also said hallo, and then went back to reading his *Hotspur* at the table, hands over his ears, humming. A few minutes later, they both decided to go out with some mates, to let off some sparklers in the school playground.

As usual, Gran was full of complaints. First of all, why wasn't Oliver there? Was he hiding from her, too? She didn't, of course, believe Letty's excuse that he was at work. She knew very well that he was having a Sunday-afternoon snooze up in the bedroom, and in any case he wouldn't come down even if he knew she were there. Oliver always kept clear when Letty and her mother got together, for it invariably ended up in an argument. Then Gran complained that Letty had ignored her and her friend Laura when they were all in the same cinema the other day. The old lady said she distinctly saw Letty sitting just behind them. She was with Oliver, Sam, and the two kids. Furthermore, she was very surprised to see them all eating sandwiches, and drinking something from a flask. Letty had to remind her mother that 'Gone With the Wind' was a very long film, and it was necessary to have refreshment during it. Gran would have none of it.

'I am *not* avoiding you, Mother!' Letty was getting irritated, as she usually did about this time during one of Gran's visits. 'But I have a husband and family to look after. My duty is to them first.'

Gran sucked her false teeth, and snapped back. 'It's yer own fault. I always told you not to marry out of your own class!'

Letty's hackles rose immediately. 'When two people love each other, there's no such thing as class!' And with that, she swept out into the scullery to make some tea.

The rest of their conversation was virtually carried on by shouting at each other through the open scullery door, for once Gran had plonked herself down at the table, she never got up. 'I hear you've gone back to scrubbing floors at that school again. It's a very degrading thing to do for someone coming from your background.'

Letty shouted back. 'Degrading it may be. But we need that extra money, for when we go on our next holiday.'

'Holiday!' Gran swung with a start. She was outraged. 'You can afford a holiday in wartime?'

'The war's coming to an end, Mother. And when it does, the first thing me and Olly are going to do is to take all the family to Southend for a week.'

'Southend! With all that sausage-and-mash and noisy funfairs?' She snorted and grunted to herself, more out of jealousy than anything else. Then she shouted, 'Your brother Nicky always takes his wife and daughter to Worthing. He says it's very select.'

Letty took no notice of this reference to Nicky, whom she hadn't seen since he'd married nearly twenty years ago. Gran usually used her son to score points over Letty. In her eyes, *he* could do nothing wrong. In reality, he very rarely came to visit the old lady. 'I'd prefer Southend any day of the week,' called Letty, 'It's the pier I like. They're bound to open it up again sooner or later.' Southend was indeed Letty's favourite place. Working-class it might well be, but

317

to her it was a place pulsating with life. And the pier – that wonderful pier! Letty remembered how, before the war, Sam used to take the kids along it on the miniature railway train. She and Olly always walked the mile or so to the end of the pier, struggling against the wind, the sea crashing against the wooden struts beneath them. Southend! If she could, she would love Oliver and her to end their days there. It was only a dream. But then, dreams sometimes come true – if you really want them to.

Gran was at her most spikey by the time Letty brought in the tea. 'If you ask me, you've changed,' she nattered, whilst noisily sipping the tea which was still too hot to drink.

'Well, come to that, Mother – so have you.' Letty was sitting upright in her chair at the table, opposite Gran. It was a clear sign that she was not going to take any nonsense from the old lady.

'It's my circumstances that have changed, not me! How would *you* like to live couped up in a tiny room, after you've been used to a different station in life.'

Letty came back at her without mercy. 'That's your own fault, Mother. You have nobody to blame but yourself. If only you and Father had –.' She suddenly stopped, realising that she had gone too far. 'I'm sorry, what I meant to say was –'

Gran knew exactly what Letty meant to say. The years had not been kind to Beatrice Alice Edginton. There was a time when she'd had everything she wanted – a fine house, servants, expensive clothes, a full social engagement diary – everything. The one thing she'd never had, however, was her husband's love. When William Edginton left her all those years ago, her world had disintegrated into a meaningless void. Only then did she realise that *he* was the centre of her life, *he* was the magnet which attracted so many

318

amusing and interesting friends to 97 Arlington Square. After William left, those friends, for her, no longer existed. At first, she had felt bitter and humiliated. Somehow, she couldn't accept that there are times when a man is still a child who needs attention, flattery, admiration, and above all, the feeling that he is wanted. It was twenty-five years now since Beatrice had left Arlington Square, and gone to live on her own in the squalid top-floor room at Bedford Terrace. She never gave William his divorce, and she never took a penny from him. But in all that time, she had not stopped thinking about him, and had not stopped loving him. As the years went by, she became resigned to the fact that she would probably never see her husband again. But at least she accepted that, in his later years, he was happy with someone he really did love. She had been totally unprepared for that day, just a couple of years before, when William's mistress, Amy Lyall, knocked twice on her front door and asked to speak to her. 'William was killed in a shooting accident at his shop, Mrs Edginton. He was cleaning a rifle when it happened. He hadn't realised it was loaded.' Beatrice could still hear Amy's words ringing in her ears. Amy'd had no need to come and tell Beatrice; she could have written. But there she was, standing on the doorstep, looking half her age and just as lovely as the time Beatrice first saw her in the pawn shop in Upper Street. Before she left, Amy had given Beatrice a letter from William, which he had left in his desk, to be delivered after his death: 'My dearest B, Forgive me all the hurt I have ever done you. Thank you for those early days of happiness. Thank you for our family. Truly with love. William.'

'I'm sorry, Mother.' For one brief moment, Letty thought the old lady had fallen asleep, for her eyes were closed. 'What I meant to say was, it was terribly sad that you and father had to split up.'

Gran's eyes sprang open. She was far from sleep. 'That's life,' she replied, cryptically.

'Lett!' The uneasy atmosphere was suddenly broken by the sound of Sam's voice, calling from the passage outside. 'The kids are 'avin' a go at young Malcolm!'

'Oh no! Not again!'

Letty rushed out into the street, where Eddie and Mick were amongst a crowd of kids who were laughing, jeering, and poking at Malcolm, a teenage mongol boy who lived in the next road. If his features had not been distorted, Malcolm would have been a good-looking boy. As Letty reached him, he was crouched in the middle of the road outside the school gates, shielding his face with his hands, crying, 'Go way! Go way!' But the more he yelled, the more the kids laughed and whooped with delight.

'Eddie! Mick! You boys! What the hell d'you think you're doing!' Letty's bellowing voice was enough to stop them dead in their tracks. Many a time they had seen her out in the street, hands on hips defiantly battling for Eddie and Mick if they were being put upon, and giving them a good whack behind the head if they were the ones in the wrong. Letty's genteel beginnings in life had certainly given way to the woman she was now, prepared to take on anyone who dared to lay a finger on her boys. But this time, her own were in the wrong, and she charged right into the middle of the crowd, pushing and pulling them out of the way as she went.

'Push me . . . boys push me.' Malcolm uncovered his soulful eyes, to reveal his bewildered face, staring wildly like a scared rabbit in a trap.

'Yes, I know they pushed you, Malcolm. I know.' Letty took his hand, gently helped him to his feet, and put a comforting arm around him. 'It's all right now, dear. You're quite safe.'

Eddie called from the crowd of kids, who had now formed

a silent circle around Letty and the boy. 'We were only having a bit of fun mum, that's all.'

'Fun!' Letty snapped back 'You call this *fun*!'

Mick was foolish enough to step forward, and poke a finger at Malcolm, who cowered. 'He's a soppy boy, mum. He hasn't got any brains.'

In a flash, Letty raised her hand, and slapped Mick hard across his face. Mick immediately burst into tears. 'Don't you ever say such things to me again, d'you hear?' Then she turned to all the kids, and shouted straight at them. 'All of you – d'you hear!'

Mick was now crying profusely. 'Malcolm can't talk properly. And he walks funny.'

Letty's eyes flashed with anger at him. 'You stupid child! What's so funny about not being able to walk properly? You can thank your lucky stars you've all got two good legs to walk on!'

'Pop's only got one leg,' sobbed Mick. 'But *he* can walk proper.'

'Now you listen to me – all of you!' Comforting Malcolm, she turned to the group, and shouted at them. Her voice was so loud, it brought a few people to their windows. 'Different people have different things to cope with, see? Just because someone's not the same as you, doesn't mean you can make fun of them. I'm ashamed of you all!' Then she turned directly to Eddie and Mick. 'And I'm ashamed of you two! I can't believe that two sons of mine could do such a mindless, horrible thing!' Mick broke down with loud sobbing. But Letty yelled above it. 'Now get out of my sight – the lot of you – before I really lose my temper!'

Eddie and Mick were the first to rush back to the house, and the rest of the children dispersed quickly into different directions.

'Push me. Boys push me.' Malcolm was still pleading with Letty.

'It's all right, Malcolm, dear. Nothing to worry about now.' She put her hand under his chin, and gently raised his head. 'My goodness. Just look at your dirty face.' She took out her handkerchief, wet it with her tongue, and rubbed off the dirt marks on his forehead and cheeks. 'Try and forgive them, Malcolm.' She was really thinking out loud. 'They know nothing about you, do they? You know far more than they think.' She finished wiping his face, then put her handkerchief away. 'Come on. Let's get you home to your mum.'

Letty started to take Malcolm home to his mother's, but had hardly turned to do so, when suddenly the whole street shook to the sound of an overpowering explosion. 'Oh my God!' she screamed out and immediately pulled Malcolm down to the ground.

It was almost a minute before Letty felt they were safe enough to look up. As she did so, a huge pall of thick black smoke was spiralling up into the early evening sky.

It was after seven o'clock in the evening when Letty, Oliver and Sam reached Grovedale Road, up near the Archway. At this time, it should have been pitch dark, but the whole road was a mass of white light, created by three enormous search-lights brought in by the Army to help rescuers dig out the dead and injured. Everyone was frantically tearing away at the debris that had once been people's homes, and the ARP had brought in Labrador and Alsatian dogs, to sniff out anyone who was still trapped beneath. Fires were burning everywhere, and the National Fire Service had four engines at the scene. Water was in short supply, because the under-ground mains had been fractured in the blast. No one was allowed to smoke, because of the danger of escaping gas, and everyone seemed to have a torch of some description, for the electricity supply had also been cut. It was a scene of devastation, and the beams of white light could be seen as far off as Wood Green, three or four miles away.

'O'Malley, you say?' A very harassed air-raid warden was being bombarded with questions by Letty and Oliver. 'No. I 'aven't 'eard that name mentioned I'm afraid, Mrs 'Obbs.'

Letty was distraught. It was only fifteen minutes after the explosion that she had been told where the Germans' horrific new secret weapon, the V-2 rocket, had dropped. 'But you must know what's happened to them. Violet and Frank O'Malley. They live with their family in Number 1. It's supposed to be a corner house. Whereabouts is it?'

The warden's expression became grim. 'Number 1, you say?' He turned, and nodded his head towards a pile of smouldering rubble. 'That was the corner house.'

Letty, Oliver, and Sam looked on in shock and horror. 'Oh my God!' gasped Letty, shaking with disbelief. Oliver put his arm around her to comfort her.

The warden looked distressed. 'Are these people relatives of yours?'

Oliver hardly dared to answer. 'Vi O'Malley's my sister.'

The Warden took off his steel helmet for a moment, and wiped the sweat from his forehead. 'Number 1 was a direct 'it, Mr Hobbs. It was a V-2 rocket. There was no warnin'. It just come outa the sky and . . . there was no warnin'.'

Letty covered her eyes, and tried to hold back the tears that were swelling up inside her. 'Oh no! Dear God – *no*! Not Vi, and Frank, and the kids!'

'Are you sure they weren't all in the air-raid shelter or somefin'?' pleaded Oliver, hopefully. 'Maybe they're all still trapped there?'

The warden shook his head gravely. 'Like I said, Mr 'Obbs – there was no warnin'. They wouldn't've 'ad time ter get ter the shelter.'

As the evening wore on, the traditional November fog began to drift across the powerful searchlight beams, and settle on the surface of the smouldering ruins. It was an ironic scene for Guy Fawkes night.

It was only just before midnight that Letty, Oliver, and Sam heard what had happened to the occupants of Number 1 Grovedale Road. When the rocket fell so unexpectedly, directly on to the house, the family had all been sitting down to tea together in the back-parlour. In the early hours the bodies of Frank O'Malley and his daughters Rosie and Doreen were all identified in the make-shift mortuary in the Archway Central Hall.

Miraculously, there was one survivor, who was said to be in a very critical condition. She was a woman in her mid-forties.

Chapter 25

St Joseph's Convent was an imposing building. Nestling comfortably on top of Highgate Hill, at the end of Archway Bridge, 'Holy Joe's' peered out at breathtaking views of bomb-scarred London. To the North and East were the suburbs of Edmonton, Waltham Cross, and Epping Forest and to the South and West, the majestic sight of the River Thames, curling its way past the Houses of Parliament, Big Ben, and a defiant St Paul's Cathedral. The RC Junior School was right next door to the convent and each day, from Monday to Friday, always echoed with the sound of children in the playground. Until the V-2 rocket fell in nearly Grovedale Road, Doreen had been one of those children.

Neither Letty nor Oliver had visited a convent before. To them, they'd always sounded such remote places. But it was Vi O'Malley's wish that she be taken to 'Holy Joe's' hospital, where, for the twenty-four hours since the rocket dropped on her house, she had been fighting for her life.

'Of course, when you realise the enormity of what's happened to this poor woman, it's God's miracle she's survived at all.'

Needless to say, the Mother Superior had a soft Irish brogue. In fact Letty and Oliver found it hard to hear what she was saying, as they were led along the stark, grey stone corridor towards Vi's hospital room. Letty found the atmosphere rather ghost-like, with the low voltage electric light bulbs and pale walls. And there was something about the silence, and the way the nuns in their black habits seemed to glide up and down the corridors. She also found it strange the way everyone, including herself, felt the need to speak in hushed voices, inside and outside the convent. Several times she had to tell Oliver to keep his voice down, to stop his words echoing along the corridor when he spoke. Olly was getting a little deaf in one ear, and couldn't judge how loud he was speaking, although he was loathe to admit it. Finally, they halted outside the small, oak-panelled door of Vi's room on which was hanging a crucifix, and a printed notice which read: *No Admission Unless Authorised.*

The Mother Superior asked Letty and Oliver to sit down and wait on a bench alongside the door for a moment, whilst she went in to check if Vi was well enough to see them. Letty asked her if Vi had been told about what had happened to her family. The Mother Superior, her voice almost a whisper, replied that Mrs O'Malley hadn't been told but that, in her opinion, she was quite sure she knew.

As Letty and Oliver watched her quietly disappear into Vi's room, Oliver thought it was more like a prison than a hospital. He was dying for a fag, but the moment he took one out, Letty scolded him and told him it was disrespectful in a holy place. Letty felt rigid with apprehension. A few minutes ago they had been told how serious Vi's injuries were. Apart from being unconscious for ten hours after the explosion, she had two broken legs, sustained a fractured collar-bone and one broken arm. Even if she survived all this, thought Letty, how would she ever come to terms with losing Frank and her two daughters? How could anyone live for the rest of their lives with such a giant cloud hanging over them? Letty's mind went back to the last time she had seen Vi, that fateful afternoon three years before, when she had brought little Doreen to Number 13 after the aerial torpedo came down in Seven Sisters Road. Letty could feel her heart thumping with emotion as she remembered how much Vi's family had come to mean to her. What was it she'd said? 'If anyone should try and take them away from me, I wouldn't want to go on living.' Now that *had* actually happened, how would she face up to it?

'I'm not goin' in there, Lett. I'm tellin' yer that right now.' Oliver's voice suddenly came at her, after both of them had sat for a moment or so in complete silence. 'It wouldn't be right. Not after all that's 'appened between me an' 'er.'

Letty turned to face him, careful to keep her voice down to a whisper. 'Olly, you must! Violet's your sister. She hasn't seen any of your other brothers for years. You're all she's got left now.'

'I tell you, I won't be a bloody hypocrite! I just won't!'

Letty quickly looked around, worried that someone might have overheard. 'Olly, listen to me – please!' She moved as close to him as she could. 'This is one time in our life when the family's got to stick together. D'you understand that? Because if there's one thing we should've learnt from all this, it's that everything can change so quickly. Vi idolised her family. To her, nothing else mattered. But all that's been taken away from her now. No home. No husband. And no kids.' She paused a moment, and looked up through the Gothic arched window, where the stars were just becoming visible despite the November fog. 'You know, I can still see her young Doreen, now – standing there in her school uniform and pigtails. Funny little thing she was. So proud, so confident. She was only a child, Olly. Just like our Eddie and Mick.' She sighed deeply, then looked back at him. 'I don't know how she's going to get through this, I really don't.' Then she took hold of his hands, and held them on her lap.

'D'you remember all those years ago – when you had your leg taken off? It took a lot of guts and determination for you to find the will to live. But you did it. Now we've got to help Violet to do the same.'

'That's all very well, Lett. But 'ow?'

'I don't know. Maybe she'll find her way through her religion – through God.'

Oliver pulled away from her angrily. 'God! You expect me ter believe there's a God, when He allows women an' kids ter be blown ter pieces in their own 'omes?'

Letty leaned forward, and gently drew his face back so that she could look at him. 'Everyone believes in what they want to believe, Olly. That's one right nobody can take away from us.'

Both of them turned and stood up as they hear the Mother Superior come out of Vi's room.

'How is she?' Letty asked anxiously.

'God's taking care of her, Mrs Hobbs.' The elderly nun was smiling as reassuringly as she possibly could under the circumstances. 'It's a bit difficult for her, poor child. Her eyes are bandaged. She can't see a thing.'

Oliver looked shocked. 'Y'mean, she's goin' ter be – blind?'

'No, I don't think so. She'll recover her sight eventually.' From her billowing sleeve she produced a delicate lace handkerchief, and gently wiped her nose on it. 'However – that's the least of our problems.' She put her handkerchief away, and looked at Letty's face first, then Oliver's. 'Mr and Mrs Hobbs. Yer not Catholics by any chance, are you?'

Letty looked awkward. 'No, we're not.'

The nun shrugged her shoulders. 'Ah well now, that's a pity. I think it would have helped Mrs O'Malley if you were. You see – that explosion – well, ter be perfectly honest with you – it's left the poor woman scarred for the rest of her life.'

'Oh!' Letty gasped with inward horror.

'The doctors estimate she has over a thousand tiny splinters of glass embedded in her face. It's a terrible thing for a woman like her.'

Oliver bowed his head for a moment. But Letty was still staring at the Mother Superior as though she hadn't heard right. *Vi of all people*, she could hear a voice saying inside her. Hadn't she suffered enough by losing her family? To think that a woman like Vi, who had always prided herself on her physical appearance, would be damaged like this.

'So you see, she's going to need all the love she can get. God's love, ours – and yours.' Then she quietly opened the door to Vi's room, and whispered, 'No more than a few minutes, please.'

Letty moved forward first, then stopped to turn and look back at Oliver. He paused a moment, without moving, just nervously fingering the rim of his cap. Then he looked up. Letty stretched out her hand to him, and they quietly went in together.

The room was bigger than they expected. But it was dimly lit, with only one central forty-watt bulb. The walls were painted white, and very stark. Apart from a coloured painting of Our Lady on the wall above the sink, and a cross beside it, there was very little cheer in the furnishings, which consisted of a bed, two wooden chairs, a bedside cabinet, and an old armchair which had been donated to the convent by a local Roman Catholic benefactor. There was only one window, which was very like the ones in the corridor, in the shape of a Gothic arch. Through it there was a perfect view of the Archway Bridge, or 'Suicide Jump', as it was known locally. Apparently, the room had once been a chapel of prayer, but since the start of the Blitz, it had been converted into one of three Intensive Care units, for patients of all denominations.

When Letty and Oliver entered the room, they found a young nun sitting at the side of Vi's bed. But she quickly got up from her chair, smiled sweetly at them, and left without a sound.

Vi's bed was at first difficult to see, being in deep shadow. Letty moved quietly forward a few paces. What she could see was Vi, propped up by pillows, her face, arms and one hand completely covered in bandages. She was being drip-fed from a bottle on one side and just behind her there were two cylinders of oxygen, with a mask hanging over the headrail. For a moment Letty just stood there, looking in distress at the pathetic figure. She didn't say a word, and it seemed clear that Vi was fast asleep.

'Letty? Is that you?' Vi's weary voice suddenly called, but it could only just be heard.

Letty was taken by surprise, and immediately moved to the side of the bed. 'Yes, Vi. It's me. How did you know?'

'I *knew*.' It was a simple reply, but, for Letty, piercing.

Letty moved closer, so that she could speak quietly into Vi's ear. It was only then that she could see Vi's lips were the only part of her face that were exposed. 'How are you feeling?'

'Bleedin' awful!' Vi tried to move her arm, but it was too painful. 'That bitch of a Mother Superior won't even let me have a fag.'

Letty was shocked by her lack of gratitude. But even so, it was so characteristic of the Vi she'd always known, and brought a smile to Letty's face. 'Vi! You mustn't talk like that about the nuns. They're being absolutely wonderful to you here.'

'Oh, I know all that,' Vi grunted, irritably. 'But they give me the creeps the way they sneak up on yer all the time. It's so quiet here. Like a graveyard. I bet yer the place is haunted.' Vi had always been scared of ghosts. When she and her brothers were young, Oliver and Sam had tried to scare her at night, by making ghostly sounds outside the room where she slept. 'It wouldn't be so bad if I could see somethin'.' Again, she tried to move. But, apart from the wounds all over her arms and shoulders, her back was badly cut and bruised, and she groaned in agony.

Letty felt helpless, for she knew that touching Vi would only increase her pain. But she was able to help her drink some Lucozade, although some of it did drip down on to her bandages.

'I was out in the scullery washin' lettuce when it happened. I don't remember anythin' – just this terrific flash of light, then a rumblin' sound. After that – I don't know.' She suddenly got a fit of coughing, but after a moment, she got her breath back again. 'Still – thank God Frank and the kids were in the parlour. They'd have been safe there.'

Letty turned to look back at Oliver, who was still standing on the other side of the room near the door.

'Oh Lett, my face feels so numb! You wait 'til I get these bleedin' bandages off. I'm goin' to buy meself a nice new lipstick and some face-powder. I've always tried to look nice. You know that – don't you, Letty?'

Letty bit her lip to try to contain her emotion. 'Yes, Vi,' she replied in a firm voice. 'I know that.'

There was another moment of silence, during which the bell from a nearby church tower struck eight times. As it was doing so, a shaft of weak moonlight began to filter in through the window, for outside, the fog was swirling in patches, which allowed a yellowy-coloured moon to show itself.

'Have you been to see Number 1?' asked Vi quite suddenly. 'Have you been to see our home?'

This was the moment Letty was dreading. All she could think of was the horrific sight she, Oliver and Sam had seen the evening before. 'Yes, Vi. I've seen it.'

To Letty's relief, Vi did not pursue the subject – at least, not out loud. But she was thinking about what Number 1 Grovedale Road had looked like when they first moved in. Rosie and Do-Do had their own rooms, lodgers upstairs, the front and back parlour knocked into one, and where the dresser had once been, Frank had bought a walnut cocktail cabinet. And then she thought about her pride and joy, the sewing-machine Frank had bought her on their tenth wedding anniversary. She remembered how she made all the kid's clothes on it; they'd never had to rely on ready-made clothes bought from a shop with ration coupons. Yes. That sewing-machine was worth its weight in gold. She hoped someone had managed to save it, because she'd have a lot of work to do on it when she got out of the Convent. 'Oliver? Are you there?' She took both Letty and Oliver by surprise with her sudden uncanny awareness.

'I'm 'ere, Vi.'

'It's good of you to come. I do appreciate it.' There was another moment's silence before she spoke again. 'Why don't yer come and sit on the bed. I can talk to you better then.'

Oliver was reluctant to do so but Letty gestured to him wildly with her hand, so he came across, and carefully sat down on the edge of her bed.

'That's better.' With effort, Vi slowly lifted up her right hand that was not bandaged. 'Take hold, Olly.'

Again, Oliver looked at Letty, puzzled, not knowing what to do. Letty nodded to him to do as Vi asked. So very carefully, he took Vi's hand.

'It's warmer than mine.' There were long pauses in between every sentence that Vi spoke. 'But then, you always *were* hot-blooded, weren't you?' Then, after another pause, she asked, 'Squeeze it, Oliver. Squeeze my hand.' Oliver did so, but reluctantly. 'Go on – squeeze it hard! Harder!' Vi's voice was suddenly showing signs of emotion.

Oliver squeezed her hand so hard, he felt as though all the blood would suddenly burst out of it.

'They're gone – aren't they, Olly?' Vi shivered, as though she were freezing cold. 'Frank. The girls. All gone!'

Letty couldn't bear it. She clutched her hand over her mouth, but tried very hard not to let Vi hear her cry.

Vi's voice then became more forceful, 'Tell me, Oliver! Tell me!'

Oliver hesitated, and thought carefully before answering. His reply was grim, but direct. 'Yes, Vi. They're all gone.'

There was a long pause. On the wall behind Vi's bed, a battalion of ants was busily making its way from a hole near the ceiling, to another hole in the floor. Beneath her bandages Vi wanted to cry, but the tears just wouldn't come. What a joke, she thought bitterly. You get married, have kids, and then it's all taken away from you. What kind of a world is it, where people have to suffer because others want to fight? She was suddenly consumed with hate. She resented every mother in the world who still had what she hadn't got any more – a husband and kids. Everyone would tell her to put the past behind her, and build a new life. But how *could* she build a new life, when she hadn't even completed the present one? There was only one thing in the whole wide world she had ever really wanted. She wanted her family.

Letty moved closer, and joined Oliver. Both of them were now holding Vi's hand. 'It'll be all right, Vi – you'll see.' Her voice was quivering with emotion. 'We'll take care of you. Won't we, Olly?'

Oliver was still squeezing his sister's hand. His reply to

Letty's question, however, was far less committed. 'We'll do our best for yer, Vi. Once the war's over—'

'The war? *What* war?' Vi's voice was firm. 'For me, the war's already over. It's diff'rent fer you two. You've got the future ter look forward to. You'll be able ter watch yer kids grow up, an' take their place in the world. But me? What 'ave I got? Nuthin'! Bloody nuthin'!' Finally, her voice was breaking up into sobs. 'It's over, I tell yer! This bleedin' war's over! I've got nowhere ter go any more!'

On the wall behind her, the last soldiers of the ant battalion disappeared into the hole they were making for. Their journey had at last come to an end.

An obstinate November drizzle had soaked the crowds lining the main road outside Holloway Road Tube Station. Some of them, like Mrs Phipps in the tobacconist's shop at the side of the station entrance, had taken up position early. Although the funeral procession wasn't due until eleven o'clock, Mrs Phipps wanted to be quite sure that she wasn't serving a customer at the time; she wanted to say farewell to her friend Frank O'Malley, and his two girls. Most of the staff from the station who weren't on duty were also there, and so, too, were officials from the London Passenger Transport Board. Frank had been a highly respected station master, popular with his regular passengers and the local shopkeepers along the Holloway Road.

By the time the poignant procession wound its way out of Hornsey Road, the crowd had swelled to almost two hundred. There were six Daimler hearses, for apart from the three O'Malleys, there was one for Rosie's boyfriend, Bryan, who'd been having tea with the family when the rocket fell, and also one each for the elderly couple who'd lived upstairs at Number 1 Grovedale Road. The smallest coffin of all contained, of course, little Doreen. There was only one wreath on top of it, a large cross of yellow and white chrysanthemums, and a card which read simply: 'For my Do-Do. Now and forever. Your loving Mum.' There were three hired Daimlers following on behind. Letty, Oliver and Sam were in the first one, together with a very solemn Eddie and Mick. They also shared it with Frank's sister, Eileen, who had travelled down from Manchester, and old Mr O'Malley, who wore a bowler hat and a black three-piece suit and bore a strong resemblance to his son. Some of Frank's other relations from Liverpool and Ireland were in the other cars, and they were followed in turn by a fleet containing friends and neighbours, some of whom were themselves survivors from Grovedale Road.

The procession continued at a snail's pace until it halted outside the entrance of Holloway Road Tube Station, where it paused for one minute, to allow the station staff to remove their hats and pay their respects. Mrs Phipps, who wasn't a Roman Catholic, crossed herself quite naturally as she tearfully blew a kiss at each one of the hearses.

It took an hour for the procession to reach Finchley Cemetery. The route took them along the Archway Road, and within sight of 'Holy Joe's' on top of the hill where some of the nuns were at the windows, watching the procession as it disappeared into the distance past Highgate Woods. In her room, Vi was lying wide awake, her one free hand clutching her own personal crucifix. No one had told her about the sad procession passing so close to the convent. But she knew.

At the cemetery, Frank O'Malley and his daughters were laid to rest in two graves dug out of the damp, heavy clay, side by side. Deprived of life before their time, they were in the company of so many families, from so many generations, whose parting would only be a temporary one.

The November drizzle streamed down from an unwelcoming grey sky, soaking the dozens of black umbrellas that were being held around the O'Malley graveside. And as Frank's heavy oak coffin was lowered out of sight, Letty felt she could see him as clearly as if it were only yesterday – raising his cap, crossing himself, and saying: 'God rest his soul'.

Letty hoped and prayed He would.

Chapter 26

'Today we give thanks to God for a great deliverance . . .
Germany, the enemy, who drove all Europe into war, has
been finally overcome.'

On the evening of Tuesday, 8th May 1945, Roden Street
interrupted its V-E Day celebrations just long enough to
listen to the King's momentous broadcast to the nation. His
words concluded five and a half years of war in a so much
more joyous message than when the war had started on that
gloomy September evening in 1939. It was the best party
Roden Street had ever had. Both sides of the street were
bristling with decorations, joined together by endless lines
of flags and home-made bunting, which were fixed to every
top-floor window-frame. Every so often a breeze came up,
and the bunting joined in the fun going on below, dancing
and flapping with joy.

As for Number 13, you could hardly see the place for huge
flags of the Allied nations, bunting, pictures of the King and
Queen and Winston Churchill, and Mick's cardboard signs,
proclaiming: *Good Old Churchill! Long Live Our Country!
God Save The King!* Mick always believed in subtle
patriotism. Old Florrie, however, wasn't at all pleased about
the hammer-and-sickle Russian flag that Eddie had mischievously draped from her top-floor window. Florrie
thought Hitler and his lot were bad enough, but, like the

true blue Tory she had always been, wasn't convinced that Stalin was much better.

Luckily, the weather had stayed fair all day. At one time during the morning it seemed as though the heavens were about to open their doors to release a torrent of unwelcome rain. But when Letty peered out of her bedroom window on the first floor she shook her fist up at the threatening dark clouds, warning them to 'go back where you come from – or else!' From that moment on, there was hardly a cloud in the sky. Just as well, for all the streets were thronging with people, amongst them, Tilly and Bill and all the Brooks family, who, to Letty's delight, had come up especially from Hertfordshire. No traffic could pass, and trestle-tables covered with cloths had been set up all along the middle of each street, and as soon as all the kids had finished their tea-parties, the adults were treated to an endless supply of cheese, spam, and fish-paste sandwiches, home-made cakes and beer.

As soon as it was dark, a bonfire was lit in the middle of the road on the corner, and hardly a person, no matter what age, was allowed to escape taking part in the dancing. Earlier in the day, Letty's old joanna was carried into the street by Sam and Bill, helped by Ted from next door and Eric from across the road. Piano music was provided by 'Big Bessie' the regular pianist at the pub in nearby Tollington Road and, fortified with frequent refills of Guinness, she performed with boundless energy from tea-time to the early hours. Everywhere, the elation was infectious. People from Roden Street mixed with their neighbours from Pakeman Street, Hertslet Road and Mayton Street. They sang together, laughed together, shared jokes together. For the first time in five and a half years, they felt free. Free to walk along the pavement without the constant fear of death, free to leave their lights on without drawing the curtains. But most of all, they were grateful that they had come through those endless dark days of war – and survived. Now all they wanted was for their husbands, and sons and lovers, to come home again. 'It's over!' That was the ecstatic cry over and over again, even when complete strangers passed each other carrying pint glasses of beer. 'IT'S OVER!'

That day Letty danced so many knees-ups that her legs began to feel like iron. Even Oliver joined in, when practically the entire street formed two huge circles either side of the bonfire to do the hokey-cokey. Gran Edginton looked on in disgust, until Mick and Eddie grabbed hold of her and dragged her into the hip-swinging line-up. After a few minutes, she was throwing herself into the fun as much as anyone, and everyone roared with laughter when in a reckless moment of singing and shouting, she briefly lifted up her dress to reveal her long white bloomers. Sam did a neat demonstration waltz with Tilly Brooks, whilst Pauline and Rita danced a variation on everything with each other. Eddie did the jitterbug with any young girl he could find and old Florrie and Oliver sang a duet together. 'Maybe It's Because I'm a Londoner' brought thunderous applause from the entire street. The only dance Mick really joined in was 'Knees Up Mother Brown'. He hated dancing with anyone, and scowled when Eddie tried to get him to join in. He felt awkward and too self-conscious.

During a lull, Letty and Oliver sat together on the coping-stone outside Number 13. Everyone was exhausted, and glad of the opportunity to put their feet up before launching into a final knees-up soon after midnight. After a few moments, they were joined by Ron and his new girlfriend, Janey Robinson, who lived in nearby Hertslet Road. For most of the war, Ron had been on active duty, serving as a signaller on board the *King George V*. During that time, he had been involved in some hair-raising naval battles, the most famous being the sinking of the *Bismarck*. Later, he was posted to a small corvette called the *Petunia*, and one night the family had been shocked to hear on the wireless that the ship had been sunk by an Italian submarine. But, even though Ron couldn't swim, he'd managed to survive several hours in shark-invested waters off the West African coast, clinging on to debris from his ship. Yes, Letty thanked the Lord all that would never happen again.

'Mum and Pop. You know Janey don't you?' Ron had been dancing energetically around the bonfire all evening, and sweat was pouring down his face. Recently he had put on quite a bit of weight, and his old flannel trousers were tugging at his waist.

Letty's face lit up immediately. 'Yes, of course I know Janey. Are you enjoying the party, dear?'

'Oh yes, it's smashing.' Janey was about eighteen. She was a goodlooking girl with a nice figure, even if it was practically bursting out of her dress. Letty liked Janey, but she did find her perpetual smile a little disconcerting, for she could never tell whether she was being sincere or not. 'Evenin', Mr Hobbs.'

Oliver had not bothered to look at her until she spoke. 'Wotcha!' was all he could reply.

Letty, embarrassed by Oliver's rude indifference to the girl, felt she had to make up for his manner, by trying to be especially nice herself. 'You must be pleased to have Ron home on leave again, aren't you? He's lucky to have a nice girl like you to go out with. Isn't he, Olly?'

Oliver merely grunted, took out a fag for himself, then gave one to Ron, and put the packet away again.

'Aren't you going to offer one to Janey?' Letty was glaring at Oliver.

Oliver looked up, surprised. 'Wot for? She don't smoke at 'er age.'

Janey giggled. 'Well, as a matter of fact, I do, Mr Hobbs. Not very often though.'

With Letty still glaring at him, Oliver reluctantly took out his packet of fags, and gave one to Janey. All three lit up, and Ron slipped his arm around Janey's waist. 'Special day today, eh Mum?' Ron was wiping the sweat from his forehead with the back of the hand that was holding his fag.

'Oh yes! It's hard to believe it's actually all over – at last.'

Ron turned to grin straight into Janey's face. 'I wasn't talkin' about the war. I was talkin' about me and Janey.'

Letty immediately exchanged a knowing look with Oliver. She half expected what was to come, for she and Olly had talked about it. But for the moment, she was prepared to feign innocence. 'Oh yes, dear. What's that?'

Ron felt awkward, and addressed his reply to his father more than to Letty. 'We've decided to get married.'

Letty leapt up in a flash. 'Ron!' She threw her arms around him, and turned to beam at Janey.

The girl blushed, and brushed her nose nervously with one finger. 'I know you'll probably think I'm still a bit young to be Ron's wife. But my mum and dad said they don't mind, if you don't.'

'Mind!' Letty moved from Ron to Janey, and hugged her. 'We're thrilled for you both. Absolutely thrilled. Aren't we, Olly?'

Oliver was stone-faced and before answering took a deep draw on his fag. 'Where yer gonna live then?'

Janey was going to answer him, but Ron got in quickly before her. 'As soon as we're married, we're going to move in with Janey's parents. They've got a spare room at the top of their house.'

'Oh, I see.' For a brief moment, Letty felt a little hurt. It seemed that Janey's parents knew far more about what was happening than Ron's own mother and father. 'Well, I'm sure you'll settle in nicely.'

'Of course, it'll only be temporary,' Ron added quickly. 'As soon as I'm demobbed, I'll be getting a job and finding us a place of our own.' He was suddenly aware that both his mother and father were looking at him. He found it unnerving. 'We won't be getting married for a year or so.'

Letty smiled bravely. 'Well, Pop and I think it's wonderful news. We hope you'll both be very happy.'

Ron felt only partly relieved. 'Thanks, Mum.'

'Thanks, Mrs—' Janey stopped, then smiled yet another smile. 'Thanks – Mum.' She leant forward, and kissed Letty on one cheek. 'Thanks – Pop.' She did the same to Oliver, who did not react. 'Don't you worry, I'll look after Ron. I promise you.' Still nothing. So Janey turned back to Letty. 'We'll never let you down, you'll see.'

A few minutes later, Ron and Janey disappeared into the crowd. Everyone around seemed to be stirring into life again, and getting ready for the last dance. At the refreshment table in the middle of the street, Letty and Oliver could hear Mick teasing his grandmother, singing tunelessly,

Gran's got a boyfriend,
Gran's got a boyfriend.
Barney. Barney,
Barnacle Bill the Sailor.

He squawked with laughter at her scolding. Poor Gran. The kids hadn't left her alone since they'd heard that she'd been given a drink by an old merchant navy captain in The Eaglet earlier in the evening. The old lady was half-cut and half-asleep, and she had been sobbing on and off all evening, saying that now the war was over, everyone would forget all about her.

'It's all changing, isn't' it, Olly?' said Letty, turning back to him. She slipped her arm around his waist, and leaned her head on his shoulder. Someone had stoked the bonfire with a huge piece of wood, and the flames were crackling up into the air amidst a profusion of sparks. 'Suddenly, everything's changing so fast.'

'You mean, because Ron's gonna marry that girl?'

'No, not just that. I mean – life seems to be moving on now. It has to. After all, nothing can stand still forever, can it?'

Both of them stared hypnotically into the bonfire, and the flames and sparks from it were reflected in their eyes. Across the road, Big Bessie had taken her seat at the piano again, and with a fag drooping from her mouth, and a glass of Guinness on the table beside her, she belted out the 'Last Waltz', Sam's favourite: 'Let the Rest of the World go by'. Oliver suddenly stood up, bowed to Letty, offered her his arm, and led her to the dance. No one could have believed that he didn't have two good legs like anyone else.

As they danced Letty rested her head on Oliver's shoulder. 'Olly,' she said in a loud whisper, 'Will you promise me something? Will you promise that, whatever happens, we'll never interfere with our kids' lives. Let's give them all the chances in life we never had. Let them make their own decisions, so they've got no one to blame but themselves. Promise?'

Oliver looked down at her. 'Come off it, Lett. When 'ave I ever interfered wiv' my kids' lives?'

Letty didn't bother to look up at him. With her head still on his shoulder, she just smiled.

When the waltz finally came to an end, everyone held hands and formed a pulsating crowd around the bonfire. 'Should Auld Acquaintance be Forgot'; they sang as one, with more meaning than ever before, and heard the words echo around the rooftops of Roden Street and her war-scarred neighbouring streets.

343

During the singing, Letty looked back at Number 13. She thought that it had never looked so proud as it did that night. To her, it was more than a house. It was a friend. A friend who had not only brought the Hobbs family safely through the war, but a wise friend who had also kept them all together. Letty hoped that it would always be like that.

'Mum. Is the war really over now?' Mick and Eddie were now safely tucked up in bed together. Eddie, of course, was already fast asleep, and snoring his head off. Mick was not going to be far behind him.

Letty switched off the light, and stooped down to talk to him in a low voice. 'Yes, Mick. It's *really* over. We've all got to try and forget about it. Now, go to sleep.'

He yawned, and rubbed his eyes. 'Will there be another one?'

Letty ran her fingers through his hair, to take it out of his eyes. 'I hope not, son. For all our sakes, I hope not.' She leaned over, and kissed him on the forehead. 'God bless.' Then she said and did the same to Eddie, 'God bless.'

For a moment she stood there in the dark at the side of their bed. The moon was popping in and out of passing night clouds, so every so often she was able to see them both, Mick breathing with his mouth wide open, and Eddie's gangling arms and legs tossing restlessly in and out of the bed-clothes. She smiled affectionately at them, then moved to the window.

In the back yard, Letty could still see the Anderson shelter, its curved aluminium roof covered in earth which was now hosting a mass of grass, dotted with a few late tulips and a lot of white daisies. There was no sound from Roden Street on the front side of the house, for the party had come to an end and everyone was now sleeping off one of the happiest days of their lives. The window was slightly open, so Letty sat on the edge of the boys' bed, and looked out. At the end of the garden, the blue lilac blossom was fluttering in a slight, warm breeze, and in the distance Letty could hear the barking and whining of a restless dog.

Suddenly, everything was silence. Letty sat there, looking out at the calm May night, and she sighed with relief. From now on, they could all sleep safely in their beds. Soon, she was speculating: looking back on those five and a half years that had cost so much in suffering and misery. But it wasn't only the past she was thinking of. What would the future hold for her, Olly and the family? Peace had to be won just the same as war. Nothing would come easy. Life would always be a challenge. Then she thought about Vi and how life for her, without Frank and the family, could never be the same. It seemed so tragic that shortly after recovering from her bomb injuries, Vi had completely cut off all contact with the Hobbs family. Without her own family around her, Vi was lost and restless, and it wasn't long before she'd returned to her trouble-making ways again, running down one person against another, and making mischievous remarks about Ron, Eddie, and Mick. Eventually, Oliver could take no more, and much to Letty's distress, he had ordered Vi out of the house, and hadn't seen her from that day to this. All they knew was that she had moved to East London somewhere, without giving anyone her address. After all that Vi had been through, Letty felt thoroughly miserable and ashamed that she and Oliver couldn't have been more tolerant as they tried to help her come to terms with life again. But Vi was Vi, and Olly was Olly, and no one would ever change them. Oh God, Letty thought, how *would* Vi cope with the future?

As she sat there, Letty prayed that this would be the last war she would have to go through in her lifetime. 'Please God,' she asked in silence, gazing up to the thousands of stars that were twinkling brightly in the dark night sky, 'give my kids the chance to grow up in a free world. Don't put them in uniforms, and give them guns to fire.' Then she thought of all the things she hoped the boys would get out of life. She wanted Eddie and Mick to discover things for themselves, to travel and marvel at the world about them, to do all the things that she and Olly had never had the chance to do. She wanted Ron to find happiness with Janey and have a family of his own, to give her and Olly grand-children. Most of all, she wanted them all to have love in their lives, like she and Olly had had since the first day they'd met. She wanted her family to get on together, not to quarrel, or fight, or resent each other. She wanted them to be – happy! Suddenly, a broad smile came across her face, and she found herself chuckling. She was thinking of all the silly, ordinary things she would like the family to go on doing for as long as they were together – like going to the pictures every Friday night and eating as many tubs of ice-creams as Pop could buy. And the seaside! She hoped they'd all go down to Southend together! They could take Gran, and they could all paddle in the water; Olly and Sam could look at the girls on the beach through their binoculars.

Letty was briefly distracted from her thoughts by the striking of two o'clock from the Emmanuel Church bells just around the corner in Hornsey Road. She got up and drew the curtains. The room still wasn't completely dark, for the three-quarter moon was obstinately popping in and out of the clouds. Quietly she moved to the door, and opened it. Then she stopped, to take one last look at the boys. 'It's up to you, now,' she said to them softly. 'You've got your chance. Please God you take it.'

Letty left the room, and closed the door. Tonight for once, she would sleep soundly.

Chapter 27

Letty was on her hands and knees scrubbing the scullery floor when Mick came in to see her. Oliver was in the back-parlour listening to a Beatles record on 'Family Favourites', the wireless turned up full volume. Now he was in his sixties, he was getting more hard of hearing than ever.

As he looked down on his mother there was a part of Mick that didn't really want to leave home. After all, he had all the comforts anyone could possibly want – a flat of his own on the top floor, a job in a travel agency, and three good meals a day cooked regularly for him by Letty. But he knew it was time for him to go. In a few years he would be thirty years old and if he continued to live at home with his parents he would become set in his ways, and never leave. In the last few months or so, he had come to realise that he was relying too much on his parents, but he was the last of the Hobbs boys still at home, and somehow his leaving seemed harder than that of his brothers.

'All ready to go, son?' Letty had been dreading this moment, but she was determined not to show it. That's why she'd embarked on scrubbing the floor.

Mick felt odd. He was excited to be moving into a new flat with two of his mates but he couldn't get rid of the constant sinking feeling in his stomach. 'Eddie's just packing the last bits into the van. We shouldn't be long now.'

'That's good.' Letty didn't look up at him; if she did, she

knew she would make a fool of herself. But as she scrubbed aimlessly over the same piece of lino all she could see was that little baby with the chubby face, whom Oliver had threatened to throw out of the window because he cried so much. Now Mick was a young man with a mind of his own. He had grown up very different from his two brothers. Apart from anything else, he was shorter, and, unlike either Eddie or Ron, he was the only son who had not married. But although Ron had remained as uninterested in Mick as ever, Letty knew that her two youngest sons would always be close.

Mick stood above her awkwardly. 'Mum, I wish you wouldn't keep scrubbing floors. It's so bad for your knees, especially with your arthritis.'

Letty straightened up. 'Hard work never did anyone any harm.' She took hold of Mick's hand, and, with obvious pain in her kneecaps, pulled herself up. She didn't look her sixty-four years. These days she had become a little plump, and had a few grey hairs. But to Mick she looked exactly the same as ever, with her curly permed hair, and loving blue eyes.

But since the end of the war, a lot of changes had taken place at Number 13 – and in the world outside, Ron had married Janey, and they lived in two rooms at the top of her parents' house in nearby Hertslet Road. After a year or so, they'd had their first child, a daughter, although it had been some time before Letty and Oliver were invited to see her. In 1951, Eddie had married his girlfriend, Mary Willis – who since the moment they'd met her had been a favourite of the Hobbs family. It had been a lovely wedding and Letty and her old pal, Tilly Brooks, cried themselves silly in the church. Mick was best man, more nervous than the bridegroom himself. The following year had seen the death of poor old King George VI, and nobody amongst his subjects was more upset than the members of the Hobbs household.

Letty had remembered with affection and pride the time during the war when the King and Queen had visited the bombed remains of Hornsey Road police station, and how she, Oliver and the kids had bowed and curtsied as the royal couple passed by. Then Coronation Day in 1953, Letty, Oliver and Sam had stayed at home and watched the celebrations on their new television set, with Mary. Mick and Eddie, however, had camped out in the Mall with Pauline and Rita Brooks and, even though it poured with rain all through the night, when Princess Elizabeth passed by in her great ceremonial procession they all agreed it had been well worth the wait. Mick remembered his mother's face as they'd told her about it when they'd got back home that evening.

'Are you sure you've got enough food in for your dinner tonight?' Letty was being her practical self again.

'Food!' Mick seized on the chance to lighten the atmosphere. 'You've packed enough to keep me going for a year!' Letty had decided that if Mick had to leave home she was going to make sure he didn't starve. For weeks she had saved enough money to stock him up with tins of ham, salmon, baked beans, peas, fruit salad, packets of tea, jars of coffee, and about twenty Mars bars, his favourite. The hall passage was piled up with cardboard boxes, filled with provisions. Mick leaned over and kissed her gently on the forehead. 'Why d'you have to go and spend your hard-earned money like that?'

Letty wiped her wet hands on her apron, 'Don't be silly! What sort of parents would we be if we let you go off empty-handed? It was Pop's idea just as much as mine. You may be leaving home, but you're still our son.'

'Oh Mum!' Mick pulled her to him, and hugged her. 'I hate doing this to you. I hate leaving you on your own.'

'On my own! Whatever are you talking about?' Letty

pulled away from him, picked up her bucket, turned on the tap, and emptied the dirty water down the sink. 'I've still got your dad – thank God!'

His mother didn't fool Mick for a moment. As he watched her busying herself at the sink, he knew how difficult these coming months were going to be for her. Number 13 Roden Street had always echoed to the laughter of the Hobbs kids. First it was Ron and his mates, then Eddie and Mick, and their schoolpals. They'd played darts in the back yard, billiards in the small front-parlour, they'd brought their girlfriends in to tea and listened to loud gramophone records of Bing Crosby and the Andrews sisters. Oliver had always pretended that he objected to his lack of privacy, but he'd loved joining the kids' games, infuriating them by cheating when he could. For Letty, it had meant slaving away cooking cakes and buns, treacle toffee and coconut ice, and chips cooked in thick lard. And she'd loved it, every single minute of it. But now it was over. And Mick knew only too well how his mother would miss it all – he was all that was left of those happy days and, now he was going, she would have to adjust to a very different life. And Mick also knew that his parents hadn't got over another loss, the sudden passing of Uncle Sam. And neither had he.

Sam had died of heart trouble during the early hours of Friday, 12th December 1958 and Mick had found his uncle, lying in his own bed, eyes fixed open, a gentle smile on his face. Sam had died as he had lived, alone, and without any fuss. Losing Sam had been like having a part of Letty and Olly's own lives taken away from them. To them, Sam was more than a brother. He had been the wise owl of the family, with an unerring instinct for what was right or wrong. And he had protected every single one of them, including Ron who had resented him so much. It had almost become a joke in Roden Street that if anyone laid a hand on any one of the

Hobbs family, Sam would batter them. Of course it very rarely came to that, but they all knew that as a 'brickie', who had knocked around quite a few tough building sites in his time, he was capable of fighting for what he thought was right. Everyone had relied on Sam. He did all the things that his brother, because of his disability, couldn't do. He helped Letty with the housework and heavy shopping. He dug the garden beds in the back yard, and built and plastered walls. He was Eddie's constant football coach, who'd taught him everything he knew about the game. And Mick, who turned out to be what most of the family called, 'the artistic one', found in his Uncle Sam someone who had an instinctive understanding of what he wanted to do in his life. When Letty had told Oliver that Mick had an ambition to become a writer, Oliver had been delighted, but he still wanted to know what the boy intended to do for a living. Sam, on the other hand, had actually read the short stories Mick had written. It would take him ages: he hadn't learnt to read until Letty taught him, when he was way into his twenties. But whether he understood the stories or not, he always told Mick how good they were, and that he was to go on writing until everyone else thought the same. And when Mick had taken over the top rooms of Number 13 after old Florrie moved in with her relations in Tottenham, it was Sam who had helped the boy to decorate the place. Sam had been fifty-two when he died. As he watched his mother at the sink, Mick couldn't help thinking of those days when he was a kid, and Sam had played cricket with him and Eddie out in the street; that time, too, when Pop had gone for Sam over their bath night. He could see his uncle's face now. Sam was always a loner. He'd never have believed that after he'd gone, everyone would miss him so much. But they did. And Mick knew his mother would miss her youngest son, now as well.

Letty turned off the tap, then looked back at Mick. 'Now

listen to me, son,' she said, with a reassuring smile. 'Pop and I have had our time. Our kids have got themselves to look after now. Nothing else matters.'

Oliver opened the scullery door, and looked in from the back-parlour, where he'd turned off his 'Family Favourites'. 'Eddie's waitin' for you in the van. You'd better get goin'. You're causin' an obstruction.'

'Thanks, Pop. Just coming.' Mick was aware that his mother was looking at him. He wanted to say something to her – and Pop. He wanted to tell them that they were the best mother and father a son could ever wish for. But the words wouldn't come out. They were stuck hard in the huge lump in his throat. So he just threw his arms around Letty, and kissed her. Then he did the same to Pop. 'Listen here, you two,' he said, before he went. 'I shall expect to see you lots of times up at the flat. After all, it's only a short bus ride. And you'd better watch out, because I intend to cook for you.'

'Take care of yourself, son,' replied Letty, with a struggling smile. 'We'll see you soon.'

Oliver tried to smile too. But he suddenly lost his confidence, and stared at the floor. He still couldn't understand why Mick had to leave home. It wasn't as if he were getting married.

The next moment, Mick was gone.

Letty rushed into the front-parlour, to watch him climb up into the furniture van alongside Eddie. After it had pulled away, she just stood there, at last allowing the tears to trickle down her cheeks. Suddenly, from behind, she felt Oliver's comforting arms hugging her around the waist. Neither said a word.

For the first time since they were married, they were now quite alone.

*   *   *

In all the years that she had been 'doing the horses', Gran Edginton had hardly ever lost any money, usually putting threepence or sixpence each way on all the favourites. She had her regular bookie, Charlie, who sold newspapers outside Finsbury Park Station, and when she placed her bets with him she behaved as though she were passing over state secrets to the enemy. Once however, her hobby had got her into trouble, and, on one of her visits to Number 13, she had heard a police message on the wireless appealing for information about an old lady criminal who was involved in illegal gambling with a bookie named Charlie. Gran had nearly had a heart-attack on the spot, and immediately accused her downstairs neighbour of shopping her. Needless to say, she was not amused when she discovered that the wireless newsreader was none other than Mick, who had fitted up a microphone in the next room. Yet, at the age of ninety-three she was still a compulsive gambler.

'Mother! You can't have noise blaring out like that. I heard it right down the other end of the street.' The moment she arrived, Letty switched off the deafening sound of the racing on the wireless. She had her own key to Number 17 Bedford Terrace, and had used it to let herself in at her mother's front door. Using a huge magnifying glass, the old woman was studying form from the racing pages of her newspaper, which was spread out over her sewing-machine.

'You turn that wireless back on!' her mother shouted. 'It's the Easter Monday three-thirty from Sandown Park.'

Letty sighed, and shook her head. 'Mother. Have you been gambling again?'

Gran struggled up from her chair, furiously accusing 'Old Mother Wolf' downstairs of splitting on her. If she called the poor woman a bitch once, she did so a dozen times. As she spoke, she heard the street door slam downstairs. In a flash, she was at the window. 'There she goes now!' she yelled.

'Just look at her. Off to the boozer for her jug of stout!' Then she thumped on the window, shouting, 'Old boozer! Old bitch!'

In the street below, Mrs Wolf held the empty jug defiantly above her head as she made her way to the pub. She was used to Edginton's tantrums.

Letty was horrified by her mother's behaviour, but then again one always was. Nowadays she rarely visited her: they always ended up arguing. Letty found it hard to believe that this foul-mouthed harridan was the same Beatrice Edginton who was once the mistress of Number 97 Arlington Square. But times had changed. It was over fifty years since Gran had moved into Bedford Terrace and, looking around her, Letty could smell the dust and grime that clung to the faded wallpaper. The room hadn't been decorated for twenty years. In the corner of the room, the old gas cooker was thick with grease, for although Gran now had a home-help, she snapped and snarled at the woman so much she invariably only stayed long enough to wash the floor, dust the piano, and peel a few vegetables. For a long time now, Letty had become acutely conscious of the awful conditions her mother was living in. She was concerned that the old lady might one day injure herself, and not be in a fit state to call for help. She looked up anxiously at the burn marks on the ceiling above the gas mantle. Even though Gran had an electric light, night after night she stubbornly continued to use the old-fashioned gas lighting.

Letty waited for her mother to settle down in her armchair by the fireplace, then put the kettle on to make some tea. 'You know, Mother, it's time you thought about making other arrangements.'

For the moment, Gran appeared not to hear her. She was still mumbling to herself. She hated having to sit staring at the same four walls day after day, never seeing anyone. She'd used to have such good times in the old days, when she and William were invited to parties, and she was always asked to play the piano. But it was the dancing she had loved most. How she missed those early days! She'd much preferred being Beatrice to 'Gran'. 'Other arrangements?' Her shrunken little body suddenly straightened up, and she swung around to glare at Letty.

'Well, just look at this place. One dingy room at the top of the house, up and down the stairs struggling with pails of water, toilet outside in the back yard.'

Gran's heavily lined face crumpled up with rage. 'This is my *home*! I'm perfectly content with it!'

Letty put the tea in the pot without turning to look at her. 'Well me and Oliver are not content with you being here. At your age, it's just not safe any more.'

Gran got up, and angrily kicked the fire-shovel into the hearth. 'Age, age, age! When people can't be bothered with you any more, they keep going on about your age!'

Letty now knew she was embarking on dangerous waters. She and her mother had had this same conversation many times before. Gran was not stupid. She knew exactly what Letty was up to. Nothing in this world was going to get her into an old people's home. But things were different now. The old woman had had many falls over the past few months, and she was bruised all over. Furthermore, Bedford Terrace had recently been issued with a demolition order, and already half the residents had been re-housed in another district. Letty had to move fast. Even though Gran was fit and well, she was beginning to smell, mainly because she hadn't the facilities to keep herself properly clean: her mother was being denied the dignity of old age. But she knew Gran would fight to the last: many a time she had told Letty that if anyone tried to put her in a home, they'd have to carry her out in her box first. Letty half believed her.

She got two cups out of the cupboard beside the fireplace. 'Oh, mother! Why d'you have to be so stubborn? There are so many nice places you could go to.'

The old lady was furiously winding the handle of her ancient gramophone. 'Is that so? Well if you're so keen to get me out of here, does that mean I can come and stay with you?'

Letty tensed immediately, but did her best not to rise to Gran's bait. This was not the first time the subject had been brought up. The old lady knew very well that now Mick had left home there was a spare bedroom at Number 13. 'Let's not go into that again, Mother, please.'

Gran snapped back. 'Don't worry, I don't want to live with *you* either!' She immediately put on a scratchy old record. 'We wouldn't want to upset your Oliver, would we?'

Letty turned with an angry start. But before she could speak, the record boomed out. It was 'The Laughing Policeman', which Gran always put on when she wanted to irritate someone. Now Letty had to shout to be heard. 'That's enough now, Mother!'

The old lady yelled back, 'You know as well as I do, Oliver's resented me ever since you two first met. He's never had a civil word to say to me all the years you've been married.'

Letty slammed down a teacup into the saucer. Battle had commenced. 'Don't you talk about my husband like that!'

'You're lucky to have a husband!'

'Well if you'd treated your own better, he'd still be with you today!'

The laughing policeman roared louder than ever, and Letty and her mother competed with each other to shout above him, screeching and barking accusations at each other. The old lady changed the record to 'See Me Dance the Polka', which she always put on when young Mick came to visit her on Sunday mornings.

'Y'know your trouble, don't you, Letty?' Gran was clapping and swaying in time to 'See Me Dance the Polka'. 'Everyone knows you wait on him hand and foot!'

Suddenly, the record finished, giving Letty the chance to be heard. 'I look after my Oliver because I love him. And he loves me. Mother, marriage needs give and take on both sides. But you wouldn't know anything about that – would you!'

Suddenly, to the old lady's genuine surprise, Letty picked up her handbag, and rushed out of the room. Gran hurried to the door, and called down the stairs. 'Letty! Letty, what's the matter with you? What have I done wrong this time?'

A moment later, the front door slammed.

Letty paused briefly on the doorstep; she needed to recover her calm before making the journey back to Roden Street. When she finally moved off, she resisted the temptation to look up at her mother's window. As she passed down the terrace, she noted that the demolition workers had already torn down two or three houses, and despairingly Letty wondered how long it would be before they reached Number 17. At the corner, a bizarre sound drifted across the pavements from where she had just come. It was the 'policeman' on Gran's gramophone record, resounding from the open window on the top floor of Number 17. Letty halted for a moment, then disappeared into the next street.

Bedford Terrace echoed to the sound of Gran's 'policeman'. These days, it was the only laughter she ever got.

Chapter 28

Midnight in Roden Street was always accompanied by twelve chimes from the clock tower of the Emmanuel Church nearby. The weather over the Easter Bank Holiday had been quite warm and, as usual, everyone streamed out of the city, and made their way to the seaside. Letty and Oliver, however, stayed at home, and watched all the Holiday programmes on television. They had the occasional visitors, of course, such as Alice and Ted Cole, who used to live next door, and Eddie and Mary had popped in for Easter Sunday lunch. But, apart from Letty's ill-fated visit to her mother up at Bedford Terrace, it was a quiet weekend for the only occupants of Number 13.

As the last of the twelve chimes rang out, Oliver turned irritably in bed. 'Cat and dog. That's what you are – you and your mother. Every time you get together, it's like the Battle of Britain all over again!'

Letty was snuggled up to him. As usual, she had kept him awake by thinking all her daily problems out loud. 'Well, it's not right, Olly! I won't have that woman running you down like that. I don't care how old she is. She's always trying to make mischief between you and me.'

'She don't like me. She never has. So why don't we forget about her, and get some kip.'

'Oh come on, Olly.' Letty kissed him on the back of his

neck, then, teasing him, bit his ear. 'You can't be as tired as all that. You don't have to get up early in the mornings any more.'

Oliver suddenly turned over. 'So what!' he snapped. 'That don't mean I don't have things to do! I'm not a bloody vegetable!'

'Olly!' Letty could have kicked herself for being so insensitive. Two years earlier, Oliver had gone into hospital for an operation to remove one of his kidneys which had had a cancerous tumour on it. Although he had completely recovered, these days he was getting a little tired. It also meant that he'd had to retire from work fourteen months early, which disqualified him from getting a pension. All he was left with was a gold wristwatch inscribed, 'London Transport. O. J. Hobbs. In recognition of 47 years' service'. Letty knew only too well what it meant to Oliver not to have his job at Manor House Station any more. To Oliver, his job had been his life, and he had loved every minute of it. For forty-seven years he had stood on one leg at that cold ticket-barrier, always immaculate in his uniform, meeting all sorts of people, telling them how to get from one station to another, collecting great bundles of tickets. Sometimes he'd open the station at crack of dawn. Other times he'd close it. Then he'd walk home, no matter what time of the day or night, smiling and waving at his regular acquaintances on the way – the newspaper man outside the station, the woman in the dry-cleaners, Reg the PC on duty outside the Astoria Cinema. For Letty and the kids, Thursday pay-day was their favourite day with Pop. Not for the money, but because they knew that Oliver would always stop at Lavells, the sweet shop in Seven Sisters Road, and arrive back at Number 13 armed with nougats, chocolate caramels, macaroons and, Letty's favourite, barley sugars. Being a

London Underground ticket collector might not be everybody's idea of the perfect job. But it was for Oliver. And how he missed it!

Letty quickly sat up in bed, and kissed him on the forehead. 'You silly thing, Olly! You know that's not what I meant. I was only thinking how lovely it is to have you home with me every day.'

Oliver, too, pulled himself up in bed. 'It doesn't feel right, Lett. I don't like sittin' around, twiddlin' my thumbs all day, no one to talk to.'

'Well – thanks very much!'

Letty leaned forward, so that he could slip his arm around her shoulders.

'You know what I mean,' he said, forlornly.

Letty knew exactly what he meant. Oliver missed his family around him. As much as he loved Letty, he found it hard to cope with the great void left behind by Ron, Eddie, Mick, and of course Sam. Several times Letty had tried to tell him that the kids were like birds – they had to feather their own nests, just like she and Oliver had done when they got married. She also reminded him how lucky they were compared to Tilly and Bill, who had lost their eldest son Jeff in a motor-cycle accident soon after the war. That loss had absolutely devastated the Brooks family, for Jeff was not only a dear boy who never seemed to have any enemies, but he was also clearly on the verge of an exciting career as a Master Chef at a London hotel. 'At least we've still got our Ron, Eddie, and Mick – thank God!' Letty said, leaning her head gently against Oliver's. 'We've got a lot to be grateful for, Olly.' She did know how proud Olly was of his kids: Eddie, with his own newspaper shop, and Mick working in a travel agency. Even Ron. But somehow, Oliver didn't feel a part of them any more.

'What did we ever do to Ron that he don't want to come and see us no more?'

Oliver's sudden question took Letty by surprise. 'Don't be silly, dear,' she said, unconvincingly. 'Ron and Janey live out in the country now. It isn't easy for them to get back and forth to London. It's expensive too.'

'We're supposed to 'ave two grandchilden. And yet we 'ardly ever see 'em.'

Letty felt she had no convincing reply to offer. Ron was just his own person, and there was nothing they could do about it. After his return from the war, he had been fussed over no end by his mother and father. They'd fitted him out with his first civvy suit; Pop gave him fifty pounds which he had saved from his weekly wages all through the war and when he got married, Letty gave him and Janey most of the sheets, pillows, and blankets they needed to start their married life. Despite all this, Ron had never really responded to anything his parents had done for him. But the thing that upset Letty most of all was Ron's total detachment from Eddie and Mick. It was true that there was a great age gap between Ron and his two younger brothers, and Letty had always thought it might be the reason for Ron's resentment of them. But she was sure they'd never favoured the two youngest. In fact, it was quite the reverse, for despite everything, Ron had always remained the one closest to Oliver's heart. Throughout the years Letty had tried to play down Ron's behaviour, but the boy's bitterness had deeply hurt his father. It was hard for Letty to see how things could ever be put right again.

'Never mind.' Letty was staring up at the plaster roses carved on the ceiling around the electric light, just visible with the help of a bright moonlit night outside. 'Just think how lucky we are to have Eddie and Mary. It's wonderful the way they come all the way down from Enfield to see us every week.'

Oliver was still grumpy. 'Yeah. And it's about time *they* had some kids. They've been married over ten years now.'

'Oliver!' Letty was shocked by his boldness. 'That's no way to talk. When Eddie and Mary decide to have children, they'll have them. You mustn't be such an old gossip.' She was just as concerned as Oliver, though, and was dying to have grandchildren from Eddie and Mary. But she also knew that they had their own reasons for waiting. After all, both of them were earning – Eddie in his newspaper shop, and Mary with her important job as a Company Secretary at an electrics firm. Letty was sure – at least she *hoped*, that as soon as Eddie and Mary had saved up enough money, they'd have a family. But, she told herself, only when they were good and ready.

'Since we're not goin' to get any shut-eye again to-night, I might as well have a fag.'

'Olly – no! You know what the doctor said. You smoke far too much.'

'To 'ell with the doctor. This is my life – not his.' Oliver stretched across to the bedside cabinet but as he did so, he let out a loud yell, enough to wake the whole street. For the second night running, a very sharp bed-spring had forced its way through the mattress covering, and was sticking firmly into Oliver's bottom.

Letty roared with laughter, so much that it gave her a coughing fit, and she had to get out of bed. She knew Oliver was exaggerating like hell, but they liked a laugh, and now the boys had left home, he relieved a lot of her depressions by fooling around. It helped her. It helped both of them.

Oliver lit his cigarette, pleased at the effect his dramatics had produced and Letty eventually stopped laughing, going over to the window to look out. Roden Street seemed very cold and empty. On the outside, nothing had changed much in the street over the years. Some of the houses had been painted up a little, and the public pig-swill bins that were used during the war had long since been removed. But the real changes had come *inside* the houses. Over the years, Letty's old neighbours and friends had gradually moved out of the district, and gone to live in the country where they could find peace and quiet in the latter part of their lives. In their place had come a new breed of neighbour, many of them from foreign countries that Letty knew hardly anything about. Some of the new children playing in the street had dark skins: some were yellow, and others seemed as though they just had a good sun tan. Letty's favourite subject at school had been geography, and she was still fascinated to learn about all the countries she was unlikely to see. And she loved meeting new people, so when the new residents moved in, she did her best to get to know them. Sometimes she greeted them as they came in or out of their front doors, other times she tried starting up a casual conversation with them in the shopping queues in the Seven Sisters Road. Sadly, it hardly ever worked. Unlike the old days, the new residents rarely stood in their front doorways passing the time of day with their neighbours. Some didn't speak English and those that did just seemed to want to keep themselves to themselves. Letty didn't even know the Greek-Cypriot family who, over two years earlier, had moved into Number 11 next door. Every time she tried to speak to them over the back-yard wall, they just smiled nervously at her and hurried back inside. Letty sighed, and shook her head sadly. She supposed people were busier nowadays. Just look at Ron and Janey. But what hope was there if people in the street couldn't even talk to each other? As she stood there at the window, looking down at the empty pavements below, she felt that she really didn't know her beloved Roden Street any more.

The smell of tobacco curled its way across the room, and reached Letty at the window. She turned to see the red glow from Oliver's fag as he inhaled deeply. She sighed helplessly, knowing that nothing in the world would persuade him to stop smoking. Night after night, Letty was woken by the dreadful struggling sound of Oliver's smoker's cough. But she could do nothing about it. After a moment, she was back in bed again, snuggling up alongside him as he continued to smoke. 'Olly', she whispered, eyes closed, dreamily. 'Wouldn't it be lovely if you and I could start all over again?'

Oliver blew out a puff of smoke, and grunted. 'Huh?'

'D'you remember when we first got married? How we used to talk about havin' our own little place down by the sea? Daffodils in the front garden, climbing roses out the back. Walks along the seashore, you feeding the seagulls.'

Oliver used the ash-tray on his bedside cabinet. 'Dreams, Lett. You spend your life livin' out dreams. Still, I tell you what.' Oliver took one last quick puff of his fag. 'Soon as I get the treble chance up on the pools, I'll get us a little place. Right?'

'Right!'

Oliver stubbed out his cigarette, and pulled himself down under the bed-clothes. He closed his eyes, and settled down, lying on his back.

After a moment, Letty whispered quietly. 'Olly.'

'What now?'

'Give us a kiss.'

Oliver grunted, turned over, kissed her briskly on the lips, then turned back again.

'Is that the best you can do?' Letty leant over him, her lips were pressed against his for so long that by the time she had pulled away, Oliver was left in no doubt about how she was feeling.

'Aren't we gettin' a bit old for this lark, Mrs Hobbs?' he asked in a whisper.

'Too old to love each other? You and me – after forty-five years?' Suddenly, Letty was like a young woman again. She snuggled up closer, her voice a barely audible whisper. 'Let me tell you something Oliver Hobbs. I fancy you now just as much as the first time I laid eyes on you. We'll never be too old to love each other – *never*.'

They kissed again, this time more passionately. But just as they were about to embrace more intimately, the room was shaken by a burst of sound, from Number 11 next door. It was a gramophone record of Greek music.

'Bloody hell!' Oliver pulled himself up with a start, as the music pierced the night air, together with the sound of people clapping in time.

After a shocked pause Letty suddenly saw the funny side of what had happened, and started to laugh. But as the music got louder and more frenzied, Oliver became angrier. 'What's the matter with all of yer?' he shouted at the top of his voice. 'Don't you lot ever go ter sleep in Cyprus!'

It was obvious that nobody else in Roden Street was going to get any more sleep that night either.

Letty thoroughly enjoyed her job as 'Milk lady' at Pakeman Street School. Her duties were very different from those of years back, when she'd spent every evening on her hands and knees scrubbing the floors in the main Assembly Hall, but now she was getting older she thought it was about time to take things just a little easier. As the school was only a stone's throw from Number 13, she was able to get to work very easily, and she was always there at least an hour before she was needed. Wearing a clean pinny every day, she laid out over five hundred half-pint bottles of free milk, and pushed a straw into the silver top of each one. As soon as the handbell rang for morning break, a great rush of children stormed into the Assembly Hall to form a disorderly queue in front of the trestle-tables where Letty was waiting to hand out the milk. Most of the children knew her as 'Mrs Hobby', but if any of the teachers were around, they were expected to call her 'Ma'am', which Letty didn't really care for. She, in turn, got to know the first names of practically all the children. In the last few years there had been a few fairly difficult ones for her to remember: Anwar and Zeinab, Dudu and Stavros.

Over the ten years she had worked there, Letty became very fond of all the children who came and went. Often if they got into trouble, or hurt themselves, they would rush to 'Mrs Hobby', sure of a sympathetic hug.

The Bank Holiday Whit Monday was unusually warm that year, so Letty decided to take her knitting, and sit on the coping-stone outside the front of Number 13. Oliver had gone off with Eddie to watch a football match at the Arsenal Stadium. She knew they'd be enjoying themselves, because every so often she could hear the massed roars and shouts from the crowds at Highbury, only a quarter of an hour's walk away. It was later in the afternoon when Letty noticed some of the children hurrying out of the school playground just across the road. They had been having a Holiday football match of their own, competing in noise with the Highbury crowds. As the last of them disappeared down the street, Letty thought it was about time to get Oliver's tea ready. Just as she was going back inside the house, however, the street suddenly echoed to the sound of a small child screaming in terror. Letty turned with a start, threw her knitting down into the hall passage, and rushed across to see what was happening. Her worst fears were immediately confirmed. One of the boys had left the school gate open, and a stray Alsatian had got into the playground where it was terrorising a small Nigerian girl called 'Anji Ukowa'. Without stopping to think, Letty rushed straight to the hysterical child and snatched her from the snarling dog. In its frustration the creature went for Letty herself and she was relieved when her cries brought a crowd of locals rushing across to the playground to help, but both she and the child had been bitten before the dog made a bolt for it. Letty hugged the screaming Anji; she took out her handkerchief, and held it over the child's wound, stroking her hair to calm her. Amongst the neighbours who had rushed to help them, Letty spotted an elderly black man shouldering his way though the crowd, saying he was the child's grandfather. Before Letty could say anything, the old man, clearly in a panic, quickly grabbed the little girl from Letty's arms, and rushed off home with her.

When Olly got home to find Letty just back from the hospital, with two stitches in her leg, he was furious. 'Bloody immigrants!' he yelled angrily, 'They come over here and take our homes, and then don't even have the decency to thank you for what you've done when you help 'em!

'That's not fair.' Letty still looked a little shaken as she reclined her injured leg on a stool. 'The old boy was scared out of his life. All he could think of was this poor kid, screaming her head off. I'd have been exactly the same if it was our Eddie or Nick. And so would you.'

Oliver was unconvinced. He resented the newcomers, positive their only interest was to drive out all the old residents so that they could take over the area for themselves. As far as change was concerned, Oliver just knew he didn't like it. He couldn't bear the Greek-Cypriot family who lived next door, even though he'd never so much as passed the time of day with them. But Letty understood why Oliver really felt so suspicious of 'foreigners': it was

367

because of the war – *his* war, which had robbed him of a stable life on two good feet. It was also a war which he wanted to forget. Greek-Cypriots; Turkish-Cypriots; West Indians; Africans; Pakistanis; Germans: they all meant the same to Oliver, and he had no time for them. And, although Letty was more open-minded, even she had to admit how surprised she was that Anji's grandfather had been so brusque.

When the street door bell rang, Oliver was in the back yard, collecting the washing that Letty had hung out earlier in the day. Letty reluctantly eased herself up from her chair, and made her way along the passage. When she opened the door, her mouth fell open: standing on her doorstep were two black people – a young couple. The man was in his Sunday best, a grey suit with a multi-coloured tie, and a black homburg. The woman looked spectacular, wearing highly coloured Nigerian national dress, complete with a bustle, and a vast, complicated headdress to match.

'Hallo lady.' The man took off his hat to reveal a head of tight black curls. In the other hand he was carrying a huge bunch of flowers, and he spoke in a deep, rich voice. 'Please can I speak Mrs Hobby?'

When she introduced herself the man broke into a smile so broad that to Letty his sparkling white teeth seemed twice the normal size. 'We Anji Mummy and Daddy,' he said, immediately pushing the bunch of flowers at Letty. 'Thank you, lady.'

Letty took the flowers, bewildered, and felt the woman take her by the hand as she launched into torrents of a language that Letty had never heard in her life.

'My lady say you very good Mummy, Mrs Hobby.' Now it was the man's turn to shake Letty's hand so hard that it nearly fell off. 'Any time you want to come tea our house, she happy lady.'

Before Letty could say thank you in return, the two of them were off down the street, the man smiling and waving his hat, and the woman blowing kisses with her hand. Eventually, clutching and smelling her flowers, Letty closed the door. As she turned to go back into the front-parlour, she saw Oliver waiting for her, holding the huge pile of washing. By the look on his face, there was no doubt he had seen and heard everything that had taken place between Letty and her unexpected visitor. But he said nothing. What *could* he say?

Chapter 29

There was a fair-sized collection of neighbours waiting for Gran Edginton on the morning she left Bedford Terrace. And, although she didn't leave Number 17 in her coffin, as she had threatened, her departure was not exactly dignified. The evening before she had fallen off a chair whilst trying to light the gas mantle, and had spent most of the night lying semi-conscious on the floor. Luckily, it was the home-help's day for a call, and she had immediately sent for an ambulance. She'd also notified Letty, who arrived just as two ambulance men were bringing Gran down the stairs. Wrapped in a red hospital blanket, the old lady cursed everything and everybody in sight. But as she was lifted up into the ambulance, her eyes drifted wistfully to the upper-floor windows of her home. When, if ever, would she see it again?

Twenty minutes later, Gran found herself being wheeled on a stretcher along the friendless corridors of the Whittington Hospital at Highgate. It was the first time she had been in such a place since her friend Laura had died over five years before, and she hated all the disgusting smells – of people and blood, of disinfectant and medicines. She also couldn't bear the false smiles she was receiving. Gran knew what folks were thinking. They thought she was being brought there to die! The old lady ignored Letty, who walked alongside her. Instead her eyes looked up at the narrow ceilings which were dark and dingy, and needed a fresh coat of paint.

For three hours, Letty sat on a half-broken chair outside Casualty, waiting for news. The young doctor who finally came out to talk to her, a bright-eyed, eager young man, whom Letty was sure had only just got out of Medical School, said that her mother was not seriously injured beyond a broken wrist, a bang on the back of her head, and quite a lot of bruises. But the patient's advanced age meant that there was always a risk of her developing pneumonia, so for that reason it was essential she stay in hospital for at least a few days. Letty was assured that Gran would fully recover; she was a tough old lady physically, and obstinate enough to survive for a good few years yet.

Letty visited her mother in hospital every afternoon, for she took longer than anticipated to recover. It was not until two weeks later that Letty was asked to call and see the lady almoner, who told her that, in the opinion of the doctor looking after Mrs Edginton, Letty's mother would never again be in a fit state to live on her own again. The news came as no surprise. Letty couldn't help feeling a sense of shame as she tried to explain to the kindly woman that her mother had never really got on with her son-in-law, so it would be out of the question that she should come to live with them. She was assured that it was a common situation, but she warned that the only solution would be for Mrs Edginton to be moved into the hospital's geriatric ward. Letty's heart was in her boots as, a week later, she went to visit her there for the first time.

'If you think I'm goin' to stay in this hole for the rest of my days, you're mistaken,' were the words that greeted her. And throughout the rest of her visit Gran made it quite clear to Letty that she loathed 'The Pit', as the ward was called by visiting relatives. Looking around her, Letty saw that about thirty old people were accommodated there, most of them either deaf, half-blind, riddled with arthritis or just pathetically senile and living in a twilight world all their own. It depressed Letty inutterably, but what could she do? Again she reflected that there seemed to be no such thing as the dignity of old age. Despite the care of the nursing staff, The Pit could be regarded as no more than a clearing house for the mortuary.

'Mark my words, Letty,' growled the old lady. 'The first chance I get to walk through that door, I'll do it!'

And when Letty returned the next afternoon she found her mother had been true to her word. Practically every day during the first week, Letty arrived at the hospital to be told that Gran had been caught in her nightie, sneaking her way down the corridor. On one occasion, she had actually managed to reach the yard outside, until a porter caught up with her, and escorted her back. His reward had been a kick on his shin, and a few choice words. Eventually however, Gran was given a tranquilliser, after which her valiant efforts to reach the outside world gradually stopped.

It took only a week for Beatrice Edginton to become a fully-fledged member of The Pit.

Oliver thought Mick's new flat was small to share with two others, but at least it was bright and airy, on the top floor of a four-storey house. He didn't like the white-painted walls, a nice flowered wallpaper would have made it look more cosy to his mind, but he kept his thoughts to himself. There were two bedrooms, one with two beds, the other just big enough to take a small-sized divan. The sitting-room, which overlooked the street, also doubled as a dining-room, with a small kitchen adjoining. The thing that impressed Letty most of all was the area they were living in, a rather posh part of Marble Arch. She could see why it needed the combined wages of all three men to pay for it. One or two pieces of furniture had come from Number 13, together with quite a lot of bed linen and towels. The rest was provided by Mick's two flatmates, who had helped to decorate the place too.

The moment Letty met Mick's two friends, she liked them, and, in no time at all, was getting them to call her 'Mum', and Oliver 'Pop'. The idea of three young men living together, looking after themselves, and pooling their resources, was a new one for Letty, and she thoroughly admired them for having a go at it. Oliver, on the other hand, was not so sure. When he saw the meal Mick had cooked for him and Letty, he looked extremely suspicious, especially when Mick teased him that the ingredients of the casserole were snails, frogs' legs, octopus tentacles and sheep's eyes. He was secretly relieved when he discovered that his meal was made with nothing more exotic than stewed beef, onions, mushrooms, and tomatoes. And Letty, couldn't believe her eyes to see her own son cooking such a lovely meal. Where had he learnt to do all these things? Mick insisted he'd simply watched her over the years, and the rest he'd got from recipes in cookery books.

What fascinated her most of all was the fact that Mick's two flatmates were so different from him. Brian and Charlie were both young actors, very cultured and worldly in their own ways. She knew Pop had been very nervous of meeting them: the only thing he knew about acting was what he saw on the telly. Letty had told him not to be so silly, that they were just ordinary boys and, to her relief, within minutes Pop was drinking and smoking with them just like he did with the lads round at the Eaglet. Charlie was clearly the extrovert one and it wasn't long before he and Pop were sharing dirty jokes, somewhat to Letty's disapproval. Brian was much more serious, but Oliver listened in awed fascination to his experiences as a child in Sri Lanka, where he was born of mixed British and European parents. Letty particularly appreciated the way Brian took the trouble to talk to Pop, especially when he explained the wonders of astronomy. As she watched them, she thought how, despite their differences, the two men responded to each other in the most unexpected way. But even so, Pop still found it difficult to believe that people actually made money by acting on a stage. It was not what he understood to be work.

Charlie quickly started filling up Oliver's glass. 'Come on, Pop! You're letting the side down!'

'No more drink for Pop, please Charlie.' Letty could see that Oliver had already had more than was good for him. It was a dangerous sign, that he was getting twitchy and over-jolly; she knew it only took one word out of place for him to turn aggressive. The last thing in the world she wanted was for him to make a fool of himself in front of Mick's friends. Also, he had never drunk wine before and, knowing that he was living on only one kidney, Letty was unsure how it would affect him.

'What d'you say, Lett?' Oliver was glaring at her, not at all pleased that Charlie had stopped filling his glass.

Letty was ill-at-ease. 'We'll be going home soon, dear. You've had quite enough to drink.'

'Who said so?'

There was a tense pause. 'I tell you what, Pop,' said Mick, suddenly, anxious to avoid any embarrassment. 'How about a cup of coffee?'

Letty quickly added, 'I think he'd prefer tea.' Then she turned to Oliver apprehensively. 'I'm right – aren't I, dear?'

The wine had made Oliver's cheeks turn a bright red, and he snapped back angrily. 'I don't want tea, and I don't want coffee! In case none of you realise, I'm not a bleedin' kid! I've done my time in the Army, mate. And this is all the thanks

I got for it!' He held out his artificial leg, and slapped it. Then, beginning to slur his words, he said, 'I've got no right ter be here. No right, d'yer hear?' He picked up his glass from the table, and held it out to Charlie, defiantly. 'Same again, please!' Then in his old army cockney-French, 'Bon Sante!' Once again, he was beaming.

Charlie and Brian thought the best thing to do was to join him, so they too picked up their glasses, and toasted him. 'Cheers! All the best, Pop!'

Mick smiled comfortingly at his mother, then took her by the arm, and led her into the kitchen, where Letty apologised for his dad's behaviour.

Letty felt crushed, as she sat at the table in the tiny kitchen, watching Mick preparing fresh coffee. 'I knew it would happen. I could see it coming.' She was close to tears. 'It's always the same when he gets a bit of drink inside him. You never know how he's going to behave.' Swallowing hard, she looked up at Mick. 'I'm sorry, son. I'm really sorry. The last thing I wanted was to show you up in front of your friends.'

Mick put the coffee percolator on the cooker, closed the kitchen door quietly, then sat with his mother at the table. 'Now listen to me, mum. Nobody's shown me up. The only thing that's happened it that Pop's got a little tight, that's all. If you're worried about Brian and Charlie, they couldn't care less. They know all about drink in their profession, you know. Sometimes it helps to cover up people's anxieties.' It wasn't easy for Mick to say that, for he didn't drink himself, but he'd seen plenty of people drunk and aggressive in his time. There were several occasions when he remembered Uncle Sam coming back from the Eaglet in a raging mood. Sam had even smashed a chair to pieces once. But he'd got over it, and the next morning couldn't even remember what had happened. Mick had often told his mother that he didn't

375

like what drink did to people. But he understood why they did it.

Letty stared at the plastic table top. 'If only he'd listen to me. If only he'd trust me.'

Mick took hold of both her hands. 'He does trust you, Mum. The trouble is – well, at times – you *could* be just a bit more tactful with him.'

Letty looked up with an indignant start. 'What d'you mean?'

'You shouldn't be so protective. People accept Pop for what he is, not what we want him to be. I know you're always worried that because he didn't have any kind of education, he might make a fool of himself in front of people who have. But he doesn't. Brian and Charlie think I'm the luckiest bloke in the world to have parents like you and Pop. As a matter of fact, so do I. But it's got nothing to do with education or class. It's to do with being who and *what* you are.'

Letty sighed. She knew Mick was right. She did worry about Oliver too much. But since the two of them had been left to live on their own, Letty felt that she'd got to know Oliver better than at any other time. There was no doubt that Pop missed the companionship of his sons, and his brother Sam. It wasn't that he didn't get on with Letty, but he could share a conversation or a joke in a different way with male company. Even though the war had scarred him, he'd loved the companionship of the men he'd shared the trenches with. Nowadays, she could tell that sometimes his heart was still back there all those years ago – in the Army. 'I suppose the trouble with your dad and I is, we're just getting old, that's all,' she said to Mick as she watched him preparing fresh coffee.

Mick laughed. 'Come off it Mum! You're not on your last legs yet!' His mother laughed too, and she quickly dried her eyes with her handkerchief. From the sitting-room, they could hear Pop was enjoying himself with Charlie and Brian, singing his old favourite, 'Red Sails in the Sunset'. The coffee percolator on the cooker had started making bubbling sounds. Mick sat back in his chair, deep in thought. There was something his father had said which had puzzled him. 'Mum. What did Pop mean about not having the right to be here? Was that something to do with his Army days?'

Letty's elbows were on the table, her chin resting on her hands. 'I wish I knew, son.'

'Has he ever talked like that before?'

'About having the right to live? Oh yes. Time and time again. Especially over the last few years.'

Mick was curious. Ever since he was a kid, he couldn't remember a time when Pop had ever talked about what happened to him during his brief period in the first war. Now Mick was intrigued. 'You know, Mum, he should tell you what he means. One of these days he'll *have* to.'

Letty lowered her hands on to the table, and clasped them together. Throughout their marriage, Oliver had always resisted talking to her in any detail about his time in the trenches. All she ever knew were the basic facts of how he was injured, and how bitter he was that so many of his friends had not returned home. Letty had always suspected that *something* had taken place that Oliver would never tell her. What it was, she didn't know. And she would never ask him. But whatever it was, he was haunted by it, and it was stuck inside him like a malignant growth. Letty looked up at Mick with a gentle smile. 'When he's ready, son. Only when he's ready.'

As Letty listened to Oliver snoring beside her that night, she thought about what Mick had said. Would Oliver *ever* tell her his secret – if there was one? And then she lay awake thinking about. Pop's behaviour in front of Mick's friends.

She turned the evening over in her mind, convinced that the following morning it wouldn't even occur to Pop that he had done anything wrong. She sighed, until eventually her anxieties sent her right off to sleep.

The following morning, Letty thought she was still dreaming. She could hear Oliver's voice calling to her gently. 'Lett. Come on Lett.' She woke up with a start, to find the sun streaming through the window, and Oliver standing over her with a cup of tea. She sat up in bed with a start. 'Olly! What's wrong?' It was the first time Oliver had got up to give her a cup of tea in bed since his early turns on the tube years ago.

Oliver put the cup and saucer down on her bedside cabinet, then leaned over to kiss her tenderly on the lips. 'I'm sorry, girl', he said, quietly. 'Forgive me?'

Smiling to herself, Letty sipped her tea. No matter how well she thought she knew Olly, he could still surprise her.

Chapter 30

Southend! Glorious Southend! Where troubles were forgotten, and hopes renewed. Where the sea could almost touch the amusement arcades, and the vinegary tang of cockles, whelks and jellied eels competed with the smell of bangers-and-mash. Southend – with a pier that could boast one of the most bracing one-and-a-half mile walks out to sea, or, for the less energetic a ride on its miniature railway. Letty called the place London-by-the-sea. So did a lot of other people, not because the Essex seaside resort looked anything like London – far from it – but during the summer months, there seemed to be more day-trippers from London than local residents.

To Letty and Oliver, Southend-on-Sea was as good as the French Riviera, not that they'd ever been to the South of France. But Southend gave them as much pleasure as a ten-times-more luxurious place could have done – perhaps even more. They preferred it any day to posh places like Bournemouth or Brighton, mainly because Oliver felt he could take his coat off and show his shirt and braces without people turning to look at him. Southend was the first place where Eddie and Mick had ever seen the sea, on a school-outing. Eddie had loved the place so much, he'd run straight into the sea with all his clothes on, much to Letty's fury when he got home. Mick was more sceptical, and preferred to wade into the sea up to his waist, then pretend that he was swimming. Letty also remembered the time when, on one Bank Holiday day-trip, Eddie and Mick had an ice-cream eating competition. Rossi's' Southend ices were famous, twirled with a spoon by hand on to a cornet, building up into a shape that resembled the roof of some Oriental Temple. Mick had won the competition, and he never let Eddie forget it. Twenty-three cornets to twenty-two.

Ever since Mick had moved out of Number 13, he hadn't had the chance to meet up very often with Eddie, and Eddie's wife, Mary. So when the family decided to have an August Bank Holiday get-together down at Southend, Letty and Oliver were overjoyed. They all travelled down in Eddie's Ford Cortina but Mary drove most of the time, so that if Eddie wanted to drink with his father he could do so. On the way they stopped for coffee and biscuits at a roadside café, and had a drink at a day-tripper's pub, sitting at a table outside in the warm sunshine. On the outskirts of the town, they slowed down to look at a new building estate of bungalows, nestled on top of a hill overlooking the sea. Letty thought to herself that whoever moved into a place like that would be the luckiest people in the world.

There were crowds of trippers along the sea-front. Everyone seemed to be eating, either fish and chips out of newspaper, or ice-cream, or sweet pink-coloured Southend rock, or great puffs of candyfloss. Letty stood out in the crowd, in a new black-and-white striped dress Oliver had bought her for her birthday, from Marks and Spencer's in the Holloway Road. As usual, Pop set the pace, marching off ahead of everyone, leaving Eddie and Mick breathless as they tried to keep up with him. Letty and Mary decided to let them get on with it, and followed on behind in their own time, chatting idly, occasionally turning their heads simultaneously to stare at some of the gawdy things people were wearing. As they walked along the Promenade, the sun was drenching the thousands of families on the beach. Everyone was so tightly packed together, it seemed an impossible task for some of them to play football or cricket. But they managed it. And as the morning wore on, the sea-front became one long Bank Holiday traffic jam, with an endless procession of cars and charabancs battling it out for parking positions.

The midday meal for the Hobbs family was in their favourite sea-front café, but not until after a long wait in the queue. The smell of sausages and onions was irresistible, and both Eddie and Mick ordered double portions, despite being scolded by Letty and Mary. As usual, the accompanying thin slices of bread were spread with only a suggestion of margarine, not butter, but it didn't matter, for the whole meal washed down very nicely with a good pot of strong tea. The only thing that marred it, was the baby at the next table, who bawled the place down. Pop said it sounded just like Mick when he was that age, but Letty stiffened with displeasure, glaring at the child so much that it eventually stopped crying, and retreated to the protection of its mother's arms.

In the afternoon, Oliver tied a handkerchief on his head and had a nap on a sea-front bench in the sunshine. After the others had wandered around a bit, they came back to find Pop's face and arms the colour of a lobster, with great puffs under his eyes. Letty, however, was fully prepared and produced a bottle of pink calamine lotion which, despite Pop's protests, she rubbed all over his face with a piece of cotton wool. By the time she'd finished, they all agreed he looked like something out of a Hammer horror film.

After a standing-up cup of tea at one of the refreshment kiosks, Eddie and Mick decided they wanted to go into the Kursaal Amusement Park, mainly because they wanted a ride on their favourite 'Scenic Railway'. Both Letty and

381

Mary snootily suggested that they were still nothing more than a couple of kids at heart. Pop, however was persuaded to keep them company. Letty realised exactly why. He had brought his binoculars with him, supposedly for spotting sea-birds, but she knew their use in the Kursaal would be put to spotting birds of a somewhat different species.

Once Letty and Mary were left to themselves, they made their way along the sea-front towards the Pier. Letty wanted to buy some sweet honeycomb for Gran, which the old lady was very fond of and which, because she had no teeth left, would melt quite easily in her mouth. They finally selected a small shop where they were served by a jolly middle-aged man wearing a hat with the words 'Hold me tight, darling' on it. Neither Letty nor Mary did anything of the sort, but they did buy the honeycomb for Gran, some chocolate fudge for Mick and Eddie, and some old-fashioned humbugs for Pop.

It was just after four o'clock by the time Letty and Mary reached the Pier where there was a queue for its railway train, but as they weren't meeting the three men back at the car park for another couple of hours or so, they decided to join it. In fact, they were on the train much sooner than they expected, and within a few minutes were bumping along in a tiny compartment on the narrow gauge railway-track, heading out towards the Pier Theatre and open sea beyond. As always, it was a memorable journey. Although it was no more than ten minutes from one end of the Pier to the other, the fresh sea-air was exhilarating, rushing seductively past the open window. For the entire duration of the journey, Letty and Mary hardly spoke a word, both staring out incredulously at the blue-grey sea, shimmering in the sunshine, the sparkling white waves rolling gently back towards the long stretch of beach far behind them. And through the window on the other side, there were occasional glimpses of those who had decided to walk it. Fathers and mothers firmly held the hands of their children, groups of senior citizens gathered beneath the sheltered benches to scold the present and lament the past, and Bank Holiday anglers lined up in rows, their menacing hooks plundering the shallow depths. Then quite suddenly, a train passed alongside from the opposite direction. Everyone waved, and shouted, and cheered. It was August Bank Holiday! No school! No work! The escape was real – until another day.

The end of the Pier was very crowded, but Mary soon commandeered a couple of deck chairs, and made room for them in a shaded corner, out of the wind, overlooking the sea. She also bought two paper cups of tea at which Letty smiled, and told her that she was a good girl, and that Eddie was a very lucky boy. Tall and erect, Mary was an attractive girl with pale blue-grey eyes and light brown hair, and she had made a deliciously lovely bride on her wedding day back in 1951. She was the daughter of a Finsbury Park Grocery Store Manager, but sadly her mother had died at the early age of fifty-two after a sudden stomach operation. For a time, Mary had looked after her father and two brothers, one older and one younger, until meeting Eddie at a dance hall, soon after he had finished two years' National Service in the RAF. Coincidentally, Mary had also served in the Forces, in the WRAF, so the two of them had shared a lot in common. Letty and Oliver had liked Mary immediately: they found her sensible to talk to, very practical, and thoughtful to them in every conceivable way. Most of all, she and Eddie clearly loved each other very much, which was, in Letty's mind, a real blessing, for the sudden death of Mary's mother had obviously been a tragic experience for the poor girl. For Letty, of course, it was a joy to have a girl in the family at last. Mary had become the daughter she had always wanted so badly.

As they sat there, sipping their tea, and watching the anglers wrestling with their fishing rods, the sound of someone playing a piano drifted out of the old end-of-Pier Theatre nearby. It immediately cast Letty's mind back to the times she and Olly used to go to concert parties there. She remembered one comedian who had been particularly smutty and another who had specialised in corny jokes. But how they'd laughed at them! Then there was 'Southend's famous International Singing Duo, Robert and Dorothy Barrington-Smith', who were very dignified performers, but who'd had to stand on tiptoe to reach the top notes. And what about that pianist! What was his name now? Henry! Henry, who always wore full white bow tie and tails, and white gloves, even during hot summer matinées! Happy times! Happy days!

Letty found herself singing 'I'll be your sweetheart', along with the rest of the deck-chair audience, who were providing a gentle, mesmerising chorus to the music from the theatre. When the song came to an end amidst gales of deck-chair applause, Mary asked, 'You really love Southend, don't you, Mum?'

'Oh yes!' Letty sighed happily. 'People often say places like this are common and vulgar. But not for Olly and me – oh no! We may not have much money in our pockets, but we can enjoy ourselves just being here.'

'But it's not the sort of place you'd want to actually live in, is it?'

'What!' Letty sat bolt upright. 'Give us half a chance! Olly and I always said we'd like to end our days down by the sea.'

Mary was really surprised. She got up from her deck chair, and threw her empty paper cup into a nearby litter bin. 'You mean, you'd leave Roden Street, give up London after all these years?'

Letty stared wistfully out to sea. Gulls were swooping down to the rolling waves below. 'There's nothing left for us in Roden Street now, Mary – not now the kids have gone. Anyway, London's not the same as it was in our day. Us old-timers feel we don't really belong there any more.'

The gulls were now shrieking madly at each other, as one of the anglers pulled in a catch. Letty and Mary leaned over the edge of the promenade, and saw a small, silver fish, struggling on the end of the angler's line. Letty couldn't bear to look. Ever since she was a child, she had hated angling, even though she knew it was a popular sport: She loathed the idea of the poor creature with its mouth stuck on a hook, and the pain it had to suffer before it was put out of its misery. Mary assured her that this one would soon recover, for the angler had found it too small, and thrown it back into the sea.

A few minutes later, they started to make their way back to the Pier Railway. On the way, they stopped to laugh with the other strollers at 'Jolly Jack the Sailor', a life-size carica-ture doll in a glass cabinet, which rolled from side to side, it's rip-roaring laugh bellowing through loud-speakers. Then Mary asked Letty quite casually what sort of place she'd like to live in if ever Pop won the football pools, and they did get the chance to move down to somewhere like Southend. Letty had no hesitation in answering: it would be on that new estate they'd seen just on the outskirts of the town – that bungalow on the corner, the one with the view down to the sea. Now *that* was really Letty's idea of absolute heaven. But then she laughed at the idea, knowing it was only another of her endless daydreams. At the train there was a queue stretching right out on to the Promenade, so Mary suggested they wait ten minutes or so for it to clear. Letty agreed and they strolled across, arm in arm, to the handrail on the other side of the Pier Promenade. On the sea below, they watched a small pleasure craft bobbing up and down on the waves, jammed tight with day-trippers. Through a loudspeaker, the skipper was rousing them all into a chorus of 'Oh I do like to be beside the sea-side'.

'Mum,' asked Mary, mainly out of curiosity. 'D'you *really* think you and Pop could settle down in a place like this? I mean, you'd be very isolated out here, away from all the people you know in London. It wouldn't be easy, starting a new life all over again at your age. You might get lonely.'

'Lonely? Me and Pop?' Letty decided to put on her cardigan, because an early evening chill was blowing up from the sea. 'It won't be long before Olly and I celebrate our Golden. Fifty years! Just think of it! How could I ever be lonely with someone I've loved practically all my life?'

'I know that, Mum,' said Mary, helping Letty on with her cardigan. 'I just don't like the idea of you getting bored, that's all.'

'Bored? Me? I tell you, I have so much to do, there are never enough hours in the day.'

Mary smiled to herself. She had to put on her sunglasses because the light reflected on the rolling white surf, below was dazzling her eyes. 'Well, I'm sorry, but over the next few months, I'm afraid you're going to have to find time. I shall need you to knit a few things for me.'

For a moment, Letty didn't catch on. She was busily doing up her buttons. 'Oh, I can't knit any more, dear. Not with this arthritis in my fingers.' She suddenly stopped, and looked up at Mary with a start. 'Knit things? *What* things?'

Mary was enjoying her moment. She had arranged the timing of it so carefully. 'Oh, one or two – baby's – woollies?'

Letty's blue eyes were sparkling more radiantly than they had ever done before. She couldn't speak. She couldn't breathe. All she could do was to throw her arms around Mary, and hug and hug her. The only thing she wanted to do now was to get back on that train, so that she could break the news to Olly. But there was no need.

In an overcrowded pub on the sea-front with Eddie and Mick, Oliver was already in high spirits. He was toasting his future grandchild.

The Pit didn't really deserve its name: in reality the ward was quite bright and airy. The worst part was, of course, the routine, which hardly changed from day to day. All the elderly patients were long-term 'residents', so they had to be woken every morning at some ungodly hour, washed, dressed, and helped into chairs. Those that were fit enough to have their breakfast at a table in the middle of the ward were helped there by the nursing staff. Others stayed in bed, and used special trays. For the rest of the day, meals were provided regularly: tea and biscuits at ten o'clock, midday meal at twelve, tea with sliced buttered bread and jam and biscuits or a cake at three-thirty, and a light supper, usually a cheese or sardine salad at five-thirty. Most residents retired to bed soon after supper, unless they hadn't been given their bath earlier in the day. Others, mainly the men, stayed up for a couple of hours, to watch the television. Sometimes, one of the die-hard women patients would sit up to join in the songs on 'The Good Old Days', the music hall programme which for some inexplicable reason was televised late in the evening, when most of its dedicated senior citizen fans were in bed. But generally by nine o'clock on most evenings, the geriatric ward was plunged into a chorus of deep snores, both male and female.

After spending six weeks in the Pit, Gran Edginton had given up all hope of leaving. The moment she got up each morning, she was made to swallow pills to calm her blood pressure. By the time she sat down to breakfast she had nothing to say to any of the other residents, and on most

387

occasions they had nothing to say to her. The rest of the day she either sat by the side of her bed, or in the Day Room, joining a circle of chairs, which were filled with silent, trembling men and women, most of whom seemed to be only just alive.

On her weekly visits, Letty found the Pit utterly depressing. There seemed to be no hope on anyone's dried-up face, and certainly no joy. Somehow, it didn't seem to be right that human beings should end their days like this. Surely there was something that one could do to make the end of a life at least tolerable? But what? Certainly, Letty had noticed that in so short a time Gran had lost all her fighting spirit. Like the others, she seemed to sleep most of the day, and when she woke up, it was only to be given a bath or be taken to the toilet. The only real treat came on Wednesday afternoons, when Letty visited. Sometimes Mick went along too, and once or twice Eddie and Mary. Letty also heard that her brother, Nicky, and his wife had been to see the old lady, but as they lived out in the country somewhere, the journey was obviously a great effort.

As usual, Gran was fast asleep in the Day Room when Letty arrived. She was sitting in her reserved chair, a blanket around her shoulders, head slumped forward on her chest, sucking her toothless gums. How she managed to sleep with the noise of a football match blaring away on the television set, Letty never knew.

'Mum. Wake up; it's me, Letty.' The old lady didn't budge, so Letty put down her shopping, and knelt on the floor in front of her. 'Wake up, dear.' She had to raise her voice above the football commentary. 'I've brought you some honeycomb from Southend.' The old lady still didn't respond, so Letty tapped her gently on the knee. 'Come on now, Mum. Wake up.'

'They took all my furniture . . .' Gran wasn't asleep at all.

But she still didn't raise her head. 'All my bits and pieces. My old piano.' She slowly raised herself, but her eyes were still closed. 'I'll never see it again.'

Letty felt shattered. She was fumbling for the right thing to say. 'Of course you will, Mum. I'll look after it for you 'til you're well enough.'

Gran's words were mumbled, and almost incoherent. 'My grandfather taught me to play on that piano. I was four years old.' Her eyes suddenly sprang open, and they seemed to stare straight through Letty. 'He had to put me on two cushions for me to reach the keyboard.'

It was only at this point that Letty realised that her mother was smelling heavily of urine. Clearly the poor old thing had had an accident in her sleep, and was sitting there in wet underclothes. Letty wanted to fetch a nurse, but her instinct told her that this was too delicate a moment for her to do so. 'I've brought you a present from Southend, Mum.' Letty dipped into her bag, and brought out the sweet honeycomb. 'It's your favourite.'

Gran looked at what Letty was holding out in her hand, but without seeming to focus on it. 'Southend. Cockles, mussels, fish and chips.' It was as though the old lady was speaking through a haze.

Letty decided to put the honeycomb in Gran's bedside locker later. 'I promise you, Mum,' she said tentatively, 'you're in good hands here. Everybody says this is the nicest ward in the hospital.' Gran just stared at her, without speaking. Somehow Letty knew that the old lady didn't believe one single word she was saying. It was awful to look into the eyes of this de-spirited old soul, who only a few weeks ago had been mistress in her own home. Now, her face was parched and yellow, the lines deeper and more numerous, and for the first time grey hairs were allowed to sprout freely from her frequently cropped hair.

Letty tried again. 'It'll take time, Mum. Once you get to know people, you'll be as cosy as if you were in your own home.'

There was a moment's pause, with both mother and daughter looking directly into each other's eyes. Then the old lady spoke. 'Home?' She turned away, and looked around some of the faces of her neighbours. Just like hers. Cold. Lifeless. Dead. Although Gran's mind was drifting in and out of reality, she was aware enough to know that this was not *her* home. It was a place where they took bets each night on which beds would be vacant by the morning. It was a place where people queued up for the graveyard. No. *Home* for Gran was now only a place she could see in her dreams.

'Well, at least you've got a nice telly you can watch.' Letty instantly hated the sound of her own voice. It sounded so bright and false.

On the other side of the room, there was crowd uproar on the television set, as someone scored a goal. This brought the first flicker of excitement from two of the old men.

For a sudden brief moment, Gran seemed to snap out of her twilight haze. 'Football! Football!' she roared, glaring at the armchair spectators. 'No horses!' Nobody took any notice of her, for they were used to her frequent bouts of anger.

Embarrassed by her mother's furious outburst, Letty quickly called over the nurse to tell her about her mother's 'accident'. Taking it all in her stride, the uniformed woman leaned over to the old lady and spoke to her in a loud, shrill schoolteacher's voice, as though Gran were a five-year-old. 'Come on now, Mrs Edginton. Shall we go and find you some nice clean undies, dear?'

Letty looked at her watch. She'd been there just twenty minutes. It seemed like two hours. 'Take care of yourself, Mum,' she said, as the nurse helped the old lady out of her chair. 'We're all thinking of you.' Then she kissed her on the cheek. 'Things'll be much better once you've made some nice friends.'

Gran didn't respond. But as the nurse led her away, Letty caught a quick glimpse of her mother's knowing eyes, which seemed to be looking straight through her again. They said so much. Before Letty left the Day Room, she turned just once more to wave and smile at the old lady. Gran only turned to look at her daughter, after she had gone. All she could see was an empty doorway.

A short time later, Gran had been changed, and was back in her usual chair at the side of her bed. The television football match had come to an end, so the Day Room at the end of the ward was mercifully silent once again. Bit by bit Gran's head cleared, and she found herself watching a baby robin, which had taken to tapping with its beak on the window pane beside her bed. It was such a small little chap, so cheeky and demanding. But at least it was free, and at the start of its life. What was it Letty had said? 'Things'll be much better once you've made some nice friends.' Friends. Gran grunted to herself, and sucked her gums. A friend was supposed to be someone you could confide in, someone you could talk to. That was something she hadn't had since William left her all those years ago. The only real friend she'd ever had was that bird on her window pane. It was her friend, because it understood her; it knew that she never meant it any harm. Everything was now churning over and over in her poor, tired brain. Even the people in the street. She remembered watching them from her window at Number 17. They always seemed to be going somewhere – but never to her. How many hours had she sat alone? How many days? So much time to think about the life she'd had, the good times – the bad times, the ups and downs, the people she'd met, and the people she never wanted to meet again. And she thought about the things she would have liked to put right, if only she'd had the chance. But it was too late for that now. She'd had all the chances she was ever likely to get. Oh, how she envied her Letty. At least *she* had friends who cared for her. But she deserved them. After all, you only get back what you give.

The robin tapped on the window pane just once more, then fluttered off up into the sky. Gran watched it go, and hoped it would come back to see her at the same time tomorrow.

Oliver had gone off to meet up with one of his old mates at Manor House Underground Station, so by the time Letty got back to number 13 Roden Street from the hospital it was she who found the telephone ringing in the passage outside. She had only just got used to the thing, even though it had been installed for nearly two years now.

Her telephone voice was rather formal, like an over-suspicious secretary. 'North 5208. Who is it, please?'

Within a few minutes, Letty was on her way back to the hospital. Soon after she left, Gran had apparently slumped forward in her chair at the side of her bed. Luckily, her favourite nurse had seen what had happened, and the ward sister had quickly called the doctor. Mrs Edginton had had a stroke, and was fighting for her life.

Mick was waiting for his mother when she arrived at the hospital. She immediately knew by the look on his face, that she was too late. The doctor assured Letty that it was the best thing for Mrs Edginton, for the stroke would have left her bed-ridden and paralysed for the rest of her life. Calmly, Letty asked to see her mother and, although Mick wanted to go with her, she insisted that this was something she had to do alone.

Gran hadn't yet been moved from her bed, which was

screened off from the rest of the ward. The sister held back the screen for Letty, and let her go in alone. Beatrice looked more peaceful than she had done for years. Memories flooded back to Letty, right back to her young days at 97 Arlington Square, when her mother hadn't been the old lady who was lying there now. She'd been Beatrice Edginton, proud and defiant, husband of William, and mother of Tom, Letty, and Nicky. Letty tried her best to think only of the good memories, not the bad ones. But it wasn't easy. So she leaned forward, whispered her farewell, and kissed her mother gently on the forehead. For one brief moment, Beatrice didn't look old at all. She looked young and beautiful and radiant. Which is how she had always wanted to be.

Beatrice Alice Edginton was buried in a communal grave in Finchley Cemetery. She was ninety-four years old. Long before she ever went into hospital, she had told Letty that when she died she didn't want to be buried in a grave all on her own. Furthermore, she threatened to come back and haunt her if she didn't carry out her last wish. Her last resting place was not all that far away from that of Sam Hobbs. Letty imagined that if the two of them should meet, they would have an awful lot to talk about.

Three months after Gran Edginton died, three large bulldozers moved in on Bedford Terrace. The site was needed, so the council said, for a new borough housing estate.

Chapter 31

The wistful sound of 'Love's Old Sweet Song' drifted along the pavements, where it was eventually drowned by the throbbing roar of the bulldozers tearing down the first block of houses in Bedford Terrace. Gran's ancient, upright piano had seen better days, but, despite its tin heart-strings, Mick still managed to coax a tune out of it. He had a soft spot for his grandmother's old piano. Every Sunday morning visit he'd made to Number 17 when he was a kid, the old lady had been waiting for him with a glass of ginger beer, and instructions to 'play a tune on the piano for your poor old Gran'. Mick was going to miss her. He didn't know why, because he knew what a fiend she'd been for a great deal of her life. But she was, after all, his grandmother, and every week she'd looked forward to his visits.

Letty didn't relish clearing out Gran's rooms: she'd put off the trauma of the task whilst Gran was still alive but she knew it now had to be done. She was only grateful that Mick was there to help her. The old lady had been dead for over a week now, and the local borough council wanted her possessions moved out as quickly as possible. It was easier said than done. Gran had been a lifelong hoarder, and her rooms were littered with photographs, ornaments that Letty and Mick had brought her back from holiday over the years, and enormous bundles of newspapers kept mainly for the horse-racing pages. The place was also filthy dirty. The gas stove was thick with grease, there were dishes that had piled up in the sink without being washed, heavy layers of dust everywhere, and cobwebs in every corner.

Letty was taking down the lace curtains, which should have been white, but were now a sickly cream colour. 'At least she died the way she always wanted to,' she was saying to Mick. 'Quick, without any fuss.'

'But not in her own home.' Mick was looking at a collection of framed photographs on the mantelpiece.

'How could she, Mick?' Letty rolled up the second set of curtains, and stuffed them into a black plastic sack. 'This place is nothing more than a slum.'

Mick turned round briefly to look at Gran's room, her home for the past forty-five years. 'It's all she had, Mum.'

Letty didn't reply, but Mick's remark clearly disturbed her. There was so much she should have done for the old lady, but just couldn't. Their relationship was always so complicated, so strained. Letty's emotions about her mother ran deep, but she didn't really know why. Obviously it had something to do with her childhood, the way Gran had treated her husband, and Tom. Maybe it was because she felt her mother had been jealous of her, which was probably the reason why the old lady never wanted Letty to do better in her life than she had done in her own. But whatever it was, at this precise moment Letty felt nothing but guilt and remorse. Inevitably, she was blaming herself for the old lady's death. During the past week she had told herself over and over again that if Gran hadn't been put into that geriatric ward, she would still be alive today. When she was in her own home Gran had felt independent, whatever her room looked like. But once she was taken away – six weeks! That's all it took for the old lady to give up the will to live. Live? Letty looked around Gran's room. Could the old lady *really* have been happy to live like this?

'Well, she certainly didn't give up her gambling instincts – right to the last!' Mick was smiling wryly, as he held up a copy of the *Racing Gazette*, complete with Gran's pen-marks, showing her 'favourites' at Newmarket. Letty looked at it, but her face just crumpled up with sadness. Mick put his arm around her. 'You've got nothing to blame yourself for, Mum. She was a good age, you know.' Letty smiled back at him gratefully, then quickly took the paper, and stuffed it into another plastic sack.

Mick left her for a moment, and went off through the archway door into Gran's tiny bedroom.

Letty started packing ornaments into a suitcase, which lay open on the table. 'If it was me,' she called, 'I'd do exactly the same thing.'

'You!' Mick called back from the bedroom. 'Bet on a horse?'

'I'm talking about if anything happened to Pop. I'd go straight into an Old People's Home. But I'd go willingly.'

Mick suddenly reappeared at the archway door. 'Mum! Don't ever let me hear you say such things! Eddie and I would never let you go into one of those places – never!'

'You wouldn't have any say in the matter. I'm over twenty-one you know. I can make my own decisions.' Letty suddenly became very busy, scurrying around the room to collect bits and pieces for the suitcase, intent on distracting Mick from what she had just said. 'Oh by the way, if you want this old gramophone, you'd better take it. Whatever we leave behind, the borough council will throw on the junk-heap.'

Mick watched her for a moment. This talk of Old People's Homes had disturbed him. He resolved to talk to Eddie about it at his first opportunity. But he knew how deter-mined his mother was. Once she'd got an idea fixed firmly in her mind, nothing would move it.

Letty started to collect the framed photographs. They

were all shapes and sizes, most of them of Letty and her younger brother Nicky when they were children. Letty was surprised that there were no photographs of her brother, Tom. Since the boy had been killed in action during the first war, the old lady seemed to have deliberately erased him from her mind. There was, however, a small oval picture of her father, William Edginton, although it had already faded quite considerably. As she sorted through the pictures Letty came across one snapshot that she decided to keep. It was of Gran on the beach at Boulogne, during their family day-visit to France. The old lady was sitting on a deck chair, eating an ice-cream cornet. Behind her, unbeknown to their grandmother, Eddie and Mick were making faces at the camera. As she looked at the photograph, Letty smiled. It gave her the feeling that, by keeping such a snapshot on her mantelpiece, her mother must have had more sense of humour than she was ever prepared to show.

'Mum!' Mick was calling from the bedroom. 'You'd better come and have a look at this.'

Letty packed the last of the photographs into the suitcase, and went off to join Mick.

He had rolled up Gran's bedclothes into a bundle on top of the mattress and in doing so, had uncovered several old cardboard boxes stuffed untidily beneath the bed. Letty checked through two or three of them: old chocolate boxes full of various brooches, bracelets, rings, and discarded National Health spectacles. It was obvious that the old lady had not retained anything of value from her former life in Arlington Square, for Letty also found quite a lot of old pawn-shop tickets for jewellery that had never been reclaimed. However, there were two boxes which did immediately fascinate her. One of them was full of Gran's private letters, including a huge wad from William, tied up with faded blue dress ribbon, and still smelling of perfume.

The other was a small black metal cash box, with a latch tied together with a piece of wire. But the intriguing thing was the label stuck on the lid, on which Gran had scribbled with a biro pen, 'My poor Tom'. Mick untangled the wire, opened the box, and gave it to Letty. The first thing she came across inside was a faded sepia snapshot of Tom, wearing his uniform as a Private in the Middlesex Regiment. She was at once moved to see again the young face of the brother she'd loved so much, and surprised to know that her mother had kept it. Even more astonishing was the fact that the box was full of momentoes of Tom when he was a little boy. There were brief, scribbled notes which he had clearly written at school, and even a couple of pencil sketches on pages from a note pad. One of them was a child's impression of Beatrice herself, with the words 'Love to Mother' scrawled across the bottom.

'So this is my Uncle Tom. Yes. I can see he's your brother. He's got the same smile.' Mick was looking at another photograph which he had taken out of the box. 'Who's the girl with him?'

Letty looked up with a start, and took the picture from him. It was a snapshot of Tom in uniform, clearly taken in France somewhere, in a cobbled town street. But with him was a pretty young girl, wearing what looked like a pinafore dress, and with long hair which hung down over her shoulders. Letty studied the photograph with intense fascination. Who was she? She turned to look at the back of the photograph, but it was competely blank. From the bottom of the box she suddenly brought out a large buff-coloured envelope, which had been folded in half. It was addressed to Mrs Edginton at Number 17 Bedford Terrace. Letty eagerly opened it, and found inside a typewritten letter, dated 14th September 1923, from the British Legion. It read:

Dear Mrs Edginton,
re: Pte Edginton, T 2079156 Dcsd
7th Middlesex Regiment
Further to our inquiry dated 5th August, 1923, we now have
pleasure in forwarding the enclosed letter from Mdme M
Edginton.
If you require any further information, please do not hesitate
to contact us.
Yours sincerely,
Peter Jackson (signed)
Bereaved Families Dept.

Letty immediately reached inside the envelope, and brought
out another, in faded blue with no stamp on it. To her
astonishment, she saw just one word scrawled on the outside, 'Letty'. Mick leaned over his mother's shoulder to look,
just as curious as she was. The envelope had already been
opened, so Letty carefully slid out the letter, and unfolded
it. The hand-written words had an unfamiliar, but rather
beautiful look to them.

Mick pressed closer. 'What does it say?'

Letty shook her head. 'I don't know. It's in French or
something.' Suddenly, her eyes widened with excitement, as
she looked to the bottom of the letter, and read out the
signature. 'Marguerite!'

Mick scratched his head. 'Who's that?'

'It was the French girl your Uncle told me about just
before he went away. He loved her very much.'

'Did they get married?'

'I have no idea.' Letty looked wistfully at the letter,
then handed it to Mick. 'Can you tell me what it says,
son?'

Mick took the letter, and looked at it. 'I'll have a go.'
Although French was one of Mick's best languages at school,
Marguerite's continental scrawl was not going to be easy

399

to decipher. So he had to work on it slowly, line by line, translating as he went.

'My dear friend, Letty,' he read. 'I don't know if this letter will ever reach you, but I hope so. It was such a little time that your brother Tom and I were together, but we loved each other so much. He talked about you, his little sister, almost every day. He had such love for you, too. So many things he told me about you, your brother Nicky and your mother and father. Why was your mother so cruel to you and Tom? Oh Letty, when Tom was killed, I wanted so many times to write to you, but I did not know how, or where to find you. So many times I wanted to tell you that Tom and I were husband and wife . . .' Mick stopped reading for a moment, and looked up at his mother. She was looking at the photograph of Tom and Marguerite, tears streaming down her face. Moved himself, Mick took a deep breath, and continued. 'Our son, Michel, was born on 14th February 1917 – Saint Valentine's Day. The name was chosen by Tom before he died. But I called him Michel Tom because he is so like his father – especially now he is growing up.

Please Letty, will you write to me? I want so much to meet you, to talk to you. Often I think of what Tom told me about you. He said that you were a very special person, and that you and me could be such good friends. You are my Tom's sister, and I am his wife. I want to be your friend, Letty. It has taken me so long to find you. I pray God this time I may succeed. I send you my great affection. Marguerite Edginton. It's addressed 6, rue des Armentières, Caen, France.'

When Mick finished reading the letter, a strange silence descended upon Gran's tiny, claustrophobic bedroom. Letty dabbed her eyes with her fingers, then Mick folded up Marguerite's letter, and handed it back to Letty. For a few moments, neither could speak. So many thoughts were going through their minds. So many questions. It was as though that handsome soldier and his young French wife in the photograph were actually right there, in the room with them.

But for Letty, the most difficult question of all was why, in all those years, she had never received Marguerite's letter.

One Saturday morning, some weeks later, Letty was on the phone to Tilly Brooks. Oliver always dreaded these endless round-ups of gossip between the two of them, for they usually led to an enormous phone bill. However, these days it was the only way the two women could speak to each other, for Bill was riddled with arthritis in his hands and knees, and found it an effort to make the journey into London. Oliver also didn't much like travelling for, now that Tilly and Bill were on their own, there was not always anyone available to meet them at the station. The two women missed their private gin and tonics and chin-wags together, especially since most of the kids had left home to get married. Letty knew only too well that Tilly had never really got over the loss of her son, Jeff, but she was glad that Pauline and Rita had turned out to be such loving, supportive daughters.

Most of this week's chat was about Marguerite Edginton. Soon after reading the undelivered letter addressed to her, Letty had been in contact with the British Legion, who had been making strenuous efforts to locate her French sister-in-law and family. However, all they had come up with so far was that Marguerite had moved in 1930 from the address shown in her letter, and they could not trace where she had gone to. They had now suggested that Letty make a trip to France, to see if the local authorities there could help. Tilly laughed at the idea of her old mate trying to make herself understood to a whole lot of 'Frogs'. But she was astonished when Letty told her she might just have a try. Finding Tom's wife had suddenly become a burning issue in her life, and she clearly wouldn't rest until she succeeded.

After she had finally finished her chat with Tilly, Letty returned to the back-parlour where Oliver was reading his newspaper for the umpteenth time. Letty started to clear the breakfast things from the table and, whilst scurrying back and forth between the scullery, she talked non-stop about her determination to find Marguerite. 'I wonder how much it would cost to go to France?' she called from the scullery. Then she came back to Oliver in the parlour. 'You know, Olly, we could probably do it on a day-trip. Shall I get Mick to find out for us?'

Oliver didn't look up from his paper. 'If you want.' It was a dour reply.

'Thing is, he'd have to come over with us. I mean, I wouldn't understand a word anyone says.' She piled up two cups and saucers on to some plates, and took them out. 'Marguerite must have been terribly upset when I didn't answer her letter. That's probably why she never tried to get in touch with me again.' She re-appeared in the scullery doorway. 'Or maybe she did. Maybe she wrote again, and Mother burnt it or something. What d'you think, Olly?'

Oliver grunted. 'I haven't the faintest idea.' His fingers were holding the edge of the newspaper so tightly, that the pages were crumpled. He had heard all this before, time and time again, and it was clearly irritating him to distraction.

Letty ignored him. She took it for granted that he wasn't really interested in anything that concerned the Edgintons, for he had never liked the old lady. But she persisted in her chatter. Coming back into the room, she sat down in her easy-chair opposite him. 'Olly. I would love to find Marguerite. After all, her son *is* my own flesh and blood. It's what Tom would want me to do, I know he would.'

To Letty's surprise, Oliver suddenly slammed the paper down on his lap. 'For Christ sake, Lett!' — He wasn't raising his voice, it was just tense and severe— 'Yer brother's dead! Yer can't bring people back from the grave!'

'Olly!'

'Well it's true! What's the point in harping back to the war? It's a long time ago.'

Letty was hurt, and perplexed. 'I'm not talking about the war, Olly. I'm talking about trying to bring the family together.'

'*Your* family – not mine.'

Letty was genuinely shocked. She was used to Oliver's indifference when it came to anything to do with the Edgintons, but she couldn't believe he was talking to her like this. 'If it was any of your side, Olly, I'd do the same thing – you know I would. I mean, you haven't seen your Vi for years. Suppose you suddenly got a letter from her and I never gave it to you. Wouldn't you want to find *her?*'

Oliver's reply was quick, and to the point. 'Never!'

'Olly! How could you!'

In one quick movement, he got up, and threw his newspaper back on to his chair. 'The past is over – gone! I never wanna to see my sister again as long as I live.'

Letty also got up from her chair. She was bewildered. 'Olly! How can you say such a thing?'

'Now you listen to me, Lett. It's not my fault your brother died.' There was a look of absolute torment in Oliver's eyes, as though he were trying to convince himself of something without believing it. 'It's not my fault that he left a widow behind. It happened to lots of my pals. *They* didn't come back neither. *They* left loved ones behind. But that's what war is all about. It's not my fault, I tell yer. It's that bleedin' war!' With tears swelling in his eyes, he quickly grabbed his coat from behind the door, and rushed out of the room.

'Olly!' Letty called after him. But when she heard the street door slam, she knew it would be unkind to follow him.

When Oliver didn't return for his midday meal, Letty began to worry. She quickly left the house, and hurried around the corner to his favourite pub, The Eaglet. She searched the public and saloon bars, but there was no sign of him. Furthermore, neither the landlord nor any of the regulars had seen him come in. Letty started to panic, and found herself practically running up the Seven Sisters Road, bumping into the Saturday shopping crowds as she went. By the time she tried The Enkel at the corner of Hertslet Road, and found Oliver hadn't been there either, she was practically beside herself with worry. Her first thought was to get back home and phone Mick. But when she got back to number 13, he was already there, bringing his weekly washing for Letty to iron.

Mick was shocked and puzzled to hear of his father's behaviour. Why should Pop want to prevent Letty from finding Uncle Tom's wife? Why, after all those years, did Pop still refuse to talk about his time in the trenches during the first war. Was he trying to hide something? And if so – what? And why? Mick was in no doubt that his father was going through some kind of crisis. Pop needed help, and had to be found as soon as possible, before something terrible happened to him. By four o'clock in the afternoon, Oliver had still not returned and so Mick said that they should go and make some inquiries about him at Hornsey Road police station.

Before doing that, however, Letty suggested that there was one place where Oliver might just be. And before they called in the police she insisted they try it.

*　　*　　*

404

The old railway footbridge in the middle of Finsbury Park was looking the worse for wear. It hadn't been repaired for years, not since Oliver used to bring Eddie and Mick up there to watch the trains, when they were kids. The iron railings were thick with rust, and the wooden tread-boards were starting to rot, so that every few yards there was a clear view to the railway line directly below. But Oliver still loved the place. It gave him such a nostalgic feeling, just standing there as the engines rushed by, obliterating the bridge from view. Not that there were too many steam engines around any more. These days it was diesel. The smell was different, uncivilised – like a paraffin stove! Soon it would all be electric. So clean, no smell, so modern. But no steam. No excitement! But the old footbridge remained a place where Oliver could escape from reality. His problems were still there, but whilst he was on that bridge, they could just drift around above the passing train engines.

'Hallo, Pop.'

Oliver turned with a start from the railings. Until now, he had been quite alone on the bridge. 'What are you doin' here, son?'

'I thought you'd like some company.'

Father and son stared at each other briefly. Then without saying a word, both turned to look out along the railway line.

Mick smiled affectionately at the track below. 'Been a long time since I came here. It's like coming back to visit an old friend.' Oliver didn't answer. So Mick continued talking, without looking at him. 'Mum's worried about you, Pop. What happened?'

Oliver hesitated before replying. 'I felt like a walk – that's all.'

'That's not what I meant.' Mick turned to look at his father. 'I'm talking about what happened in the war – *your* war. In the trenches.'

Oliver turned, and snapped back. 'The war! The war! It's over! Gone! Forgotten! Why does everyone have to keep askin' questions about the bleedin' war!'

'I don't know. Maybe it's because we feel ashamed or something.'

'Bein' ashamed won't bring back the men you left behind. It won't bring back the men you shot down in cold blood.'

A cold shiver ran up and down Mick's spine. This was the first time he'd realised that his own father could have actually taken someone's life. But then, so did thousands of other fathers, husbands, boyfriends, or lovers. On the battlefield you kill or you are killed. Nevertheless, it was an odd feeling for Mick to know that all his life he had lived under the same roof as someone who had deprived a man, or maybe many men, of life. 'You know, Pop, you have no need to feel guilty. What you did during the war, you had to do. It was your duty.'

'Duty!' Oliver grunted dismissively. 'Is it your duty to send one of your own blokes to face a Jerry machine-gun? Is it your duty to send a man to his death, a man who meant more to your own wife than anyone else in the world. It should have been me, I tell you – me!'

Mick was stunned into silence. All he could do was to watch his father as he quickly took out a fag and lit it, the tears beginning to seep from the corners of his eyes. Mick was only too aware that this was probably one of the most critical moments in his father's life. For the first time, the old soldier was thinking aloud about what had happened all those years ago. For these few moments, every fibre in Pop's body was exposed. One word out of place, and his mind could collapse like a pack of cards. Slowly, and gradually, without any pressure from Mick, Pop began to talk. Everything came out, the full horror of his brief time in the trenches. The relentless rain, the mud, the bully-beef rations, the mice and rats running over their legs. The hours of silence, of waiting, and of deafening heavy artillery gunfire. The smell of death, of blood, severed limbs, and the cries of the injured, the pleas to the Almighty for mercy. And finally, the meeting with Tom Edginton. That brief, unexpected, one and only meeting with his own future brother-in-law. The tossing of a coin. Over the top. Machine-gun fire. Death. By the time he had finished his fag, Pop was staring at Mick as though he couldn't see him. He was ashen-faced, and could only say again, 'It should have been me. That coin was meant for me.'

Mick felt as though his legs would give way beneath him. He moved forward to his father, and threw his arms around him. 'It's all over now, Pop,' he whispered quietly. 'Let's go home.'

Pop was in tears. 'I can't tell your mother, Mick. It would hurt her. I won't do it. I'll never tell her. I love her too much. It's all wrong, I tell yer. Don't you understand? It should have been me.'

Mick shook his head, and held his father close. 'No, Pop. That's not how it was meant to be. Never forget that.' He pulled away, and gave him his own handkerchief to wipe his eyes on, and blow his nose.

A few moments later, father and son left the old footbridge. As usual, Oliver walked without any sign of a limp. It was hard to believe that he had ever fought in a war.

Letty was peering out anxiously through the window of the front-parlour, when she suddenly caught sight of Oliver and Mick just turning around the corner from Pakeman Street. She quickly rushed out to the street door to greet them. Mick decided to leave them together as soon as possible, so he kissed his mother, then left immediately. Letty could see that Oliver had been crying, for his eyes were still very red. But she made no mention of it: it was the last

407

thing Oliver would have wanted. Without saying anything, she just hugged him, led him into the back-parlour, and helped him take off his jacket. She told him that she'd saved his dinner for him, and she would heat it up right away. But he asked her to sit down for a moment.

'I've got somethin' to say to you, Lett,' he said. And then he told her.

Chapter 32

The 1960s had brought a fair share of excitement and tragedy to the world. The Russians put the first man into space, in the United States President Kennedy was gunned down, the Beatles exploded on the pop music scene, there was a bloody war in Vietnam, and in 1965 Britain and the world mourned the passing of Winston Churchill.

For Letty and Oliver, the arrival of Jonathan Adam Hobbs in their lives brought them the greatest possible joy. On the day he was born, they had been more anxious than if it had been their own child. The first moment Letty held the baby in her arms, she pronounced he looked like his mother. Mary disagreed. She thought he was a Hobbs if ever she saw one. When Eddie held the baby, he said that it couldn't possibly grow up to be as handsome as him. Jonathan's response to that was to give him the wet lap he deserved. As he got older, both Eddie and Mary thought Jonathan resembled photographs of his Uncle Mick at that age. But whoever he reminded anyone of, Jonathan had certainly inherited one obvious characteristic of the Hobbs side – the Roman nose!

The birth of Jonathan Hobbs was not the only event of note in the second half of the decade, what with the assassination of the South African Prime Minister, a six day Arab-Israeli war in the Middle East, the first human heart transplant, and, almost as important, Letty and Oliver's Golden Wedding.

On Saturday, 3rd August 1968, absolute pandemonium descended on Number 13 Roden Street. Although Letty and Oliver's fiftieth anniversary wasn't officially until the following day, the post was bulging with cards and letters, and the North 5208 telephone number in the passage never stopped ringing. During the morning, bouquets of flowers seemed to be arriving every few minutes, which prompted Oliver to remark that the place was 'lookin' more like a funeral parlour'. One or two of the old, long-time neighbours popped in for a cup of tea, and even the Greek-Cypriot couple from Number 11 next door, called 'Happy Anniversary' over the back garden wall. Letty didn't know herself. All this attention was more than she had ever dreamt of, and she was only grateful that God had allowed her and Olly to reach this day.

The preparation for the 'Golden' had, of course, started weeks before the big day. Mick had decided that, as his mother had not been able to afford a traditional wedding dress when she was married, he would buy her an evening dress for the special outing that he, Eddie, and Mary were planning for the Saturday evening. At first, Letty was embarrassed by the idea. She had never had an evening dress in her entire life and was sure, she said, she would look like 'mutton dressed up as lamb'. But when Mick took her along to Selfridges in Oxford Street, she found a dress she absolutely fell in love with at once, all organza, silk, and lace, and in one of her favourite colours – midnight blue. Pop was not allowed to see Letty's dress until *the* day, but he never stopped teasing her about dressing herself up to look like the Queen Mum. But Pop's laughter soon faded when Mick told him that, as they would be going to a West End show, followed by a meal at a very smart London restaurant, he would have to hire himself a dinner suit for the evening. As the great day approached, Letty and Oliver lay in bed at night, rocking with laughter at the prospect of them both dressed up to the nines. But beneath the laughter Oliver was unnerved by the whole thing: people in their class of life shouldn't go around acting up like Dukes and Duchesses. But Letty insisted that if the kids were taking the trouble to celebrate their mum and dad's anniversary, the least they could do was to appreciate it, and grudgingly Olly agreed.

At about five-thirty on the Saturday evening, Mick arrived at Number 13 to discover that his mother had locked herself away in the bedroom for about two hours, getting herself ready for her special evening out. Pop was banished to the front-parlour downstairs, and when Mick arrived, he was cursing the black bow tie which he had been wrestling with for over half-an-hour. But Mick succeeded in tying it for him and by the time he was fully dressed, and looking at himself in the mirror, Pop didn't recognise what he saw. If only his old mates in the 'Shiney Seventh' from his Army days could see him now! Before Mum appeared, Mick handed over the present Pop had asked him to get for her, a small packet which Mick had wrapped in gold paper. It was about six o'clock when Letty finally came down the stairs. When Oliver saw her, he couldn't believe his eyes. She looked just like Audrey Hepburn in 'My Fair Lady', only better. Eddie had paid for her to have a perm at her local hairdressers, and the dress fitted like a dream. And when she saw Oliver, Letty's eyes lit up with sheer love: he was even more handsome than her favourite film star, Spencer Tracey.

Before they left the house, Mick told his mother that Pop had something he wanted to say to her. Leading Letty into the back-parlour, Oliver reached into his jacket pocket and took out the small, gold-wrapped packet. 'Happy Anniversary, Lett,' he said shyly, handing it to her. 'It's been a long time coming out of pawn, but better late than never.'

Letty was taken aback. She took the packet, and slowly,

methodically, undid the gold wrapping. Inside was a smart jewellery box. Letty excitedly lifted the lid, and gasped. It was a small, but delicate gold brooch, in the shape of a heart, embedded with an array of different coloured stones, not expensive, but exceptionally pretty. Letty immediately looked at Mick.

'It was nothing to do with me,' said Mick, quickly. 'It was all Pop's idea.'

Letty turned to Oliver, and stared straight into his eyes. She knew only too well what he had done. He had remembered the small, valuable brooch her mother and father had given her when she was sixteen years old, the brooch she had pawned when she and Olly were close to being evicted by Mr Cotton from their room in Citizen Road, all those years ago at the end of the first war.

'Well, go on then, Pop!' Mick suddenly felt he was an intruder, for he could see his mother and father were sharing a very private moment with each other. 'Pin it on for her.'

Letty gave Oliver the brooch, and he pinned it on her dress. Then she threw her arms around him, and kissed him. 'Thank you, dear. Thank you – for everything.'

A few minutes later, 'Audrey Hepburn' and 'Spencer Tracey' were on their way in Mick's car for their special evening out. Although he only drove an old Ford Anglia, Mick insisted that he act as chauffeur, so he put both his mother and father in the back seat. As they left Roden Street, Letty made quite sure all the neighbours could see her, and when they did, she smiled and gave a gracious royal wave.

Ten minutes later Letty and Oliver began to grow puzzled, for the car was heading not towards the West End, but in the direction of Edmonton, in North London. They finally pulled into the courtyard of a rather grand looking building called The Cambridge Hotel, just off the North Circular Road.

'What's this place then?' Oliver looked very suspicious, as he let Mick help him out of the car.

'We're just stopping off to collect Eddie and Mary. We thought you'd like a quick drink before we all go off to the theatre.'

Letty was more uneasy than suspicious. 'Looks a bit posh, son. Are you sure this is the right place?'

Mick helped her out of the car, then slammed the car door. 'Of course it's the right place. Now stop looking so nervous, you two!'

After locking the car, Mick led the way into the front entrance of the hotel. Letty held on to Oliver's arm tightly as she went in, and became even more uneasy when she saw that there were very few people around.

The lobby was rather large and plush, with extravagant Persian carpets, and a huge chandelier. There were two people on the reception desk, a young man and a young woman. Both of them swung a quick, intimate glance at Mick, then carried on with their work.

'I don't see Eddie or Mary anyway,' said Letty, anxiously looking around the deserted lobby. 'Are you *sure* this is right, Mick?'

'I said we'd meet them in the bar. This way.' Mick led them across towards a huge pair of unmarked doors. When they got there, he stopped, and turned back to them. 'Right both of you. Take a deep breath.'

Letty exchanged an anxious look with Oliver, and squeezed his arm even tighter. What was going on?

Mick raised his hand, and thumped on the doors three times. As he did so, they were opened from inside with a great flourish.

Letty and Oliver gasped, for as the doors opened, to their absolute astonishment there came from inside the most tumultuous sound of cheering, applause, and whistles.

Then, Eddie and Mary stepped forward.

'Happy Anniversary, Mum!' Eddie threw his arms around his mother, and hugged her. Then he did the same to his father. 'Happy Anniversary, Pop!'

Letty was too overwhelmed to speak. All she could say was, 'Oh, Eddie! And Mary!'

Mary was there immediately, hugging and kissing first Letty, then Oliver. 'Happy Golden, both of you!'

Suddenly, from inside the room, somebody started to sing, 'For they are jolly good fellows'. Then a whole crowd of people joined in, and as Letty and Oliver passed through the doors, they found themselves inside a vast ballroom, with a sea of familiar faces waiting to greet them. Over a hundred and fifty relations, friends, and old neighbours were there, all flanking their path into the room. For Letty and Oliver, it was breathtaking to see everyone around them in beautiful evening dresses and suits, singing, clapping, smiling, all wishing them on. Oliver found it all too much, and his face crumpled up into tears immediately. But Letty was determined not to let her kids down, and, holding tightly on to Oliver's arm, and with her head held high, she practically marched them both through the lines of guests, and straight into the vast room, which was laid out with dining-tables, all covered with bright white table-cloths. On the way, Tilly Brooks, tears streaming down her cheeks, rushed forward to kiss and hug her old mate. So did Bill Brooks, momentarily forgetting all about his arthritic fingers and knees. Alice and Ted Cole were there. Then there were dear old Winnie and Bert Bracknell from Number 9; the school caretaker, Mr Mitchinson and his wife; Mary's father and her two brothers, and dozens more. By the time Letty and Oliver reached the centre of the room, Letty's favourite adopted niece from the Brooks family, young Pauline, was waiting to welcome her with a huge bouquet of joyful summer flowers, and a hug that was as warm and affectionate as the hot August evening. After a huge cheer from everyone in the room, an amateur three-piece band struck up from a small, nearby stage, which immediately prompted a massed chorus of 'You Were Meant For Me'.

It took Letty and Oliver a long time to take in what was happening. Only when they got into conversation with Tilly and Bill did they hear how, for the past few months, Mick, Eddie, and Mary had been preparing the surprise Golden Wedding celebration. Letty was so excited as she fluttered from one guest to another, feeling like a hostess at a Society Ball. There were so many people to talk to, some of whom she had met only briefly before. It was thrilling for her to see Eddie and Mary's friends mixing so happily with Mick's friends, many of whom were actors and actresses, or producers and directors from radio and television. It was music to Letty's ears to hear everyone laughing and joking in small groups together. And when she and Oliver were taken to a long table, overflowing with gifts, she had to bite her lip firmly to make sure she didn't cry. The centrepiece of the gifts on display was from Eddie and Mary – an upright vacuum-cleaner, wrapped up with gold paper and ribbons. Now Letty had got a vacuum-cleaner, she wouldn't need a broom to wallop Olly with any more! yelled one of the guests and a few minutes later, a bright- eyed young reporter from the *Islington Gazette* came to talk to both of them, telling them that he always got the job of covering anniversaries, weddings, and funerals. Oliver caused a laugh when he assured the reporter that he wasn't quite ready for his box just yet! After they had finished having their photograph taken, Letty told the journalist how proud she was of her boys. She boasted about everything – Eddie, with his own newspaper shop in Enfield, and Mick, who was now writing plays for the radio and television full-time. The only sad

415

moment was when the reporter asked Letty about her third son, Ron. Letty's reply was evasive. All she could say was that, much to her great regret, she didn't see much of her eldest son and his family these days.

'Ladies and gentlemen. Please be seated!'

The head waiter's announcement brought everyone bustling around the dining-tables, looking for their own individual name-card. Eddie, Mary and Mick had deliberately mixed the guests, so that all of them would have a chance to get to know each other. It turned out to be more successful than they dared hope, for within a few minutes the ballroom was ringing with the sound of chatter and laughter. Letty and Oliver, were, of course, Guests-of-Honour at the long top table, which Mary and Pauline had beautifully decorated with flowers and a large golden horseshoe. Mick sat beside his mother, and Eddie and Mary beside Pop. The only other guests at their table were Tilly and Bill Brooks, and Pauline. Letty had to put on her spectacles to read the menu. The cover had gold lettering on it, and read, 'LETTY and OLIVER. 50 GOLDEN YEARS'. And the menu itself had all the things that both Letty and Oliver loved the most: Minestrone soup, Roast Beef and Yorkshire Pudding, followed by Lemon Meringue Tart, and a cheese board. When Letty read out the menu to Oliver, quietly, into his only good ear, he was greatly relieved to know that it did not contain any of Mick's threatened snails and frogs' legs!

And so dinner began. As the sipping of minestrone soup hissed across the ballroom, the air was also filled with the buzzing of chat, and the occasional excited yells from some of the guests' children. From time to time, Letty looked out at them all. She just felt so happy, almost as though she were dreaming. She had her boys with her, and Mary, and her dearest mates Tilly and Bill and Pauline. She had all those people out there, in their fine dresses and suits, who had come together for one evening just for them, Letty and Oliver. So many different faces. So many different personalities. But all with smiles on their face. It was amazing, she thought. A supreme act of friendship. A genuine show of affection. But most of all, Letty had the one person at her side, who meant more to her than anyone else in the whole wide world. She turned to look at him, Oliver Jubilee Hobbs. What a name! Oliver had always cringed with embarrassment at both the names his mother and father had given him, 'Oliver' – after Oliver Cromwell's statue in Parliament Square, and 'Jubilee' after Queen Victoria's Diamond Jubilee, which took place in the year of his birth. If anyone asked, he always insisted to Letty, she was to tell them that his middle name was 'John'. As she watched him enjoying his soup, Letty chuckled to herself. How she loved her 'Jubilee'. Yes, everything was perfect for her, thought Letty, as her eyes constantly roamed the happy faces around the dining-tables. There was nothing, absolutely nothing more that she could have hoped for. Or was there? For one brief moment, she felt a strange emptiness in her stomach. Something – someone *was* missing out there. Oh, if only Ron could have been one of the faces at those tables. No matter what had happened, she could never forget that she and Olly had three sons, not two. Eddie and Mick had no need to explain why they hadn't invited their elder brother and his family to the 'Golden'. Ron had his own reasons for not wanting to keep in contact with his parents. He had his own reasons for being resentful of his two brothers. The divisions were too strong. As in so many other families, the inexplicable barrier of hate could not be broken down. Of Oliver's Vi, there was no sign either, but then that was only to be expected nowadays.

By the time the cheese boards had been demolished, most

417

of the guests were in fairly high spirits, and exchanging bawdy comments with Oliver about having a second honeymoon. But just when Letty thought everything was over, a great cheer from everybody heralded the arrival of a huge, double-decker wedding cake, piped in white and gold icing, with 'Letty loves Oliver loves Letty' inscribed on top. It took Letty's breath away, and when she and Oliver stood up to cut the cake, the whole ballroom erupted into loud, sustained applause and cheering. After posing for everyone to take photographs, Letty called out that she felt like a newlywed, which prompted more bawdy remarks from Bill Brooks and some of the men guests.

Then the wine glasses were put to one side, and a team of waitresses came round with clean ones, into which they poured champagne. Once that little task was complete, Mick got up from his seat beside Letty, and thumped the table. Apart from one or two of the kids laughing and playing together at the back of the ballroom, everyone suddenly went quiet.

'Ladies and gentlemen.' Mick looked so stern, some people thought he was going to make some earth-shattering announcement. 'First of all, on behalf of Eddie, Mary and myself, I want to thank you all for joining us on this very special evening for Mum and Pop.'

Letty agreed, with a loud 'Hear! Hear!' But when Oliver didn't join her, she nudged him in the ribs, and to laughter from the guests, he said likewise.

For the rest of his speech, Mick flicked his attention back and forth between the guests, and his parents. 'You know, to me, it seems an incredible achievement that two people can not only live together for fifty years, but still be on speaking terms with each other!'

'Me and my old woman ain't been on speakin' terms since the day we married!' yelled Bill Brooks, who received a whack on the head from Tilly for his cheek.

Mick waited for the rumpus to die down, then continued. 'People often ask me what's so special about my mother and father, why I'm so proud when I talk about them. Well, *they* would tell you that they're just two ordinary people like anyone else. And so they are. Let's face it, to all of us here tonight, Letty and Oliver are just simply – Mum and Pop.'

This brought affectionate calls of 'Hear! Hear!' from the guests, during which Letty squeezed Olly's hand under the table.

'They are typical of so many mums and dads, who want nothing for themselves, only for their kids. And, as most of you here tonight know Letty and Oliver as "Mum and Pop", I'm sure you'll agree that includes all of you too.'

This brought thunderous applause and sustained cheering from the guests. Letty and Oliver looked at each other in astonishment. Neither of them could identify themselves as the same people Mick was talking about.

Mick tried to raise his voice above the applause, but decided it was best to let it fade before continuing. For the rest of his speech, he turned to look at his mother and father, speaking directly to them. 'Mum and Pop. You've often told us that on the day you were married, you didn't have the money to buy three things that most newly-weds these days would expect to have. Well, I think we can say that tonight you've at last got all those three things – the wedding dress, the horseshoe, and, even though it's been baking in the oven for fifty years – the wedding cake!

Once again, the guests broke out into wild applause, cheers, and laughter, leaving Pop to raise one of his thumbs up at Mick in agreement. 'Dinky-Dink!' he called, with a cheeky wink at Letty.

'But, Mum and Pop,' continued Mick, now sounding more and more like a comedian's impression of an after-dinner

419

speaker, 'this evening we have just one extra thing that we'd like to add to that collection . . .'

There was an immediate buzz of speculation from the guests. Letty shot a puzzled glance at Oliver, then turned back to Mick again.

'As most of you know, Mum and Pop have been living in good old 13 Roden Street since soon after they were married. Number 13 turned out to be a lucky number, because it's been a happy house for all the family. But – like all good things – there comes a time for change, a breath of fresh air. So, Mum and Pop, Eddie and I got together, and we bought you both a rather special extra Golden Wedding present.' From his inside jacket pocket he took out an envelope, which he gave to Letty.

She took the envelope, and looked at it suspiciously. 'What is it?'

'Open it, and have a look.'

The mystery sent more waves of excited speculation around the room.

Letty put on her spectacles, and ripped open the envelope. She tipped out three yale keys on to her hand. 'Keys?' She was still baffled.

Mick smiled, and exchanged a quick, knowing look with Eddie, who was sitting at the side of Pop. 'D'you both remember that little bungalow we once saw near the sea down at Southend? It was the one you liked so much, on top of the hill, on the corner. When we saw it, they'd only just started building the estate. Well, they've finished it now. Those are the keys of that bungalow – number 12 Sea View Drive. It's *your* bungalow now.'

There were gasps from Letty and Oliver, and then the guests, who suddenly erupted into wild applause.

When it was quiet enough, Mick continued, sounding more and more like Eamonn Andrews on 'This is your life'.

'We've given your new home the name you always wanted, "Rendezvous" and, when you're ready, she's just waiting for you to move in.'

Letty and Oliver stared at the keys in Letty's hand as though they were magic.

'And so, Mum and Pop. On behalf of Eddie, Mary, and myself – and everyone here tonight, we'd like to offer you our congratulations, our admiration, and our love.' Then Mick picked up his glass of champagne, despite the fact that he didn't drink alcohol. Turning to the guests in the ballroom, he called, 'Ladies and gentlemen. May I ask you to join us in a toast.'

This immediately prompted everyone to pick up their glasses, and rise from their seats. Letty and Oliver wanted to do likewise, but Eddie told them to remain seated.

Holding his glass up high, Mick called, 'Happy Anniversary – Letty and Oliver. Happy Anniversary – Mum and Pop!'

Everyone in the room roared back, including the kids playing at the back of the room. 'Mum and Pop!' Then they sipped or gulped down their champagne, all enjoying the occasion. Letty and Oliver sat there, utterly bewildered, not knowing what had hit them. Finally Oliver dissolved into tears, while Mary teased him that she had never known anyone who could turn the waterworks on so quickly. Further along the table, Tilly Brooks was also in tears, a sure sign she was happy! Then pandemonium broke out in the room, for the guests were thumping their tables, someone called for three cheers, and when they came, even the rather snooty head waiter and his smiling waitresses joined in. In the middle of it all, some of the more rowdy elements bawled out to Oliver to make a speech which soon became a general chorus of 'Speech! Speech!' Oliver's tears immediately dried up, for he was suddenly chilled with terror by such a suggestion. Over and over again, he shook his head, and waved his hands, until finally Letty had to come to his rescue.

'Oh goodness!' said Letty, rising anxiously from her seat. 'What *am* I going to say?'

This brought affectionate laughter from the guests, and a guilty look from Oliver.

Letty was still looking with incredulity at the set of keys in the palm of her hand. 'A bungalow by the sea! A place of our own – our very own – for the first time in our lives! Oh my goodness! Who said dreams don't come true?'

There was gentle laughter from everyone, but then, for the first time, a strange silence descended upon the room. Letty looked out at the sea of faces watching her. She found it difficult to understand why they'd all shown such affection for them both. After all, she thought, she and Olly hadn't done anything special. Of course, they *had* been married for fifty years. But so had a lot of people. And not all of them had the chance to have a do like this. In those few seconds before she started to speak, so much danced across Letty's mind. She thought of all the people who had meant so much to her during her life with Olly, and who'd gone now. She felt she could almost see some of them, sitting at the tables amongst the other guests, with warm, fixed smiles just like anyone else. There was her mother, Beatrice – poor old Gran, such a complicated, unhappy soul, whose own life was so insular and tortured. And her father, William, who had so wanted a long, happy married life like Letty's. Then there were Olly's mum and dad, old Annie and Ernie Hobbs. And Sam. Dear, honest, caring Sam. Letty knew *he* was there, because she could visualise him, laughing proudly at all the attention his brother and sister-in-law were getting. And what about Tom? Her own brother? Oh, he was there all right, smiling lovingly just like everyone else. But how sad that his Marguerite and her son knew nothing about all this, for despite Letty's latest efforts, this time with Ollie's support, Tom's French wife had not been traced.

Letty's suddenly pulled herself out of her brief daydream. All those faces were waiting for her to say something. 'Oh, its so good of you all to come here to be with Olly and me tonight,' she said, eventually. 'I remember my poor old mother telling me just before she died, "Letty," she said, "You're lucky to have friends who care for you." ' Letty looked around the room, and sighed. 'She was right. We *are* lucky.'

She turned briefly to Oliver, who again raised his thumb in agreement, with a 'Dinky-Dink'.

'Having you all here with us tonight is *the* most wonderful thing. Family and friends mean so much to us. Without you – well, I don't know what we'd do. Mind you, when you come to think of it, our family's no different to any other, really. We all do much the same things, like getting up in the morning, going to work, coming home and having tea, watching telly, going to bed. To some people, that might sound, well – dull. Maybe it is, I don't know. But not to me. Since I married Olly, every day has been different – sometimes good, sometimes bad – but always different. That's the way I look at it anyway.' She paused a moment, to smile at a child who had fallen asleep in his mother's arms at one of the tables. 'But I tell you this,' she continued, 'neither Olly nor me ever dreamt we'd live to see this day. Fifty years!' She turned to Oliver again. 'Doesn't seem possible, does it, dear?'

Oliver, who seemed to be staring mesmerised at the tablecloth, shook his head.

'But then, we never dreamt we'd be lucky enough to have kids who'd care for us, and love us, as much as we love them. Eddie and Mick have been two sons anyone would be proud of.'

423

There was a murmur of agreement from the guests, leaving Eddie and Mick looking embarrassed.

Letty looked out at the room, and somehow felt that there was one more face she could picture there. 'Of course, I can't deny how sad we are not to have all our three boys with us here tonight. Sad, because Olly and I have always loved them – all three of them. We've never made flesh of one and fowl of another. But then – well, I suppose every family has its problems.'

By now, it was so silent in the room, you could hear a pin drop. One of Mick's friends, a young actress, was listening so intently, the ash on her cigarette dropped on to the table-cloth without notice.

The champagne had made Letty's mouth a little dry, so she quickly picked up a glass of water, and sipped some of it. 'Anyway, it's been a good life. Not easy mind you – oh, no. We've had our ups and downs, just like anyone else. But it's been worth it.' She turned to Oliver with an affectionate smile. 'Worth every moment of it. I never wanted anyone but Olly, and as far as *I* know, he never wanted anyone but me.' Then she added with a chuckle, 'At least I *hope* he didn't!'

The silence was finally broken, as everyone laughed, and jeered at Oliver, who guiltily covered his face with his hands, then grinned back mischievously at Letty.

Once again, Letty looked at the set of keys in the palm of her hand, and a huge lump rose in her throat. But she quickly took a deep breath, looked back at everyone around her, and said firmly, 'Anyway – I can't really say much more, because if I do, I shall make a fool of myself. It's hard for me to tell you just how Olly and I are feeling right now. You've all been so – kind and wonderful.' She swallowed hard to get rid of that lump in her throat. 'But before I finish, there's one thing I'd like to say to you – Eddie and Mick.'

Eddie and Mick both looked up at her.

'Years ago, when you were both at school, I remember someone in the street tried to give me a lecture on how I ought to bring up my children. I replied, "Don't talk to me about kids, I've had three of my own!" All I want to say to you both is – thank God we did!'

Letty sat down, to thunderous shouts of 'Good old Letty! Well done, girl!'

A few minutes later, the dining-tables were cleared, and the three-piece band started playing. It seemed that practically everyone took to the dance floor, apart from Mick, who felt far too self-conscious. Regardless of dinner suits and evening dresses, 'Knees up Mother Brown' was not forgotten, nor was the hokey-cokey or the 'Paul Jones'. Eddie succeeded in getting to the microphone for another song, but the jeering and catcalls ensured that the pain he was inflicting was somewhat muted. The evening ended with Letty and Oliver dancing to the 'Anniversary Waltz'. For several minutes, everyone kept off the floor and just watched them, all humming and swaying together in time to the music. When everyone joined them, the band were quite happy to play the same song more times than they had ever known. Letty leaned her head on Oliver's shoulder, and they both closed their eyes, swaying to the music – *their* music – in absolute oblivion.

This had been an evening that the two seventy-year-olds would never forget.

Chapter 33

A few days before Letty and Oliver were to move from Number 13 Roden Street, Letty was invited to have afternoon tea with the teaching staff at Pakeman Street School. She hated the thought of having to say goodbye to all the teachers and pupils, for in one way or another, she had been associated with the school for the best part of fifty years, first as a cleaner, then as Mrs Hobby the milk lady.

At exactly ten minutes to three in the afternoon, Letty left Number 13, to walk across the road to the school. She was wearing her favourite blue felt hat, matching cotton dress and cardigan, and she smelt of fresh eau de Cologne. It was a lovely early September day, and Letty watched the rows of sparrows and pigeons which had settled on the high school wall to preen in the warm afternoon sun. She opened the school gate, but was surprised to find nobody around, for at this time of day during the nice weather, Miss Buchanan the PT teacher usually took her classes in the playground. A few minutes later, she was climbing the worn stone steps inside the building, which led up to the staff-room on the first floor. Apart from the echo of her own footsteps, she was puzzled by the almost total silence throughout the school, which was usually alive with the sounds of children. She was a little puffed by the time she actually reached the staff-room, and was relieved to find Miss Wainright waiting to meet her. A tall, well-built woman in her fifties, who taught English and loved ballet, Miss Wainright was Letty's favourite teacher at the school. The two of them had become firm friends over the years, and Letty had often given her motherly advice whenever she had a problem. But she was taken aback to be told that before they had tea, Miss Neville, the headmistress, would like to see her. Miss Wainright took hold of Letty's arm, and led the way upstairs to the older children's Assembly Hall on the top floor; Letty had to take it slowly, for she was getting bad arthritis in her knees these days, and climbing stairs was quite an effort.

On the top-floor landing, Letty had to pause to get her breath back. It was only then that she discovered the reason for the unnatural silence throughout the building. As Miss Wainright opened the Hall doors for Letty to enter, there was a great roar of children's voices, cheering so loudly that the walls of the entire school seemed to vibrate. Letty stopped dead in her tracks, and looked around the Hall. Every pupil from the entire school was gathered there and on the platform Miss Neville was waiting to greet her, together with all her teaching staff.

During the next hour, Letty was dazzled by all the fuss and affection shown her. Miss Neville made a speech about how sad Pakeman Street School was to be losing their dear, loyal, hard-working friend, Mrs Hobbs. One fourth-form boy played 'La Golondrina' on the piano; the girls of the fifth form, rehearsed by Miss Wainright, danced an excerpt from 'The Nutcracker Suite', and another small boy from the third form read a composition, written by Mick Hobbs when he was the same age, all about spending his birthday in the air-raid shelter during the war. The highlight of the after-noon was a presentation to Letty of a huge painting of the school, drawn and painted by over a hundred pupils of all ages. All its forefront was the figure of a lady holding up a bottle of milk, under which was scrawled, 'Our Mrs Hobby'.

Even more poignant for Letty was the elegant, middle-aged lady who presented the gift. A former pupil of the school, Rosie Layton had been a tiny five-year-old when she had once wandered into the school where Letty was scrubbing the floors, to offer her a barley sugar. Although that was way back at the end of the first war, Letty remembered the moment as though it were only yesterday. 'My mum works in Stagnells the Baker's,' Rosie had said. 'I don't have a dad – not any more. He got killed in the war.' The elegant lady with slightly greying hair bent forward and kissed Letty on each cheek. 'God bless you, my dear,' she said, affectionately. 'We'll never forget you.'

Later, during tea with the teachers, Letty was presented with a gold-leaf china tea-pot. Then, as she made her way back home across the playground, clutching her gifts and a huge bouquet of red roses, the sound of children, singing songs to her from 'The Sound of Music', still rang in her ears. She hadn't even reached the gates before the tears started streaming down her cheeks.

Moving out of Number 13 Roden Street seemed to Letty like leaving behind a loyal and trusted friend. It had been almost forty years since Mr Cotton had first brought them through the door, and now they were about to go out through it for the very last time. Memories! Memories! Letty's head was full of them as she went from one room to another saying her own private thank you and farewells. In those forty years, she had got to know every nook and cranny of the place, every mark on the wall and every chip in the woodwork made by her family. Mick had been born in Letty and Oliver's own bedroom, and all three boys had spent their early years in the house, before moving out to start up homes of their own. What was happening now was a painful experience for Letty, for Number 13 had always been so good to the Hobbs family. She just hoped and prayed that whoever moved in after them would know that it was a house which protected those who gave it love and care.

'The van's just leavin', Lett.' Oliver found Letty out in the back yard, picking a late-flowering pink rose from her favourite bush. 'Mick's waitin' for us in the car.'

Letty was taking a last look at the tiny back yard, which, over the years, she had lovingly kept sown with flower seeds from Woolworth's. During the summer months there had been an abundance of colour, but as it was now September, all that was left were a few asters, some antirrhinums, and some marigolds. Letty's great pride and joy, the blue lilac tree, seemed to have grown fuller than ever over the past year or so, and the flat green colour of its huge leaves were almost blocking out the view of the neighbours' windows beyond the back-yard wall. 'It's hard to believe there was once an air-raid shelter out here, isn't it?'

Oliver didn't answer. He knew how she was feeling. After standing with his arm around her waist for a moment or so, he led her back into the house.

'I bet you'll be glad to get out of the place,' said Mick, helping his mother into the back seat of his car. 'Roden Street's not the same as it used to be.' He didn't believe a word he said, but he thought it would help if he said it.

Whilst Mick was helping his father to get his artificial leg into the front passenger seat of the car, Letty looked up at Number 13. In her mind's eye, she could still see it as it was on V-E Day in 1945, with flags and bunting fluttering from every window, and the walls holding Mick's patriotic cardboard slogans. Memories! Memories! But Letty, practical as ever, quickly turned her eyes away. It was no good looking back.

Mick's car drove off, and quickly disappeared out of sight

around the corner. It took only a few seconds for Letty and Oliver to leave Roden Street for the last time.

Southend sometimes feels like the sunniest place on earth. If you walk along by the sea, you quickly get a tan and the combination of sunshine and sea is a real tonic, stripping years off even the most weary. At least, that's what Letty always thought. Situated at the tip of the Thames Estuary, the town is flanked on either side by residential suburbs such as Westcliff, Thorpe Bay, and Shoeburyness. Number 12 Sea View Drive was part of a new cluster of bungalows, part of an estate built on a high position overlooking the sea, situated between Southend town centre and Westcliff. From the lawn of their new front garden, Letty and Oliver had magnificent views of Canvey Island to the east, and on the other side of the Estuary, the Isle of Grain, and beyond that, the North Downs of Kent. It was obvious from the start that they were going to be very exposed to the sea winds, and they would have to learn to cope with the effects of salt on their garden plants. But even on dull days the light was so bright, nothing else seemed to matter.

Moving in to Number 12 Sea View Drive was not nearly so difficult as moving out of Number 13 Roden Street. For a start, it was a bungalow, so there were no stairs to haul furniture up. Not that there was very much furniture left over, for the bungalow was much smaller than number 13, and a lot of it had either been sold or given away. Letty was glad that Mick had taken her old upright piano to his place, for she herself had taught him to play it when he was a child, and she'd have hated to see it go. Eddie and Mary were already supervising the removal men when Letty and Oliver arrived with Mick. The three of them had a bouquet of flowers and a bottle of champagne waiting to greet Mum and Pop, and once the workmen had left, everyone toasted

Number 12 in high style. And, judging from the gurgling sounds coming from Mary and Eddie's new baby in his pram, he also was joining in the celebration. Now six months old, Jonathan was the pride and joy of his Grandma and Grandad, and was clearly enjoying his first visit to their new home.

With Mick and Eddie's help, Letty soon set about arranging the furniture where she wanted it. The bungalow had four good-sized rooms, including a kitchen which was big enough to have meals in. When Letty saw the bathroom, she scared the life out of everybody by bursting into tears, saying it was the first bathroom of their very own that she and Olly had ever had in their entire married life. Furthermore, the tiles and bathroom suite were all in Letty's favourite colour, blue, and Mick had even bought them a magnum-size bottle of bubble-bath to start them off. There was a main bedroom for Letty and Oliver, and another smaller one for guests. Both rooms overlooked the back garden, which had a lawn just big enough for Oliver to tackle with his new electric mower. The sitting-room was large, bright and airy, so Letty's heavy oak sideboard fitted nicely against one wall, and the settee against another. There was a small open fireplace with grey-coloured tiled surrounds, and a narrow mantelpiece that was just big enough to take the chiming clock, a couple of photographs, and some ornaments. Letty and Oliver's easy-chairs were comfortably placed either side of the fireplace and, after much grumbling, puffing, and blowing, Eddie and Mick unrolled the two-tone carpet, which fitted the floor perfectly, leaving only a narrow gap around the edge of the room. Oliver announced he didn't like the plain white walls, and as soon as he could, he would paint them a different colour, which immediately provoked a chorus from everyone of, 'When Father painted the parlour, you couldn't see Pa for paint!'. But the greatest treat in the world for both Letty and Oliver was, without a doubt, the spectacular panoramic view from the large bay window. From the small front lawn in front of the bungalow, they could see how the hill they were on swept down to the seafront, where sea-birds swooped down endlessly for any scraps of food that might be left on the pavement.

When Mary went out to buy some fish and chips for lunch, Eddie joined his mother at the window, where she was staring out with incredulity at the view. 'Well, Mum, think you're going to like living down by the sea?'

'*Like*!' Letty sighed, and sat down on the window bench seat. 'Oh Eddie, your dad and I are going to be in our seventh heaven. I mean, just look at that sun shining out there.'

'The sun doesn't always shine by the sea, you know.' Eddie turned to look at his mother. 'It's a long way way from London, Mum. I hope you won't get lonely – especially on those long winter evenings.'

Letty looked at him, puzzled. 'Lonely? Me? With your dad around?'

'It's a big step to take. You and Pop have lived all your life in London. It's different here. You don't know anyone. You have to get on a bus to go to the nearest shops.'

'We've got a lovely little shop just round the corner. We can get anything we want there.'

'That's not what I mean, Mum. This is a lovely place, but you're very cut off. Of course, we'll come and see you as often as we can, but no matter how you look at it – down here, you're on your own.'

Letty hesitated before answering. There was clearly an element of truth in what Eddie was saying. This was the first time in forty years that she and Olly had moved house. Although Roden Street had changed over the years, at least there were lots of people around, and plenty of shops within easy walking distance. There was also the Odeon Cinema just around the corner in Holloway Road, where she and Olly had got in practically free on their pension-cards in the afternoons. Yes. Everything *was* going to be different. It was going to take all their perseverance to get used to a new way of life. 'Don't worry about us, son,' Letty said suddenly. 'Your dad and I'll be all right, just you wait and see. In a year or so's time, we'll have forgotten we ever lived in London.'

A moment later Mary rushed in with the lunch, shaking with laughter with what she had just seen along the road outside. Apparently one of Letty and Oliver's new neighbours was using a vacuum-cleaner on his front lawn. Needless to say, nobody believed her, but when they all dashed to look out of the kitchen window, Mary's story was proved absolutely true. What they saw in the front garden of the semi-detached bungalow just two doors way, was a man, probably in his late sixties, using an upright vacuum-cleaner on his small lawn, which had already been mown down to the last blade of grass. To complete the picture, the man was wearing a flat, brown-and-white checked cap, bright green overalls, and white gardening gloves. Behind him was a woman, about the same age, in a housecoat, with a turban tied around her head, using furniture polish on the outside windowsills. For nearly ten minutes, Letty, Oliver, Eddie and Mary laughed and giggled at the extraordinary goings-on at Number 8 Sea View Drive. A little later, after the performance was over, and the Hobbs family had settled down to their fish and chips in the kitchen, a tap on the door brought a puzzled exchange of looks from everyone. Letty got up from the table, wiped her mouth on a piece of paper kitchen-towel, and opened the door.

'Mrs Hobbs?' It was the wielder of the vacuum-cleaner in person. The window-polisher was with him.

Letty gulped hard. 'Yes.'

The brown-and-white checked cap was raised, a hand

outstretched. 'Pleased to meet you, Mrs Hobbs. Fred Golding. And this is my wife, Gladys. We're your neighbours from Number 8.'

The window-polisher smiled effusively, and shook hands. As she did so, she screwed up her shoulders, giving the impression for a moment that she had no neck. 'Welcome to Sea View Drive, my dear.'

The fish-and-chip plates were quickly cleared away, and after brief introductions, the Hobbs family were given a lengthy history of Sea View Drive and its inhabitants, of whom Fred and Gladys had been first to move in just over a year before. There were stories of 'skeletons in the cupboard' at number 17, the ex-colonial sisters in Number 22, and the family of Jehovah's Witnesses in Number 14. The Goldings had very little time for most of the neighbours who had moved in so far, especially some of the 'riff-raff' from the rougher parts of London. They were delighted, they said, that a nice class of person had arrived at last, for they wanted to keep Sea View Drive a select neighbourhood. To Letty and Mary's embarrassment, they could see Eddie and Mick sending the new neighbours up behind their backs, imitating them with twitches and nods. And it soon became clear that Gladys didn't approve much of Mick either; she expressed disdainful surprise that someone in their thirties had not yet found himself a wife. Furthermore, the Goldings' enthusiasm was somewhat diminished when Fred, himself a retired civil servant from the Water Board, was told that Oliver had spent his working life as a ticket collector on the London Underground. Jonathan wasn't much help either. When Mrs Golding bent over his pram to introduce herself as 'your Aunty Gladys', he started crying at the top of his voice. At which Fred was not amused, 'We don't have any children of our own,' he said, acidly. 'We've never felt the need.' However, before Fred and Gladys went home, they had left behind promises to invite their new neighbours to tea and clearly expected, if not demanded, a similar return invitation.

As Letty waved to them through the sitting-room bay window, she felt sure that from now on life was going to be very different for her and Olly, down by the sea.

It was the silence Letty noticed more than anything else. As she lay propped up in bed at the side of Oliver, listening to the sound of waves gently rolling on to the distant seashore, she gradually realised that she had never known such silence before. Although in comparison to other areas in London, Roden Street was very quiet at night, there was always something you could hear: either gangs of cats fighting in someone's front garden; or the distant rumble of traffic from the Seven Sisters Road; or the chimes of the clock-tower bells from the Emmanuel Church in Hornsey Road. But here, on their first night in the bungalow, Letty had heard nothing for over two hours apart, she thought, from the hoot of an owl on the other side of the estate. Even Oliver couldn't sleep. And, as the doctor had finally *forbidden* him to smoke any more, all he could do was to sit up in bed and listen for a sound – *any* sound, that would tell him there were people living around them. But in Sea View Drive there was no Greek music coming from next door, no 'old Polly' at the top-floor window of the house across the road to gawp into the window of Number 13 whilst Oliver was taking off his artificial leg. It felt strange: although they had always longed for peace and quiet at night, now they actually had it, it seemed unnatural.

But the first few weeks turned out to be very exciting, especially for Letty, and in no time at all she had got to know some of the other neighbours. She particularly liked the young couple next door in Number 10, who offered them a lift into Southend town centre any time they wanted. The people who ran the small shop and sub-post office on the estate were also very warm and friendly to Letty. Whenever she collected her pension on a Wednesday afternoon, they always stopped to have a little chat, and pass on any information about local events. Oliver soon discovered that there was a pub called the King's Arms just around the corner and he equally soon got used to a pre-lunchtime pint and a game of dominoes with some of the older country locals in the public bar.

Inside the bungalow itself, Oliver had his way and painted the walls a pale yellow in a matt finish. The woodwork was painted in a gloss finish, even if more of it ended up dripping on the floor than anywhere else. Letty got to work on their gardens, both front and rear. She spent hours weeding, and planting daffodil bulbs, but she left the lawn-cutting to Oliver. It was a new job for him to learn and it turned out to be one of his favourite. Occasionally Fred Golding stopped by to talk to him, but Oliver usually pretended he was just about to go in for his morning tea or afternoon nap. Only the once did Letty and Oliver get an invitation to Number 8 for afternoon tea and it was a most nerve-racking visit for them both, for they discovered Fred and Gladys walked around their bungalow wearing plastic bags tied round their feet. Once again they had to stifle their giggles as they made polite conversation over the Battenburg cake.

The most exhilarating experience for Letty and Oliver, however, was their daily walk to the path at the top of the cliff overlooking the sea-front. Within the first few days of their arrival, they discovered a bench seat on a corner of the cliff and, until the autumn winds started to turn chilly, they would sometimes take sandwiches and a flask of tea to the bench, and watch the glistening waters of the Thames Estuary spread out before them. Oliver always made sure he never ate the breadcrusts, so that he could feed his friends the seagulls, who soon got to know him and swooped down to snatch anything he was holding up to them in between his fingers. Letty got to love these moments, sitting alone with Oliver on the sea-bench, watching the great ships making their way down the Estuary towards the Pool of London. Sometimes, they would sit there until the sun set and turned the sea into a dazzling spectacle of crimson light, as though the whole world were on fire. And when the dying sun finally gave way to a soft twilight, they would make their way back along the winding path to Number 12 Sea View Drive, hand-in-hand, like young lovers out on their first date.

The gentle brown hues of October, eventually gave way to the grey sea-mists of November. It was time for the young lovers to prepare for the long, dark nights of winter.

Chapter 34

Winter or summer, the first few years at Number 12 Sea View Drive turned out to be some of the happiest of Letty's life. The bungalow almost became an obsession with her, and both she and Oliver kept it spotlessly clean. Every morning in the winter she lit a fire with smokeless coal, so that by the time Oliver got up, the sitting-room was already nice and warm. In the really cold weather, the other rooms did tend to be a bit chilly from time to time, so after Letty and Oliver had been there for a year or so, Eddie and Mary bought them some electric central heating, which stored the heat up overnight. Even so, Oliver tried to keep it turned down as much as he could, maintaining that they shouldn't 'waste the juice'. Before going to bed at night, Letty always switched on her electric blanket, so that by the time they turned in, Oliver complained that he was getting into a 'blinkin' greenhouse'. Luxury for Letty, however, was the tea-making machine Mick had bought them for a Christmas present, and which she kept on her own bedside cabinet. No more getting up on those cold winter mornings to put the kettle on! Oh, the wonders of modern science! Sometimes she couldn't believe how the world had changed – and for the better!

Spring had always been Letty's favourite time of the year, and she was thrilled to see the first daffodils she had planted suddenly showing their shy yellow heads when she least

438

expected them. After the first year, each side of the front-garden path bulged with a sea of yellow faces, all swaying to and fro in the cold spring breeze. Letty never left or entered the bungalow without stopping to look at them: 'It's like looking at the sun itself,' she would say. Summer brought an abundance of roses – all kinds of them. Some were moving-in and birthday gifts from Eddie, Mary and Mick. Others came from Mick's actor friend, Brian, who loved gardening, and knew a great deal about it. During the summer months, Letty got up early every morning and from her bay window in the sitting-room, she watched the sun rise. The light over the sea was just too beautiful for words, for the surface seemed to be transformed into a galaxy of glittering stars. Letty sat there, in her seventh heaven, and only came down to earth with a bump when Oliver, getting the first smell of toast being made next door, announced that he was ready for his breakfast. For Letty, life in Sea View Drive turned out to be absolute bliss. That is, until the morning she received a rather unexpected telephone call.

The news of her brother Nicky's death, from cancer, affected Letty more than she could have anticipated. She didn't know why, for she hadn't seen him for years, and had only spoken to him once or twice on the telephone. But it was those blasted memories again. She could still see him as a small boy all those years ago, in 97 Arlington Square. In those days he'd been a scoundrel, totally self-centred and very determined, more able to stand up to their mother than Letty ever was. Of course, she never felt the same for Nicky as she did for Tom: in many ways, she thought Nicky was selfish and lacking in sensitivity. But on the few occasions she had spoken to him since, it was clear that the responsibility of marriage and family had mellowed him considerably. When the telephone call came from Nicky's married daughter, Eileen, Letty felt a sick feeling inside her stomach, as though a part of her had disappeared in a flash. After all, Nicky was younger than her. By the law of averages, *she* should have gone first.

From that moment on, Oliver began to notice a change in Letty. She had become more withdrawn, less animated about things she had seen, or people she had talked to. Most days she was restless, and would go out with her purse and shopping bag, even though there was nothing she really needed to buy. Worst of all, Oliver noticed that she became irritable very easily, and that was so unlike her. There were times when she would snap at him for no reason at all. In fact, on occasions, everything he said seemed to irritate her. In such a very short time, she had begun to look older. The arthritis in her knuckles, back, and knees was getting worse, and she took to using a walking stick and basket-trolley when she went out to do her shopping. It all came to a head one wintry day when, drenched with rain after being caught in a thunderstorm, Letty returned home from collecting their pensions, to find Oliver watching a children's programme in the sitting-room. 'What's the matter with you, Olly!' she snapped, taking off her sopping wet coat as she came in. 'Haven't you got anything else better to do than watch rubbish like this on telly all day!'

Oliver looked at her as though she'd brought the thunderstorm in with her. 'What else is there ter do on a day like this?'

'What about going out in the pouring rain to collect the pensions for a change?'

Oliver got up and, switching off the television set, turned to face her. 'I've told you a hundred times I'll collect the pensions. It's not my fault if you always insist on doin' it yerself.'

Letty ignored him, hung her coat up on a hook on the passage wall, then went off to the kitchen to put the kettle on for tea. Oliver followed her in, took the kettle from her, and put it down on the sink unit. 'What's this all about, Lett?' he asked, turning her to face him. 'What's the matter with yer?'

'I don't know what you're talking about.'

'Oh yes, you do.' He held her chin up, and looked directly into her eyes. 'What're you snappin' and snarlin' for?' She tried to pull away, but he held on to her chin. 'Everything I say seems to upset yer. Why, Lett? Why?'

Letty bit her lip, her face crumpled up, and tears started to fill her eyes. 'I don't know, Olly. I just don't know. I seem to get so lonely sometimes, with you sitting here reading the newspaper all day long. You hardly ever open your mouth to me.'

Oliver sighed despondently, and shook his head. 'Come off it, Lett. You know I've never been much of a talker.'

'You used to be, when we first got married.'

'Bleedin' 'ell! That was over fifty years ago!'

'That's what I mean.' Letty pulled away, and picked up the kettle again. 'Everything's in the past. There's nothing to look forward to.' She put the kettle on the stove, and lit the gas. Then she went back into the sitting-room, followed once again by Oliver. She sat on the bench seat by the bay window, staring out at the torrential rain, which was now pounding down furiously on to the concrete path outside. Oliver came into the room, and stood beside her. 'I never thought that being old meant we had to live such a quiet life,' said Letty, without turning from the window.

Oliver put a comforting hand on her shoulder. 'Well, I suppose we could always join a formation team on "Come Dancing".' Almost as he said it, he wished he hadn't. Letty was in a state that he had never seen before, and to tease her at this time was unwise. Oliver knew that she had spent a great deal of their married life helping him through one crisis or another. Now she was having one of her own, and he didn't know how to cope with it. An angry clap of thunder made the bungalow vibrate, and a streak of jagged lightning darted across the dark, menacing sky over the Estuary. Oliver waited for it to calm down, then sat beside Letty on the bench seat. As they both stared out at the violent storm, the reflection in their eyes was of rain, dribbing down the windowpanes. 'You know, girl,' he said, awkwardly. 'Everybody has ter get old sooner or later. It's the one thing we can't get out of.'

Letty was still staring out through the window. 'Oh, it's not that I mind getting old, Olly. But it's this feeling of hanging on I can't bear, as though we're just marking time. Day after day we sit in this bungalow. We never go anywhere, we hardly ever see anyone. All our old friends and relations are dying off, the people we used to know and love. It makes me feel so – cut off'. She finally turned to look at him. 'There's nothing to look forward to, Olly – absolutely nothing.

Oliver lowered his eyes. He knew what Letty meant. People of their own generation *were* getting few and far between. Every week they seemed to hear about someone they used to know in the old days who had passed away. It was bound to make them feel as though they themselves were now living on borrowed time. But he also knew the real reason why Letty had been so upset for the best part of a year now. It wasn't only because of hearing about Nicky's death, for, to be absolutely truthful, she had never really felt very close to him. It was the passing of Tilly Brooks, from a sudden and unexpected heart attack over a year before, that had depressed her, deep down. Tilly had been her old mate for over fifty years, the one woman she could always share a problem with in confidence. If Tilly had been there now she could have talked things over and ended up laughing.

Her being gone just made everything worse. With Tilly's passing, Letty had felt that a chunk of her own life had been taken away. She and Til had nattered on the telephone practically every week, and had a family gathering as often as they could. They told each other everything, and always looked on the bright side of life, even when it wasn't particularly bright. Every week, Oliver had listened to giggles and hoots of laughter coming from Letty, as she and her pal shared a joke, or recalled incidents from their past. Tilly and Bill had always been there. They were around when Ron, Eddie, and Mick were born, and Letty and Oliver were in Number 22 Leslie Street when Tilly and Bill's own kids, Jeff, Pauline, and Rita were born. Now Tilly had gone. No more laughs for Letty. No more bread pudding, and a song on the old joanna. It was all over. The past. Even poor old Bill was so crippled with arthritis, he had had to move into an Old People's Home. Yes. Oliver knew exactly how Letty felt. It *was* sad and lonely for her. After sitting there with her in silence for a moment, he suddenly raised his eyes and looked at her. 'Have we made a mistake, Letty? Did we make the right decision by moving down here?'

Letty looked genuinely surprised and shocked. 'Olly! How can you say such a thing? I love this bungalow.'

'That's not what I asked, Lett. You and I are Londoners born and bred. Maybe people at our time of life shouldn't just give up everything they've been used to. Starting all over again is for the young 'uns, not for us old creakin' doors.'

'It's not that I mind starting over again, Olly. It doesn't matter where you go, as long as you're with the ones you love. No. What I find hard is that when you get old, everything's – different. People you've known all your life start dying off, others forget you even exist. Nothing's the same as it used to be. Everything, everybody changes. Even you.'

'Me?'

Letty's eyes were tearful again. 'Sometimes, we seem to be living separate lives. We go in and out of rooms without looking at one another. There's no contact, no warmth.' She swallowed hard, 'I can't remember the last time you put your arms around me and said, "I love you".'

'Love's just a word, Lett. It don't really mean anyfin'.'

Letty didn't turn to look at him. 'It means a lot – to me.'

Oliver was bewildered, totally out of his depth. He rubbed his hands through his short-back-and sides haircut. 'All right,' he said, finally. 'I love yer. OK?'

The brusque, almost casual way Oliver said it only upset Letty even more. 'Oh Olly . . .' As the tears came, her body started to shake, and she swung round on the seat with her back to him, covering her face with one hand.

Seeing her cry like this upset Oliver terribly. 'What is it, Lett? What have I said wrong now?'

Letty couldn't say anything to him. He was so clumsy, so totally incapable of expressing warmth and affection like other people. Surely old people could say they loved each other – and mean it?

A brief moment passed without a word between them. Outside, the dark storm clouds were gradually giving way to patches of a thinner, brighter grey sky. It was getting much quieter, for the rain pounding down on the tiles of the bungalow roof was now reduced to a drizzle. Oliver looked crestfallen, like a lost child. Then he edged close to her on the bench seat, and with her back still turned towards him, he wrapped his arms around her waist, and whispered into her ear. 'I *do* love you, Lett. You *know* I do.'

Letty leaned her head back on his shoulder, her eyes closed, tears running down her cheeks into her mouth. 'Oh Olly! Do you? Do you – *really*?

As he held her in his arms, Oliver couldn't understand

why there should ever have been a moment's doubt in Letty's mind. In his own way – his own funny, complicated way, of course he loved her, he always had done, and always would. But to Oliver, love was something he couldn't put into words. To him, it was a feeling, a gut reaction – like watching Letty on the other side of the kitchen-table as she ate her meal, spectacles perched on the end of her nose. Like seeing her shake with laughter when Eddie knocked his elbow on the door, or her cheeky smile, or the way she moved her hands as gracefully as any young girl. Like staring into her eyes – those blue, blue eyes that had melted Oliver the first day Letty walked into his ward at the military hospital in Richmond. To this old soldier, Letty was more radiant and desirable than any young girl. In fact, in *his* eyes, she was still a young girl. And yes, he loved her. He loved her more than anything else in the whole wide world, so much so that he never wanted to be apart from her. How *could* she ever doubt him? 'Yer know, Lett,' he whispered. 'Old age doesn't have to be lousy. Yes, I know we have all the aches and pains that go with it. But after all you and me've been through in our time, we can cope with it.' He released his arms from around her waist, and pulled her round to face him. 'Yer know our trouble, don't yer? We're lettin' ourselves get stale. It's time we got out of this place once in a while, had a bit of fun in our old age. From now on, we're goin' to stop starin' out of windows all day and watchin' telly. We're goin' to enjoy ourselves! Dinky – dink?'

For the first time, Letty broke out into a broad smile. 'Dinky – dink!'

With one finger, Oliver wiped the tears away from her eyes. 'Right then. For a start, you can do somethin' for me.'

'What's that?'

'Give us a kiss!'

'Olly!' She had no time to object, for he quickly tightened

445

his arms around her, and covered her lips with a firm kiss.

When their lips finally parted, Oliver stared straight into Letty's eyes. 'Shall I tell you somethin', Mrs 'Obbs. I may be a bit creaky in me old age, but I don't arf fancy you!'

Over the next few weeks and months, Letty became more and more like her old self. Thanks to Oliver's gentle understanding, she found a new meaning to everyday life. In fact, each day was not really long enough for her, for she always had something to do, whether it was going into Southend with the young couple next door, or making currant cakes for the local church bazaar, or just weeding in the garden. Both she and Oliver took a lot more interest in local activities, such as joining a Senior Citizens sponsored walk along the clifftops, to raise money for the children's ward at the hospital in Southend. They supported the local amateur dramatics group by going to see one of their plays, and Letty attended the regular Tuesday afternoon meetings of the WVS in the church hall, in which, for the first time in her life, she learnt how to make fig rolls. Letty and Oliver didn't much care for the local 'Derby and Joan Club', for by the time they'd listened to endless tales about everyone's ailments, they came out of the get-togethers feeling far older than when they went in! Of course, weekend visits from Eddie and Mary, or Mick and any of his friends, were still Letty and Oliver's greatest joy, and when they all turned up together, Letty thought it was just like the good old days back at Number 13. In December, everyone was surprised when she and Oliver went on a coach trip to London, to do some Christmas shopping. They had a wonderful time, buying shirts for Eddie and Mick, and an acrylic cardigan for Mary, who was allergic to wool. Then they finished up by having fish and chips cooked by a Chinese man, which they ate in a busy café in Soho, before walking down Regent Street to gaze in awe at all the Christmas lights and decorations. On the way home, Oliver fell asleep and snored loudly, much to the irritation of an indignant lady sitting just in front of him. And he kept waking up with a nasty hacking cough, which had been troubling him for the past couple of weeks.

One morning in June, months later, Letty was in the kitchen listening to the radio, whilst getting their breakfast ready. There was a lot of fuss about the miners going on strike, and the news bulletins were full of talk about whether the Labour government should resign or not. Oliver was fed up with the way everyone was at each other's throats, and Letty said she hoped they never televised the goings-on in Parliament, because it sounded as though they all behaved like a lot of children. In reality, neither of them had ever taken any real interest in politics. In his young days Oliver had voted for the Labour Party, mainly because he believed they were 'for' the working class. Most times, Letty had given her vote to the Liberals which, during her time, seemed to be the most neutral thing to do. But both of them had swapped and changed whatever allegiance they had, although neither of them would ever divulge to the other how they had actually voted. However, their breakfast-time political debate was suddenly curtailed by the arrival of the postman, who slipped an unexpected letter through their letter box. Letty went to pick it up, and found that the envelope was addressed to Oliver, and written in a rather shaky scrawl. She took it into the kitchen to him, but as he hadn't his spectacles with him, he went off to read it in the sitting-room.

'Lett!'

The sound of Oliver's voice yelling at her told Letty that he was angry. She rushed in, and found him waving the

opened letter at her. 'Get rid of this bleedin' thing! Throw
it out the window – anythin'!'

Letty was flustered. 'What is it? What's wrong?'

Oliver practically threw the letter at her. 'Bleedin' bitch!
Who does she think she is!'

Letty took the letter, which was written on blue
notepaper. But it was difficult to read, because the writing
and spelling was so awful:

6/6/'76

29 Mallard Road,
Bethnal Green,
E1

Dear Oliver,

I got your address from the cairtaker at Pakeman School. He
said you moved out a long time ago. I offen think about you
and Lett, and wonder how you are getin on. I got married
again in 1958. His name's Harold Shenfield, and he's very
good to me. I offen come and see his married daughter, Lil.
She lives down your way in Shoeburyness. Oh Ol, it would
be realy luvly to see you and Lett again after all these years.
The next time I come down to your part of the world, can
I come and call on you to talk over old times? A lot of waters
past under the bridge since I saw you last and I'd like to put
things right with us. Could you call me on the phone? I've
put my number on the back of this letter. I look forward to
hearing from you. Please give my love to Lett. Is she still
alive?

I am,

Your loving sister,

Vi (now Shenfield)

PS I hope *you* are still alive!

Letty finished reading, and took off her spectacles. 'Well!
That's a surprise. I didn't think *she* was still alive. But you
mustn't be unkind, Olly. If Vi's taken the trouble to look us
up, the least we can do is to ask her over for tea.'

448

Oliver's eyes were blazing with fury. 'Over my dead body!'

'But she's your own sister, Olly. Just think of all she's been through.'

Oliver got up from his easy-chair, snatched the letter from her, tore it up into small pieces, and threw it into the empty fire-grate. 'I never wanna see that woman again, d'yer hear? I tell yer, she's got a reason why she wants to contact us again.'

'But she can't do us any harm now – not after all these years. She must be almost eighty by now. After what happened to her in the war, she deserves a little kindness and understanding. She's old, Olly – like you and me. We should try to forgive and forget.'

Oliver knew Letty was right, but no matter how hard he tried, he could neither forgive nor forget how Vi had tried to stir up trouble when Sam was living with them in Roden Street all those years ago. To Oliver's way of thinking, Vi had a spiteful tongue that would never be clean. Even after her husband Frank and the family had been killed during the war, Vi still hadn't found a decent word to say for either Letty or himself, despite everything they had tried to do for her. No. Oliver's bitterness towards his sister ran too deep. There was no way he was ever going to forgive *or* forget her. 'I'm tellin' you straight, Lett,' he said, forcibly. 'I won't have that woman back in our lives. Not now. Not never!'

Oliver's obstinacy and lack of compassion distressed Letty. That night, she lay in bed wide awake, thinking of what she could do about his refusal even to acknowledge Vi's letter. No matter how hard she tried, Letty felt she couldn't just turn her back on her own sister-in-law, not after all the poor woman had been through. After all, she had lived a life of hell on earth, and it was only by the grace of God that she had survived that V-2 bomb which fell on her home, killing all her family. The last time Letty had seen Vi was

449

a couple of years after the war, when Vi had just moved into a one-bedroom flat in Stepney. In those days, she was still having to visit the hospital each week, to have splinters of glass removed from her face, arms, and hands, caused by the shattering of windows during the explosion. It had been a deeply disturbing experience to see Vi so appallingly disfigured, especially when she had always been a woman who was so vain about her looks. Letty couldn't help wondering how she was now, and whether the advances in the medical world over the years had helped her. After all, Vi had found herself a new husband, so she couldn't be looking too bad. Letty's curiosity conflicted sharply with her sense of loyalty to Oliver. But, as she turned to look at him, lying alongside her, snoring loudly, she made an instant decision. Quietly getting out of bed, she crept into the sitting-room next door, and retrieved the shreds of Vi's letter, which Oliver had thrown into the grate.

The following morning, whilst Oliver was having his daily pre-lunch drink in the King's Arms, Letty dialled the telephone number which Vi had scrawled on the back of her letter.

When Letty first saw Vi, sitting at a table in the café on the Southend sea-front, she was astonished at how young and well she looked. True, she was wearing spectacles, but they were very stylish tinted ones, and her clothes looked really expensive – a kind of basket-weave cartwheel hat (which Letty noted didn't really suit her long face), and a two-piece, powder-grey cotton suit, with matching gloves. Not bad for a woman of that age, thought Letty. She's clearly married well.

'Allo, Lett. 'Fanks fer comin'. I appreciate it.'

It was only when Letty leaned forward to kiss Vi on the cheek, that she saw the scars on her face – dozens of them, maybe hundreds, tiny, like minute potholes, all disguised with a thick layer of powder. Combined with the deep, heavy lines which criss-crossed her skin, it was a sad, strange mixture. 'It's good to see you, Vi. You're looking really wonderful.'

Vi smiled weakly behind her spectacles, only too aware of Letty's well-intentioned, but unfortunate remark. Then she ordered another pot of tea, some bread and butter and jam, and a plate of assorted cakes. 'I can't believe it's all those years since we last met,' she said, her voice only a little gruff and deeper in old age. 'You ain't changed much, Lett. Filled out a bit, that's all.'

Letty suddenly felt a little self-conscious, and was glad her stomach was now concealed behind the table. 'I don't worry too much how I look, Vi. As long as I feel all right.'

'And do yer?'

'By and large – yes. Except for a bit of arthritis and some diabetes. The doctor says I have a touch of angina. But I keep it down with tablets.'

'What about Oliver?'

Letty hesitated briefly, then said brightly, 'He's fine. Well – more or less. He has a rotten cough though. Bronchitis. He gets it from the Hobbs family, y'know.' She tried to make light of it, but was not very convincing. 'Anyway, that's why he can't make it to see you. But he sent his very best.' Nervous that Vi was going to ask more questions about Oliver, she quickly changed the subject. 'So, tell me what you've been doing with yourself all these years, Vi. I'm so pleased you got married again. I think it's wonderful.'

'Oh, it's all right,' Vi replied, rather wryly, Letty thought. 'It's better than sittin' around pickin' me nose on me own all day. Mind you, I 'ad a rough time fer a few years after the last time I saw yer. All I got was me widow's pension. Nothin' from the Underground though, in spite of Frank workin' on the tube all those years. Anyway, I got a job in this sewin' factory down Stepney. That's where I met Harold Shenfield.' And she added pointedly, 'He owns the place.'

It was only now that Letty noticed the cupid's-bow shape of Vi's lipstick, just like the old days. She also noticed again the thin cotton gloves that Vi was wearing, clearly with no intention of taking them off. 'He's a very lucky man to have someone like you for a wife, Vi. He must love you very much.'

'We don't do anyfin', yer know.' Vi's sudden, blunt reply totally shocked Letty. 'In fact we've never done anyfin'.' Twenty-five years ago, I told 'im I'd only marry 'im as long as we didn't do anyfin'. That's 'ow it's always been. He lost 'is wife in a car accident, and I lost my Frank in the war. We stay tergevver fer company, nuffin' more. A bargain's a bargain, I say. Yer don't 'ave ter live wiv someone ter love 'em.' She lowered her eyes briefly to add, 'I've only ever loved once in my life.'

Letty was fascinated by Vi's frank admission and she had to admit, she couldn't help but admire her honesty. When the tea arrived, Letty listened to Vi's account of her life over the years since they'd last met, how she still continued to visit the family grave in Finchley cemetery every week, and how, despite the fact that her second husband was Jewish, she had remained a devoted Catholic. Time and time again Vi would return to talk of Frank and their two girls, Rosie and little Do-Do. After five minutes' conversation, Letty knew exactly where Vi's heart was, and would always be. It was right there in the family grave, back in Finchley. But the two women had lots to talk over, and plenty of memories of the old days to exchange. During it all, Letty watched in awed fascination as Vi tackled a thick cream slice, which she managed to eat without once dropping a blob of cream on to her plate.

It was only when they had finished their tea, that Vi returned to the one subject that Letty had carefully tried to avoid. 'Yer know, Lett, yer don't 'ave to pretend ter me about Oliver,' she said, delicately wiping her lips on a paper napkin. 'I don't blame 'im for not wantin' ter see me.'

Immediately Letty tried to cover up for Oliver, assuring Vi that that wasn't the situation at all; Oliver really wasn't *well* enough to come out that day. But Vi discreetly ignored her explanation and, to Letty's surprise, she took a cigarette out of a silver case, and lit it. To her knowledge, Vi had given up smoking when she married Frank. 'Oll's got every right to feel the way 'e does about me,' Vi continued, blowing out her match, and dropping it into an ashtray. 'I've been a real bitch in my time. I probably still am. It's not surprisin' I was punished. Though I wish the good Lord had taken it out on me, and not Frank an' my girls.' She turned her head away from Letty to blow smoke from her mouth. But she quickly turned back again, to look her straight in the eyes. 'But I would 'ave liked just one last chance to tell Oll – I'm sorry.'

Letty lowered her eyes, awkwardly. She just didn't know what to say.

Vi leaned across the table, and lowered her voice. 'Yer see, Lett. I *do* 'ave a reason why I wanted to see 'im. Not just to make my peace wiv 'im, but to try and explain that I really couldn't stop myself from doin' all those 'fings that upset you, and 'im, and everyone else. I've never admitted that to anyone in the whole wide world, Lett, and I won't do again. But who knows 'ow much longer we'll all be around. I'ave to get it off my chest – I just 'ave to.' She took only one more puff of the cigarette, then stubbed it out. There was a ring of lipstick left on the upright tip. 'Anyway, when yer see 'im, tell 'im – tell 'im, if 'e can find room in 'is 'eart ter forgive me, 'e'd be doin' me a great favour.'

A few minutes later, Vi insisted on paying the bill, and

they left. The two women kissed and hugged each other, and said goodbye. As they walked off in opposite directions to catch their buses, Letty peered back over her shoulder. The tall figure of Vi was just disappearing into the boisterous crowds of London day-trippers who were thronging the pavements along the sea-front. Letty thought she looked pretty good for an eighty-year-old, slower in her movements, but firm and erect as ever.

Since she'd last seen her, Vi seemed as though she'd grown much taller – in more ways than one.

Chapter 35

When Letty got back from Southend, she didn't tell Oliver about her meeting with Vi. She knew she was doing wrong, but she felt that she had to wait for the right moment. Oliver's relationship with his sister had always been such a complicated one, and he was prone to fits of temper at even the mention of her name. To Letty's way of thinking, bitterness seemed to be such a waste of time and energy. Everyone had their faults, some worse than others. But it was no use living in the past. Each day was too precious for that. However, Letty's dilemma only increased, for as the weeks rolled by, then months, she still couldn't bring herself to tell him. On one occasion she almost told Eddie, but she suddenly lost her nerve at the last moment, worrying that it might cause a heated family debate. Both Eddie and Mick knew Aunty Vi when they were young, but hadn't really liked her very much, thinking that she was eccentric and highly strung. And so, as almost a year went by, Letty found herself keeping a secret which was beginning to take on the same proportions as the one Oliver had kept from her for so many years, the secret of his one and only wartime meeting in the trenches with her brother, Tom Edginton.

The following year, Letty and Oliver spent Easter with Eddie and Mary, who were still doing good business in their newspaper shop in Enfield. With Mick, and Mary's father joining them, they all had the most wonderful time, for it

455

was Jonathan's ninth birthday and his grandparents had bought him a new pair of football boots which he was so excited about Mary was sure he would want to sleep in them. During his first nine years, Jonathan, or 'Jonty' as he was nicknamed had, like his father, Grandpop Hobbs and late Uncle Sam, developed into a sports fanatic. Every time she saw him, Letty bought him either a pair of football socks or a T-shirt, and his poor mother and father spent a fortune on kitting him out with a cricket bat, white trousers, and knee-pads. When watching football matches on television together, Jonathan and his Grandpop Hobbs frequently engaged in heated discussions with Eddie about who should have made which pass, and how their latest hero was performing. On all occasions, Letty took Jonathan's side against his father and Grandpop, regardless of who was in the right or wrong. Whenever she discovered that Grandpop was cheating Jonty at cards or Ludo, she would expose him, to jeers and thumps on the head with a newspaper by his grandson. But when it came to which football club to support, there was complete solidarity in the Hobbs family, who remained fiercely loyal to Arsenal, a throwback to the good old days at Number 13 Roden Street. Mick, who was certainly no football or cricket enthusiast, thought his family was idiotic, and couldn't wait for the Saturday afternoon sports marathon to finish, before getting to the most important part of television viewing – the old feature film!

With all her family around her, the Easter weekend in Enfield was an idyllic time for Letty. The only snag was that Pop's bronchitis was playing up a bit, and he had to have heavy doses of cough mixture in order to get a good night's sleep. On the last night before they went back home, however, Letty and Oliver became embroiled in an unexpected row with Eddie and Mick. Soon after Jonty had gone to bed, Letty reiterated what she had said before, that if anything should ever happen to Pop, she would move into an Old People's Home. And when Pop said that he would do exactly the same thing if anything happened to Letty, Eddie blew his top, angrily supported by Mick. But, despite assurances from her two sons and daughter-in-law that there would always be a place for them with them, Letty insisted that she and Oliver would never allow themselves to be a burden on their own children. That, she said firmly, was the end of that and, tight-lipped, she went into the kitchen to help Mary make their bedtime drinks.

The Saturday evening after Easter Letty sat up late watching a horror film on television, but, she was up bright and early the next morning, collecting the Sunday paper from the newsagent's round the corner, then preparing Oliver's bacon and tomatoes on toast for breakfast. Oliver decided to have a lie-in for a bit, so he listened to the morning service on the radio at the side of his bed, and joined in with the hymn-singing. He particularly enjoyed it when they sang his favourite, 'Amazing Grace', even though it wasn't really a hymn. After he'd got up, he put on his artificial leg, and had his breakfast with Letty in the kitchen, then went into the bathroom to have his wash and shave. As had happened so many times before, he had a coughing fit, and cut one of the moles on his face with his razor. As usual, Letty came to the rescue with cotton wool and, after dabbing on some disinfectant, the bleeding stopped. While he was getting dressed, Oliver heard the sound of a lawn-mower coming from one of the front gardens along the road. It was a bit premature for someone to be cutting their lawn at this time of year, for it was still only April, but there had been a lot of rain in March; the weather was very warm, and the grass had grown fast. So, out he went through the street door to investigate. Needless to say the lawn cutter was none other than Fred Golding, down the road at Number 8.

Oliver looked at his own front lawn. The grass was already an inch high. Should he or shouldn't he? Without much hesitation, he made his way around the side of the bungalow into the back garden, where he collected his small electric mower from the garden shed. But when he asked Letty to 'plug-in' for him in the sitting-room, she protested strongly at his doing such an unnecessary job so early in the year. She didn't want him to tire himself whilst still trying to recover from the after-effects of his recent attack of bronchitis, which still left him coughing and sweating in bed at night, but she always knew she was fighting a losing battle once Olly had made up his mind to do something, so she duly 'plugged-in' the extension wire for him.

For the next hour Oliver, in shirt-sleeves and braces, was in his element, pushing his machine up and down the front garden of number 12, manoeuvring difficult curves around the rose-beds. Every blade of grass was dealt with, every daisy, every weed. Once or twice, he would stop the mower and bend down to pull out an obstinate thistle. But he never touched any of the buttercups that strayed into the beds: buttercups were very special to both him and Letty. Occasionally one of the neighbours would pass by, wave to him, and marvel at the way he could do such a job, on one leg. Every so often, Letty would peer out of the window to check that he wasn't overdoing it. She roared with laughter when a stray mongrel roamed into the garden, piddled against the hedge where Oliver was mowing and, with Oliver shaking his fist at him, made a quick getaway down the street. Letty always loved to see Oliver enjoying himself, and as she watched him through the kitchen window, with the sweat pouring through his vest and shirt, she felt a surge of love and admiration for him. Before he had finished, Oliver had two visitors. One was a robin who sat on a large stone in the middle of one of the flowerbeds, darting in and out of the grass cuttings for an exposed worm. The other was Fred Golding.

'I must say Oliver, old chap, you've made a good job of this lawn.' Oliver's neighbour was today wearing a different coloured pair of overalls, bright blue this time. But the brown-and-white checked cap was the same as ever, so, too, were the white gardening gloves. 'Me and Gladys were just saying, it's a miracle the way you get 'round on that one leg of yours.'

Oliver ignored him, and carried on pulling up lawn weeds. Almost immediately, Letty appeared at the front door of the bungalow. 'Morning, Mr Golding,' she said, politely but coldly. Then she called straight to Oliver 'Lunch is almost ready, dear.'

'Be right wiv yer.' Oliver carried on weeding.

Uninvited, Golding came up the path, and cast a critical eye over the garden. 'I must say, I'm amazed you don't get any help with all this. It wouldn't hurt your two boys to give their dad a hand with the mowing from time to time.'

Oliver looked up and shot him a resentful glance. 'My boys 'ave to earn their livin'. They 'ain't retired like you and me.'

Letty, still standing in the front doorway, drew herself up haughtily. 'We can hardly expect Eddie and Mick to come up all the way here just to cut a lawn. But I'm sure you noticed, Mr Golding, they did it quite a few times for us last year.'

Golding was immediately on the defensive. 'Oh, don't get me wrong, Letty. I wasn't criticising. As a matter of fact, I like your sons – both of 'em.' His fingers unconsciously nipped at a new, young rose shoot, and it came off into his hand. To Letty's irritation, her unwelcome neighbour continued to nose around, knowing that she was in the middle of serving up lunch. He was always the same, making any excuse to call on them, to gossip about anything or anybody on the estate. For nearly ten minutes, Letty and Oliver had to listen to Golding; his questions about Eddie's newspaper shop in Enfield, and how he was sure that he would want to better himself one of these days; about how Eddie had such a lovely wife in Mary, in direct contrast, of course, to Mick. Eventually, he came to the point. 'You must be very disappointed with the way things have turned out with him.'

Oliver, sweat still streaming down his face, fixed Golding with an icy glare. 'What d'you mean by that?'

'Oh nothing, nothing Oliver,' Golding added quickly. He was on dicey ground – and knew it. 'It's just that – well, he must be getting on a bit now. I mean, he's not a youngster any more, is he?'

Oliver was still glaring. 'So what?'

Golding was beginning to feel the heat now, so he took off his cap and wiped his forehead with his other hand. The only hair remaining on his head had been combed straight back past his ears. 'You would have thought that by now, Mick would have found himself a nice little wife – like your Eddie.'

Letty cut in like a flash, 'If Mick had wanted to get married, Mr Golding, he'd have done so a long time ago.'

'Oh, quite so, Mrs H, quite so. I just wondered whether he'd ever – well, ever talked it over with you, that's all.'

Oliver was holding the garden rake in his hand. He looked as though he might use it. 'What d'yer mean – talk it over wiv us?'

'As far as *we're* concerned, Mr Golding,' said Letty, 'our Mick has nothing to talk over with us about how he wants to live his *own* life.'

Golding smiled back at her quickly, and ingratiatingly. 'Couldn't agree with you more, dear. And anyway, they live peculiar lives in the business he's in, don't they?'

Letty glared back at him, angrily. 'Peculiar lives?'

Oliver took a few menacing steps towards Golding, eyes blazing. He knew exactly what he was trying to get at, and he wasn't having any of it, especially from a little squirt like this. 'What d'you mean by that?'

Golding was now fighting to get out of a difficult spot. 'Don't get me wrong, Oliver. It's not Mick I'm talking about. It's all those actors and actresses he has to mix with. I mean, they don't care what they get up to, do they?'

'You bleedin' double-dyed 'ypocrite!' The bubble of anger had burst in Oliver and he moved so close to Golding, he was practically nose to nose with him. 'Let me tell you somethin', mate. I'm proud of my two sons. Proud of anythin' they care to do wiv their lives. If they wanna run a shop – good luck to 'em. And if they don't wanna get married and settle down – that's up ter them.' He suddenly lifted up his finger and pointed it menacingly at Golding, who ducked back thinking Oliver was going to hit him. 'You know you're trouble, don't yer? You wanna 'ave some kids of yer own!'

Golding straightened back his shoulders in haughty protest. 'Now just one moment please! All I was trying to do was to be neighbourly.'

'Right then!' Oliver's voice was now raised so high, that faces were already peering out from behind curtains along the street. 'Sling yer bleedin' 'ook out of 'ere, before I ferget just 'ow good a neighbour you are!'

'Well!' The outraged Golding drew himself up angrily but when Oliver started to raise the rake at him, he quickly retreated back to the safety of the street, calling back, 'If that's the way you feel, we want nothing more to do with you – *or* your family!'

Letty came down to join Oliver, and together they

461

watched Fred Golding strut up the street, doing his best to retain whatever dignity he had left. By the time he had disappeared into Number 8, the young couple from next door were both holding up their thumbs in recognition of Oliver's defiant outburst. But no one was more proud of him than Letty. She usually tried to keep the peace between him and the Goldings, but this time, the poisonous insinuations had gone too far. For Letty, Oliver's spirited defence of his son was music to her ears. She was sick of hearing people say that she was the trousers in the family, that if it wasn't for her Oliver wouldn't be able to cope. Of course he would! He could cope with *anything*. Letty was absolutely sure about that. Today, Oliver had shown, not for the first time, that *he* was the head of the Hobbs family. He had a mind of his own, and would speak it any time his wife or sons were threatened. Letty gave him a hug, and reminded herself of the one thing they had decided long ago – that they would never interfere in any of their kids' lives. 'I don't know, Oliver Hobbs,' she said, proudly. 'What *will* the neighbours think?'

'To 'ell wiv the bleedin' neighbours!' he scowled.

Letty laughed, and soon she was shaking up and down with helpless giggles. Gradually, Oliver saw the funny side of what had just happened and joined in too. Soon, the pair of them were just standing there in the middle of the lawn, hugging each other, and rocking with laughter. And all along the street, eyes were watching them from behind curtains, secretly admiring what they themselves had been longing to do. But, as Letty took hold of Oliver's arm to lead him back into the bungalow, he suddenly started to cough. This time, it was more than the hacking he had been plagued with for the past few months. This time, she realised with a wave of horror, he was struggling for breath.

'Olly!' Letty immediately panicked. 'Olly, what is it?'

Oliver grabbed hold of her shoulder. All the colour was drained from his face, his eyes were watering, and he was struggling to breathe. 'Can't . . . breathe!' To Letty's distress he gradually started to slump to the ground, holding on to her as he did so. 'Can't . . . breathe!'

'Help! Somebody – please help me!' Over and over again, Letty yelled out at the top of her voice. By the time a group of neighbours had reached her, Oliver was laid out on the ground, holding on to her, almost choking, struggling desperately for breath.

A short time later, an ambulance arrived outside Number 12 Sea View Drive, and, with Letty by his side, Oliver was rushed off to hospital.

It was several days before Oliver came out of Intensive Care at the Southend General Hospital. Most of the time he was there he wore a plastic oxygen mask, for the bad bronchial attack he had suffered was in danger of turning to pneumonia. However, by the time he was transferred to a public ward, he had a little more colour in his cheeks, and his eyes were brighter. Even so, a huge cylinder was placed at the head of his bed, and every time he felt as though he were having any trouble breathing, he clipped on the plastic mask, operated the switch on the cylinder, and gave himself a little whiff of oxygen. After another ten days he was getting impatient to go home, saying he'd spent enough of his life in hospitals, and hated the places. But the doctors said they wanted him to stay on a bit, so that they could carry out some tests, just as a precaution.

Letty came to see Oliver every day, and as visiting hours on most days were from two-thirty in the afternoon until eight o'clock in the evening, she invariably stayed for as much time as she possibly could. It was tiring for her, waiting each day for the bus, and when she got home in the evening, she usually went to bed straight away.

At the beginning of his third week in hospital, Oliver was delighted, if somewhat surprised, to have a visit from all the family. It was a Monday afternoon, and both Letty and Oliver thought they should all have been at work. But Eddie and Mary explained that they were using up some holiday days that were owed them, and as Mick did his writing at home most of the time, he could come any time he wanted. As usual, Letty brought Oliver a packet of his favourite liquorice allsorts, and Mary's contribution was some tea-biscuits, oranges, and bananas. Brian sent along a pictorial book about astronomy, which Oliver loved, and another of Mick's friends sent him an old book of photographs of Queen Victoria's Diamond Jubilee celebrations, which he knew had taken place in the year Oliver was born. After they had all been there about an hour or so, Eddie and Mick said they thought they would go and have a chat with the ward sister, just to see how soon their father would be getting out of hospital. Letty stayed at Oliver's bedside, but whilst Mary was telling him about how well Jonathan had been playing in his school football team, Letty's eyes kept flicking over her shoulder, to the room at the end of the ward, where Eddie and Mick were in deep discussion with a doctor. After about twenty minutes, they came out with the news that Oliver was going to be allowed to leave the following day. Letty was overjoyed, and said she wanted to get home as soon as possible, so that she couldn't get the bungalow ready for his return.

After they had left the hospital, Letty, Eddie, Mick and Mary made their way to the car park. On the way, Letty bubbled with delight that Oliver was at last coming home, and was greatly relieved that he was clearly on the mend. 'I must say, he's looking so much better,' she said eagerly, to the others.

Eddie was looking a little sombre, until Mary glared at him. 'Yes, Mum,' he answered, brightly. 'Much better.'

As they reached the entrance of the open car park, Letty turned back briefly, half expecting to see Oliver at the window of his third floor ward. But, after smiling hopefully up at the building, she took Mary's arm again and followed her sons to Eddie's car, cursing the bronchitis that had plagued Oliver for so many years. 'If only he'd given up smoking when I told him,' she added, ruefully, chuckling at Olly's obstinacy. But gradually, her initial excitement to hear that Oliver was coming out of hospital was replaced by a growing doubt. 'Poor Olly,' she said to Mary, 'he looks so tired. It's all that treatment they've been giving him – radio something, or whatever they call it. Still, he's eating well. That's always a good sign. Mind you, he's lost a lot of weight.' As if seeking confirmation, she asked, 'What d'you think, Mary? *Has* Pop lost weight?'

Mary's reply was as casual as she could make it. 'It doesn't mean anything, Mum. Pop needed to lose a few pounds. He was far too heavy.'

When they finally got to the car, Letty paused for a moment before getting in. 'What did the doctor say about Pop?' she asked Eddie and Mick, suddenly, and unexpectedly, gazing clear-eyed at them over the vehicle's roof.

Eddie and Mick exchanged a quick, anxious glance. 'Oh, it was nothing important, Mum,' said Mick, cautiously. 'Just more or less what they've already told you. Pop's had a bad chest infection. He needs a lot of rest.'

But Letty was no fool. 'Was that all?' she asked quietly, still gazing directly at her sons.

'There's nothing to worry about, Mum,' Eddie assured her. 'Pop's going to be just fine. Once you get him home, a bit of home cooking'll soon put him right again.'

Letty smiled gently, but did not reply. Then she let Mary help her into the back seat.

A few minutes later, the car was lost in the heavy afternoon traffic, heading its way along the Southend sea-front, and out towards the upper reaches of Sea View Drive.

Chapter 36

May had always been Letty's favourite month. There was
such an explosion of beautiful, colourful new flowers everywhere, and it was warm enough for her not to have to light
a fire each day in the sitting room. Even so, Oliver still felt
the cold slightly, for since coming home from hospital two
weeks earlier, he had lost another half-stone. From the
moment Mick had collected Oliver and brought him back
home to Number 12, Letty was determined to look after him
herself. She had cushions ready for his easy-chair by the
fireplace, a blanket to cover his knees, and the television set
moved out from the wall so that he could have a clear view
of it. She collected two newspapers for him every day, and
he was provided with hot cups of coffee and biscuits every
morning, and either rock cakes or Chelsea buns for tea in
the afternoon: Letty's way of getting him well again was to
feed him up as much as she could. At lunch time, regardless
of how warm the weather was, she would always cook him
a hot meal. Sometimes it was a beef stew with dumplings,
or it might be a pork chop with apple sauce, or even home-
made mince-pie with onions. And when Mick, Eddie, Mary
and Jonty came at the weekends, Letty invariably made her
speciality for 'afters', roly-poly roll, filled with either
currants and raisins, or home-made strawberry jam. Oliver
had his last snack of the day around six o'clock, before
turning in to bed about an hour later. Letty always gave it

to him on a tray whilst he watched the telly, and most times it was skinned tomatoes fried in oil and vinegar, served on toast, or just a chunk of cheese, some chutney, and bread. Each morning, Letty made Oliver stand on the bathroom scales, to see if he had put on any weight but after a week or so Mick discreetly removed the scales, telling his parents that they were broken.

During the first week after he'd left hospital, Oliver's local GP called in to see him. He told Letty that now the weather was beginning to warm up, they should both try to take a little exercise each day. And so, every afternoon, soon after Oliver had had his nap, she plonked his flat cap on his head, wrapped him up in the woollen scarf she'd knitted him from one of his old stump socks, helped him on with his parka, and strolled slowly with him down to their favourite bench overlooking the sea, at the end of the street. Oliver now leaned heavily on a walking stick, and every step he took was a shaky one. But his wife held on to his arm every inch of the way.

One afternoon, Letty decided that the time was right to tell Oliver her long-kept secret about her meeting with Vi. She didn't know how she was going to do it, but she felt if she didn't do it now – well, she just knew it was wrong to keep it from him any longer. The weather was warm and sunny but there was a gentle breeze twisting in from the Estuary, so that afternoon the two of them snuggled up together on the sea-view bench, with a blanket covering their knees. Letty had brought some left-over stale bread with her, and, enjoying himself, Oliver threw bits of it to the endlessly greedy cluster of screeching sea-birds who had descended upon them. Letty relished these few moments each day. It reminded her so much of all those Sunday mornings when she and Olly used to take the kids to feed the seagulls in St James's Park. What happy days they'd been!

Letty's opportunity came soon after they'd watched a Coast Guard helicopter buzzing high above the shoreline and speeding off in the direction of Canvey Island further down the Estuary. It made her think how much progress she and Olly had seen in their lifetime. 'Tell me something, Olly,' she said, leaning her head on his shoulder. 'If you had the chance to live your life all over again, would you want to change anything?'

'Yeah. There's plenty I'd like to change.'

Letty looked up at him with a start. His reply took her by surprise. 'Really, Olly?'

'For a start, I'd make sure you didn't 'ave such a bad time of it.'

'Silly old thing! What are you talking about now?'

'You, Letty. I'm talkin' about you. I don't know how I'd 'ave got through my life without you. You've been so – strong.'

Letty gave him a dismissive laugh. 'Strong! *Me?*'

Oliver didn't actually look at her. His eyes were still watching the helicopter disappearing in the far distance. 'Oh yes. You've been strong, and I've been weak.'

'Oliver Hobbs – look at me!' He turned to look at her. His eyes were different now, so tired, lacking their usual cheeky sparkle, almost as though they were bulging out of the sockets of his yellowy, parched face. 'Don't ever say things like that to me, d'you hear? You've been a wonderful husband, and a wonderful father to your kids. I'm a lucky woman!'

They were briefly distracted by a fat middle-aged couple, unwisely attired in floral T-shirts, shorts, and sandals. Soon after they passed, Letty shook up and down sniggering and, infected by her laughter, Oliver did the same. After they had recovered, Letty rested her head on Oliver's shoulder again, and they both stared out towards the Estuary. The tide was out, and in the distance they could see children playing on the thick, muddy beaches. 'Olly.' Letty finally plucked up courage to say what she had to say. 'There's something I've been wanting to tell you.' She paused before continuing. 'It's about your sister – Vi.'

To Letty's surprise, Oliver's reaction was a mere, quiet, 'What about her?'

'You remember that letter she wrote you – almost a year ago it must be. Well, the fact is, Olly, I – went to meet her.'

There was a few second's pause before Oliver answered, but without turning to look at her. 'Yes. I know.'

Letty sat up with a start. 'You know? *How* did you know?'

He finally turned to look at her. 'Because I know you, Lett.'

Letty was totally shocked, and taken by surprise. 'And you didn't *tell* me?'

Oliver grinned. He always loved it when she looked puzzled or anxious. 'I knew the moment I saw you'd cleared the torn pieces of letter from the fireplace.'

Letty couldn't believe she was hearing right. After all the agony she'd been through, trying to keep this from Oliver. A whole year of agony and guilty conscience! 'And you never told me? Why, Olly? Why?'

'Because you were right, Lett. You've always been right, and I've always been wrong. I've never been able to make out what you ever saw in me. I've never had much of a brain.' Letty was still staring at him, so he took hold of her hand, which was freezing cold. 'I wish I'd had the guts to put things right between me and Vi,' he said, rubbing her hand to warm it up. 'She's 'ad such a lousy life, and I've 'ad such a good one.'

Letty didn't mention the subject again. She was just content to sit there with him in the warm sunshine, the two of them wrapped up as though it were mid-winter. For several

470

minutes not a word passed between them. They just sat there, staring out towards the mud flats on the distant shore below, where a young teenager was tugging at the string of a huge red kite, its tailpiece fluttering against the deep blue sky.

'Lett.' Oliver's eyes were closed as he spoke. 'If anything should happen to me—'

The moment he said it, Letty shut her eyes quickly. She had been anticipating, and dreading, what she knew he would eventually say. 'No, Olly! I don't want to hear it!'

Oliver stretched his arm around her shoulders, and held her tightly. Both of them now had their eyes closed as he talked. 'Be sensible now, Lett. We have to talk. You *know* we do.' The light breeze was carrying the smell of mud and seaweed up from the shore below. That smell that was, to both of them, the undeniable essence of their beloved Southend. 'If anything should happen,' Oliver persisted, 'I want you to promise me one thing. I want you to promise – that you'll accept it.'

Letty felt that her heart was about to burst apart. But she kept her eyes closed tightly in an effort to hold back tears.

'Go on livin', Lett. Live a full life. 'Cos if yer don't, I'll come back an' haunt yer!'

Letty could take no more. She sat up quickly, and re-tied her scarf around her head. 'Please, Olly. It's getting chilly. We've got to get home . . .'

Oliver was determined that she should face up to the inevitable. He grabbed hold of her, turned her towards him, and looked straight into her eyes. 'Mick and Eddie love you, Lett. You've got to go on livin' for them – for our kids.'

Letty was shaking her head, refusing to take in what he was saying. 'This is absurd, Olly! You're talking as though you're going to die. You're *not* going to. You've had a bad attack of bronchitis, a really bad attack. But you're getting better now. You're getting better every day. The doctor told me so.'

'You've got blue eyes.' Oliver wasn't listening to her, merely looking.

Letty stopped what she was saying, and looked straight at him. 'Olly – don't. Please don't.'

'They're just as blue as they ever was. Bright blue . . . just like the sea . . . just like the day we first met.'

For the next few minutes, they just sat there in silence, staring long and hard into each other's eyes. It was all there, right there in those two pairs of eyes – their life together, their hardships, their trials and tribulations, their tears, and their laughter. But most of all there was their bond, that very special bond which had brought them together, and would never keep them apart.

An afternoon stroller walking along the clifftop at the bottom of Sea View Drive that sunny afternoon would have seen an elderly couple sitting on a public bench, holding hands, and looking at each other. And that would have been all. What they wouldn't have seen was a soldier-boy in uniform, handsome, with short, dark greased hair. And his girlfriend, with a tight-fitting daffodil-coloured hat, and matching cotton dress. What they wouldn't have seen were two young people from a world so long ago, who were ridiculously, impossibly, and hopelessly – in love.

Over the next few weeks, Oliver's condition deteriorated rapidly. He continued to lose weight, and was becoming so weak that he had to stay in bed day and night. Letty absolutely supported Oliver's decision not to go back into hospital, but as he was having difficulty breathing for a lot of the time, the local GP arranged for the delivery of an oxygen cylinder, which was placed at the head of their bed. The district nurse called once a day, to shave and bed-bath Oliver but, although she was quite young, she was a tyrant, so unlike most of her profession, rough, ill-mannered and impatient. Both Letty and Oliver dreaded her visits, for she bossed them around and usually left Oliver feeling exhausted after she had finished with him. Each night, Letty slept alongside her husband, but she was awake most of the time, listening to his hacking cough, and hurriedly helping him on with his oxygen mask to ease the congestion in his chest. Then she would get back into bed, and gently stroke his forehead with her hand until he gradually fell asleep again. Despite their now legendary row with Fred Golding in their front garden, Letty and Oliver's neighbours from Number 8 rallied around in their hour of need, and immediately offered to help in any way they could. Gladys Golding did bits and pieces of shopping for Letty, and Golding himself did all sorts of odd jobs for her, like repairing the roof gutter outside, or mending a fuse. In fact, all the neighbours turned out to be kindness itself, always offering help, and coming in to spend just a few minutes with Oliver, or keep Letty company over a cup of tea in the afternoon.

Eddie, Mary, Jonty and Mick all paid frequent visits to Number 12. Everyone felt the strain tremendously, for Letty still insisted that Oliver would eventually take a turn for the better, and get well again. As always, Eddie fooled around a lot, but it helped a great deal, for he managed to make his mother laugh at his antics several times, and just occasionally he even brought a welcome, if exhausted, smile to Pop's face. The big occasion came on Oliver's eightieth birthday, when all the family gathered around his bed for a special celebration with a bottle of champagne. For months before, Eddie and Mick had been planning a surprise party for him, but this had to be abandoned in favour of something more low-key. However, the day before his birthday, Oliver managed to sit up in bed to listen to an hour-long comedy play on the radio, written by Mick to commemorate the Queen's Silver Jubilee, and inspired by Pop's own middle name.

As each day passed, Oliver seemed to sleep more, and eat less. Most times, the only thing he felt like eating was fried tomatoes on toast, and even that, he hardly ever finished. And Letty's morale was getting low, her confidence gradually ebbing away. Mick was aware of this, and drove up from London to see her every other day. But one evening he arrived late, and when he let himself into the bungalow with the key Letty had given him, he found his mother in the sitting-room, alone, and in the dark. 'Mum?' he called, switching on the light. 'What are you sitting in the dark for?'

Letty was perched on the bench seat by the bay window. The curtains weren't drawn, and all evening she had clearly been watching the small sailing-boats, bobbing up and down on the incoming tide along the Estuary. As the light came on, she immediately shielded her eyes. 'Not for the moment, if you don't mind, son,' she said, quietly. 'I've got a bit of a headache.'

Mick turned off the light, put his car keys down on the sideboard, then went across and sat with his mum, and put one arm around her. 'What all this about then?' he said in a lowered voice. 'Is Pop all right?'

It wasn't completely dark outside, and Mick could just see the outline of his mother's face, partly lit by the soft glow of late evening light coming from across the vast expanse of the Estuary. 'He's going to die, Mick.' The gentle tone of Letty's voice seemed to explode out of the darkness. 'Your dad's got lung cancer.'

For a brief moment, Mick could say nothing. The fact that his mum had told him the news came as a complete surprise. 'Who told you?' His voice was no more than a whisper.

'The doctor stopped by. I asked him to. I wanted to know.' Letty turned to face Mick in the dark. 'You knew, didn't you? You *and* Eddie?' Mick didn't answer. He just held on to his mum, and hugged her. 'It's all right, son,' she assured him. 'I'm not afraid.'

So much was going through Mick's mind. This was the first time he had ever had to face a situation like this, and he felt so helpless. But one thing he had learnt from both his parents. When something is a fact, you can't run away from it. This was going to be a time that his mother was going to need all the love and support he and the family could give her. Even so, he couldn't rid himself of the sinking feeling inside his stomach. Ever since he could remember, Pop had always been there, chasing him and Eddie around the garden beds at Number 13, when they'd been too cheeky to Mum, or being scrubbed by him in the old aluminium bath in the scullery. But if it was going to be hard for him, Mick, to cope with losing his father, just imagine what Mum must be feeling. She and Pop had spent almost an entire lifetime together. They had lived through two world wars, eaten together, slept together, and weaved their dreams together. And now, for the first time since they were married, they were to be parted. What would it do to his mum? How would she adjust to life on her own? 'Now listen to me, Mum,' Mick whispered. 'I want you to know that you won't have to face up to this alone. Eddie, Mary, and I – we're all behind you.'

Letty suddenly became very practical. She got up, crossed the room and switched the light on. Then she closed the door, but knew Oliver couldn't hear them, for he had become increasingly deaf now, in both ears. 'The doctor can't tell me exactly how long it'll be. It could be any time from now.' Only now could Mick see how tired and strained his mum was looking. 'He wanted Pop to go back into hospital, but I said no. This is Olly's home, *our* home. If he's got to die, he'll. die here.' She paused only briefly before asking, 'Can I get you something to eat, son?'

Mick shook his head. 'No thanks, Mum.' Her apparent coolness and refusal to show emotion, disturbed him. She was bottling it all up inside her, which was the worst thing she could do. For a moment Mick watched her, bustling around the room quite unnecessarily, tidying newspapers and punching up cushions on the settee. So he went across to her, took hold of her arm to stop her doing anything more, and turned her round to face him. 'Does he know?'

'Nobody's told him. They don't have to. You can see it in his eyes.' Her mind wandered briefly for a moment, then she said, 'It'll be a good thing when it's all over. Best for him.'

'We'll look after you, Mum, you know that, don't you? You'll have nothing to worry about, I promise.'

Letty smiled affectionately at him. She knew only too well what all this meant to both her sons. 'You're a good boy, Mick. You and Eddie. But I'm quite prepared. Your dad took care of that.'

Mick didn't really understand what she meant by that. All he knew was that if he was going to see his mum through this hell, he must be as practical as she was. 'If you don't mind, Mum, I'd like to stay the night.'

'This is your home as much as ours, son. But you don't have to. I shall be perfectly all right.'

Mick followed her to the kitchen and, from the open doorway, he watched her every movement as she filled the kettle at the sink, and put it on the stove to make some tea. As he looked around the room, everything Mick saw reminded him of Mum and Pop – both of them. On the dresser that Eddie and Mary had bought them, there were two large cups and saucers, which they had used for years, right back to their time in Number 13 Roden Street. Mick always knew which cup was Pop's, for a few years ago he had broken the handle, and Letty had glued it back on again. And even though Oliver had been confined to bed for the past few weeks, the kitchen-table was still laid for two, just as always. Letty paused for one brief moment, brushed aside a greying hair-curl which was hanging over one of her eyes, and flashed a warm smile at Mick. He smiled back, then came into the kitchen, and hugged her. 'You know, Mum,' he whispered quietly into her ear. 'It would help if you cried.'

'I know,' she replied. 'But not yet. I wouldn't know how.'

A few minutes later, Mick quietly opened the door of his parents' bedroom, and peered in. He was grateful that Pop was sleeping soundly, even though the plastic oxygen face-mask was placed on the bed close to his hand, just in case of an emergency. He crept into the room, made his way to the window, and looked out. The moon was just making its presence known over the top of the bungalow rooftops on the other side of the Estate, enabling him to see the back garden quite clearly. Unfortunately, it was showing signs of neglect; Fred Golding hadn't liked to help out on such a private patch and it was some time since Pop was able to get out there to mow the lawn, so the grass was already covered with small daisies and weeds. Mick bit his lip anxiously. He knew only too well that from where he was lying in bed, Pop could see straight out into the back garden, and would be very depressed each day by what he could see.

There and then, Mick decided what his first job would be the following morning.

Chapter 37

The district nurse was pushing and pulling at Oliver as she tried to bed-bath him. But he was very weak, and though he had the plastic face-mask on, the oxygen supply was giving him limited help to breathe. 'Come on now, Mr Hobbs! If you want to be washed properly, then for goodness sake keep still!'

Oliver, stripped of his pyjamas and clearly distressed, tossed and turned in the bed. 'Leave me alone!' he spluttered, breathlessly, his voice muffled behind the mask. 'Don't wanna bath!' He could hardly be heard above the sound of the oxygen, snaking its way out of the cylinder, and hissing into his mask.

'You stupid man! You're behaving like a spoilt child!' The nurse was pulling at Oliver's arm, trying to turn him on one side so that she could wash his back. For a young woman, who had to nurse probably a dozen or more bed-ridden men and women in their home every week, she showed a surprisingly aggressive way of handling her patients. Letty couldn't bear her, and over the past month had twice asked her GP to replace her. But the doctor's helpless response was that home nursing care on the National Health Service was difficult to come by and that, regretfully, there was nothing he could do about it. Letty found it difficult to understand how a woman like this should want to do such work for, apart from the rough way she handled Oliver, she didn't even have the compassion to stop for a few minutes' friendly chat with her patient's own wife.

'If you don't keep still, you're going to pull off your mask!' the nurse yelled, angrily.

Oliver's anguished protests brought Letty rushing into the room. 'What's going on in here?' She stopped dead, and gasped in shock at what was happening. 'Olly!' Drained of all energy, Oliver, his poor body now showing the bones through his flesh, was literally fighting to keep the bullying nurse away from him. And then, in one sudden movement, he ripped off the oxygen mask from his face, and yelled breathlessly, 'Get . . . away . . . from me!'

The nurse pushed him away roughly, and shouted, 'In all my professional career I've never seen such immature behaviour from a grown man!' Then she turned to Letty, eyes blazing with fury. 'He should be back in hospital! They'd have no nonsense with him there!'

'Get away from him!' Letty rushed across the room, and pulled the nurse away from the side of the bed. 'You have no right to be let loose with sick people.'

'Now just one moment, Mrs Hobbs—'

'I won't ask you again, nurse – or whatever you are! Get out of here! Right out! I don't want you near my husband ever again.'

Suddenly the nurse realised that she was being edged towards the door. 'Your husband needs a bath!' she spluttered, shuffling backwards.

'From now on, I'll bath him myself!'

'Don't be ridiculous!' The nurse found herself standing in the open doorway. 'You don't have the training.'

Letty picked up the nurse's holdall from the floor, pushed her out into the passage, and followed her. 'If you call this

479

training, then we can do without it!' She closed the bedroom door, and stood with her back to it. 'My husband's a sick man, not a lump of rag!'

'Of course, I intend reporting this to your doctor. You'll be getting a letter from the DHSS.'

'*If* they don't get a letter from me first!' Letty pushed past her, opened the front door, and pointed to the street outside. 'Out!'

The nurse didn't hang around to argue. She left the bungalow, rolling down her sleeves as she went, and called back. 'In case you've forgotten, Mrs Hobbs, the National Health Service provides this facility free for people like you, absolutely free.'

Letty yelled back. 'I know! Thank God we don't have to pay for it!' She didn't wait to see the nurse get into her car. She slammed the door, took a deep breath, then rushed back in to see Oliver.

To her horror, Letty found Oliver hanging over the side of the bed, fighting for breath, trying to reach the oxygen mask on the floor. She quickly used what little physical strength she had to help him back on to the bed again, retrieved his face-mask, and clipped it on for him. Then she covered him over with the duvet for, although it was the middle of June and a hot, sunny day outside, he was shivering. As soon as she was sure he was comfortable, she told him she was just going to the sitting-room, to ask the doctor to come straightaway. But Oliver begged her to stay with him, indicating that he was feeling much better, so Letty sat on the side of the bed with him, and after a few minutes of heavy breathing through the mask, Oliver seemed to calm down. Although he was not asleep, he closed his eyes, every breath still an effort. In the past month or so since he had come out of hospital, the bones of his cheeks had become more pronounced than ever, and his lips were permanently dry, white and sore. But he looked peaceful and Letty quietly got up from the bed, found the flannel which the nurse had been using to bathe him, and dipped it into the bowl of water beside the bed. She wrung it out, then leaned over Oliver, to dab his forehead gently with it. As she was doing so, Oliver's eyes slowly opened, and he smiled. 'Thanks, girl,' he said, from behind the face-mask, his breathing a little slower, but deeper. 'That's better.'

Letty leaned forward close, and with her fingers gently removed some of his still greasy, but now completely grey hair, which had fallen across his forehead and into one eye. 'I'm sorry, dear. I'm so sorry. I won't let her near the place again.'

'Bleedin' woman!' Oliver had lost none of his old tetchiness, and there was the suggestion of a mischievous twinkle in his tired eyes. 'She tried ter kill me.'

'Relax, dear.' Letty found his pyjama top, and helped him on with it. 'Don't think about her. I'll look after you.' She straightened his pillow, and tucked in his sheet.

With the oxygen still hissing into his plastic face-mask, she propped Oliver up into a sitting position in bed. Whilst Letty was making him comfortable, his eyes were closed; when she had finished, he opened them again, and looked around the walls of the bedroom. 'Needs a coat of paint, Lett.' His voice was muffled behind the mask. 'Better get Mick and Eddie ter do it . . .'

Letty perched on the side of the bed, and held his hand. 'No, Olly. That's your job. I'm waiting for you to do it. You're the best painter I know.'

Oliver's head was resting on several pillows which Letty had banked up against the wall behind him. He turned his head towards the window, through which he was able to see quite a lot of the back garden. 'Young Mick . . . made a good job of that lawn.' The back garden had been transformed from what it was a month before. The lawn was as smooth and green as a billiard table and, thanks to Mary and Eddie, who'd spent most of their weekends at the bungalow, the garden beds were free of weeds. The roses, the sweet william and the early summer stocks were in full bloom and the creamy-coloured honeysuckle trailed down over the timber roof of the tiny garden shed. But it was his lawn that Oliver was most proud of: it was something he'd never dreamt of having during those days when he was a kid, sharing a bed on the bare floorboards of his parents' small, scruffy terraced house in Upper Holloway. Oliver turned to look at Letty. Although he was in the shade, a beam of dazzling sunlight through the window accentuated the deep, crystal-blue of Letty's eyes. 'Don't leave me, girl,' he said, his voice barely audible behind the face-mask. 'Don't ever leave me – will yer?'

Letty, still holding his hand, smiled straight back at him. 'Don't be silly, dear. Of course I won't leave you.' She let go of his hand for a moment, got up, and lay beside him on the bed. She took hold of it again, and turned her head towards him. 'You don't have to worry about a thing, dear. I'm right here – just like always.'

Oliver turned to look at her, and just managed a smile. 'I love yer, girl.'

'I love you too, Olly.' Although she was clearly aware of his heaving breath, she kissed his hand, and, moving very close to him, started to sing in a very soft voice:

> 'You are my honey, honey-suckle,
> I am the Bee,
> I'd like to sip the honey sweet
> from those red lips you see . . .'

Whilst Letty was singing, she suddenly felt Oliver's hand stiffen in hers. She sat up with a start. His eyes were open, fixed and staring, and his body was absolutely still. 'Oh, Olly! No, Olly,' she cried. Then she lay there for a moment or so, hugging him, and listening to the seemingly endless hiss of oxygen filtering into his plastic mask. Only then did the tears start rolling down her cheeks. And as the tears came, Letty was determined to finish her song – *their* song:

> I love you dearly, dearly
> and I want you to love me,
> You are my honey, honeysuckle,
> I am the Bee.

Oliver's funeral was a very quiet affair. He'd always said that he didn't want too much fuss, and Letty carried out his wishes to the full. It was held in the small parish church on the far side of the estate, which had a wonderful view of the sea and Southend Pier. Both Letty and Oliver had at one time thought they should be buried alongside Sam, back in Finchley Cemetery, but after they'd spent a few years at Number 12 Sea View Drive, they knew it would be much nicer to lay together in the peace and quiet of the lovely little local church's graveyard. The service was quite simple. About twenty people came, including the Goldings and some of the other neighbours. Mick, Eddie, and Mary came up from London, and sat with Letty in the front pew. She looked very pretty in the new dress Mary had helped her to buy: black had never been one of her favourite colours and regardless of what anyone thought, she insisted on wearing the daffodil-coloured hat Oliver had always liked seeing her in. It wasn't a very fashionable one, but she looked like Eddie and Mick's mum in it, like Oliver's Letty. Everyone was surprised how well Letty stood up to the ordeal of the service. She listened to readings from the Bible by one or two of

Mick's actor friends, an address from the vicar on how loyal a husband Oliver had been, and, although her voice was too grieved to sing some of the hymns, she managed to join in with everyone in the church, as the organ played 'Onward Christian Soldiers'. It was only when they came to sing Oliver's great favourite, 'Amazing Grace', that it all became a little too much for her. All through the singing of it, her eyes never left that flag-draped coffin on the pedestal in front of the altar. In her mind's eye, she could still see Oliver sitting there in front of the telly at home, singing his heart out. She could see him in the front-parlour at Number 13 Roden Street, belting out 'Red Sails in the Sunset', whilst dear old Tilly Brooks banged it out on the piano. And she saw him at their golden wedding party, dancing the 'Anniversary Waltz' with her, and singing out his love and joy at just being with her.

After the service, the vicar led Oliver's coffin and its bearers into the small graveyard. Letty, flanked on either side by Mick and Eddie, followed on behind with Mary, Jonty and the rest of the congregation. One of Oliver's most fervent wishes over the years had been that when he died he wanted to be buried like a soldier. And so Mick went to an Army surplus store and bought Pop a soldier's rubber cape, and the day before the funeral, the undertaker had wrapped it around Oliver's shoulders. The Union Jack draped over Oliver's coffin was the final touch: a fitting tribute to a dedicated old soldier who had never ever spent his King's shilling.

Oliver's coffin was lowered into his chosen resting place. The vicar read the blessing, and Brian bid everyone's farewell with a reading from Mick's radio play about his father. Finally, the church bell tolled, slowly and sadly. It didn't sound exactly like the bell from the old Emmanuel Church in Hornsey Road close to Roden Street. But to Letty and her sons, it seemed like it.

Letty stepped forward to take one last look down at the coffin of the man she had loved so much, who she would continue to love until the end of her days. Then she scattered her own personal offerings into his grave. Slowly they floated down and settled majestically on the top of his coffin: a handful of grass cuttings from the back lawn of Number 12 Sea View Drive.

Oliver Jubilee Hobbs had died on a brilliantly sunny, mid-summer day. It was 20th June 1977. It was the eightieth year of his birth.

During the following months, Letty was very rarely left on her own. Eddie, Mary, and Jonty came up to spend practically every weekend with her, and occasionally she went down to Enfield to spend a week or so with them. Mick spent a lot of his time at the bungalow: it took things off Letty's mind to cook for him, and if she knew he was coming she would force herself to go shopping and choose all the food he liked most. Once a week, Mick took his mum to a cinema in Southend. Both of them loved horror films, and they would sit in the stalls, chocolate and ice-cream on their laps, eyes wide at the ghosts, monsters and studio-manufactured blood pouring out on the screen. By spring the following year, Mick had saved up enough money to move in to an old, thatched country cottage, and, as it was only a few miles down the road from Sea View Drive, Letty often stayed with him. However, Letty had made a vow to herself that she would not be a burden on her children so when either Eddie or Mick telephoned to invite her for a visit, she would often decline, saying that she was feeling too tired to come out. She was determined to keep her promise to herself.

In the summer of the following year Letty had her eightieth birthday, and Mick, Eddie, and Mary held a surprise party for her in the garden of Mick's cottage. There were eighty guests, one for each year of her life, and like Letty and Oliver's golden wedding celebration ten years before, there was a great variety of people there: Eddie and Mary's friends from Enfield, Mick's friends from radio and television, and even one or two neighbours from the old days at Number 13 Roden Street, whom Letty hadn't seen for years. It was a wonderfully happy day, and Letty was overwhelmed by it all. But, even though she was grateful for all the love shown her by her family and friends, it was easy to see that she was no longer her old self: the one person she wanted at the party more than anyone else wasn't there.

And so, for over a year, Letty coped with Oliver's death in the only way she knew how. She was practical, coolheaded, and carried on with her life in as normal a way as possible, which was the way Oliver had wanted it. Most days, the young couple in Number 10 next door called in to see how she was, and to find out if she needed anything. So did either Fred or Gladys Golding. All the neighbours did their bit, stopping to chat to her as she passed by on her way to do her little bit of shopping, or collect her pension at the sub-post-office. Over the years she had become a regular sight, a small figure, her shoulders more stooped than before, never without her walking stick, pushing her shopping-basket-on-wheels to the small shop on the estate, now a mini-market. Some people remarked to her that she had lost a little weight, and that she should make sure she ate properly each day. But Letty always assured them that she 'never went without anything', and ate more than enough for her needs.

The Hobbs bungalow itself remained very much the same as when Oliver was alive. Letty still slept in their double bed, and always kept three pillows on either side. And she refused to get rid of his own personal cup and saucer, even though she wouldn't allow anyone else to use them. On a

486

couple of occasions, Mick tried to persuade her to change the furniture around, but Letty always resisted. 'Why should I change things at my time of life?' she asked. 'Your dad and I like them the way they are.' It wasn't the first time she'd referred to Oliver as though he were still alive. For Mick, Eddie and Mary, it was a disturbing development. After her eightieth birthday, she started collecting papers together that Eddie and Mick might need after her own death. There were a few letters from the Social Security about her pension, her post office savings book, which had no more than a few hundred pounds in it, and some business correspondence relating to the purchase of the bungalow. There were also a few personal letters: some addressed to Gran Edginton, others from Letty's neighbours back in Holloway, and one or two from her old friend, Miss Wainwright – her favourite teacher at Pakeman Street School. She kept every Christmas and birthday card that Oliver had ever sent her since they first got married, and tied them all up in neat piles with red curtain ribbon, just like all the other papers. Everything had to be neat and tidy. Letty wanted to make quite sure that, after she'd gone, she didn't leave a mess for Eddie and Mick to have to clear up.

As one year tumbled into another, Letty carried out a constant routine, which hardly ever wavered from one day to the next. Without being fully conscious of what she was doing, she kept everything the way it used to be when Oliver was alive, including a regular stroll to their bench overlooking the sea, at the end of the road. Summer or winter she was there, throwing out handfuls of breadcrumbs to the sea-birds who swooped down to join her, talking to them as though they understood exactly what she was saying. One late October afternoon as she was sitting on the bench, emptying the last of the breadcrumbs from her bag, Letty was approached by a young man she had never seen before. She looked quizzically at him as he came to a halt before her.

'Please. I'm looking for Mrs Hobbs.'

She couldn't quite see his features; he was no more than a silhouette, standing with his back to the sun. But he seemed young, quite tall, with fair hair which just fell over his shoulders. He was casually dressed in jeans and a white polo-necked sweater, and over this he was wearing a very long fawn-coloured raincoat. 'Yes. I'm Mrs Hobbs.'

'I was told to find you here. It was the people in the next house where you live.' As he spoke again, Letty detected a slight burr in his voice, some kind of accent. 'May I sit here – please?'

Letty stared at him nervously for a brief moment. But she nodded and he sat down beside her. Now she could see his features clearly, and she immediately thought there was something vaguely familiar about them – a round face, pastel-blue eyes, long thin nose, and, but for one or two freckles, a clear skin.

The young man smiled warmly at her. He had the most friendly eyes. 'My name – it's Edginton.'

Letty was confused. '*Edginton!*'

The boy's voice was soft, gentle and so sensitive. 'My family – we 'ave been looking so long for you.' Then, to Letty's shocked surprise, he took hold of both her hands, and stared straight into her eyes. 'My name is Christian. I am the grandson of your brother, Tom Edginton.'

Letty was overwhelmed. The earth seemed to tilt around her as the boy raised her hands to his lips and kissed them. 'Oh God!' she said, and then said it again. She could say no more, but she knew what to do: immediately she threw her arms around him and for several minutes they hugged each other, the boy whispering over and over again into her ear, 'Letty! Ma chère, chère grand'tante – Letty!'

As they sat there, the seagulls swooped down low, and in the distance a large boat sounded its horn, as it made its way out of the River Thames and into the Estuary.

After a few moments they just sat there looking at each other, Letty's grandnephew dabbing her tears away with his handkerchief 'Christian?' said Letty, her voice choking. 'It's such a pretty name.'

'Christian Michel Edginton. It's after my father. I have a sister also. She is two years born after me. Her name is Ann-Marie Marguerite. It's after my grand'mère Marguerite.'

The name sent a warm glow through Letty's veins. She could see Tom, just before he went away. She could still hear him say, 'I love her, Letty. I knew the moment I saw her. It's not like the way I love you. With Marguerite – it's different.' For the next few minutes, she listened to what seemed like the entire history of Tom's family in France. She heard how Tom had married his Marguerite only days before he was killed on special assignment during the Battle of the River Somme. And then there had been the birth of their son, Michel Thomas in 1917. As Christian spoke in his carefully measured French accent, Letty watched his every movement. What *was* it about him that reminded her of Tom? The eyes? That devastating smile? Whatever it was, the years suddenly rolled back in just a few minutes, and Letty felt a flood of joy that in the final years of her life Tom's loved ones had found her at last.

A few minutes later, Letty and Christian were walking back, arm-in-arm, to Number 12 Sea View Drive. Letty cooked her grandnephew a huge meal of sausages, ham, chips, and baked beans, and for the rest of the day they talked of nothing else but the family – the Hobbs family, and the Edgintons. Letty wanted to hear everything about Christian's parents, Michel and Patrice: where they lived; what they did; their friends; their relations in France. She

489

heard how, before his grand'mere Marguerite had died, Christian had promised that he would never give up trying to find grand'pere Tom's sister and her family. Quietly, Letty decided not to tell the boy about the letter, that Gran Edginton had kept from her all those years. Things had come right now. There was no point in passing on old wrongs. By the end of the evening, Letty was as animated as she'd ever been, telling Christian the entire history of the Hobbs family, of Eddie and Mick and Mary, and how he would *have* to meet with his cousin, Jonty, for they would have so much to talk about.

It was almost ten o'clock in the evening before Christian left Number 12 to start his journey back to London. To Letty's disappointment, it was the last day of the boy's trip to England, and the following day he had to return to France, where he was training to be a teacher. But he promised to return very soon, and the next time he would bring his fiancée, Jeni, to meet his English 'grand'tante'. Before he bid her farewell, he stopped on the doorstep of the bungalow, took hold of Letty's hands, and kissed them. 'Dear grand'tante Letty,' he said, rubbing her hands affectionately against his cheek. 'I feel as though I have known you all my life.'

Letty was torn between joy and tears. 'I'm very proud to have met you, Christian. God bless you, boy.'

Christian kissed her on both cheeks, hugged her, then he was gone. Letty watched him striding off down the street, a lengthening shadow, stretching along the pavement beneath the fluorescent street lamps. 'Oh Olly,' she sighed to herself, almost as though he were there. 'Just look at him.' Eventually, Christian stopped at the corner of Sea View Drive, turned, and waved to her. Letty waved back, and waited for him to disappear. Afterwards, she went back into the bungalow, closed and bolted the front door, and turned off her outside light. Inside, she could still feel the boy's presence, as though she had lived through a wonderful dream.

A few minutes later, exhausted by the excitement of her day, Letty turned off the lights in the kitchen, passage, and hall, and after a quick wash in the bathroom, she went to bed. But, tired as she was, she lay awake, and in her mind she discussed with Olly everything she had heard from Christian that day. As her eyes closed, and she gradually drifted into sleep, she thought how lucky she was that her life had come full circle. But would she ever see Christian again? About that, she was not at all sure. But to have seen him once was an experience that would help to sustain her for the rest of her life.

Less than a week later, a letter arrived with a French postage stamp on the envelope. It was from Christian, who told her that he would be returning to England in a few weeks' time, and that he would be bringing his mother, father, and fiancée with him. Letty felt as if she had won the pools.

Chapter 38

The next two years brought Letty more moments of happiness than she'd ever thought possible. Christian kept his promise, and brought his young fiancée, Jeni, and his sister, Anne-Marie, to meet her. Letty also met her brother Tom's son, Michel, and his wife, Patrice. It was an emotional moment, for although her nephew was now in his early sixties, he looked so like she imagined Tom would look had he been allowed to live to such an age. Suddenly, so many memories came flooding back.

Michel's wife, Patrice, turned out to be much younger than her husband, and hadn't started a family until she was just turning thirty. But she and Letty got on famously, or at least they thought they did, for Patrice spoke very little English and Letty no French. And when Eddie tried to help out, things didn't become clearer, even though he pretended he understood everything his newly discovered relatives said. But on every occasion the Hobbs and the French Edgintons met, Letty was overjoyed to see them all getting on so well together. During those two years, Michel and Patrice came several times to England to see Letty and the English side of the family, and they always stayed with either Eddie and Mary in Enfield, or with Mick in his country cottage. On one or two occasions they even brought other relations with them, including Patrice's younger sister, Rosalie, who was divorced and so attractive that

Eddie's spectacles appeared to steam up every time he looked at her – much to Mary and Letty's amusement. Eddie, Mary, Jonty and Mick also paid visits to Michel and Patrice, at their home near Lille in Northern France. Letty was always invited too, but insisted she didn't want to start travelling at her time of life. This was not entirely true, for during the past two years, Letty had been working out other plans for her future.

It was a combination of events that finally made up Letty's mind. It started one evening, when she had just locked up the bungalow for the night and was having a wash in the bathroom before going to bed. Somehow, her legs just suddenly seemed to give way beneath her, and she fell with a thump to the floor, hitting her thigh against the edge of the bath as she did so. With great difficulty, she managed to pull herself to her feet again, and make her way to bed. But the following morning she awoke to excruciating pain, and a massive bruise.

Over the next months, Letty had more falls and with every little accident she was reminded more and more of her mother in the last years or so of her life. And she worried that she was becoming absent-minded and forgetful. On several occasions, she left the tap running in the sink, allowed meat in the oven to cook to a cinder and she frequently left the television turned on overnight. Gradually, she got to wondering what would happen if she should have an accident at home and be unable to call for help. During the hours she spent alone in the bungalow, her worries started to become an obsession. Desperately, she needed to talk to someone about her dilemma, but who? Certainly not Eddie, Mick, or Mary. They had enough problems of their own without having the burden of their old mother hanging around their necks. But there was always someone else. The idea of asking Oliver's advice came as no real surprise to her, for since his death nearly three years before she had often appealed to him when she felt low, or in difficulty. Sometimes she spoke to him when she was putting fresh flowers on his grave in the churchyard, other times when she was lying awake in bed at night, as she always had when he was alive. It seemed perfectly natural to talk to him, even though it was only in her own mind: after all, to her, Olly was still around, keeping an eye on her. 'What d'you think we should do about it, dear?' was her usual question. And even though she never actually *heard* Olly's reply, she always seemed to get the gist of what he was advising.

Despite the new lease of life given to her by the emergence of Tom's French family, Letty made up her mind about what her course of action should be. One morning early in spring, Eddie and Mary arrived to find her outside the kitchen door of the bungalow, filling the dustbins with all kinds of household items and personal effects.

'Mum! What are you doing out here in the cold?' Eddie couldn't believe his eyes: the dustbins were overflowing with old LPs, ornaments, bits and pieces of kitchen china, and photograph albums, all stuffed into black plastic bags.

Letty threw Oliver's own cup and saucer into one of the bags. Without looking up, she answered him. 'Now don't fuss, Eddie. I'm just throwing out a few old bits of rubbish, that's all.'

'Rubbish!' Eddie reached into one of the bags and brought out a small wooden chiming clock, which, until now, had been in the centre of the mantelpiece above the sitting-room fireplace. 'Isn't this the clock Pop bought you for your birthday?'

'It's no use to me any more. There's no point in hoarding things you can't use.' She snatched the clock from him, and dropped it back into the plastic bag again.

'Mum!' Now it was Mary's turn. Sorting through another

plastic bag, she brought out two photograph albums. 'You can't get rid of these.' She flicked through the pages. They were full of old family snapshots. 'There are some wonderful photos here.'

Letty knew what Mary was holding up but, for her own reasons, she avoided looking at them. 'What's the point in trying to hold on to memories? The past is the past. It's up to you young people to build your own lives now.'

'Well, thank you very much!' Mary closed the albums, and tucked them under her arm. 'I'll hang on to these if you don't mind.'

Eddie put the lids on the dustbins, and confronted his mother. 'Just what d'you think you're up to, eh?'

Letty sniffed, haughtily. 'I've told you. I'm sick of hoarding stuff. And in any case, I won't have room for a lot of old junk where I'm going.'

Eddie and Mary exchanged an immediate, startled look. 'I *beg* your pardon?' growled Eddie, eyes bulging.

'What d'you mean, Mum?' asked Mary, quietly.

Letty took out of her pocket a paper tissue, wiped her nose on it, and answered quite casually. 'Oh – didn't I tell you? They've accepted my application.' She smiled sweetly, seemingly unaware of the impact her reply would have on them. 'To the Old People's Home in Southend. I'm moving in next Tuesday – at ten o'clock in the morning.'

'What!' Eddie and Mary's horrified response came in unison. 'Mum! What the hell have you been up to!' Eddie snapped, angrily.

Letty, embarrassed, glanced anxiously along the bungalows in Sea View Drive. 'Keep your voice down, son! I don't want all the neighbours to know my business.' She turned quickly, and made her way back into the kitchen.

Eddie and Mary exchanged another look of disbelief, then followed her in. When they got inside, they were in for yet

495

more shocks. Apart from the furniture, the kitchen had been stripped nearly bare. The shelves had been cleared and scrubbed, curtains taken down, and there were tea chests bulging with kitchen china, cooking utensils, and goodness knows what else. Worse was to follow, for when they entered the sitting-room, it was exactly the same; even the pictures had been taken down from the walls. The small, second bedroom was completely bare, with no curtains up at the windows, and all that was left in Letty's bedroom was her dressing-table, a chair and the bed itself. Eddie and Mary couldn't believe their eyes, wandering around in a state of shock. It had only been a couple of weeks since they'd last seen Letty, and she had done all this without their knowing anything.

'You can get rid of the furniture and put the bungalow up for sale. I don't want any of the money. You and Mick can split everything you get between you. Better wait a week or so though. Just to make sure I settle in all right.'

Letty's matter-of-fact way of dismissing her whole life in just a few seconds completely shattered Eddie. 'Mum!' he barked angrily. 'Mick and I will not allow you to lock yourself away in an Old People's Home. I absolutely forbid it!'

'Well I'm sorry, son. I've already agreed to give up my pension to pay for it.' She picked up a cloth duster, and started wiping the top of the sideboard.

Mary went across to Letty, took the duster away, and led her to her easy-chair by the fireplace. 'Now then, Mum. Tell us what this is all about.'

Letty looked at her wide-eyed with innocence. 'There's nothing to tell, dear. I told you years ago, I'd never be a burden on my children.'

Eddie sat on the bench seat by the bay window, and Mary sat in Oliver's easy-chair facing Letty. Then, for the next half-hour or so, they listened to how she had first decided

496

that it was too risky for her to go on looking after herself. The residential home for senior citizens that she had signed up for was very modern, she said. And as for the gardens – well, they were absolutely beautiful, and there was even a bench there, overlooking the sea, just like the one she and Oliver used to sit on. She said the matron and staff were all lovely, and had guaranteed that she would spend a very happy time there.

After she had finished talking, Eddie covered his face despondently with one hand. 'Mum. How could you do such a thing?'

Letty's reply was direct, as practical as ever. 'There's no point in my hanging around here any longer.' She looked around the pastel-yellow walls of the sitting-room, which were still fresh from the last time Oliver had painted them. And for the first time she didn't sound too convincing. 'It's too nice a bungalow to waste on one person.'

Upset, Eddie went to his mum, and squatted down on the floor at her feet. 'Oh Mum,' he sighed, despairingly. 'You *know* both Mick and I have made room for you in our own homes. Why can't you let your own sons take care of you?'

Letty smiled at him affectionately, then rubbed her hand through his hair. 'Because Pop and I love you both too much.'

Later in the day, when they were driving back home through Southend, Eddie and Mary began to understand Letty's last remark. Number 12 Sea View Drive meant little to her without Pop there to share it with her. There was no use pretending otherwise.

'Oh God,' sighed Eddie, 'I hope she knows what she's doing.' He still couldn't fully come to terms with his mother's decision.

'Don't worry,' replied Mary, as the car passed the winding path which led down to Letty and Oliver's favourite bench.

'Your mum knows what she's doing all right. She always has.'

On Tuesday morning, Letty got up bright and early and, taking her walking stick for support, made her way on foot to the church on the other side of the estate. Before she went, she picked a bunch of daffodils from the front garden, and a few blades of grass that were just beginning to grow in between. Oliver's grey gravestone was clean and tidy, for she'd attended to the grave only a week before. After taking out the dead tulips from the vase, she replaced them with the daffodils and blades of grass from Number 12 Sea View Drive. 'There we are, dear,' she said, softly, as she arranged them so that they gave a splash of colour against Oliver's name inscribed on the headstone. 'All dinky-dink again.' She stood in silence at the foot of the grave for a moment or so, but she knew Oliver could still hear her. 'I don't think I'll be able to come any more for a bit, dear,' she went on. 'But I'll see you again – sooner or later.'

In ten minutes she was back at the bungalow, packing the last of her personal things into a suitcase before Mick was due to pick her up at nine-thirty. She had already stripped the bed, tucked all the bed-clothes into several black plastic bags, and given most of her dressing-table ornaments to the young girl next door in Number 10. She had left until last her framed photograph of Oliver and herself. It was the best of those taken at their golden wedding party some years before, the one of them both looking a picture of happiness in their swish evening clothes. By nine o'clock she had nothing more to do. Over the past few days she had scrubbed and dusted and polished everything, so that the bungalow was dazzling with cleanliness, ready for its future occupants. The day before, she had said cheerio to all the neighbours, cancelled the milk, given the postman her new address, and put all the remaining rubbish out for the dustmen for when they called later in the week. So, with a little time to spare before Mick was due to arrive, she sat on her seat by the bay window, and gave herself up to a few moments of private reflection.

As Letty looked out through the window the vast, majestic sweep of the Thames Estuary seemed to disappear. In her mind's eye it was replaced by a huge cinema screen, on which her entire life was played out before her. And what an extraordinary life it had been, floating down the twentieth century like a balloon packed full of people and events. And so much had happened in her eighty years. There were the two dreadful wars, taking their grim toll of the Hobbs, the Edgintons, and so many other families. Gas lamps had been replaced by electricity. People had their own bathrooms. Airliners were carrying passengers around the world every day. More wars – in Korea, Vietnam, and the Middle East. Men had climbed the highest mountain, and others had even walked on the moon. Brave people had crossed the Antarctic to the South Pole, or sailed single-handed around the oceans of the world. And now Britain had its first woman Prime Minister. Letty tried to imagine what Oliver would have thought about *that*! As she sat there, day-dreaming as ever, she cast her mind back to some of the people she had met – those she had admired, those she had pitied, those she had fought with – and those she had loved. There was her mother, Beatrice – old Gran Edginton, proud and defiant in life, but incapable of showing love, even to her own husband and children. And Oliver's brother, Sam Hobbs, who gave so much more to people than he ever got back from them. Then there were Letty's in-laws, old Annie and Ernie Hobbs, working their fingers to the bone. They'd had hard lives! And, of course, her brother Tom. Dear, sadly-missed Tom, so cruelly deprived of the joy of growing old through the years with his Marguerite. But to Letty, her lifetime had always been about one thing – her family. As she sat there, and watched that ballroom of her life drifting across time, she was more convinced than ever that she could not have survived the awe-inspiring twentieth century without Olly and the family around her. Despite the estrangement from Ron, she had loved her kids – all three of them – and had lived her life only for Olly and them. But why *was* her family so important to her, she wondered? After all, they were no different from any other family. They had their highs and lows, their ups and downs. They had arguments, disagreements, and jealousies – just like anyone else. Surely it wasn't just the tie of blood that kept them together? No. It was the feeling that they were a unit – 'the good old Number 13 Roden Street brigade' – as Oliver used to call them. It was the feeling that each member of the family *cared* about the others, cared even if they were hurting one another, cared about what they were doing or thinking, cared about their ambitions, and hopes for the future. Without that, it could all have been so very different.

'It's almost half-past nine, Mum. Time we were leaving.'

Letty snapped out of her daydream immediately. She hadn't realised that Mick's car had arrived outside, and he was now in the room. 'I'm all ready, son,' she said, easing herself up from the bench seat at the bay window. 'I'll just go and put on my hat.'

Mick followed her to her bedroom, where she quickly packed the framed photograph of her and Oliver into the suitcase, and locked it. 'Only one suitcase?' he asked.

Letty smiled to herself, as she put on her camel-coloured coat. 'Yes. Seems very little to take after a lifetime of collecting things, doesn't it? Still, I only need what's necessary. Don't want to mess up my new room with a whole lot of rubbish.'

Mick watched her whilst she put on her daffodil-coloured hat, the one she had worn at Pop's funeral, the one she had worn for goodness knows how long. He remembered Pop buying it for her. It was for her birthday over ten years ago, before they'd left Roden Street. Letty often told the story of how she had dragged Pop into the Ladies' Wear department of Jones Brothers in the Holloway Road, and how he had laughed at every shape, size, and style of hat she had tried on. But when she came to try on this particular one, he'd stopped laughing, and paid up for it immediately. It cost three pounds exactly.

Mick waited for her to finish putting in the hat pin, then went up behind her as she was looking into the dressing-table mirror. 'Mum . . .'

Letty looked at his reflection in the mirror behind her. She knew he was upset. 'Don't say anything, son. I know how you feel.'

'I hate this!'

'So do I.'

'Then why are you doing it?'

Letty turned round to face him. 'Because I want to get settled, have some time to think for myself.'

'Don't you understand, Mum? Seeing you leave your own home like this makes me and Eddie feel so helpless, as though we're turning our backs on you.'

'No, Mick! Don't ever say things like that – neither you nor Eddie. What I'm doing is my own idea. Pop and I talk it over lots of times.' She took hold of his shoulders, and held them firmly. It was the first time she'd really realised what blue eyes he had, too. 'Now listen to me, son. You and Eddie have been more wonderful to Pop and I than any parents have the right to expect. But I've had a good run for my money, and now it's time to get things sorted out.' She turned away from him, picked up a big, buff envelope from

501

the dressing-table, and held it out for him. 'Take this please, son.' She was brisk and businesslike.

Mick looked suspiciously at the envelope. 'What is it?'

She pushed it at him so that he had to take it. 'It's my post-office savings book. It's for you and Eddie after I'm gone.'

Mick was horrified. 'Mum!'

Letty collected her umbrella, which was still hanging on a hook behind the door. 'Now don't be silly about it, Mick. There's enough there to pay for my funeral, and whatever's left over I want you to split between you. And don't forget to buy something nice for Mary and Jonathan. It's not much, I'm afraid, but it might help out on a rainy day.'

'Oh God, Mum!' Mick, desperate not to let her see that he was fighting back tears, turned his back to her, and looked out of the window, which now had no curtains. 'Why d'you have to talk about funerals? You're not going to die!'

Letty put her handkerchief into her handbag on the dressing-table, and closed it. 'Don't be silly, dear! Of course I'm going to die – one day. We all are. But it's only right to tidy up things first.'

Distressed and trying hard to swallow the huge lump in his throat, Mick stared out of the window into the small back garden. The grass was already starting to grow on Pop's lawn, and Mick realised that he wouldn't be cutting it this year. Letty crept up behind him, and put her arms around his waist. 'Don't upset yourself, son,' she whispered, affec-tionately. 'If you start me off, we'll flood the place!' She moved alongside him, and now the two of them were staring out into the back garden together. In the distance, they could just see smoke curling up from the chimneypot of one of the bungalows: someone was not using smokeless fuel. Letty leaned her head on Mick's shoulder, just like she used to do with Oliver. 'All I want you to do, son, is to get on with your life. You and Eddie have got a lot of good times to look forward to – and, yes, bad times too. But you'll survive. Just like me. Just like Pop.'

Mick felt himself breathing deeper, and swallowing more frequently. 'There'll never be anyone like you,' he assured her, his voice barely audible. 'One of these days, Mum, I'm going to write about you. You *and* Pop.'

Letty turned to look at him, and gently laughed. 'Write about Olly and me? Don't be silly, dear! Who wants to know about us? We're nobody special.' She broke away from him, and collected her handbag from the dressing-table. 'Come on now. Better be going. I don't want to get into Matron's bad book on my first day!'

Letty left the room, leaving Mick to pick up her suitcase from the bed, now stripped down to its mattress. Before he followed her out into the passage he stopped at the door to take one last look round at the bedroom.

Mick, carrying Letty's suitcase, came out of the bungalow first. Letty followed, then paused briefly to double-lock the door. 'Do me a favour please, son,' she said, turning to Mick who was waiting for her. 'Before we go, just run these down to the letter box on the corner. I shall forget them otherwise. I'll wait here for you.' She handed him three letters to post. Mick took them, and started to walk off. 'Mick.' He stopped as she called, and turned. 'Better take these. They belong to you and Eddie now.' She held out the keys to the bungalow. 'Take good care of them.' Mick put down the case, and took the keys from her. For a brief second, he squeezed them tightly in the palm of his hand, then quickly picked up the suitcase again, turned, and hurried off without speaking.

Letty watched him go to the car, put her case into the boot, close it, then walk off briskly down the street to post her letters. For these last few moments she stood on the bunga- low doorstep, gazing at the mass of yellow-head daffodils swaying to and fro in the chilly, spring breeze. And laid out in front of her in the distance was the sea. Calm now, and with the March morning sun getting stronger by the minute, high in the sky above. Soon, there would be white surf on the undulating waves, and it wouldn't be long before the small sailing-boats would cut their way in and out of the Estuary, all the way from Canvey Island to the far tip of Southend Pier itself. And the Estuary! The majestic sweep of the great Thames Estuary, with its adorable muddy shorelines cluttered with seaweed, and the air pierced with the smell of salt, cockles and whelks, and the distant fumes from the funnels of great ocean freighters passing back and forth along the English Channel. Letty stood there, took a deep breath of invigorating fresh sea air, and marvelled how lucky she had been to have seen all this. Then she sighed wistfully. 'Oh Olly. Partings are never easy, are they, dear?' She paused for a moment, thinking back again. 'I remember how I used to hate it every time you went off to work your late-night turns at the tube station. I couldn't bear being parted from you, not for a single minute. I still can't bear it.' She smiled to herself. In her mind's eye she could see Oliver standing there in his uniform, soon after he got out of hospital. What a handsome man he was. 'Still, we've been lucky, Olly – oh yes. Lucky to have kids like ours, lucky to have good friends. Oh, we've come through some good times together, haven't we, dear?' Her eyes suddenly looked up at the sky, to watch the Coast Guard helicopter skimming high above. 'But what will the future be for our kids, eh Olly? Sometimes I wonder.' She sighed, and lowered her eyes again, because the sun was brighter than she thought. 'But then, you and me managed to get through it all, didn't we? No. They'll manage all right.' Her attention suddenly focused on the daffodils all around her in the garden. She could almost hear them, calling to her, like bells, peeling out a message in the breeze. Only now did her cheeks feel warm, for the sun was heating up, determined to do well by her. So she turned around, to take a parting glance at the bungalow, the last home of her own she would ever have. The clematis, climbing up the wooden trellis on the red brick wall, looked as though it had survived the winter. She was very proud of that clematis, for she and Oliver had planted it there together. 'Olly. D'you remember you once said that *I* was strong? Well, let me tell you something. No one can ever be strong unless they've got someone to be strong for.' She smiled, and her eyes scanned every brick on the front of the bungalow, every drainpipe, every window. Everything there was so precious to her. 'Oh Olly. I can't wait to see you again, to hold you in my arms, and keep you awake by gabbing and singing with you all through the night.' And as she turned to take one last look out at the Estuary, their two voices sang out in unison within her mind:

> You are my honey, honey-suckle,
> I am the Bee,
> I'd like to sip the honey sweet
> from those red lips you see;
> I love you dearly, dearly
> and I want you to love me,
> You are my honey, honeysuckle,
> I am the Bee.

The sound of Mick's car horn brought her out of her day-dream. 'Coming!' she called. And after taking a deep breath of good sea air, she straightened her shoulders, and held up her head. 'Right then, Letty,' she said to herself, firmly. 'Let's get on with it!

Off she went then, down the garden path, leaning only slightly on her walking stick. And as she went, she was given a rousing send-off by a host of yellow-head daffodils, swaying in the breeze. Mick helped her into his car, and in a matter of seconds, she was gone. For a few moments, it looked as though the sun was going to remain behind the clouds. But it soon reappeared again, and the Estuary became a galaxy of dazzling light.

Clearly, it was going to be yet another beautiful day outside Number 12 Sea View Drive.